WITNESS
IN
DEATH

*Also by Nora Roberts
in Large Print:*

Born in Shame
Captivated
Daring to Dream
From the Heart
Homeport
Inner Harbor
The Reef
River's End

Written as J. D. Robb:

Naked in Death
Loyalty in Death

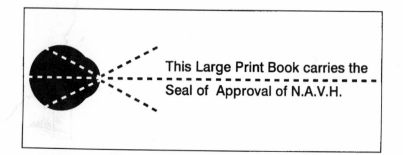

This Large Print Book carries the
Seal of Approval of N.A.V.H.

WITNESS IN DEATH

J. D. Robb

Thorndike Press • Thorndike, Maine

Published in 2000 by arrangement with The Berkley Publishing Group, a member of Penguin Putnam, Inc.

Thorndike Press Large Print Americana Series.

The tree indicium is a trademark of Thorndike Press.

The text of this Large Print edition is unabridged. Other aspects of the book may vary from the original edition.

Set in 16 pt. Plantin by Minnie B. Raven.

Printed in the United States on permanent paper.

Library of Congress Cataloging-in-Publication Data

Robb, J. D., 1950–
    Witness in death / J.D. Robb.
      p. cm.
     ISBN 0-7862-2715-X (lg. print : hc : alk. paper)
     ISBN 0-7862-2716-8 (lg. print : sc : alk. paper)
    1. Dallas, Eve (Fictitious character) — Fiction. 2. Police
  — New York (State) — New York — Fiction. 3. New
York (N.Y.) — Fiction. 4. Policewomen — Fiction.
5. Large type books. I. Title.
PS3568.O243 W58 2000
  813′.54—dc21   00-032535

The play's the thing.

— WILLIAM SHAKESPEARE

This reasonable moderator,
and equal piece of justice, Death.

— SIR THOMAS BROWNE

chapter one

There was always an audience for murder.

Whether it took its form in horror or glee, in dark humor or quiet grief, mankind's fascination with the ultimate crime made it a ripe subject for exploration in fact and in fiction.

At its bottom line, murder sold tickets and had packed theaters throughout history. Romans had pushed and shoved their way into the Coliseum to watch gladiators hack each other to bloody bits. Or, to alleviate the boredom of the day, by catching a matinee where a few hapless Christians were pitted against happy-to-oblige lions for the amusement of a cheering audience.

Since the outcome of these uneven matches was pretty much a sure bet, the crowd hadn't packed the stands to see if maybe this time the Christians would win the day. They wanted the results and all the blood and gore they offered.

People could go home pleased that they'd gotten their money's worth — and more, that they themselves were alive and whole.

Vicarious murder was a simple way of reassuring yourself that your personal problems weren't really so bad after all.

Human nature, and the need for such entertainment, hadn't changed very much in a millennium or two. Lions and Christians might have been passé, but in the last gasp of winter in the year 2059, murder still sold strong and bumped the ratings in the media.

In a more civilized way, of course.

Families, wooing couples, the sophisticated, and their country cousins continued to queue up and plunk down hard-earned credits to be entertained by the *idea* of murder.

Crime and punishment was Lieutenant Eve Dallas's business, and murder was her specialty. But tonight she sat in a comfortable seat in a packed house and watched the canny business of murder play out onstage.

"He did it."

"Hmm?" Roarke was every bit as interested in his wife's reaction to the play as he was the play itself. She leaned forward in her chair, her arms crossed on the gleaming rail of the owner's box. Her brandy-colored eyes scanned the stage, the players, even as the curtain came down for intermission.

"The Vole guy. He killed the woman. Bashed her head in for her money. Right?"

Roarke took the time to pour them each a glass of the champagne he had chilling. He hadn't been certain how she'd react to an evening with murder as the entertainment and was pleased she'd gotten into the spirit. "Perhaps."

"You don't have to tell me. I know." Eve took the flute glass, studied his face.

And a hell of a face it was, she thought. It seemed to have been carved by magic into a staggering male beauty that made a woman's glands hum a happy tune. The dark mane of hair framed it, those long, sculpted bones; the firm, full mouth that was curved now in the faintest of smiles as he watched her. He reached out, ever so casually, to skim those long fingers over the ends of her hair.

And those eyes, that brilliant, almost burning blue, could still make her heart stumble.

It was mortifying the way the man could turn her inside out with no more than a look.

"What are you staring at?"

"I like looking at you." The simple phrase, delivered with that musical hint of Ireland, was a power all its own.

"Yeah?" She angled her head. Relaxed by the idea of having the entire evening to do nothing but be with him, enjoy him, she let him nibble on her knuckles. "So, you want to fool around?"

Amused, he set his glass down and, watching her, ran his hand up the long line of her leg to where the slit in her narrow skirt ended at the hip.

"Pervert. Cut it out."

"You asked."

"You have no shame." But she laughed and handed him back his glass. "Half the people in this fancy joint of yours have their spyglasses on this box. Everybody wants a look at Roarke."

"They're looking at my very nifty wife, the homicide cop who brought me down."

She sneered at that, as he knew she would. It gave him the opening to lean over and sink his teeth lightly into her soft bottom lip. "Keep it up," she warned. "We'll have to sell tickets."

"We're still basically newlyweds. It's perfectly acceptable for newlyweds to neck in public places."

"Like you care about what's acceptable." She put a hand on his chest, nudged him back to a safe distance. "So, you've packed them in tonight. I guess you figured you would." She turned back to look out on the audience again.

She didn't know much about architecture or design, but the place dripped with class.

She imagined Roarke had employed the best minds and talents available to rehab the old building into its former glory.

People wandered in and out of the enormous, multilevel theater during the break, and the sound of their voices rose in a low roar of humanity. Some were dressed to kill, so to speak. Others were decked out in the casual wear of airboots and oversized, retro flak jackets that were all the rage that winter.

With its soaring, muraled ceilings, its miles of red carpet and acres of gilt, the theater itself had been redone to Roarke's exacting specifications. Everything he owned was done to his specifications — and, Eve thought, he owned damn near everything that could be owned in the known universe.

It was something she still wasn't used to, something she doubted she'd ever be fully comfortable with. But that was Roarke, and they'd taken each other for better or worse.

In the year since they'd met, they'd had more than their share of both.

"It's a hell of a place you've got here, pal. I didn't get the full punch of it from the holo-models."

"Models only provide the structure and elements of ambiance. A theater needs people, the smell and sound of them, to have impact."

"I'll take your word for it. What made you pick this play for the opening?"

"It's a compelling story, and, I think, has timeless themes as the best stories do. Love, betrayal, murder, all in a layered and untidy package. And it's a stellar cast."

"And it all has your stamp on it. Still, Leonard Vole's guilty." She narrowed her eyes at the shimmering red-and-gold drawn curtain as if she could see through it to measure and judge. "His wife's a very cool customer, with some trick up her sleeve. The lawyer guy's good."

"Barrister," Roarke corrected. "The play takes place in London, mid–twentieth century. Barristers plead criminal cases in that particular system."

"Whatever. The costumes are cool."

"And authentic, circa 1952. When *Witness for the Prosecution* came out on film, it was a huge hit, and it's proven an enduring one. They had a stellar cast then, too." He had it on disc, of course. Roarke had a particular fondness for the black-and-white films of the early– and mid–twentieth century.

Some saw black-and-white as simple and clear cut. He saw shadows. That, he thought, his wife would understand very well.

"They've done a good job casting actors

who reflect the original players while maintaining their own style," he told her. "We'll have to watch the movie sometime, so you can judge for yourself."

He, too, scanned the theater. However much he enjoyed an evening out with his wife, he was a businessman. The play was an investment. "I think we're in for a good, long run with this."

"Hey, there's Mira." Eve leaned forward as she spotted the police psychologist, elegant as always, in a winter-white sheath. "She's with her husband, and it looks like a couple of other people."

"Would you like me to get a message down to her? We could invite them for a drink after curtain."

Eve opened her mouth, then slid her gaze to Roarke's profile. "No, not tonight. I've got other plans."

"Do you?"

"Yeah. Got a problem with that?"

"None whatsoever." He topped off their wine. "Now, we have a few minutes before the next act. Why don't you tell me why you're so sure Leonard Vole is guilty."

"Too slick not to be. Not slick like you," she added and made Roarke grin. "His is a — what do you call it — a veneer. Your slick goes down to the bone."

"Darling, you flatter me."

"Anyway, this guy's an operator, and he does a good job with the honest, innocent act of a hopeful, trusting man who's down on his luck. But great-looking guys with beautiful wives don't piddle time away with older, much less attractive women unless they have an agenda. And his goes a lot deeper than selling some goofy kitchen tool he invented."

She sipped her champagne, settling back as the houselights flickered to signal the end of intermission. "The wife knows he did it. She's the key, not him. She's the study. If I were investigating, she's the one I'd be looking into. Yeah, I'd have myself a nice long talk with Christine Vole."

"Then the play's working for you."

"It's pretty clever."

When the curtain rose, Roarke watched Eve instead of the courtroom drama.

She was, he thought, the most fascinating of women. A few hours before, she'd come home with blood on her shirt. Fortunately, not her own. The case that caused it had opened and closed almost immediately with the dead she stood for and a confession she'd drawn out within an hour of the crime itself.

It wasn't always that *simplistic*. He supposed that was the word. He'd seen her drive herself to exhaustion, risk her life, to bring justice to the dead.

It was only one of the myriad facets of her he admired.

Now she was here, for him, dressed in sleek and elegant black, her only jewelry the diamond he'd once given her, dripping like a tear between her breasts, and her wedding ring. Her hair was short, a careless cap of dozens of shades of brown.

She watched the play with those cool cop's eyes, dissecting, he imagined, evidence, motive, and character, just as she would a case that landed in her lap. Her mouth was unpainted — she rarely remembered or thought of lip dye. Her strong face with its take-me-on chin and its shallow cleft didn't need it.

He watched that mouth thin and those eyes narrow and gleam as the character of Christine Vole took the stand and betrayed the man she'd called her husband.

"She's up to something. I told you she was up to something."

Roarke danced his fingers over the back of Eve's neck. "So you did."

"She's lying," Eve murmured. "Not all the way. Pieces of lies. Where does the knife come into it? So he cut himself with it. It's not a vital point. The knife's a red herring. Not the murder weapon, which, by the way, they haven't introduced into evidence. That's a flaw. But if he cut himself slicing bread with the knife — and everyone agrees he did — why do they need it?"

"He either cut himself on purpose to explain the blood on his sleeves or by accident as he claims."

"Doesn't matter. It's smoke." Her brow furrowed. "Oh, he's good." Her voice lowered, vibrated with the intense dislike she'd developed for Leonard Vole. "Look at him standing in the . . . what is it?"

"The dock."

"Yeah, standing in the dock looking all shocked and devastated by her testimony."

"Isn't he?"

"Something's off. I'll figure it out."

She liked putting her mind to it, looking for the angles and the twists. Before her involvement with Roarke, she'd never seen an actual live play. She'd passed some time in front of the screen, had let her friend Mavis drag her to a couple of holograph acts over the years. But she had to admit watching live performers act out the scenes, deliver the lines, and make the moves took the whole entertainment aspect to a higher level.

There was something about sitting in the dark, looking down on the action that made you a part of it, while separating you just enough that you didn't have a real stake in the outcome.

It removed responsibility, Eve thought. The foolish and wealthy widow who'd gotten her skull bashed in wasn't looking to Lieutenant Eve Dallas to find the answers. That made looking for those answers an interesting game.

If Roarke had his way — and it was rarely otherwise — that rich widow would die six nights a week, and during two matinees, for a very, very long time for the amusement and entertainment of an audience of armchair detectives.

"He's not worth it," she muttered, drawn in by the action enough to be annoyed by the characters. "She's sacrificing herself, performing for the jury so they look at her as an opportunist, a user, a cold-hearted bitch. Because she loves him. And he's not worth a damn."

"One would assume," Roarke commented, "that she's just betrayed him and hung him out to dry."

"Uh-uh. She's turned the case on its ear, shifted it so that she's the villain. Who's the jury looking at now? She's the center, and he's just a sap. Damn smart thinking, if he was worth it, but he's not. Does she figure that out?"

"Watch and see."

"Just tell me if I'm right."

He leaned over, kissed her cheek. "No."

"No, I'm not right?"

"No, I'm not telling, and if you keep talking, you'll miss the subtleties and the dialogue."

She scowled at him but fell silent to watch the rest of the drama unfold. She rolled her eyes when the not guilty verdict was read. Juries, she thought. You couldn't depend on them in fiction or in real life. A panel of twelve decent cops would have convicted the bastard. She started to say so, then watched Christine Vole fight her way through a crowd of spectators, who wanted her blood, into the nearly empty courtroom.

Eve nodded, pleased when the character confessed her lies and deceptions to Vole's barrister. "She knew he was guilty. She *knew* it, and she lied to save him. Idiot. He'll brush himself off and dump her now. You watch."

Eve turned her head at Roarke's laugh. "What's so funny?"

"I have a feeling Dame Christie would have liked you."

"Who the hell is that? Ssh! Here he comes. Watch him gloat."

Leonard Vole crossed the courtroom set,

flaunting his acquittal and the slinky brunette on his arm. *Another woman,* Eve thought. *Big surprise.* She felt both pity and frustration for Christine as she threw herself into Vole's arms, tried to cling.

She watched his arrogance, Christine's shock and disbelief, Sir Wilfred's anger. It was no less, no more than she expected, however well played. And then, she came straight up out of her chair.

"Son of a bitch!"

"Down girl." Delighted, Roarke dragged Eve back into her seat while onstage, Christine Vole plunged the knife she'd snatched from the evidence table into her husband's black heart.

"Son of a bitch," Eve said again. "I didn't see it coming. She executed him."

Yes, Roarke thought Agatha Christie would have enjoyed his Eve. Sir Wilfred echoed those precise words as people rushed out onstage to huddle over the body, to draw Christine Vole away.

"Something's wrong." Again, Eve pushed to her feet, and now her blood was humming to a different beat. This time she gripped the rail tight in both hands, her eyes riveted to the stage. "Something's wrong. How do we get down there?"

"Eve, it's a performance."

"Somebody's not acting." She shoved the chair out of her way and strode out of the box just as Roarke noted one of the kneeling extras scramble to his feet and stare at the blood on his hand.

He caught up with Eve, grabbed her arm. "This way. There's an elevator. It'll take us straight down to backstage." He keyed in a code. From somewhere, down below, a woman began to scream.

"Is that part of the script?" Eve demanded as they stepped into the elevator.

"No."

"Okay." She dug her communicator out of her evening bag. "This is Dallas, Lieutenant Eve. I need a medi-vac unit. New Globe Theater, Broadway and Thirty-eighth. Condition and injury as yet unknown."

She tossed the communicator back in her bag as the elevator opened onto chaos. "Get these people back and under control. I don't want any of the cast or crew to leave the building. Can you get me a head count?"

"I'll take care of it."

They separated, with Eve shoving her way through to the stage. Someone had had the presence of mind to drop the curtain, but behind it were a dozen people in various stages of hysteria.

"Step back." She snapped out the order.

"We need a doctor." The cool-eyed blonde who'd played Vole's wife stood with both hands clutched between her breasts. There was blood staining her costume, her hands. "Oh my God. Somebody get a doctor."

But Eve crouched beside the man sprawled facedown on the floor and knew it was too late for doctors. She straightened, dug out her badge. "I'm Lieutenant Dallas, New York Police and Security. I want everyone to step back. Don't touch anything, don't remove anything from the stage area."

"There's been an accident." The actor who played Sir Wilfred had pulled off his barrister's wig. His stage makeup ran with sweat. "A terrible accident."

Eve looked down at the pool of blood, the gored-to-the-hilt bread knife. "This is a crime scene. I want you people to step back. Where the hell is security?"

She tossed out a hand, slapped it on the shoulder of the woman she still thought of as Christine Vole. "I said back." When she spotted Roarke come out of the wings with three men in uniform, she signaled.

"Get these people offstage. I want them sequestered. You've got dressing rooms or whatever. Get them stashed, and keep the guards on them. That goes for crew as well."

"He's dead?"

"That or he wins best actor award for the century."

"We need to move the audience along to a safe area. Keep it controlled."

"Go ahead and make it happen. See if you can find out if Mira's still around. I could use her."

"I killed him." The blonde staggered back two steps, holding up her bloody hands, staring at them. "I killed him," she said again and fainted.

"Great. Terrific. Roarke?"

"I'll take care of it."

"You." She jabbed a finger at one of the guards. "Start moving these people into dressing rooms. Keep them there. You," she ordered the second guard, "start rounding up the crew, the techs. I want the doors secured. Nobody comes in, nobody goes out."

A woman began to sob, several men began to argue in raised voices. Eve counted to five, lifted her badge in the air, and shouted, "Now, listen up! This is a police investigation. Anyone refusing to follow the directives will be interfering with that investigation and will find themselves transported to the nearest station house where they will be kept in holding. I want this stage cleared, and cleared now!"

"Let's move." The brunette with the bit part as Vole's tootsie gracefully stepped over the unconscious Christine. "A couple of you big strong men pick up our leading lady, will you? I need a goddamn drink." She glanced around, her eyes cool, clear, and green. "Is that allowed, Lieutenant?"

"As long as it's not on my crime scene."

Satisfied, Eve pulled out her communicator. "Dallas, Lieutenant Eve." Once more she crouched beside the body. "I need a crime scene unit dispatched immediately."

"Eve." Doctor Mira hurried across the stage. "Roarke told me . . ." She trailed off, looked down at the body. "Good lord." She let out a long breath, shifted her gaze back to Eve. "What can I do?"

"Right now, you can stand by. I don't have a field kit. Peabody's on the way, and I've sent for the crime scene team, and the ME. But until they get here, you're both the doctor on-scene and a designated police and security official. Sorry to screw up your evening."

Mira shook her head, started to kneel by the body.

"No, watch the blood. You'll contaminate my scene and ruin your dress."

"How did it happen?"

"You tell me. We all watched it. Using my acute powers of observation, I identify that knife as the murder weapon." Eve spread her hands. "I don't even have a damn can of Seal-It. Where the hell is Peabody?"

Frustrated that she couldn't begin a true examination or investigation without her tools, she spun around and spotted Roarke. "Would you hold here for me, Dr. Mira?"

Without waiting for an answer, Eve strode stage left. "Tell me, the bit with the knife in the last scene. How does it work?" she asked Roarke.

"Dummy knife. The blade retracts when it's pressed against a solid surface."

"Not this time," Eve murmured. "The victim, what's his real name?"

"Richard Draco. A very hot property. I suppose he's cooled off considerably now."

"How well did you know him?"

"Not well. I've met him socially a few times, but primarily I knew his work." Roarke tucked his hands in his pockets and rocked back on his heels as he studied Draco's stunned and staring eyes. "He's a four-time Tony Award winner, garnered excellent reviews in the films he's done. He's a top box office draw, stage and screen, and has been so for a number of years. He has a rep," Roarke continued, "for being difficult, arrogant, and childish. Juggles women, enjoys a certain amount of chemical enhancements that might not meet the police department's code."

"The woman who killed him?"

"Areena Mansfield. Brilliant actress. A rare untemperamental type, and dedicated to her art. Very well respected in theater circles. She lives and works primarily in London but was persuaded to relocate to New York for this role."

"By who?"

"Partially by me. We've known each other for a number of years. And no," he added, dipping his hands in his pockets again, "I've never slept with her."

"I didn't ask that."

"Yes, you did."

"Okay, if I did, we'll have the follow-up. Why haven't you slept with her?"

A faint smile lifted his mouth. "Initially because she was married. Then, when she wasn't . . ." He ran a fingertip along the dent in Eve's chin. "I was. My wife doesn't like me to sleep with other women. She's very strict about it."

"I'll make a note of that." She considered her options, juggled them. "You know a lot of these people, or have impressions of them anyway. I'm going to want to talk to you

25

later." She sighed. "On the record."

"Of course. Is it possible this was an accident?"

"Anything's possible. I need to examine the knife, and I can't touch the fucker until Peabody gets here. Why don't you go back there, do a pat and stroke on your people? And keep your ears open."

"Are you asking me to assist in an official police investigation?"

"No, I am not." And despite the circumstances, her lips wanted to quiver. "I just said keep your ears open." She tapped a finger on his chest. "And stay out of my way. I'm on duty."

She turned away as she heard the hard clop of what could only be police-issue shoes.

Peabody's were shined to a painful gleam Eve could spot across the length of the stage. Her winter-weight uniform coat was buttoned to the throat of a sturdy body. Her cap sat precisely at the correct angle atop her dark, straight hair.

They crossed the stage from opposite ends, met at the body. "Hi, Dr. Mira." Peabody glanced down at the body, pursed her lips. "Looks like a hell of an opening night."

Eve held out a hand for her field kit. "Record on, Peabody."

"Yes, sir." Because it was warm under the stage lights, Peabody shrugged out of her coat, folded it, set it aside. She clipped her recorder to the collar of her uniform jacket.

"Record on," she said as Eve coated her hands and evening shoes with Seal-It.

"Dallas, Lieutenant Eve, on-scene, stage set of New Globe Theater. Also in attendance, Peabody, Officer Delia, and Mira, Dr. Charlotte. Victim is Richard Draco, mixed race male, late forties to early fifties."

She tossed the Seal-It to Peabody. "Cause of death, stabbing, single wound. Visual exam and minimal amount of blood indicate a heart wound."

She crouched, and with her coated fingers picked up the knife. "Wound inflicted by what appears to be a common kitchen knife, serrated blade approximately eight inches in length."

"I'll measure and bag, Lieutenant."

"Not yet," Eve murmured. She examined the knife, dug out microgoggles, examined it again from hilt to tip. "Initial exam reveals no mechanism for retracting the blade on impact. This is no prop knife."

She shoved the goggles up so they rested on the top of her head. "No prop knife, no accident." She passed the knife to Peabody's sealed hand. "It's homicide."

27

chapter two

"I could use you," Eve said to Mira while the sweepers worked over the crime scene. Draco's body was already bagged, tagged, and on its way to the morgue.

"What can I do for you?"

"We've got a couple of dozen uniforms logging names and addresses of audience members." She didn't want to think about the man-hours, the mountains of paperwork that would go into interviewing over two thousand witnesses. "But I want to start the interview process on the main players before I kick them clear for the night. I don't want anybody lawyering on me until I get a better handle on the setup."

Right out in the open, Eve thought as she studied the stage, the set, the tiers after tiers of plush velvet seats that had held a rapt audience.

Someone was cool and cocky. And smart.

"People are comfortable with you," she went on. "I want Areena Mansfield comfortable."

"I'll do what I can."

"Appreciate it. Peabody, you're with me."

Eve crossed the stage, moved into the wings. There were uniforms scattered throughout the backstage area. Civilians were either tucked behind closed doors or huddled in miserable little groups.

"What do you give our chances of keeping the media locked out of this until morning?"

Peabody glanced over at Eve. "I'd say zero, but that's optimistic."

"Yeah. Officer." Eve signaled a uniform. "I want guards posted at every entrance, every exit."

"Already done, sir."

"I want the guards inside. Nobody leaves the building, not even a cop. Nobody comes in, especially reporters. Clear?"

"Yes, sir."

A corridor bent off the wing, narrowed. Eve scanned the door, vaguely amused by the gold stars affixed to several of them. Name plaques were displayed as well. She stopped by the door marked for Areena Mansfield, knocked briefly, then walked in.

She only lifted her eyebrows when she saw Roarke sitting on a royal blue daybed, holding Areena's hand.

The actress had yet to remove her stage makeup, and though tears had ravaged it, she was still stunning. Her eyes darted to

29

Eve and were instantly full of fear.

"Oh God. Oh my God. Am I going to be arrested?"

"I need to ask you some questions, Ms. Mansfield."

"They wouldn't let me change. They said I couldn't. His blood." Her hands fluttered in front of her costume, fisted. "I can't stand it."

"I'm sorry. Dr. Mira, would you help Miss Mansfield out of her costume? Peabody will bag it."

"Of course."

"Roarke, outside please." Eve stepped back to the door, opened it.

"Don't worry, Areena. The lieutenant will sort this out." After giving Areena's hand a comforting squeeze, he rose and walked by Eve.

"I asked you to keep your ears open, not to cozy up with one of my suspects."

"Trying to keep a hysterical woman lucid isn't particularly cozy." He blew out a breath. "I could use a very large brandy."

"Well, go home and have one. I don't know how long I'll be."

"I believe I can find what I need here."

"Just go home," she said again. "There's nothing for you to do here."

"As I'm not one of your suspects," he

added in a quiet voice, "and I own this theater, I believe I can come and go as I please."

He ran a finger down her cheek and strolled off.

"You always do," she muttered, then went back into the dressing room.

It seemed to Eve that *dressing room* was a lowly term for a space so large, so lush. A long, cream-toned counter held a forest of pots, tubes, wands, bottles, all arranged with soldierly precision. Over it all gleamed a wide triple mirror ringed with slim white lights.

There was the daybed, several cozy chairs, a full-sized AutoChef and friggie unit, a trim, mini–communication system. Wardrobe hung in a long closet area, open now so that Eve noted the costumes and street clothes were as precisely arranged as the makeup.

On every table, in groupings on the floor, were flowers. The overfragranced air made Eve think of weddings. And funerals.

"Thank you. Thank you so much." Areena shivered slightly as Mira helped her into a long white robe. "I don't know how much longer I could have stood . . . I'd like to clean off my makeup." Her hand reached for her throat. "I'd like to feel like myself."

"Go ahead." Eve made herself comfortable in one of the chairs. "This interview will be recorded. Do you understand?"

"I don't understand anything." With a sigh, Areena sat on the padded stool in front of her makeup mirror. "My mind seems numb, as if everything's happening one step after it should be."

"It's a very normal reaction," Mira assured her. "It often helps to talk about the event that caused the shock, to go over the details of it so they can be dealt with. Set aside."

"Yes, I suppose you're right." Shifting her gaze in the mirror, she watched Eve. "You have to ask me questions, and it has to be on the record. All right. I want to get it done."

"Record on, Peabody. Dallas, Lieutenant Eve, in interview with Mansfield, Areena, in subject's dressing room at the New Globe Theater. Also present are Peabody, Officer Delia, and Dr. Charlotte Mira."

While Areena creamed off her stage makeup, Eve recited the revised Miranda. "Do you understand your rights and responsibilities, Miss Mansfield?"

"Yes. It's another part of the nightmare." She closed her eyes, tried to envision a pure white field, tranquil, serene. And could see only blood. "Is he really dead? Is Richard really dead?"

"Yes."

"I killed him. I stabbed him." The shudder ran from her shoulders down. "A dozen times," she said, opening her eyes again to meet Eve's in the center of the triple mirror. "At least a dozen times, we rehearsed that scene. We choreographed it so carefully, for the biggest impact. What went wrong? Why didn't the knife retract?" The first hint of anger showed in her eyes. "How could this have happened?"

"Take me through it. The scene. You're Christine. You've protected him, lied for him. You've ruined yourself for him. Then, after all that, he blows you off, flaunts another woman, a younger woman, in your face."

"I loved him. He was my obsession — my lover, my husband, my child, all in one." She lifted her shoulders. "Above all else, Christine loved Leonard Vole. She knew what he was, what he did. But it didn't matter. She would have died for him, so deep and obsessive was her love."

Calmer now, Areena tossed the used tissues into her recycle chute, turned on the stool. Her face was marble pale, her eyes red and swollen. And still, she radiated beauty.

"In that moment, every woman in the audience understands her. If they haven't felt that kind of love, in some part of themselves they wish they had. So when she realizes that after all she's done, he can discard her so casually, when she fully understands what he is, she grabs the knife."

Areena lifted a fisted hand, as if holding the hilt. "Despair? No, she is a creature of action. She is never passive. It's an instant, an impulse, but a bone-deep one. She plunges the knife into him, even as she embraces him. Love and hate, both in their highest form, both inside her in that one instant."

She stared at the hand she'd flung out, and it began to tremble. "God. God!" In a frantic move, she yanked open a drawer of her dressing table.

Eve was on her feet, her hand clamped over Areena's wrist in a flash.

"I — it — a cigarette," she managed. "I know I'm not supposed to smoke in the building, but I want a cigarette." She pushed at Eve's hand. "I want a damn cigarette."

Eve glanced in the drawer, saw the pricey ten-pack of herbals. "We're on the record. You'll get an automatic fine." But she stepped back.

"My nerves." She fumbled with the lighter until Mira stepped over, gently pried it from her fingers, and flicked it on. "Thanks. Okay." Areena took a deep drag, blew it out slowly. "I'm sorry. I'm not usually so . . . fragile. The theater smashes the fragile to bits, and quickly."

"You're doing very well." Mira kept her voice low, calm. "Talking it through with Lieutenant Dallas will help."

"I don't know what to say." Areena stared back at Mira with the trust Eve had wanted to see radiating in her eyes. "It just happened."

"When you picked up the knife," Eve interrupted, "did you notice anything different?"

"Different?" Areena blinked as she focused on Eve again. "No. It was exactly where it was supposed to be, hilt toward me to make the movement fast and smooth. I swept it up, to give the audience that one shocked instant to see the blade. The lighting's designed to catch it, to glint off the edges. Then I charged. It's only two steps from the table to Richard. I take his right arm, between the elbow and the shoulder, with my left hand, holding him, draw back with the right, then . . . the impact," she said after another long drag, "of the prop knife against his chest releases the pack of stage blood. We hold there for an instant, just two beats, intimately, before the others onstage rush forward to pull me away."

"What was your relationship with Richard Draco?"

"What?" Areena's eyes had glazed.

"Your relationship with Draco. Tell me about it."

"With Richard?" Areena pressed her lips together, her hand running up between her breasts to massage the base of her throat as if words were stuck there, like burrs. "We've known each other several years, worked with each other before — and well — most recently in a London production of *Twice Owned*."

"And personally?"

There was a hesitation, less than a half beat, but Eve noticed and filed it away.

"We were friendly enough," Areena told her. "As I said, we've known each other for years. The media in London played up a romance between us during that last work. The play was a romance. We enjoyed the benefit of the interest. It sold tickets. I was married at the time, but that didn't discourage the public from seeing us as a couple. We were amused by it."

"But never acted on it."

"I was married, and smart enough, Lieutenant, to know Richard wasn't the kind of man to throw out a marriage for."

"Because?"

"He's a fine actor. Was," she corrected, swallowed hard before she drew one last time on her cigarette. "He wasn't a particularly fine human being. Oh, that sounds vicious, horrible." Her hand lifted to her throat again, fingers restless against flesh. "I feel vicious and horrible saying it, but I — I want to be as honest as I can. I'm afraid. I'm terrified you'll think that I meant this to happen."

"At the moment, I don't think anything. I want you to tell me about Richard Draco."

"All right. All right." She drew in a breath, sucked on the cigarette as if it were a straw. "Others will say it in any case. Richard was very self-interested and egocentric, as many . . . most of us are in this business. I didn't hold it against him. And I jumped at the chance to work with him in this play."

"Are you aware of anyone else who, believing him not a particularly fine human being, might have held that against him?"

"I imagine Richard insulted or offended everyone attached to this production at one time or another." She pressed a fingertip to the inside corner of her eye, as if to relieve some pressure. "Certainly there were bruised feelings, complaints, mutters, and grudges. That's theater."

The theater, as far as Eve was concerned, was a screwy business. People wept copiously, gave rambling monologues when any half-wit lawyer would have advised them to say yes, no, and shut the hell up. They expounded, they expanded, and a great many of them managed to turn the death of an associate into a drama where they themselves held a starring role.

"Ninety percent bullshit, Peabody."

"I guess." Peabody crossed the backstage area, trying to look everywhere at once. "But it's kind of cool. All those lights, and the holoboard, and there're some really mag costumes if you're into antique. Don't you think it'd be amazing to be standing out front and having all those people watching you?"

"Creepy. We're going to have to let some of these people go before they start whining about their civil rights."

"I hate when that happens."

Eve smirked, scanned her memo pad. "So far, we're getting an interesting picture of the victim. Nobody really wants to say so, but he was well disliked. Even when they don't want to say so, they do anyway, while they dab tears from their eyes. I'm going to look around back here. Go ahead and have the uniforms cut these people loose. Make sure we have all pertinent data on them, that they're issued the standard warning. Set up interviews for tomorrow."

"At Central or in the field?"

"Let's keep it light and go to them. For now. After you've set them up, you're relieved. Meet me at Central at oh eight hundred."

Peabody shifted her feet. "Are you going home?"

"Eventually."

"I can hang until you do."

"No point in it. We'll do better with a fresh start tomorrow. Just scramble the interviews in. I want to talk to as many people as possible as soon as possible. And I want a follow-up with Areena Mansfield."

"Yes, sir. Great dress," she added as she tucked her memo log away. "You're going to have to get the blood and sweeper gunk off the skirt before it sets in."

Eve looked down, scowled at the elegant black column. "Damn it. I hate not being dressed for the job." She turned, strode deeper backstage, where a uniform stood by a huge, locked cabinet.

"Key." She held out a hand while the uniform took out a key in an evidence bag. "Anybody try to get in this thing?"

"The prop master came back — old guy, pretty shaky. But he didn't give me any hassle."

"Fine. Go out front and tell the sweepers they'll be cleared to run this area in about ten minutes."

"Yes, sir."

Alone, Eve unlocked the cabinet and pulled the double doors open. She frowned, noting the box of cigars, the old-fashioned telephone, and a few other items neatly arranged in an area marked Sir Wilfred's Office.

Another section held props that had been used in the bar scene. The courtroom section was empty. Apparently, the prop master was very careful about replacing and arranging his props, and did so directly after the scene where they were needed was wrapped.

Someone that meticulous wouldn't have mistaken a kitchen knife for a dummy.

"Lieutenant Dallas?"

Eve glanced back and saw the young brunette from the last act moving from the shadows of the wings into the lights of backstage. She'd changed from her costume and wore a simple black jumpsuit. Her hair had been combed out of its tight waves and fell straight and richly brown down the center of her back.

"I hope I'm not disturbing your work." She had the faintest accent, soft and southern, and an easy smile on her face as she walked closer. "I was hoping to have a word with you. Your aide told me I was free to go, for the moment."

"That's right." Eve cast her mind back over the program she'd scanned after the murder. "Miss Landsdowne."

"Carly Landsdowne, Diane in this tragic production." She shifted her large blue eyes to the cabinet. "I hope you don't think Pete had anything to do with what happened to Richard. Old Pete wouldn't hurt a fly if it was buzzing in his ear."

"Pete would be the property master?"

"Yes. And as harmless as they come. That can't be said for everyone in this little circus."

"Obviously. Is there something specific you want?"

"Only to say what I doubt most of the others will, at least initially. Everyone hated Richard."

"Including you?"

"Oh, absolutely." She said it with a bril-

41

liant smile. "He'd step on your lines every chance he got, cut off your mark, anything that would draw the attention onto him and off anyone else. Offstage, he was a vicious little worm. His world revolved around one thing, his own ego."

She gave a delicate shrug. "You'll hear it from someone eventually, so I thought it would be best if you heard it from me. We were lovers for a brief period. It ended a couple of weeks ago, in a nasty little scene. Richard was fond of nasty little scenes and staged this one for the biggest impact. During our first full dress rehearsal."

"I take it he broke things off."

"He did." She said it carelessly, but the gleam in those green eyes told Eve the resentment still simmered. "He went out of his way to charm me, and once I was charmed, he went out of his way to humiliate me in front of the cast and crew. This was my first Broadway production."

She glanced around, and though her lips were curved, the smile was sharp as broken glass. "I was green, Lieutenant, but I ripen fast. I won't bother to say I'm sorry he's dead, but I will say I don't think he was worth killing."

"Were you in love with him?"

"I don't have room for love at this point in

my career, but I was . . . dazzled. Much, I think as my character was dazzled by Leonard Vole. I doubt there's anyone involved in this production who didn't have some grudge against Richard. I wanted to be up front about mine."

"I appreciate that. You said he humiliated you. In what way?"

"In his last scene, the one where I come down with him into the courtroom and he confronts Christine, he broke off my lines to her, stormed around the stage, claiming my delivery was flat."

Her lips compressed, her eyes slitted. "He compared its lack of passion and style to my performance in bed. He called me a brainless rube who was trying to trade her lack of talent on mildly attractive looks and a good pair of breasts."

Carly brushed back her hair, a lazy gesture in direct contrast with the bright fury in her eyes. "He said I was boring, and while I'd amused him for a while, if I couldn't pretend to act in my minor capacity, he'd see I was replaced with someone who could."

"And this came as a complete surprise to you?"

"He was a snake. Snakes strike quickly, because they're cowards. I gave back a few shots, but they weren't my best. I wasn't prepared, and I was embarrassed. Richard stalked offstage, locked himself in his dressing room. The assistant director went off to try to placate him, and we ran the scene again with Richard's stand-in."

"Who's the stand-in?"

"Michael Proctor. He's very good, by the way."

"And if the play goes back into production, would he step into the part?"

"That's a question for the producers, I imagine. But it wouldn't surprise me, at least in the short term."

"I appreciate the information, Miss Landsdowne." And that much information, unbidden, was always suspect.

"I've got nothing to hide." She moved her shoulders again and kept those big green eyes on Eve's face. "And if I did, I imagine you'd dig it out. I've heard quite a bit about Roarke's cop wife over the last few months. It took a certain arrogance, don't you think, to choose a night you'd be in the audience to do murder?"

"Arrogance is required to take another's life. I'll be in touch, Miss Landsdowne."

"I don't doubt it."

Eve waited until the woman was nearly to the wings. "One thing."

"Yes?"

"You don't care much for Areena Mansfield either."

"I don't have strong feelings about her one way or the other." Carly tilted her head, lifted one eyebrow in a high arch. "Why do you ask?"

"You weren't very sympathetic when she fainted."

The smile came back, bright enough to play to the back rows. "A damn graceful faint, wasn't it? Actors, Lieutenant Dallas, you can't trust them."

With a casual toss of her hair, she made her exit.

"So," Eve murmured, "who's performing?"

"Lieutenant." One of the sweepers, a young, fresh-faced woman, marched up to Eve. Her baggy protective jumpsuit made little swishing noises with each step. "Got a little toy here I think you'll want to take a look at."

"Well, well." Eve took the evidence bag, pursed her lips as she studied the knife. Through the clear plastic she fingered the tip of the blade, felt it retract. "Where'd you find this, ah . . ." She scanned the name stitched on the breast of the dull gray jumpsuit. "Lombowsky."

"In a vase full of genuine long-stemmed

red roses. Nice flowers. The room was packed with them like it was a state funeral or something. Areena Mansfield's dressing room."

"Good work."

"Thanks, Lieutenant."

"Do you know where Mansfield is?"

"She's in the cast lounge. Your man's with her."

"Peabody?"

"No, sir. Your husband." Lombowsky waited until Eve scowled down at the prop knife before she dared to raise her eyebrows. It had been her first up-close look at Roarke, and she considered him worth two big eyesful.

"Finish the sweep, Lombowsky."

"On it, Lieutenant."

Eve strode offstage and caught Peabody coming out of a dressing room. "I've got four of the interviews scheduled."

"Fine. Change of plan for tonight." Eve held up the dummy knife. "Sweepers found this in Mansfield's dressing room, tucked in with some roses."

"You going to charge her?"

"Her lawyer'd get her bounced before I got her into Central. It's awfully damn pat, isn't it, Peabody? She kills him in front of a packed house and stashes the prop knife in her own dressing room. Very neat or very stupid." Eve turned the evidence bag over in her hands. "Let's see what she has to say about it. Where's the cast lounge?"

"Lower level. We can take the stairs."

"Fine. You know anything about actors?"

"Sure. Free-Agers are big on all the arts. My mother did some little theater when I was coming up, and two of my cousins are actors. Live stage work and small screen stuff. And my great-grandmother was a performance artist in San Francisco before she retired. Then there's my —"

"Okay, all right." Shaking her head, Eve clattered down the stairs. "How did you stand all those people crowding into your life?"

"I like people," Peabody said cheerfully.

"Why?"

Since it wasn't a question that required an answer, Peabody gestured to the left as they came to the bottom of the steps. "You like them, too. You just pretend to be snarly."

"I am snarly. If and when I cut Mansfield loose, or she lawyers, I want you to stick with her. If she goes home, settles in, call for a couple of uniforms to watch her place. We've got enough for a surveillance clearance. I want to know where she goes and what she does."

"Want me to run the background check on her now?"

"No, I'll take care of it."

Eve pulled open the door to the lounge. As with anything Roarke had his fingers in, it was far from shabby. Obviously he wanted the talent comfortable and had spared no expense to insure it.

There were two separate seating areas with plush sofas flanked by serving droids. The room bent into an ell, with the short leg offering an AutoChef she assumed was fully stocked, a clear-fronted friggie holding a variety of cold drinks, and a small, separate table with a slick little computer setup.

Roarke sat, cozily to Eve's mind, beside Areena in the sitting area on the right, swirling a snifter of brandy. His gaze; that lightning-strike blue, shifted to his wife's face, gleamed there, and reminded her of the first time she'd seen him, face-to-face.

He hadn't been baby-sitting a murder suspect then. He'd been one.

His lips curved in a lazy, confident smile. "Hello, Peabody," he said, but his eyes remained on Eve's face.

"I have a few more questions for you, Miss Mansfield."

Areena blinked up at Eve, fluttered her hands. "Oh, but I thought we were finished

48

for the evening. Roarke's just arranged my transportation back to my penthouse."

"The transpo can wait. Record on, Peabody. Do you need me to refresh you on your rights and obligations as pertains to this investigation, Miss Mansfield?"

"I —" The fluttering hand landed on her throat, rested there. "No. I just don't know what else I can tell you."

"Recognize this?" Eve tossed the sealed prop knife onto the table between them.

"It looks like . . ." Her hand, still restless, reached out, then fisted, drew back. "It's the dummy knife. It's the prop that should have been on the set when . . . Oh, God. Where did you find it?"

"In your dressing room, buried in red roses."

"No. No." Very slowly, Areena shook her head from side to side. She crossed her arms over her breasts, fingers digging into her shoulders. "That's not possible."

If it was an act, Eve mused, it was damn good. The eyes were glazed, the lips and fingers trembled. "It's not only possible, it's fact. How did it get there?"

"I don't know. I tell you, I don't know." In a sudden spurt of energy, Areena leaped to her feet. Her eyes weren't glazed now, but wild and wheeling. "Someone put it there.

Whoever switched the knives put it there. They want me to be blamed for Richard. They want me to suffer for it. Wasn't it enough, God, wasn't it enough that I killed him?"

She held out her hand, a Lady Macbeth, staring at blood already washed away.

"Why?" Eve's voice was cold and flat. "Why not just toss the prop away, into a corner, a recycling bin. Why would anyone hide it in your dressing room?"

"I can't think . . . who would hate me so much. And Richard . . ." Tears shimmered, fell gorgeously as she turned. "Roarke. You know me. Please, help me. Tell her I couldn't do this terrible thing."

"Whatever the answers are, she'll find them." He rose, letting her come into his arms to weep as he watched his wife over her head. "You can be sure of it. Can't she, Lieutenant?"

"Are you her representative?" Eve snapped back and earned a lifted brow.

"Who, other than yourself, has access to your dressing room, Miss Mansfield?"

"I don't know. Anyone, really, in the cast and crew. I don't keep it locked. It's inconvenient." With her head still resting on Roarke's shoulder, she drew steadying breaths.

"Who sent you the red roses? And who brought them into the room?"

"I don't know. There were so many flowers. My dresser took the cards. She would have marked the type on each. One of the gofers brought some of the deliveries in. People were in and out up till thirty minutes before curtain. That's when I cut off visitors so I could prepare myself."

"You were back in your dressing room after your initial scene and again for costume changes throughout the play."

"That's right." Calmer, Areena drew back from Roarke, faced Eve. "I have five costume changes. My dresser was with me. She was in the dressing room with me each time."

Eve drew out her memo. "Your dresser's name?"

"Tricia. Tricia Beets. She'll tell you I didn't hide the prop. She'll tell you. Ask her."

"I'll do that. My aide will see you back to your penthouse."

"I can go?"

"For the moment. I'll be in touch. Record off, Peabody. See Miss Mansfield back to her home."

"Yes, sir."

Areena grabbed the coat she'd draped over the arm of the sofa, passed it to Roarke

51

in a way Eve had to appreciate. So female, so smoothly confident a man would be right there to wrap her up warm.

"I want you to catch who did this, Lieutenant Dallas. I want that very much. And even then, even when whoever arranged for this to happen is punished, I'll always know it was my hand that caused it. I'll always know that."

She reached back, touched the back of Roarke's hand with her fingers. "Thank you, Roarke. I couldn't have gotten through tonight without you."

"Get some rest, Areena."

"I hope I can." Head bowed, she walked out with Peabody trailing sturdily behind.

Frowning, Eve picked up the evidence bag, put it in her field kit. "She'd like to rectify the fact that you didn't sleep with her."

"Do you think so?"

The faint trace of amusement in his voice was just enough to put her back up. "And you just lap that up, don't you?"

"Men are pigs." He stepped forward, brushed his fingers over her cheek. "Jealous, darling Eve?"

"If I was jealous of every woman you've had sex with, compounded by every woman who wishes you did or would, I'd spend my life green."

She started to turn, shoved at his hand when he grabbed her arm. "Hands off."

"I don't think so." To prove it, he took her other arm, pulled her firmly against him. The humor was in his face and so, damn him, was a tenderness she had no defense against. "I love you, Eve."

"Yeah, yeah."

He laughed, leaned down, and bit her bottom lip gently. "You romantic fool."

"You know your trouble, ace?"

"Why don't you tell me?"

"You're a walking orgasm." She had the pleasure of seeing his eyes widen.

"I don't believe that's entirely flattering."

"It wasn't meant to be." It was very rare to sneak under that slick polish and hit a nerve, she thought. Which was why she enjoyed it so much. "I'm going to talk to Mansfield's dresser, see if she confirms the story. Then I'm done here for tonight. I can start some background runs on the way home."

He retrieved his coat and hers, and his equilibrium. "I believe you're going to be too busy to do background runs on the way home."

"Doing what?"

He held her coat up before she could take it and shrug into it herself. Rolling her eyes, she turned, stuck her arms in the sleeves.

Then let out a choked sound when he whispered a particularly imaginative suggestion in her ear.

"You can't do that in the back of a limo."

"Want to bet?"

"Twenty."

He took her hand to lead her out. "Done."

She lost, but it was money well spent.

"If it were done when 'tis done, then 'twere well it were done quickly."

Well, it is done, done well and done quickly. And I dare quote from the Scottish play as I sit alone. A murderer. Or, as Christine Vole was in our clever play, am I but an executioner?

It's foolish of me to record my thoughts. But those thoughts are so loud, so huge, so brilliantly colored I wonder the world can't see them bursting out of my head. I think this speaking aloud where no one can hear might quiet them. Those thoughts must be silenced, must be buried. This is a precarious time. I must steel my nerve.

The risks were weighed before the deed was done, but how was I to know, how could I have imagined what it would be like to see him dead and bleeding center stage? So still. He lay so still in the white wash of lights.

It's best not to think of it.

It's time now to think of myself. To be cautious, to be clever. To be calm. There were no mistakes made. There must be none now. I will keep my thoughts quiet, tucked deep inside my heart.

Though they want to scream out in jubilation.

Richard Draco is dead.

chapter three

Given the state of the equipment at her disposal at Cop Central, Eve saved herself considerable frustration and ran her initial background checks at home. Roarke loved his toys, and the computer and communications systems in her home office made the junk at Central look like something out of the second millennium.

Which it very nearly was.

Pacing her office with her second cup of coffee, she listened while her computer listed the official details of Areena Mansfield's life.

Areena Mansfield, born Jane Stoops, eight November, 2018, Wichita, Kansas. Parents, Adalaide Munch and Joseph Stoops, cohabitation union dissolved 2027. One sibling, male, Donald Stoops, born twelve August, 2022.

She let it run through education data for form — all standard stuff as far as Eve could tell right through her enrollment in New

York's Institute of Dramatic Arts at the age of fifteen.

Got the hell out of Kansas first chance, Eve mused, and couldn't blame her. What did people do out there with all that wheat and corn, anyway?

Areena's professional credits started young. Teen model, a scatter of plays, a brief stint in Hollywood before a return to live theater.

"Yeah, yeah, blah blah." Eve wandered back to her machine. "Computer, search and list any criminal record, all arrests."

Working . . .

The computer hummed with quiet efficiency. Comparing it to the useless pile of chips she was cursed with at Central made her sneer.

"Gotta marry a billionaire to get a decent tool these days."

Search complete . . .
Possession of illegals, New Los Angeles, 2040.

"Now we're talking." Intrigued, Eve sat behind the desk. "Keep going."

Plea bargain resulted in probation with

standard obligatory rehabilitation. Obligation satisfied at Keith Richard Memorial Rehabilitation Center, New Los Angeles.

Consumption of illegals with secondary charges of indecent exposure, New York City, 2044. Second rehabilitation ordered and satisfied, New Life Clinic, New York City.

No further criminal activities noted in subject file.

"That's good enough. What was her drug of choice?"

Working . . . File indicates Ecstasy/Zoner combination in both counts.

"That'll get you off, won't it?"

Please rephrase query.

"Never mind. Search and list cohabitation and/or marriage data."

Working . . . Formal cohabitation license issued in New Los Angeles for Areena Mansfield and Broderic Peters from June 2048 to April 2049, union mutually dissolved. Marriage license issued in London, England, for Areena Mansfield and Law-

*rence Baristol September 2053. Divorce pe-
titioned, Mansfield v. Baristol January
2057, unopposed and granted. No children
resulted from marriage or cohabitation
unions.*

"Okay. Search and list any professional
credits in productions that involved Richard
Draco."

*Working . . . Off-Broadway production of
drama* Broken Wings, *from May through
October 2038. Subject and Draco, Richard,
in secondary roles through run of play.
Small-screen video production,* Die for
Love, *starring subject and Draco, Richard,
taped New Los Angeles, 2040. Video production, New York,* Check Mate, *starring
subject and Draco, February 2044. London
Arts production of drama,* Twice Owned,
*starring subject and Draco, Richard, from
February 2054 through June of that year.*

"Interesting timing," Eve murmured,
reaching over idly to scratch the ears of the
plump cat that leaped onto her desk. As
Galahad made himself comfortable directly
in front of the computer screen, Eve
watched Roarke stroll in through the door
connecting their personal offices.

"You didn't mention Areena had an illegals habit."

"*Had* being the operative word. Is it relevant?"

"Everything's relevant. Are you sure her affection for illegals is past tense?"

"To my knowledge, she's been clean more than a dozen years." When he sat on the edge of the desk, Galahad slithered over to bump his head against Roarke's long-fingered hand. "Don't you believe in rehabilitation, Lieutenant?"

"I married you, didn't I?"

Because it made him grin, she angled her head. "You also didn't mention that she and Draco were in some productions together over the years."

"You didn't ask."

"The timing of two of their acting connections coincide down the line with her illegals convictions."

"Ah. Hmmm." Roarke sent Galahad into feline ecstasy with one slim finger over fur.

"How tight were they, Roarke?"

"They may have been involved. Gossip ran that way during their last project together in London. I didn't meet Areena until a few years ago when she was married and living in London. And I never saw her and Richard together until we were casting this play." He lifted a shoulder, helped himself to what was left of Eve's coffee.

"When I do my run on the victim, am I going to find illegals charges?"

"Probably. If Areena was still using, she was discreet and professional. No missed rehearsals, no temperamental scenes. I wouldn't use the term *discreet* in the same sentence with Draco, but he did his job. And if they were involved in a romantic or sexual fashion, they kept it behind locked doors."

"Nobody's ever discreet enough. If they were banging each other, someone knew. And if they were rolling around sweaty together or popping illegals, it adds some angles."

"Do you want me to find out?"

She got to her feet, leaned forward until her nose bumped his. "No. Now, if there's any part of that you didn't understand, let me repeat. No. Got it?"

"I believe I do. I have a meeting in San Francisco in a few hours. Summerset knows how to reach me if you need to."

Her scowl at the mention of Roarke's tight-assed aide de camp was instant and heartfelt. "I won't need to."

"I should be home before nine." He rose, sliding his hands up the sides of her body, then down again to her hips. "I'll call if I'll be any later."

She understood he was reassuring her she wouldn't be alone at night — alone where the nightmares chased her. "You don't have to worry about me."

"I like to."

He bent his head to give her a light kiss, but she changed the tone, the texture, by pulling him close, her mouth hot and greedy. Her hands were fisted in his hair, and her blood was up before she released him.

There was satisfaction in seeing his eyes had darkened and his breath quickened. "Well. What was that for?"

"I like to," she said and picked up her empty coffee cup. "See you." She gave him a smile over her shoulder as she went to the kitchen for a refill.

Eve screened her calls on her home unit, her palm unit, her vehicle, and her equipment in her office at Central. If her math held, she'd received twenty-three calls from reporters, which ran the gamut from charm, pleas, vague threats, and minor bribes, since midnight. Six of them, at varying locations and with increasing levels of frustration and urgency, were from Nadine Furst at Channel 75.

They might have been friends, which never failed to surprise Eve, but for both of them business was business. Nadine wanted an exclusive one-on-one with the primary investigator in the death of Richard Draco. Eve just wanted his killer.

She dumped each and every one of the calls from the media, signaled Peabody to stand by, and played the terse message from her commanding officer.

That one was simple enough. His office. Now.

It was still shy of eight A.M.

Commander Whitney didn't keep her waiting. His aide gestured Eve straight into his office where Whitney sat behind his desk, juggling his own communications.

His big hands tapped the surface of his desk impatiently, one lifting to jab a finger at a chair as she entered. He continued to man his tele-link, his broad, dark face betraying nothing, his voice calm and brisk.

"We'll brief the press at two. No, sir, it cannot be done any sooner. I'm well aware Richard Draco was a prominent celebrity and the media is demanding details. We'll accommodate them at two. The primary will be prepared. Her report is on my desk," he said, lifting a brow at Eve.

She rose quickly, set a disc at his fingertips.

"I'll contact you as soon as I've analyzed

the situation." For the first time since Eve entered, irritation rippled over Whitney's face. "Mayor Bianci, whether or not Draco was a luminary of the arts, he's dead. I have a homicide, and the investigation will be pursued with all energy and dispatch. That is correct. Two o'clock," he repeated, then ended the transmission and pulled off his privacy headphones.

"Politics." It was all he said.

He leaned back, rubbed at a line of tension at the base of his neck. "I read the prelim report you filed last night. We have a situation."

"Yes, sir. The situation should be in autopsy right about now."

His lips stretched in what was almost a smile. "You're not much of a theater buff, are you, Dallas?"

"I get my quota of entertainment on the street."

" 'All the world's a stage,' " Whitney murmured. "By now you're aware that the victim was a celebrity of considerable note. His death in such a public, and shall we say, dramatic venue, is news. Major news. The story's already hit on and off planet. Draco to Mansfield to Roarke to you."

"Roarke isn't involved." Even as she said it, a dozen curses ran through her head.

"He owns the theater, he was the primary backer for the play, and from the information that's come to me already, he was personally responsible for wooing both Draco and Mansfield into the production. Is that accurate, Lieutenant?"

"Yes, sir. Commander Whitney, if every crime that took place in a property Roarke owns or has interest in was connected to him, he'd be tied to every cop and perpetrator on planet, and half of them off."

This time Whitney did smile. "That's quite a thought. However." The smile vanished. "In this case his connection and yours is considerably more tangible. You're among the witnesses. I prefer to look at that as an advantage in this instance. The fact that you were on-scene and were able to contain it quickly keeps this from being more unwieldy than it is. The media's going to be a problem."

"Respectfully, sir, the media is *always* a problem."

He said nothing for a moment. "I take it you've seen some of the early headlines."

She had. Running right after the flash of "Draco Dies for Art" had been annoying little tidbits such as: "Murder Most Foul! Renowned actor Richard Draco was brutally stabbed and killed last night, the murder committed under the nose of top NYPSD homicide detective, Lieutenant Eve Dallas."

So much, she thought, for plugging media leaks.

"At least they didn't refer to me as Roarke's wife until the third paragraph."

"They'll use him and you to keep the story hot."

She knew it. Detested it. "I've worked under media heat before, Commander."

"True enough." As his 'link beeped, he pushed its All Hold button and silenced it. "Dallas, this isn't an ordinary murder or even an extraordinary one. It's, as my grandchildren say, got juice, and you're part of it. You'll need to prepare carefully for the press conference at two. Believe me, the actors involved will play to the cameras. They won't be able to help themselves, and as they do, the story adds layers."

He leaned back, tapping his thigh. "I'm also aware you're not particularly interested in the public and media end of this. You'll have to consider that end, in this case, part of the job. Don't grant interviews or discuss any area of the case with any reporter prior to the press conference."

"No, sir."

"I want this to move fast. I've already requested the ME put a rush on the autopsy. The lab's on alert. We go by the book here, but turn those pages quickly. Has Areena Mansfield requested her lawyer or representative?"

"Not as yet."

"Interesting."

"I don't expect that to last long. She was shaken, but my impression is she'll want a rep once her mind clears. Her dresser confirms she was in the dressing room with Areena at every costume change. I don't put complete faith in her statement. The woman worships Mansfield. Meanwhile, I'm running background checks on all members of cast and crew. It's going to take some time. There are a lot of players here. Interviews are starting this morning."

"Are the estimates of three thousand witnesses in the ballpark?"

Just thinking about it made Eve's head throb. "I'm afraid they are, Commander. Obviously, we couldn't hold the audience members in the theater for long. We did a person-by-person ID for name and residence as each was released. Some statements were taken because, basically, some people couldn't shut up. Most of those, which I've reviewed, were disjointed and essentially useless."

"Divvy up the audience witnesses in the squad. I'll pull in some detectives from other areas. Let's run some eliminations to get those numbers down."

"I'll start that today, Commander."

"Delegate it," he ordered. "You can't be spared for drone work. Tag Feeney for the backgrounds on cast and theater personnel. I want this to close. He's to prioritize the backgrounds over his current caseload."

He'll moan over that one, Eve thought, but she was pleased to be able to pass that part of the load over to the e-detective. "I'll communicate that to him, Commander, and send him the list."

"Copies to my attention. After the press conference, I'll need you to clear any and all media interviews with me before confirmation. Dallas, you can expect to see yourself and your husband on-screen, in print, and blasted out of the goddamn tourist trams until this matter is satisfactorily closed. If you require a larger team, let me know."

"I'll start with what I have. Thank you, Commander."

"Be here, this office, at thirteen-thirty, for premedia briefing."

It was dismissal, and acknowledging it, Eve headed out of the office and down the glide. Before she reached her level, she pulled out her communicator and contacted Feeney in the Electronic Detective Division.

"Hey, Dallas. Heard you caught a hell of a show last night."

"The reviews were a killer. Okay, got that out of my system. I've got direct orders from the commander. I'll be shooting you a full list of cast and crew from the play, and additional theater personnel. I need full backgrounds, with correlation runs. Any and all connections of any and all individuals with Richard Draco and/or Areena Mansfield."

"Love to lend a hand, Dallas, but I'm up to my nostrils here."

"Direct from the commander," she repeated. "He tagged you, pal, not me."

"Well, hell." Feeney's already hangdog face filled the screen with sorrow. She watched him drag a hand through his wiry rust-colored hair. "How many backgrounds we talking?"

"Including nonspeaking roles, walk-on, tech and talent crew, concessions, maintenance, and so on? Four hundred, give or take."

"Jesus, Dallas."

"I've done Mansfield, but you could go deeper." Instead of sympathy, she felt amusement that lightened her step as she passed through the bullpen and gave Peabody the come-ahead sign. "Whitney wants it prioritized and rushed. Media conference at fourteen hundred. I need all I can get by then. You're authorized to put as many hands on the team as you need."

"Isn't that just dandy?"

"Works for me. I'll be in the field. Peabody'll get you the list ASAP. Look for sex, Feeney."

"You get to be my age, you slow down on that some."

"Ha ha. Sex and illegals. I've got a tie already. Let's see if it spreads out any. I'll be in touch."

She pocketed her communicator, leading the way down to the lower level where her vehicle was parked. "Shoot the witness and suspect lists to Feeney. We're dumping backgrounds on EDD."

"Good for us." Peabody drew out her palm unit and began the transfer. "So . . . is he using McNab?"

"I didn't ask." Eve slid her gaze toward Peabody, then shook her head and coded open the locks on her vehicle.

"You want to know, don't you?"

Eve strapped in, started the car. "I don't know what you're talking about."

"About me and McNab."

70

"As far as I'm concerned, there is no you and McNab. It does not exist in my world. My aide is not having some weird-ass sexual fling with the fashion plate from EDD."

"It is weird," Peabody admitted, then let out a long sigh.

"We're not talking about it. Give me the first address."

"Kenneth Stiles, aka Sir Wilfred, 828 Park Avenue. And it's really good sex."

"Peabody."

"You were wondering."

"I was not." But she winced as a distressingly clear image of Peabody and McNab popped gleefully into her head. "Keep your mind on the job."

"I have lots of compartments in my mind." With a happy sigh, Peabody settled back. "Room for everything."

"Then make room for Kenneth Stiles and give me a rundown."

"Yes, sir." Obediently, Peabody took out her PPC. "Stiles, Kenneth, age fifty-six, a rare New York City native. Born and bred in midtown. Parents were entertainers. No criminal record. Educated by private tutor through secondary level with additional classes in drama, stage design, costuming, and elocution."

"Whoopee. So we've got a serious thespian on our hands."

"First performance at age two. Guy's won a pot load of awards. Always live stage. No video. An artist, is my guess. Probably temperamental and emotional."

"Won't this be fun. Has he worked with Draco before?"

"Several times. A couple of times with Mansfield. Last time in London. He's unmarried at the moment. Had two spouses and one formal cohabitation partner. All female."

Eve scanned for a parking place, rejected the idea, and pulled up to the front of the post–Urban War building on Park. Before she'd climbed out, the uniformed doorman was at her side.

"I'm sorry, madam, this is a nonparking zone."

"And this is a badge." She held up her shield. "Kenneth Stiles?"

"Mr. Stiles occupies the apartment on the fiftieth floor. Five thousand. The deskman will clear you. Madam —"

"Does this say madam?" Eve asked and waited for the doorman's eyes to skim down, read her badge.

"I beg your pardon, Lieutenant, might I arrange to have your vehicle garaged during your visit? A valet will return it when you're ready to leave."

"That's a nice offer, but if I gave you the ignition code, I'd have to arrest myself. It stays right here."

Eve kept her badge out and walked into the building, leaving the doorman staring sadly at her pea-green police issue.

It was hard to blame him. The lobby area was lush and elegant, with gleaming brass and spearing white flowers. Huge squares of polished black tiles covered the floor. Behind a long white counter, a tall, slim woman sat gracefully on a stool and beamed welcoming smiles.

"Good morning. How may I direct you?"

"Kenneth Stiles." Eve laid her badge on the counter beside a brass pot teeming with flowers.

"Is Mr. Stiles expecting you, Lieutenant Dallas?"

"He'd better be."

"Just one moment please." She swiveled to a 'link, her smile never dimming, her voice maintaining that same smooth and pleasant tone of an expensive and well-programmed droid. "Good morning, Mr. Stiles. I have a Lieutenant Dallas and companion at the lobby desk. May I clear them?" She waited a beat. "Thank you.

Have a lovely day."

Turning from the 'link, she gestured toward the east bank of elevators. "The far right car is cleared for you, Lieutenant. Enjoy your day."

"You bet. I used to wonder why Roarke didn't use more droids," she said to Peabody as they crossed the black tiles. "Then I run into one like that, and I understand. That much politeness is just fucking creepy."

The ride up to the fiftieth floor was rapid enough to have Eve's stomach jump and her ears pop. She'd never understand why people equated height with luxury.

Another droid was waiting for them when the doors slid open. One of Stiles's serving units, Eve concluded, done up in such stark and formal attire he made the dreaded Summerset look like a sidewalk sleeper. His steel gray hair was slicked back and matched with a heavy mustache that dominated his thin, bony face. The black of his slacks and long jacket was offset with snow-white gloves.

He bowed, then spoke in a fruity voice with a rolling English accent. "Lieutenant Dallas and Officer, Mr. Stiles is expecting you. This way, please."

He led them down the hall to double

doors that opened into the corner apartment. The first thing Eve saw when she entered was the sweeping window wall that opened onto New York's bustling sky traffic. She wished Stiles had drawn the privacy screen.

The room itself was wild with color, rubies and emeralds and sapphires tangled together in the pattern on the wide U-shaped conversation pit. Centered in it was a white marble pool where fat goldfish swam in bored circles among lily pads.

A strong scent of citrus spread out from the tidy forest of dwarf orange and lemon trees, heavy with fruit. The floor was a violent geometric pattern of color that on closer look shifted into an erotic orgy of naked bodies in inventive forms of copulation.

Eve strode across blue breasts and green cocks to where Stiles lounged — posed, she thought — in a saffron ankle-duster.

"Some place."

He smiled, a surprisingly sweet expression on his craggy face. "Why live without drama? May I offer you anything before we begin, Lieutenant?"

"No, thanks."

"That will be all, Walter." He dismissed the droid with a wave of his hand, then gestured Eve to sit. "I realize this is routine for you, Lieutenant Dallas, but it's new and, I confess, exciting territory to me."

"Having an associate murdered in front of you is exciting?"

"After the initial shock, yes. It's human nature to find murder exciting and fascinating, don't you think? Else why does it play so well through the ages?" His eyes were deep, dark brown, and very shrewd.

"I could have taken any number of tacks with this interview. I'm a very skilled actor. I could be prostrate, nervous, frightened, confused, sorrowful. I chose honesty."

She thought of Carly Landsdowne. "It seems to be going around. Record on, Peabody," she said, and sat.

And sank into the clouds of cushions. Biting off an oath, Eve shoved herself up, sat on the edge of the couch. Balanced, she read off the pertinent data and issued the standard warning.

"Do you understand your rights and obligations in this matter, Mr. Stiles?"

"I do indeed." That sweet smile spread over his face again. "Might I say you read your lines with authority and panache, Lieutenant."

"Gee, thanks. Now, what was your relationship with Richard Draco?"

"Professional associates. Over the years, we worked together from time to time, most recently in the play that had its unusual opening night yesterday."

Oh yeah, Eve thought. *He's enjoying this. Milking this.* "And your personal relationship?"

"I don't know as we had one, in the way I assume you mean. Actors often . . ." He made a vague gesture with his hand and set the multicolored stone cuff bracelet on his wrist to winking cheerfully. "Gravitate toward each other, you might say: 'Like minds, like egos.' We marry each other with a kind of distressing regularity. It rarely lasts, as do the temporary friendships and other intimacies between players on the same stage."

"Still, you knew him for a number of years."

"Knew him, certainly, but we were never chums, let's say. In point of fact . . ." He paused again, his eyes glittering as happily as his bracelet. "I despised him. Loathed him. Found him a particularly vile form of life."

"For any particular reason?"

"For any number of very particular reasons." Stiles leaned forward, as if imparting confidences. "He was selfish, egocentric, rude, arrogant. All of those traits I could forgive, even appreciate as we who act require a certain sheen of vanity to do what we do. But under Richard's sheen was a sheer nastiness of spirit. He was a user, Lieutenant, one who not so quietly rejoiced at crushing hearts and souls. I'm not the least bit sorry he's dead, though I regret the method of his oh-so-timely demise."

"Why?"

"The play was brilliant, and my part one I relished. This incident will postpone if not cancel the rest of the run. It's very inconvenient."

"It's going to get a lot of publicity. That won't hurt you."

Stiles ran a fingertip down his chin. "Naturally not."

"And when the play resumes, it'll pack the house, night after night."

"There is that."

"So his death, in so dramatic and public a way is, on some levels, an advantage."

"Clever," he murmured, eyeing her more closely now. "That's cleverly thought out. We have a play within a play here, Lieutenant, and you're writing it well."

"You had access to the prop knife. And enough time to make the switch."

"I suppose I did. What a thought." He

blinked several times as if processing new data. "I'm a suspect. How entertaining! I had seen myself as a witness. Well, well. Yes, I suppose I had opportunity, but no real motive."

"You've stated, on record, you hated Richard Draco."

"Oh, my dear Lieutenant, if I arranged the death of every person I disliked, the stage would be littered with bodies. But the fact is, however much I detested Richard on a personal level, I admired his talent. He was an exceptional artist, and that is the only reason I agreed to work with him again. The world might have rid itself of a nasty, small-minded man, but the theater has lost one of its brightest lights."

"And you, one of your toughest competitors."

Stiles's eyebrows lifted. "No indeed. Richard and I were much different types. I don't recall that we ever competed for the same role."

Eve nodded. It would be easy enough to check that data. She shifted tactics. "What's your relationship with Areena Mansfield?"

"She's a friend, one I admire as a woman and as an associate." He lowered his eyes, shook his head. "This business is very difficult for her. She's a delicate creature under it all. I hope you'll consider that."

His eyes, darker now, with hints of anger in them, came back to Eve's. "Someone used her horribly. I can tell you this, Lieutenant. If I had decided to kill Richard Draco, I would have found a way to do so that wouldn't have involved a friend. There were two victims on stage last night, and my heart breaks for her."

"An operator," Eve murmured as they rode down to lobby level. "Slick, smart, and self-satisfied. Of all the actors, he's the one with the most experience. He knows the theater in and out."

"If he's really a friend of Mansfield's, would he have set it up so she killed Draco? Planted the weapon in her dressing room?"

"Why not?" Eve strode out of the building, flipped the doorman a sneer. "It's theatrical, and if you wind it all around, the plant was so obvious it looks like a plant. So . . ." She climbed behind the wheel, drummed her fingers on it, and frowned. "Whoever planted it wanted us to find it, wanted us to know it was put there to toss suspicion on Mansfield. Otherwise, it's just stupid, and whoever set the murder up isn't. I want to know who worked backstage who wanted to be on it. Let's see how many frustrated actors were doing tech duty on this thing."

Eve pulled away from the curb. "Toss that ball to Feeney," she ordered Peabody, and used her car 'link to contact the morgue.

Morse, the chief medical examiner, came on-screen. His luxurious hair was slicked back to show off a duo of gold and silver hoops in his right ear. "I was expecting you, Dallas. You cops are damned demanding."

"We get our rocks off hassling dead doctors. What have you got on Draco?"

"He's most sincerely dead." Morse smiled thinly. "Single stab wound to the heart did the job quickly and neatly. No other wounds or injuries. He's had some excellent body sculpting work over the years, and a recent tummy toner. A superior practitioner, in my opinion, as the laser marks are microscopic. His liver shows some rehabilitation. I'd say your guy was a serious drinker and had at least one treatment to revitalize. He did, however, have a lovely little mix of illegals in his system at time of death. Exotica and Zing, with a soupçon of Zeus. He chased that with a double shot of unblended scotch."

"Hell of a combo."

"You bet. This guy was a serious abuser, who continued to pay to have his body put back in shape. This kind of cycle eventually takes its toll, but even at this rate, he likely had another twenty good years in him."

"Not anymore. Thanks, Morse."

"Any chance of getting me seats when this play goes back on? You got the connections," he added with a wink.

She sighed a little. "I'll see what I can do."

chapter four

The trip from Stiles's rarified uptown air to Alphabet City's aroma of overturned recyclers and unwashed sidewalk sleepers was more than a matter of blocks. They left the lofty buildings with their uniformed doormen, the pristine glide-carts and serene air traffic for prefab, soot-scarred complexes, blatting maxibuses, and sly-eyed street thieves.

Eve immediately felt more at home.

Michael Proctor lived on the fourth floor of one of the units tossed up haphazardly after the devastation of the Urban Wars. At election time, city officials made lofty speeches about revitalizing the area, made stirring promises to fight the good fight against neglect, crime, and the general decay of that ailing sector of the city.

After the elections, the entire matter went back in the sewer to rot and ripen for another term.

Still, people had to live somewhere. Eve imagined a struggling actor who managed bit parts and understudy roles couldn't afford to pay much for housing.

Eve's initial background check revealed that Michael Proctor was currently six weeks behind on his rent and had applied for Universal Housing Assistance.

Which meant desperation, she mused. Most applicants to UHA became so strangled, so smothered in red tape reeled out by the sticky fingers of bureaucrats, they stumbled off into the night and were pitifully grateful to find a bed in one of the shelters.

She imagined that stepping into Draco's bloody shoes would considerably up Proctor's salary. Money was an old motive, as tried as it was true.

Eve considered double-parking on Seventh, then, spotting a parking slot on the second level street side, went into a fast vertical lift that had Peabody yelping, and shot forward to squeeze in between a rusted sedan and a battered air bike.

"Nice job." Peabody thumped a fist on her heart to get it going again.

Eve flipped on the On Duty light to keep the meter droids at bay, then jogged down the ramp to street level. "This guy had something tangible to gain by Draco's death. He's got a good shot at the starring role — if only temporarily. That gives him an ego, a career, and a financial boost all rolled into one. Nothing popped on his record, but every criminal has to start somewhere."

"I love your optimistic view of humanity, sir."

"Yeah, I'm a people-lover all right." She glanced at the street hustler on air skates, eyed his wide canvas shoulder bag. "Hey!" She jabbed a finger at him as he hunched his shoulders and sulked. "You set up that game on this corner, I'm going to be insulted. Take it off, two blocks minimum, and I'll pretend I didn't see your ugly face."

"I'm just trying to make a living."

"Make it two blocks over."

"Shit." He shifted his bag, then scooted off, heading west through the billowing steam from a glide-cart.

Peabody sniffed hopefully. "Those soy dogs smell fresh."

"They haven't been fresh for a decade. Put your stomach on hold."

"I can't. It has a mind of its own." Glancing back wistfully at the glide-cart, Peabody followed Eve into the grimy building.

At one time the place had boasted some level of security. But the lock on outer doors had been drilled out, likely by some enterprising kid who was now old enough for retirement benefits. The foyer was the width of a porta-john and the color of dried mud. The old mail slots were scarred and broken. Above one, in hopeful red ink, was M. Proctor.

Eve glanced at the skinny elevator, the tangle of raw wires poking out of its control plate. She dismissed it, and headed up the stairs.

Someone was crying in long, pitiful sobs. Behind a door on level two came the roaring sounds of an arena football game and someone's foul cursing at a botched play. She smelled must, urine gone stale, and the sweet scent of old Zoner.

On level three there was classical music, something she'd heard Roarke play. Accompanying it were rhythmic thumps.

"A dancer," Peabody said. "I've got a cousin who made it to the Regional Ballet Company in Denver. Somebody's doing jetés. I used to want to be one."

"A dancer?" Eve glanced back. Peabody's cheeks were pretty and pink from the climb.

"Yeah, well, when I was a kid. But I don't have the build. Dancers are built more like you. I went to the ballet with Charles a couple of weeks back. All the ballerinas were tall and skinny. Makes me sick."

"Hmmm." It was the safest response

when Peabody mentioned her connection to the licensed companion, Charles Monroe.

"I'm built more like an opera singer. Sturdy," Peabody added with a grimace.

"You into opera now?"

"I've been a few times. It's okay." She blew out a relieved breath when they reached the fourth floor and tried not to be irritated that Eve wasn't winded. "Charles goes for that culture stuff."

"Must keep you busy, juggling him and McNab."

Peabody grinned. "I thought there was no me and McNab in your reality."

"Shut up, Peabody." Annoyed, Eve rapped on Proctor's door. "Was that a snort?"

"No, sir." Peabody sucked it in and tried to look serious. "Absolutely not. I think my stomach's growling."

"Shut that up, too." She held her badge up when she heard footsteps approaching the door and the peephole. The building didn't run to soundproofing.

A series of clicks and jangles followed. She counted five manual locks being disengaged before the door opened.

The face that poked into the crack was a study of God's generosity. Or a really good face sculptor. Pale gold skin stretched taut and smooth over long cheekbones and a heroic, square jaw that boasted a pinpoint dimple. The mouth was full and firm, the nose narrow and straight, and the eyes the true green of organic emeralds.

Michael Proctor framed this gift with a silky flow of rich brown hair worn with a few tumbling, boyish curls. As his eyes darted from Eve to Peabody and back, he streamed long fingers through the mass of it, slicking it back before he tried out a hesitant smile.

"Um . . . Lieutenant Houston."

"Dallas."

"Right. I knew it was somewhere in Texas." Nerves had his voice jumping over the words, but he stepped back, widening the opening. "I'm still pretty shaken up. I keep thinking it's all some kind of mistake."

"If it is, it's a permanent one." Eve scanned what there was of the apartment. The single room held a ratty sleep chair Proctor hadn't bothered to make up for the day, a skinny table that held a low-end telelink/computer combo, a pole lamp with a torn shade, and a three-drawer wall chest.

For some, she supposed, acting wasn't lucrative.

"Um . . . let me get . . . um." Coloring slightly, he opened the long closet, fumbled inside, and eventually came out with a small folding chair. "Sorry. I don't do much more than sleep here, so it's not company friendly."

"Don't think of us as company. Record on, Peabody. You can sit, Mr. Proctor, if you'd be more comfortable."

"I'm . . ." His fingers danced with each other, tips to tips. "I'm fine. I don't really know how to do this. I never worked in any police dramas. I tend to be cast in period pieces or romantic comedies."

"Good thing I've worked in a number of police dramas," Eve said mildly. "You just answer the questions, and we'll be fine."

"Okay. All right." After glancing around the room as if he'd never seen it before, he finally sat on the chair. Crossed his legs, uncrossed them. Smiled hopefully.

He looked, Eve thought, like some schoolboy called down to the principal's office for a minor infraction.

"Dallas, Lieutenant Eve, in interview with Proctor, Michael, in subject's residence. Peabody, Officer Delia, as aide."

Watching Proctor, she recited the revised Miranda. As he listened, he tapped his fingers on his knees and succeeded in looking as guilty as a man with six ounces of Zeus in each pocket.

"Do you understand your rights and obligations in this matter?"

"Yes, I think. Do I need a lawyer?" He looked up at Eve like a puppy, one hoping not to be whacked on the nose for spotting the carpet. "I've got a representative, a theatrical rep. Maybe I should call her?"

"That's up to you." And would waste time and complicate matters. "You can request one at any time during the interview. If you prefer, we can move the process down to Central."

"Well now. Gosh." He blew out a breath, glanced toward his link. "I don't guess I'll bother her now. She's pretty busy."

"Why don't you start by telling me what happened last night."

"You mean . . ." He shuddered visibly. "I was in the wings. Stage left. It was brilliant, just brilliant. I remember thinking that if the play had a long run, I'd get a chance to be Vole. Draco was bound to miss a performance or two along the way . . ."

He trailed off, looked stunned, then appalled. "I don't mean to say . . . I never wished for anything bad to happen to him. It was more thinking that he'd catch a cold or something, or maybe just need a night off. Like that."

"Sure. And what did you see from the wings, stage left, in the last scene?"

"He was perfect," Proctor murmured, those deep green eyes going dreamy. "Arrogant, careless, smooth. The way he celebrated his acquittal even as he cast Christine off like a leftover bone. His pleasure in winning, in circumventing the system, fooling everyone. Then the shock, the shock in his eyes, in his body, when she turned on him with the knife. I watched, knowing I could never reach that high. Never find so much in myself. I didn't realize, even after everyone broke character, it didn't sink in."

He lifted his hands, let them fall. "I'm not sure it has yet."

"When did you realize that Draco wasn't acting?"

"I think — I think when Areena screamed. At least, I knew then that something was horribly wrong. Then everything happened so quickly. People were running to him, and shouting. They brought the curtain down, very fast," he remembered. "And he was still lying there."

Hard to jump up and take your bows with eight inches of steel in your heart, Eve thought. "What was your personal relationship with Richard Draco?"

"I don't suppose we had one."

"You had no personal conversations with

91

him, no interactions?"

"Well, um . . ." The fingers started dancing again. "Sure, we spoke a couple of times. I'm afraid I irritated him."

"In what way?"

"You see, Lieutenant, I watch. People," he added with another of those shaky smiles. "To develop character types, to learn. I guess my watching him put Draco off, and he told me to keep out of his sight or . . . or he'd, hmmm, he'd see to it that the only acting job I got was in sex holograms. I apologized right away."

"And?"

"He threw a paperweight at me. The prop paperweight on Sir Wilfred's desk." Proctor winced. "He missed. I'm sure he meant to."

"That must have pissed you off."

"No, not really. I was embarrassed to have annoyed him during rehearsal. He had to take the rest of the day off to calm down."

"A guy threatens your livelihood, throws a paperweight at you, and you don't get pissed off?"

"It was Draco." Proctor's tone was reverent. "He's — he was — one of the finest actors of the century. The pinnacle. His temperament is part — was part — of making him what he was."

"You admired him."

"Oh yes. I've studied his work as long as I can remember. I have discs and recordings of every one of his plays. When I had a chance to understudy Vole, I jumped at it. I think it's the turning point in my career." His eyes were shining now. "All my life I dreamed of walking the same stage as Richard Draco, and there I was."

"But you wouldn't walk that stage unless something happened to him."

"Not exactly." In his enthusiasm, Proctor leaned forward. The cheap chair creaked ominously. "But I had to rehearse the same lines, the same blocking, know the same cues. It was almost like *being* him. In a way. You know."

"Now, you'll have a shot at stepping onto his — what do you call it — his mark, won't you?"

"Yes." Proctor's smile was brilliant, and quickly gone. "I know how awful, how selfish and cold that must sound. I don't mean it that way."

"You're having some financial difficulties, Mr. Proctor."

He flushed, winced, tried that smile again. "Yes, ah, well . . . One doesn't go into the theater for money but for love."

"But money comes in handy for things like eating and keeping a roof over your head. You're behind on your rent."

"A little."

"The understudy job pays enough to keep you current with your rent. You gamble, Mr. Proctor?"

"Oh, no. No, I don't."

"Just careless with money?"

"I don't think so. I invest, you see. In myself. Acting and voice lessons, body maintenance, enhancement treatments. They don't come cheap, especially in the city. I suppose all that seems frivolous to you, Lieutenant, but it's part of my craft. Tools of the trade. I was considering a part-time job to help defray the expenses."

"No need to consider that now, is there? With Draco out of the way."

"I suppose not." He paused, considering it. "I wasn't sure how I was going to manage the time. It'll be easier to —" He broke off, sucked in a breath. "I don't mean that the way it sounds. It's just that following your line of thinking, it takes some strain off my mind. I'm used to doing without money, Lieutenant. Whatever else, the theater's lost one of its finest, and one of my personal idols. But I guess I'd feel better if I said — if I was honest and said — that there's a part of me that's thrilled to think that I'll play Vole. Even temporarily."

He sighed, long and loud, closed his eyes. "Yeah, yeah, I do feel better. I wish he'd just caught a cold, though."

Eve's head was throbbing lightly as she walked back up the steps to her car. "Nobody's that naive," she muttered. "Nobody's that guileless."

"He's from Nebraska." Peabody scanned her pocket unit.

"From where?"

"Nebraska." Peabody waved a hand, vaguely west. "Farm boy. Done a lot of regional theater, some video, billboard ads, bit parts on-screen. He's only been in New York three years." She climbed into the car. "They still grow them pretty guileless in Nebraska. I think it's all that soy and corn."

"Whatever, he stays on the short list. His fee for walking into the part of Vole is a big step up from watching in the wings. He's living like a transient in that dump. Money's a motivator, and so's ambition. He wanted to be Draco. What better way than to eliminate Draco?"

"I've got this idea."

Eve glanced at her wrist unit to check the time as she zipped down into traffic. Goddamn press conference. "Which is?"

"Okay, it's more of a theory."

"Spill it."

"If it's good, can I get a soy dog?"

"Christ. What's the theory?"

"So, they're all actors in a play. A good actor slides into the character during the performance. Stays there. It's all immediate, but another part of them is distant — gauging the performances, remembering the staging, picking up vibes from the audience and stuff like that. My theory is whoever switched the knives was performing."

"Yeah, performing murder."

"Sure, but this is like another level. They could be part of the play and watch it go down without actually doing the crime. The objective's reached, and it's all still a role. Even if it's a tech who did it, it's all part of the play. Vole's dead. He's supposed to be. The fact that Draco's dead, too, just makes it all the more satisfying."

Eve mulled it over, then pulled over at the next corner where a glide-cart smoked and sizzled.

"So it's a good theory?"

"It's decent. Get your soy dog."

"You want anything?"

"Coffee, but not off that bug coach."

Peabody sighed. "Wow, that sure stirs my appetite." But she got out, beelined through the pedestrian traffic, and ordered the double wide soy dog and a mega tube of Diet Coke to convince herself she was watching her weight.

"Happy now?" Eve asked when Peabody dropped back into the passenger seat and stuffed the end of the dog into her mouth.

"Ummm. Good. Wanna bite?"

Peabody was saved from a scathing response by the beep of the car 'link. Nadine Furst, reporter for Channel 75, floated on-screen. "Dallas. I need to talk to you, soon as you can manage."

"Yeah, I bet." Eve ignored the transmission and whipped around the corner to head back to Central. "Why she thinks I'll give her an exclusive one-on-one before a scheduled press conference, I don't know."

"Because you're friends?" Peabody hazarded with her mouth full of soy dog and rehydrated onion flakes.

"Nobody's that friendly."

"Dallas." Nadine's pretty, camera-ready face was strained, as Eve noted with mild curiosity, was her perfectly pitched voice. "It's important, and it's . . . personal. Please. If you're screening transmissions, give me a break here. I'll meet you anywhere you say, whenever you say."

Cursing, Eve engaged transmission. "The

Blue Squirrel. Now."

"Dallas —"

"I can give you ten minutes. Make it fast."

It had been a while since she'd swung through the doors into the Blue Squirrel. As joints went, there were worse, but not by much. Still, the dingy club held some sentimental attachment for Eve. At one time, her friend Mavis had performed there, slithering, bouncing, and screaming out songs in costumes that defied description.

And once, during a difficult and confusing case, Eve had gone in with the sole purpose of drinking her mind to mush.

There Roarke had tracked her down, hauled her out before she could accomplish the mission. That night, she'd ended up in his bed for the first time.

Sex with Roarke, she'd discovered, did a much better job of turning the mind to mush than a vatful of screamers.

So the Squirrel, with its debatable menu and disinterested servers, held some fond memories.

She slid into a booth, considered ordering the hideous excuse for coffee for old times' sake, then watched Nadine come in.

"Thanks." Nadine stood by the booth, slowly unwinding a brilliant multicolored scarf from around her neck. Her fingers plucked at the long, dark fringe. "Peabody, would you mind giving us a minute here?"

"No problem." Peabody pushed herself out of the booth, and because Nadine's eyes were clouded, gave the reporter a quick, reassuring squeeze on the arm. "I'll just go sit at the bar and watch the holo-games."

"Thanks. Been a while since we've been in here."

"Never long enough," Eve commented when Nadine took her seat across the wobbly table. At a server's approach, Eve merely took out her badge and set it in clear view on the table. She didn't think she or Nadine were in the mood for a snack, much less possible ptomaine. "What's the problem?"

"I'm not sure. Maybe there isn't one." Nadine closed her eyes, shook back her hair.

She'd added some blonde streaky things in it, Eve noticed. She could never figure out why people were always changing colors. All that maintenance baffled her.

"Richard Draco," Nadine said.

"I'm not going to discuss the case with you." Eve scooped up her badge with one impatient swipe. "Press conference at fourteen hundred."

"I slept with him."

Eve paused in the act of getting out of the booth, settled back, and took a closer look at Nadine's face. "When?"

"Not long after I got the on-air job at 75. I wasn't doing the crime beat then. Mostly fluff stories, social gigs, celebrity profiles. Anyway, he contacted me. Wanted to tell me how good I was, how much he enjoyed watching my reports. Which were pretty damn solid, considering I hated every fucking minute of it."

She picked up her scarf, wound it around her hand. Unwound it. Set it down again. "He asked me to dinner. I was flattered, he was gorgeous. One thing led to another."

"Okay. That would have been, what, five years ago?"

"Six, actually, six." Nadine lifted a hand, rubbed her fingers over her mouth. It was a gesture Eve had never seen her make before. On-air reporters didn't like mussing their makeup.

"I said one thing led to another," she continued, "but it led there romantically. We didn't just jump into bed. We dated for a couple of weeks. Quiet dinners, theater, walks, parties. Then he asked me to go away with him for the weekend, to Paris."

This time Nadine simply dropped her head in her hands. "Oh Jesus. Jesus, Dallas."

"You fell for him."

"Oh yeah. I fell for him. All the way. I mean I was gone, stupid in love with the son of a bitch. We were together for three months, and I actually . . . Dallas, I was thinking marriage, kids, the house in the country. The whole ball."

Eve shifted in her seat. Emotional declarations always made her feel clumsy. "So, I take it things didn't work out."

Nadine stared for a moment, then let her head fall back with a long, shaky laugh. "Yeah, you could say things didn't work out. I found out he was two-timing me. Hell, three- and four-timing me. I caught a gossip report right before I went on air, and there was Richard cuddled up with some big-breasted blonde at some swank club up-town. When I confronted him about it, he just smiled and said he enjoyed women. So what?

"So what," she murmured. "The fucker broke my heart and didn't have the decency to lie to me. He even talked me back into bed. I'm ashamed of that. I let him talk me back into bed, and when I was still wet from him, he takes a call from another woman. Makes a date with her while I'm lying there naked."

"How long was he hospitalized?"

Nadine managed a weak smile. "There's the pity. I cried. I sat there in his bed and cried like a baby."

"Okay, I'm sorry. It was a raw deal. But it was six years ago."

"I saw him the night he was killed."

"Oh hell, Nadine."

"He called me."

"Shut up. Just shut up right now. Don't say another word to me. Get a lawyer."

"Dallas." Nadine's hand shot out, and her fingers dug into Eve's wrist. "Please. I need to tell you everything. Then I need you to tell me how much trouble I could be in."

"Fuck. Fuck. Fuck." Eve jabbed at the menu, ordered coffee after all. "I haven't read you your rights. I'm not going to. I can't use anything you say to me."

"He called me. Said he'd been thinking about me, about old times. He wondered if I'd like to get together. I started to tell him to go to hell, but I realized, even after all that time, I wanted some of my own back. I wanted to burn his ass in person. So I agreed to drop by his hotel. They'll have me on the security discs."

"Yeah, they will."

"He'd ordered up a dinner for two. The bastard remembered what we'd had on our first date. Maybe he orders it on all his first dates. It would be just like him. May he rot in hell."

She blew out a breath. "Well, I pulled out the stops myself. I'd really put myself together. New dress. New hair. I let him pour me champagne, and we made small talk while we drank. I knew his moves. I remembered every one of them. And when he ran his fingertips down my cheek, gave me that long, soulful look, I threw my champagne in his face and said everything I wish I'd said six years ago. We had a terrible fight. Broken glass, vicious words, a couple of slaps on both sides."

"He got physical with you?"

"More the other way around, I guess. I slapped him, he slapped me back. Then I punched him in the gut. That took the air out of him. While he was wheezing, I walked out, feeling really good."

"Will the security disc show you looking disheveled, emotional?"

"I don't know." She rubbed her fingers over her mouth again. "Maybe. I didn't think of that. But no matter what, I'm glad I went. I'm glad I finally stood up for myself. But then, Dallas, I made a really big mistake."

The coffee slid greasily through the serving slot. Eve simply pushed it toward

Nadine, waited until her friend gulped it down.

"I went to the theater last night. I wanted to prove to myself that I could go, see him, and feel nothing." The coffee was barely lukewarm, but it managed to take the worst chill out of her belly. "I did. I felt nothing. It was like a celebration to finally have that bastard out of my system. I even, oh God, I even went backstage — used my press pass — at intermission to tell him."

"You talked to him backstage last night?"

"No. When I got back there, started toward his dressing room, it occurred to me that confronting him again made him too important. It would only feed his ego. So I left. I went out the stage door, and I took a long walk. I did some window-shopping. I stopped off at a hotel bar and bought myself a glass of wine. Then I went home. This morning, I heard . . . I panicked. Called in sick. I've been sick all day, then I realized I had to talk to you. I had to tell you. I don't know what to do."

"When you went back, you headed for the dressing rooms. Nowhere else?"

"No, I swear."

"Did anyone see you?"

"I don't know. I imagine. I wasn't trying to be invisible."

"I want to do this formally, putting it on record that you came to me with this information. That's the best for you. Meanwhile, I want you to get a lawyer, a good one. Do it quietly and tell the rep everything you told me."

"Okay."

"Did you leave anything out, Nadine? Anything?"

"No. That's all. I only saw him that once in his hotel room, then again onstage. I might have been a sap, Dallas, but I've come a long way. And I'm no coward. If I'd wanted the son of a bitch dead, I'd have killed him myself, not pawned it off on someone else."

"Oh yeah." Eve picked up the coffee, finished it up. "I know it. Talk to the lawyer. We'll do the interview tomorrow." She rose, then after a slight hesitation, patted Nadine's shoulder. "It'll be okay."

"You know what sucks here, Dallas? I was feeling so damn good about everything. Ever since — you know I do the therapy thing with Mira."

Eve shifted her feet. "Yeah."

"One of the things we got down to is I haven't been open to love — not the real thing — since Richard. He really messed me up. Then last night, when I was in that hotel bar, I realized that now I could be. I wanted to be. Lousy timing all around. Thanks for listening."

"Don't mention it." Eve signaled for Peabody. "Nadine, take that literally."

chapter five

The calendar claimed spring was just around the corner, but it was taking a slow walk. Eve drove home in a thin, spitting sleet that was nearly as nasty as her mood.

Press conferences annoyed her.

The only good thing about it, as far as she was concerned, was that it was over. Between that and a day spent in interviews that gave her no more than a murky picture of people and events, she was edgy and dissatisfied.

The fact was, she shouldn't be going home. There was more field work that could be, should be done. But she'd cut Peabody loose, much to her aide's undisguised delight.

She'd take an hour, she told herself. Maybe two. Do some pacing, juggle her thoughts into some sort of order. She chugged and dodged through bad-tempered traffic and tried to block out the irritatingly chirpy sky blimp shouting about the new spring fashions on sale at Bloomingdale's.

She got caught at a light, and in a stinking

stream of smoke from a glide-cart currently on fire and being sprayed with gel foam by its unhappy operator. Since the flames seemed reasonably under control, she left him to it and tagged Feeney via her car 'link.

"Progress?"

"Some. I got you backgrounds and current locations, financial data, and criminal records on cast and crew, including permanent theater personnel."

Eve's voice calmed. "All?"

"Yeah." Feeney rubbed his chin. "Well, I can't take full credit. Told you we were backed up here. Roarke passed it on."

Her agitation returned. "Roarke?"

"He got in touch early this afternoon, figured I'd be doing the search. He had all the data anyway. Saved me some time here."

"Always helpful," she muttered.

"I shot it to your office unit."

"Fine, great."

Feeney kept rubbing his chin. Eve began to suspect the gesture was to hide a grin. "I started McNab on running patterns, probabilities, percentages. It's a long list, so it's not going to be quick. But I figure we should have simple eliminations by tomorrow, with a most-likely list to shuffle in with your interview results. How's it going?"

"Slow." She inched her way across the intersection, spied a break in traffic, and went for it. The chorus of horns exceeded noise pollution levels and made her smile thinly. "We managed to make the murder weapon. Standard kitchen knife. It came right out of the sublevel kitchen at the theater."

"Open access?"

"To cast and crew, not to the public. I had a uniform pick up the security discs. We'll see what we see. Look, I'm going to run some probability scans myself, see if they jibe with yours. I should have some profile from Mira tomorrow. Let's see if we can whittle this down from a few thousand suspects. How far's McNab gotten?"

"He got a ways before I sprang him for the day."

"You let him go?"

"He had a date," Feeney said and grinned.

Eve winced. "Shut up, Feeney," she ordered and broke transmission.

She brooded, because it made her feel better, then shot through the gates of home. Even in miserable weather, it was magnificent. Maybe more magnificent, she thought, in that gloom and gray.

The sprawling lawns were faded from winter, the naked trees shimmering with wet. *Atmosphere,* she supposed Roarke would say. It was all about atmosphere, and it showcased the glorious stone-and-glass structure with its towers, its turrets, its sweep of terraces and balconies that he had claimed as his own.

It belonged on a cliff somewhere, she mused, with the sea boiling and pounding below. The city, with its crowds and noise and sneaky despair couldn't beat its way through those tall iron gates to the oasis he'd built out of canniness, ruthlessness, sheer will, and the driving need to bury the miseries of his childhood.

Every time she saw it, her mind was of two conflicting parts. One told her she didn't belong there. The other told her she belonged nowhere else.

She left the car at the base of the front steps, knowing Summerset would send it lumbering into the garage on principle. The pea-green city issue offended his sensibilities, she supposed, nearly as much as she did herself.

She jogged up the steps in her scarred boots and walked inside to the warmth, the beauty, and all the style money could buy and power could maintain.

Summerset was waiting for her, his thin face dour, his mouth in a flattened line. "Lieutenant. You surprise me. You've arrived home in a timely fashion."

"Don't you have anything better to do than to clock me in and out of here?" She stripped off her jacket, tossed it on the newel post to annoy him. "You could be out scaring small children."

Summerset sniffed and to annoy her, picked up her damp leather jacket with the delicate tips of two fingers. He examined it with dark, disapproving eyes. "What? No blood today?"

"That can still be arranged. Roarke home yet?"

"Roarke is in the lower-level recreation area."

"A boy and his toys." She strode past him.

"You're tracking wet on the floor."

She glanced back, glanced down. "Well, that'll give you something to do."

Well satisfied with their evening exchange, Summerset went off to dry her jacket.

She took the steps, then wound her way through the pool house where wisps of steam danced invitingly over water of deep, secret blue. She thought fleetingly about stripping to the skin and diving in, but there was Roarke to deal with.

She bypassed the gym, the dressing area, and a small greenhouse. When she opened the door of the recreation area, the noise poured through.

It was, in Eve's opinion, a twelve-year-old's wet dream. Though she herself had long since ceased dreaming of toys by the age of twelve. Perhaps Roarke had, too, which was why, she supposed, he indulged himself now.

There were two pool tables, three multiperson VR tubes, a variety of screens designed for transmissions or games, a small holodeck, and a forest of brightly colored, noisy game stations.

Roarke stood at one, long legs comfortably spread, elegant hands on either side of a long, waist-height box with a glass top. His fingers were tapping rhythmically on what seemed to be large buttons. The top of the box was a riot of lights.

Cops and Robbers, she read and had to roll her eyes as a high-pitched siren began to scream. There was an explosion of what she recognized as gunfire, the wild squeal of tires on pavement, and blue and red lights crowned the vertical length of the box as it began to spin.

Eve hooked her thumbs in her front pockets and strolled over to him. "So this is what you do with your downtime."

"Hello, darling." He never took his eyes

off the duo of silver balls that raced and ricochetted under the glass. "You're home early."

"Only temporarily. I want to talk to you."

"Mmm-hmm. One minute."

She opened her mouth to object, then nearly jumped as bells began to clang and lights shot like lasers. "What the hell is this thing?"

"Antique — prime condition. Just — fucker — just got it in today." He bumped the machine lightly with his hip. "It's a pinball machine, late–twentieth century."

"Cops and Robbers?"

"How could I resist?" The machine ordered him to "Freeze!" in menacing tones, and Roarke responded by zipping his remaining ball up a chute where it banged and bumped against a trio of diamond shapes, then slid into a hole.

"Free ball." He stepped back, rolled his shoulders. "But that can wait." As he leaned down to kiss her, she slapped a hand on his chest.

"Hold on, ace. What do you mean by calling Feeney?"

"Offering my assistance to New York's finest," he said easily. "Doing my duty as a concerned citizen. Give us a bite of this." So saying, he drew her against him and nipped at her lower lip. "Let's play a game."

"I'm primary."

"Darling, you most certainly are."

"On the case, smart guy."

"That, as well. And as such, you'd have requested the data from the theater's files and funneled it to Feeney. Now it's done. Your hair's damp," he said and sniffed at it.

"It's sleeting." She wanted to argue but didn't see the point when he was exactly right. "Why do you have deep background and extensive data on everyone involved with The Globe and this production?"

"Because, Lieutenant, everyone involved with The Globe and this production works for me." He eased back, picked up the bottle of beer he'd set beside the machine. "Had an annoying day, have you?"

"Mostly." When he offered the bottle, she started to shake her head, then shrugged and took a small swig. "I wanted to take a couple of hours to clear my mind."

"Me, too. And I've the perfect method. Strip pinball."

She snorted. "Get out."

"Oh well, if you're afraid you'll lose, I'll give you a handicap." He smiled when he said it, knowing his wife very well.

"I'm not afraid I'll lose." She shoved the beer back at him. Struggled. Lost. "How

114

much of a handicap?"

Still smiling, he toed off both his shoes. "That, and five hundred points a ball — seems fair, as you're a novice."

She considered, studying the machine. "You just got this in today, right?"

"Just a bit ago, yes."

"You go first."

"My pleasure."

And as he enjoyed watching her fume, compete and lose herself in the moment, it proved to be. Within twenty minutes, she'd lost her boots, her socks, her weapon harness, and was currently losing her shirt.

"Damn it! This thing is rigged." Out of patience, she threw her weight against the machine, then hissed when her flippers froze. "Tilt? Why does it keep saying that to me?"

"Perhaps you're a bit too aggressive. Why don't I help you with this," he offered and began unbuttoning her shirt.

She slapped his hands away. "I can do it. You're cheating." While she tugged off her shirt, she scowled at him. She was down to a sleeveless undershirt and her trousers. "I don't know how, but you're cheating."

"It couldn't be that I'm just the superior player."

"No."

He laughed, then pulled her in front of him. "I'll give you another go here, and help you out. Now." He placed his fingers over hers on the control buttons. "You have to learn to finesse it rather than attack it. The idea is to keep the ball lively, and in play."

"I got the idea, Roarke. You want it to smash up against everything."

Wisely, he swallowed a chuckle. "More or less. All right, here it comes."

He released the ball, leaned into her, watching over her shoulder. "No, no, wait. You don't just flip madly about. Wait for it." His fingers pressed over hers and sent the little silver ball dancing to the tune of automatic weapon fire.

"I want the gold bars over there."

"In time, all in good time." He leaned down to skim his lips over the back of her neck. "There now, you've evaded the squad car and racked yourself up five thousand points."

"I want the gold."

"Why am I not surprised? Let's see what we can do for you. Feel my hands?"

He was pressed into her back, snug and cozy. Eve turned her head. "That's not your hands."

His grin flashed. "Right you are. These are." Slowly, he skimmed those clever hands up her body, over her breasts. Beneath the thin cotton, he felt her heart give one fast leap. "You could forfeit." His mouth went to the curve of her neck this time, with the light scrape of teeth.

"In a pig's eye."

He caught the lobe of her ear between his teeth, and the resulting jolt to her system had her fingers jabbing into the buttons. Even as she moaned, the machine exploded under her hands.

"What? What?"

"You got the gold. Bonus points." He tugged at the button of her trousers. "Extra ball. Nice job."

"Thanks." Bells were clanging. In the machine, in her head. She let him turn her so they were face-to-face. "Game's not over."

"Not nearly." His mouth came down on hers, hot and possessive. His hands had already snaked under her shirt to cup her breasts. "I want you. I always want you."

Breathless, eager, she dragged at his shirt. "You should've lost a few times. You wouldn't be wearing so many clothes."

"I'll remember that." The need reared up so fast, so ripe, it burned. Her body was a treasure to him, the long, clean lines of it, the sleekness of muscle, the surprising delicacy of skin. Standing, wrapped tight, he sank into her.

She wanted to give. No one else had ever made her so desperate to give. Whatever she had. Whatever he would take. Through all the horrors of her life, through all the miseries of her work, this — what they brought to each other time and time again — was her personal miracle.

She found his flesh with her hands — firm, warm — and sighed deeply. She found his mouth with hers — rough, hungry — and she moaned.

When she would have pulled him to the floor, he turned, stumbled with her until her back was pressed against something cool and solid.

"Look at me."

His name caught in her throat as those skilled fingers slid over her, into her, and sent her spinning as madly as the silver ball under glass.

He watched her eyes cloud, then the rich brown of them go opaque as she came. "More. Again." While she shuddered, while her hands gripped his shoulders, he took her mouth, swallowed her cry of release.

His breath was as tattered as hers as he took her hips, lifted them, and plunged.

He pinned her, pummeled her system with a pleasure too outrageous for reason. Energized her so that she fought to give it back, beat for beat. When her hands slipped from his shoulders, she lifted them to his hair, fisted her fingers in all that black silk.

They drove each other up, and over.

"I didn't lose."

Roarke glanced over, smiled at the view of her pretty naked butt as she gathered up her clothes. "I didn't say you did."

"You're thinking it. I can hear you thinking it. I just don't have time to finish playing that stupid game."

"It'll hold." He fastened his trousers. "I'm hungry. Let's have something to eat."

"It'll have to be quick. I've got work. I want to go over and take a look at Draco's hotel room."

"That's fine then." Roarke wandered to the AutoChef, considered, and decided a cool, sleety night called for something homey. He ordered beef and barley stew for both of them. "I'll go with you."

"It's police business."

"Naturally. Just doing my civic duty again, Lieutenant." Because he knew that would irritate her, he offered her a bowl and a smile. "It's my hotel, after all."

"It would be." Because she knew he *meant* to irritate her, she scooped up a bite. And scalded her tongue. It wasn't a crime scene, she thought as she blew some of the heat from the second spoonful. And she could use Roarke's eyes, his mind, not that she wanted to admit it.

"Fine." She shrugged. "But you stay out of my way."

He nodded agreeably. Not that he had any intention of doing what she asked. Where was the fun in that? "Will we be picking up Peabody?"

"She's off. She had a date."

"Ah. With McNab?"

Eve felt her appetite take an abrupt nose-dive. "She doesn't date McNab." At Roarke's look of surprise, she stubbornly stuffed more stew in her mouth. "Look, maybe, in some alternate universe far, far away, they have sex. But they're not dating. That's it."

"Darling, there comes a time, however sad for Mum, when the children must leave home."

"Shut up." She jabbed her spoon at him. "I mean it. They are *not* dating," she insisted, and polished off her stew.

Some might have called Ian McNab's ramshackle apartment on the Lower West Side an alternate universe. It was a guy's space, badly decorated, heavy on the sports memorabilia, and scattered with dirty dishes.

While he did, occasionally, think to stuff some of the worst of the debris in some dusty closet when female company was expected, it was a long way from the sumptuous space of Roarke's home, and it smelled a great deal like overcooked veggie hash. But it worked for him.

At the moment, with his heart stuttering and his skin slick from sex, it worked just fine.

"Jesus, Peabody." He flopped over on his back, much like a landed trout. He didn't bother to gasp for air. He had a lush, naked woman in his bed. He could die a happy man. "We had to break a record that time. We ought to be writing this down."

She lay where she was, stunned as she always was when she found herself in this situation with Ian McNab. "I can't feel my feet."

Obligingly he propped himself on his elbow, but as they'd ended up crosswise on the bed, he couldn't see past her knees. She had, he noted, really cute knees. "I don't think I bit them off. I'd remember." But with a grunt, he scooted down, just to be sure. "They're there, all right, both of them."

"Good. I'm going to need them later."

As the shock wore off, she blinked, stared at McNab's pretty profile, and wondered, not for the first time, when she'd lost her mind.

I'm naked in bed with McNab. Naked. In bed. McNab.

Jesus.

Always self-conscious about body flaws, she tugged at the knotted sheets. "Cold in here," she muttered.

"Bastard super cut the main furnace back first of March. Like it's his money. First chance I get, I'm rerouting the system."

He yawned hugely, dragged both hands through his long and tangled blond hair. His narrow shoulders seemed weighed down by the mass of it. Peabody had to order her fingers not to reach up to play with the long loops of reddish gold. He had skinny hips, with the right one currently decorated with a temp tattoo of a silver lightning bolt. It matched the four earrings winking in his left earlobe.

His skin was milk white, his eyes a cagey green. She still couldn't figure out why anything about him attracted her on a physical level, much less how she'd ended up having regular and outrageous sex with him when out of bed they spent most of their time annoying each other.

She'd liked to have said he wasn't her type, but she didn't think she actually had a type. Her luck with men was usually, distressingly, piss-poor.

"I'd better get going."

"Why? It's early." When she sat up, he leaned over and nipped suggestively at her shoulder. "I'm starving."

"Christ, McNab, we just finished having sex."

"That, too, but I was thinking more of pizza, loaded." He knew her weaknesses. "Let's fuel up."

Her taste buds stirred to attention. "I'm dieting."

"What for?"

She rolled her eyes, yanking the rumpled sheet around her as she climbed out of bed. "Because I'm pudgy."

"No, you're not. You're built." He caught the edge of the sheet, surprising her with his quickness, and pulled it down to her waist. "Seriously built."

As she fumbled for the sheet, he sprang up, caught her around the waist with an affectionate squeeze that both disarmed and worried her. "Come on, let's eat, then see what happens next. I've got some wine around here."

"If it's anything like the wine you had last time, I'd as soon dip a cup in the sewer."

"New bottle." He picked his bright orange jumpsuit off the floor, stepped into it. "You want some pants?"

The fact that he would offer her his pants made her want to pinch all four of his cheeks. "McNab, I couldn't have squeezed into your pants when I was twelve. I actually have an ass."

"True. That's okay; I love a woman in uniform." He strolled off, struggling not to brood. He always had to talk her into staying.

In the corner of the living area that doubled for his kitchen, he pulled out the bottle of wine he'd bought the day before when he'd been thinking of her. He thought about her just often enough to be demoralized. If he could keep her in bed, they'd be fine. He didn't have to think about his moves there, they just happened.

He flipped on his 'link. The pizza joint was keyed in on memory, in the primo position due to frequency of transmissions. He ordered a mongo pie, loaded, then dug out a corkscrew.

The damn wine had cost him twice what he usually spent. But when a guy was competing with a slick, experienced LC, he needed to hold his own. He didn't doubt Charles Monroe knew all about fine wines. He and Peabody probably took baths in champagne.

Since the image infuriated him, he glugged down half a glass of wine. Then he turned as Peabody came out of the bedroom. She was wearing her uniform pants with her shirt open at the throat. He wanted to lick her there, just there where the stiff cotton gave way to soft flesh.

Goddamn it.

"What's the matter?" she asked, noticing the scowl on his face. "They run out of pepperoni?"

"No, it's coming." He held out her glass of wine. "I was thinking . . . about work."

"Mmm." She sipped the wine, pursed her lips at its smooth and subtle fruity taste. "This is pretty good. You're running backgrounds on the Draco case, right?"

"Already done. Dallas should have them by now."

"Quick work."

He answered with a shrug. He didn't have to tell her Roarke had dropped the data in his lap. "We in EDD aim to please. Even after eliminations and probability scans, it's going to take days to shift the list down to a workable number. Guy gets his heart jabbed in front of a couple thousand people, it's complicated."

"Yeah." Peabody sipped again, then wandered off to drop into a chair. Without being aware of it on a conscious level, she was as comfortable in McNab's mess of an apartment as she was in her own tidy one. "Something's going on."

"Something's always going on."

"No, not the usual." She struggled with herself, brooded into her wine. If she didn't talk to someone, she'd explode. And hell, he was here. "Look, this is confidential."

"Okay." Since the pizza wouldn't arrive for a good ten minutes more, McNab snagged an open bag of soy chips. He settled on the arm of Peabody's chair. "What's the deal?"

"I don't know. Nadine Furst tagged the lieutenant today, and she was razzed. Nadine, I mean." Absently, Peabody reached into the bag. "You don't see Nadine razzed very often. She makes a meet with Dallas — a personal meet. It was serious. They stashed me across the room, but I could tell. And after, Dallas didn't say a word about it."

"Maybe it was just personal shit."

"No, Nadine's not going to ask for a meet like that unless there's trouble." Nadine was her friend, too, and part of Peabody was bruised that she'd been brushed aside. "I think it ties to the case. Dallas should've told me." Peabody crunched on chips. "She should trust me."

"Want me to poke around?"

"I can do my own poking. I don't need an E Division hotshot running plays for me."

"Suit yourself, She-Body."

"Just lay off. I don't even know why I told you. It's just sitting in my gut. Nadine's a friend. She's supposed to be a friend."

"You're jealous."

"Bullshit."

"Yeah, you are." He was beginning to have an intimate relationship with the feeling. "Dallas and Nadine are playing without you, so you're jealous. Girl Dynamics one oh one."

She shoved him off the arm of the chair. "You're an asshole."

"And there," he said as his security bell rang, "is the pizza."

chapter six

"Don't touch anything, and stay out of the way."

"Darling." Roarke watched Eve slip her master into the security lock on Penthouse A. "You're repeating yourself."

"That's because you never listen." Before she opened the door, she turned, met his eyes. "Why does a man whose primary residence is New York, whose main source of work is New York, opt to live in a hotel rather than a private residence?"

"First the panache. 'Mr. Draco keeps the penthouse at The Palace when in the city.' Next, the convenience. At the crook of a finger, whatever you need or want done for you can be. Is. And lastly, perhaps most tellingly, the utter lack of commitment. Everything around you is someone else's problem and responsibility."

"From what I've learned of Draco so far, that's the one I go for." She opened the door, stepped inside.

It belonged to Roarke, she thought, therefore it was plush and lush and perfect. If you went for that kind of thing.

The living area was enormous and elegantly furnished with walls of silky rose. The ceiling was arched and decorated with a complicated design of fruit and flowers around a huge glass and gold chandelier.

Three sofas, all in deep, cushy red were piled with pillows bright as jewels. Tables — and she suspected they were genuine wood and quite old — were polished like mirrors, as was the floor. The rug was an inch thick and matched the ceiling pattern grape for grape.

One wall was glass, the privacy screen drawn so that New York exploded with light and shape outside but couldn't intrude. There was a stone terrace beyond, and as the flowers decked in big stone pots were thriving, she assumed it was heated.

A glossy white piano stood at one end of the room, and at the other, carved wood panels hid what she assumed was a full entertainment unit. There were plants of thick and glossy foliage, glass displays holding pretty dust catchers she concluded were art, and no discernable sign of life.

"Housekeeping would have come in after he left for the theater," Roarke told her. "I can ask the team on duty that evening to come up and let you know the condition of the rooms at that time."

"Yeah." She thought of Nadine. If she knew the reporter, the condition of the rooms had been something approaching the wake of a tornado. She walked over to the panels, opened them, and studied the entertainment unit. "Unit on," she commanded, and the screen flickered to soft blue. "Play back last program."

With barely a hiccup, the unit burst into color and sound. Eve watched two figures slide and slither over a pool of black sheets. "Why do guys always get off watching other people fuck?"

"We're sick, disgusting, and weak. Pity us."

She started to laugh. Then the couple on the bed rolled. The woman's face, soft with pleasure, turned toward the camera. "Goddamn it. That's Nadine. Nadine and Draco."

In support, Roarke laid a hand on Eve's shoulder. "It wasn't taped here. That's not the bedroom. Her hair's different. I don't think it's recent."

"I'm going to have to take it in, prove it isn't. And I've got a damn sex tape of one of the media's cream as evidence on a murder case." She stopped the play, ejected the disc, and sealed it in an evidence bag from her field kit.

"Damn it. Damn it."

She began to pace, to struggle with herself. All this relationship stuff was so complicated and still so foreign to her. Nadine had told her what she'd told her as a friend. In confidence. The man currently, and patiently, watching her from across the room was her husband.

Love, honor, and all the rest of it.

If she told him about Nadine and Draco, was she breaching a confidence and the trust of a friend? Or was she just doing the marriage thing?

How the hell, she wondered, did people get through life juggling all this stuff?

"Darling Eve." Sympathizing, Roarke waited until she'd stopped prowling the room and turned to face him. "You're giving yourself a headache. I can make it easier on you. Don't feel you have to tell me something that makes you uncomfortable."

She frowned at him, narrowed her eyes. "I hear a *but* at the end of that sentence."

"You have very sharp ears. But," he continued, crossing to her, "I can deduce that Nadine and Draco were involved at one time, and given your current concern, that something happened between them a great deal more recently."

"Oh hell." In the end she went with the

gut and told him everything.

He listened, then tucked Eve's hair behind her ear. "You're a good friend."

"Don't say that. It makes me nervous."

"All right, I'll say this: Nadine didn't have anything to do with Draco's murder."

"I know that, and there's no hard evidence indicating any different. But it's going to be messy for her. Personally messy. Okay, what else is in this place?"

"Ah, if memory serves. Kitchen through there." He gestured. "Office, bath, bedroom, dressing room, bath."

"I'll start in the office. I want to run his 'links and see if he had any conversations that involved threats or arguments. Do me a favor." She handed him her kit. "Bag the rest of the video discs."

"Yes, sir. Lieutenant."

She smirked but let it ride.

She worked systematically. He loved watching her at it: The focus, the concentration, the absolute logic of her method.

Not so long before in his life if anyone had suggested he could find a cop and her work sexy, he'd have been both appalled and insulted.

"Stop staring at me."

He smiled. "Was I?"

She decided to let it pass. "Lots of com-

132

munications in and out. If I were a shrink, I'd guess this was a guy who couldn't stand being alone with himself. Needed contact on a constant basis. Nothing out of the ordinary though, unless you count some pretty heavy 'link shopping — eight pairs of shoes, three snazzy suits, antique wrist unit." She straightened. "But you wouldn't count that."

"On the contrary, I'd never buy snazzy suits via 'link. Fit is everything."

"Ha ha. He did have a short, pithy kind of conversation with his agent. Seems our boy discovered that his leading lady was pulling in the same salary for the run of the play. He was pretty pissed off about it, wanted his rep to renegotiate and get him more. One credit more per performance."

"Yes, I knew about that. No deal."

Puzzled, she turned away from the neat little desk. "You wouldn't give him a credit?"

"When dealing with a child," Roarke said mildly, "you set boundaries. The contract was a boundary. The amount of the demand was inconsequential."

"You're tough."

"Certainly."

"Did he give you trouble over it?"

"No. He may have planned to push it, but

we never had words over it. The fact is, his agent went to my lawyers, they to me, me back to them, and so on. It hadn't progressed beyond my refusal before opening night."

"Okay, that keeps you clean. I want to check out the bedroom." She moved past him, across a small, circular hallway and through the door.

The bed was big, elaborate, with a high, padded wall behind and covered with sheer, smoky gray. It looked like a bank of soft fog.

She moved briefly into the adjoining dressing room, shook her head at the forest of clothes and shoes. A built-in, mirrored counter held a chorus line of colored bottles and tubes: enhancers, skin soothers, scents, powders.

"Okay, we've got vain, selfish, egocentric, childish, and insecure."

"I wouldn't argue with your assessment. All those personality traits are motive for dislike, but for murder?"

"Sometimes having two feet's a motive for murder." She moved back to the bedroom. "A man that full of ego and insecurity wouldn't sleep alone very often. He dumped Carly Landsdowne. I'd say he had someone else lined up to take her place." Idly, she pulled open the drawer of the bedside table. "Well, well, look at the toys."

The drawer was fitted with compart-ments, and each was jammed with various erotic enhancers suitable for partnership or solo bouts.

"Lieutenant, I really think you should take these in for further examination."

"No touching." She slapped Roarke's hand away as he reached in.

"Spoilsport."

"Civilian. What the hell does this do?" She held up a long, cone-shaped piece of rubber. It made cheerful tinkling noises when she shook it.

Roarke tucked his tongue in his cheek and sat on the bed. "Well, in the interest of your investigation, I'd be happy to demonstrate." Smiling, he patted the bed beside him.

"No, I mean it."

"So do I."

"Never mind." But she was still pon-dering when she put the cone back and opened the bottom drawer. "Ah, here's a little gold mine. Looks like a month's supply of Exotica, a bit of Zeus, and . . ." She opened a small vial, sniffed cautiously, then shook her head like a dog coming out of a pool of water. "Shit. Wild Rabbit."

She fumbled the stopper back in, grabbed for an evidence bag, and sealed the vial.

"Pure, too." She blew out a breath. "If

he's using that on his dates, no wonder they all think he's a sex god. One or two drops of Rabbit, and you'd screw a doorknob. Did you know he was into this?"

"No." All humor fled, Roarke rose. "I don't have particularly strong feelings about most of the illegals. But this one is the same as rape, as far as I'm concerned. Are you all right?"

"Yeah. Yeah." A little dizzy, she thought, and annoyingly horny. And that was only from a quick whiff of the fumes. "Stuff this pure goes for ten thousand an ounce, minimum, and it isn't easy to come by. It only works on the female system," she murmured. "Only takes a drop too many to overdose."

Roarke cupped a hand under her chin, lifted it to examine her eyes. Clear enough, he decided. "There was never any talk about him using anything like this. If there had been, and I'd discovered it was true, I'd have broken his contract. And very likely, his arms."

"Okay." She lifted a hand to his wrist, squeezed. "That's enough in here for now. I'm going to need you to keep this room vacant another day or two. I want an Illegals unit to run through it."

"All right."

She slipped the vial into her kit, and

hoped to lighten his mood. "So, how much is it costing you?"

"Excuse me?"

"To keep this place vacant? How much does it run a night?"

"Oh this little place? I believe it's in the neighborhood of eighty-five hundred a night, though I imagine we have weekly and monthly rates as well."

"Chump change. Mansfield has a unit in here, too, right?"

"Penthouse B, the other tower."

"Let's pay her a visit. She and Draco had an illegals history in common," Eve began as she gathered her field kit and started out. "She may know his sources. It could all come down to a bad drug deal."

"I don't think so."

"Okay, I don't think so either, but the majority of cop work is eliminating." She locked the door, started to reach for a police seal in her kit.

"Must you do that?" He eyed the seal with dislike. "It's very off-putting to the other guests."

"Yes, I must. Besides, it'll give them a secret thrill. Oooh, look, George, that's where the dead actor lived. Get the vid cam."

"Your attitude toward society at large is sadly cynical."

"And accurate." She stepped into the elevator ahead of him, waiting for the doors to close. Then pounced. "Just give me a quick — God —" Desperate for release, she rubbed herself against him, bit his lip, moaning as her hands squeezed hard on his butt.

"Whew." On a long breath, she pushed him away, circled her shoulders. "That's better."

"For you maybe." He made a grab for her, but she slapped a hand on his chest.

"No games in public elevators. Don't you know that's a violation of city code? Tower A, penthouse level," she ordered, and the car slid seamlessly into motion.

"You'll definitely have to pay for that."

She leaned back against the wall as the elevator started its horizontal ride. "Please, you're scaring me."

He only smiled and slipped his hands into his pocket. Toyed idly with the rubber cone he'd palmed out of the drawer. "Be afraid," he murmured, and made her laugh as the car came to a stop.

"I had to clear my head before talking to a witness, didn't I?"

"Mmm-hmmm."

"Listen, you know Mansfield fairly well. I'd like your observations when this is done."

"Ah, there I am. Useful again."

She stopped, turned, and laid a hand on his cheek. Love for him reared up and bit her at the oddest times. "You do come in handy." When he turned his head and brushed his lips over her palm, she felt the thrill of it right down to her toes. "No mushy stuff," she ordered and strode to Areena's door.

She pressed the buzzer, waited.

Areena, dressed in a white lounging robe, opened the door. She looked flushed, obviously surprised, and not altogether pleased. "Lieutenant Dallas. Roarke. I . . . I wasn't expecting —" Then those limpid eyes went wide, went bright. "Is there news? Have you caught whoever —"

"No. I'm sorry to disturb you, but I have a few questions."

"Oh. I thought, I hoped, it might all be over. Well." She lifted a hand, pressed pink-tipped fingers under her eye as if to soothe an ache. Indeed, there were faint bruises of fatigue under it. "I'm afraid this isn't really a good time. Is this absolutely necessary?"

"I'm sorry it's inconvenient, but it won't take long."

"Of course. This is awkward. You see, I'm not alone. I . . ." In surrender, Areena let her hand fall, stepped back. "Please, come in."

Eve stepped inside. The penthouse was very like its opposite in setup, in size. The furnishings were softer, more female somehow, and the colors a symphony of blues and creams.

And seated on one of the trio of sofas, looking sleek and gorgeous in black, was Charles Monroe.

Terrific, Eve thought, and immediately wanted to kick his expensive balls into his throat.

He grinned, a quick snap of pleasure, then seeing the chill in her eyes, the look shifted into lazy amusement as he got languorously to his feet. "Lieutenant. Always a delight to see you."

"Charles. Night work still keeping you busy?"

"Fortunately. Roarke, nice to see you again."

"Charles."

"Can I freshen your drink, Areena?"

"What?" Her eyes had whipped back and forth between faces, and her fingers twirled and twisted the silver links at her throat. "No. No, thank you. Ah, you know each other."

The flush that had pinked prettily on her face deepened. She lifted her hands again in that feminine gesture of helplessness.

"The lieutenant and I have met a number of times. We even have a mutual friend."

"Watch your step," Eve said, very quietly. Temper had already stormed into her eyes and was ready to snap. "Is this a social call, Charles, or are you on the clock?"

"You should know a man in my position doesn't discuss such matters."

"Please, this is embarrassing." Areena lifted her hand to toy restlessly with her necklace again and didn't notice Charles's mouth twist in a thin, cynical line, but Eve did. "Obviously, you're aware Charles is a professional. I didn't want to be alone, and I needed . . . some simple companionship. Charles — Mr. Monroe came highly recommended."

"Areena." Smooth as silk, Roarke stepped forward. "I'd love some coffee. Would you mind?"

"Oh, of course. Forgive me. I can . . ."

"Why don't I see to it." Charles brushed a hand over Areena's arm and started toward the kitchen.

"I'll just give him a hand." With a last look at Eve, Roarke strolled away.

"I know how this must look to you," Areena began. "It must seem very cold and very self-interested for me to have hired a sexual partner the night after . . ."

"It seems odd to me that a woman like you would have to hire anyone to be with her."

With a light laugh, Areena picked up a glass of wine and, sipping, began to pace. The silk whispered around her legs. "A pretty compliment wrapped in barbed suspicion. And well delivered."

"I'm not here to pay you compliments."

"No." Areena's eyes lost their light of humor. "No, of course not. The simple answer to your underlying question is that I keep to myself a great deal. It comes, I suppose, from spending too much of my youth at parties, in groups. You'll have learned about my indiscretions, my difficulties with illegals. That's behind me now."

She turned back, lifted her chin. "It wasn't easy to put it behind me, but I did. In doing so, I lost a number of what I once considered friends. I ruined relationships that mattered to me because of addictions, lost those that shouldn't have mattered when I beat the addictions. And now I'm at a point in my life where my career needs all my attention. It doesn't leave much time for socializing or for romance."

"Were you romantically involved with Draco?"

"No. Never. We had sex a lifetime ago, the sort hearts and minds have nothing to do with. For some time, we've had nothing in common but the theater. I came back to New York, Lieutenant, because I wanted this play, and I knew Richard would shine in his part. I wanted that. There'll never be another like him onstage. God."

She squeezed her eyes shut, shivered. "It's horrible. Horrible. I'm more sorry to have lost the actor than the man. I'm sorry to know that about myself. No, I can't be alone." She sank down on the sofa. "Can't bear it. I can't sleep. If I sleep, I wake up, and my hands are covered in blood. Richard's blood. The nightmares."

She lifted her head, and her eyes swam as they met Eve's. "I have horrible nightmares every time I lie down, they leap into my head, and I wake up sick, wake up screaming, with his blood all over me. You can't imagine. You can't."

But Eve could. A small, freezing room, washed in the dirty red light from the sign across the street. The pain, the sheer hideousness of the rape, of the bone he'd broken in her arm when she'd fought him. The blood, his blood everywhere, slicked on her hands, dripping from the blade of the knife as she crawled away.

She'd been eight. In her nightmares, Eve was forever eight.

"I want you to find who did this," Areena whispered. "You have to find who did it. When you do, the nightmares will stop. Won't they? Won't they stop?"

"I don't know." Eve forced herself to step forward, forced herself to step away from her own memories and stay in the present. Stay in control. "Tell me what you know about the illegals. Who were his contacts, who supplied him, who played with him?"

In the kitchen, Charles sipped his wine, and Roarke made do with the reasonably decent faux coffee the AutoChef offered.

"Areena's having a difficult time," Charles began.

"I imagine she is."

"There's no law against paying for comfort."

"No."

"My job is as viable as hers."

Roarke inclined his head. "Monroe, Eve has no personal vendetta against licensed companions."

"Just against me, in particular."

"She's protective of Peabody." With his eyes clear and direct, Roarke sipped again. "So am I."

"I'm fond of Delia. Very fond. I'd never hurt her. I've never deceived her." On a sound of disgust, Charles turned away to stare through the window at the lights. "I lost my chance to have a relationship outside my job — to have a life outside my job — because I deceived a woman. Then because I cared enough about her to be honest. I've come to terms with that. I am what I am."

He turned back, and his lips curved. "And I'm good at what I do. Delia accepts that."

"Perhaps. But women are the oddest creatures, aren't they? A man never really knows. And that, I think, is part of their continual appeal. A mystery's more interesting, isn't it, before it's completely solved."

With a half laugh, Charles looked over his shoulder, and Eve walked through the door.

She couldn't have said, precisely, why it annoyed her to see Charles and her husband sharing a moment of what couldn't be mistaken for anything but male amusement. But since it did, she scowled at Roarke.

"Sorry to break up the boy talk, but could you keep Areena company for a moment while I speak to Charles?"

"Of course. The coffee's reasonably good."

She waited until he'd walked out, then moved to the AutoChef more to give herself a moment to settle than out of a desire for hotel coffee. "When did Ms. Mansfield make the appointment for your services?"

"This afternoon. About two, I believe."

"Isn't that late notice for you?"

"Yes."

Eve pulled the coffee out, leaned back against the wall, with the steam rising from her cup. "No bookings tonight?"

"I rearranged my schedule."

"Why? Areena indicated you hadn't met before, socially or professionally. Why go to that trouble for a stranger?"

"Because she doubled my fee," he said simply.

"What did she buy? Straight sex? An overnighter?"

He paused, stared down at his wine. When he lifted his gaze again, his eyes had gone cool. "I don't have to answer that. And won't."

"I'm investigating a homicide. I can pull you in for an interview at Central."

"Yes, you can. Will you?"

"You're making this sticky." She set the coffee down, paced up and down the narrow space between the wall and the counter. "I have to put you in my report as it is. That's bad enough. But you make me take you in, formalize this, it's right up Peabody's nose."

"And neither of us want that," he murmured, then sighed. "Look, Dallas, I got a call. A client of mine gave my name to Areena as someone who could give her a comfortable evening. She was obviously upset. I'd heard about Draco, so I didn't have to ask why. She wanted a companion for the night. Dinner in, conversation, sex. To compensate for my inconvenience, she doubled my usual overnight fee. It's simple."

"Did you talk about Draco?"

"No. We talked about art, we talked about theater. She's had three glasses of wine and half a pack of herbals. Her hands stopped shaking about twenty minutes before you got here. She's an emotional wreck who's trying to hold on."

"Okay. I appreciate it." She jammed her hands in her pockets. "Peabody's going to see the report."

He could feel his own hackles rise. "Delia knows what I do."

"Right." It stuck in her craw like barbed wire.

"She's a grown woman, Dallas."

"Grown, my ass." She gave up and kicked the wall. "She's out of her league with an operator like you. Damn it, her family's Free-Agers. She grew up out in bumfuck somewhere." A vague gesture took care of the

Midwest. "She's a good cop. She's a solid cop, but she's still got blind sides. And she's going to get really pissed off when she finds out I said anything to you about it. She'll jam that stick up her ass and freeze me out, but damn it —"

"She matters," he shot back. "She matters to you. Doesn't it occur to you that she could matter to me?"

"Women are a business to you."

"When they pay me to be my business. It isn't like that with Delia. For Christ's sake, we don't even have sex."

"What? She can't meet your fee?" As soon as it was out, she hated herself. Hated herself more when she saw those cool eyes register simple hurt. "I'm sorry. I'm sorry. That was wrong. That was way off."

"Yeah, it was."

Suddenly tired, she scooted down and sat on the floor with her back against the wall. "I don't want to know this stuff. I don't want to think about this stuff. I like you."

Intrigued, he lowered to the floor, his back to the counter so their knees almost brushed. "Really?"

"Yeah, mostly. You've been seeing her since before Christmas, and you haven't . . . What's wrong with her?"

He laughed, and this time it was easy and

rich. "Jesus, Dallas, which way do you want it? I have sex with her, I'm a bastard. I don't, I'm a bastard. Roarke was right."

"What do you mean, Roarke was right?"

"You can't figure women." He took a drink of his wine. "She's a friend. It just happened that way. I don't have many friends who aren't clients or in the business."

"Watch yourself. They start to multiply when you're not paying attention. It complicates your whole damn life."

"You're a good friend. One more thing," he said and gave her foot an easy pat. "I mostly like you, too, Lieutenant Sugar."

The nightmare came. She should have expected it. Areena's talk of dreams and blood and terror triggered it. But even knowing, she could never stop it once it slid into her mind.

She saw him come into the room. Her father. That nasty little room in Dallas, so cold, even with the temperature gauge stuck on high. But seeing him, smelling him, knowing he'd been drinking, but not drinking enough, had sweat popping out on her chilled arms.

She dropped the knife. She'd been so hungry, so hungry it had been worth the risk of finding a snack. Just a little piece of cheese. The knife fell out of her hand, took days, years, centuries to reach the floor. And in the dream, the clatter of it was like thunder that echoed. Echoed. Echoed.

Across his face as he walked to her, the red light from the sign washed red, then white, then red.

Please don't please don't please don't.

But it never did any good to beg.

It would happen again and again and again. The pain of his hand smashing almost casually across her face. Hitting the floor so hard it rattled her bones. And then his weight on top of her.

"Eve. There now. Eve, come back to me. You're home."

Her breath burned in her throat, and she struggled, bucking, shoving against the arms that held her. And Roarke's voice seeped into the dream, warm, calm, lovely. Safe.

"That's right. Hold on to me." He gathered her closer in the dark, rocking her as he would a child until her shudders quieted. "You're all right now."

"Don't let go."

"No." He pressed his lips to her temple. "I won't."

When she woke in the morning, the dream only a vague smear on her mind, his arms were still around her.

chapter seven

Eve beat Peabody into Central. It was deliberate, and it cost her a full hour's sleep that morning. She hoped to file her updated report, then move on, before her aide showed up. If she was lucky, there would be no discussion involving Charles Monroe.

The detective's bullpen was buzzing. It turned out that Detective Zeno's wife had given birth to a baby girl the night before, and he'd celebrated by bringing in two dozen donuts. Knowing detectives, Eve snagged one before the unit fell on them like hyenas on scavenged meat.

"Who won the pool?"

"I did." Baxter grinned around a cinnamon twist with raspberry jelly. "Six hundred and thirty smackeroos."

"Damn it. I never win the baby pool." Consoling herself, Eve snagged a cruller. Taking the first bite, she grinned at him. *Good old Baxter*, she thought. He could be a pain in the ass, but he was meticulous and sharp with details.

He was just perfect. "Looks like this is

your lucky day."

"No shit. I've had my eye on this new auto-entertainment system. The six bills plus is going to go a long way toward putting that baby in my ride."

"That's great, Baxter, but I mean it's *really* your lucky day." She pulled a clear file of discs out of her bag, those gathered from the uniforms and detectives who'd logged witness names the night of the Draco homicide. "You get the grand prize. Run standard backgrounds and probabilities on these individuals, re Draco. We got close to three thousand names here. Grab a couple of detectives, a few uniforms if you need them, and get statements. Let's see if you can cut that number in half by the end of the week."

He snorted. "Very funny, Dallas."

"I have orders from Whitney to tag somebody for this duty. Tag, Baxter. You're it."

"This is bullshit." When she dropped the file on his desk, his eyes wheeled. "You can't dump this nightmare on me, Dallas."

"Can, have, did. You're dropping crumbs, Baxter. You should remember to always keep your area clean."

Pleased with the morning's work, she headed for her office with his curses following her.

The door was open, and the sounds of riffling came clearly into the hall. Eve pressed her back to the wall, danced her fingers over her weapon. The son of a bitch. She had him this time. The sneaking candy thief's ass was hers at last.

She charged into the room, leading with her fist, and caught the intruder by the scruff of the neck. "Gotcha!"

"Hey, lady!"

She had six inches and a good twenty pounds on him. Eve calculated she could squeeze him through her skinny window without too much trouble. He'd make an interesting smear on the pavement below.

"I'm not going to read you your rights," she said as she bounced him against the file cabinets. "You won't need them where you're going."

"Call Lieutenant Dallas!" His voice piped out like a rusty flute. "Call Lieutenant Dallas."

She hauled him around, stared into his jittery eyes, doubled in size behind microgoggles. "I *am* Dallas, you candy-stealing putz."

"Well, jeez. Jeez. I'm Lewis. Tomjohn Lewis, from Maintenance. I got your new equipment."

"What the hell are you talking about? Let

me smell your breath. You got candy breath, I'm going to pull out your tongue and strangle you with it."

With his feet dangling an inch from the floor, he puffed out his cheeks and blew explosive air in her face. "Cracked wheat waffles down to the Eatery, and — and the fruit cup. I ain't had candy. Swear to God."

"No, but you might want to consider a stronger mouthwash. What's this about new equipment?"

"There. Right there. I was just finishing the transfer."

Still holding him off the floor, she turned her head. Her mouth fell open seconds before she dropped Lewis in a heap and leaped on the industrial gray shell of the computer. "Mine. It's mine."

"Yes, sir, Lieutenant sir. She's all yours."

With her arms possessively circled around the unit, she looked back at him. "Look, maintenance boy, if you're toying with me, I'll bite your ears off and make them into stew."

"I got the order right here." Moving cautiously, he reached in his pocket for his logbook, punched in the code. "See, here, Dallas, Lieutenant Eve, Homicide Division. You got yourself a new XE-5000. You requisitioned it yourself."

"I requisitioned it two goddamn years ago."

"Yeah. Well." He smiled hopefully. "Here she is. I was just hooking her to the mainframe. You want I should finish?"

"Yeah, I want you should finish."

"Okay. Have it done in a wink, then get right out of your way." He all but dived under the desk.

"What the hell kind of name is Tomjohn?"

"It's my name, Lieutenant. You got your complete owner's manual and user's guide in that box over there."

She looked over, snorted at the foot-high box. "I know how it works. I have this model at home."

"It's a good machine. Once you're linked to the main, all we gotta do is transfer your code and data from your old equipment. Take about thirty minutes, tops."

"I got time." She skimmed her eyes over her old unit, dented, battered, despised. Some of the dents had been put into it by her own frustrated fist. "What happens to my old equipment?"

"I can haul it out for you, take it down to recycle."

"Fine — no. No, I want it. I want to take it home." She'd perform a ritual extermination, she decided. She hoped it suffered.

"Okay by me." Since he figured his tongue and his ears were safe again, he began to whistle with his work. "That thing's been obsolete for five years. Don't know how you managed to get anything done with it."

Her only response to that was a low, throaty growl.

When Peabody came in an hour later, Eve was sitting at her crowded desk, grinning. "Look, Peabody. It's Christmas."

"Whoa." Peabody came in, circled around. "Whoa squared. It's beautiful."

"Yeah. It's mine. Tomjohn Lewis, my new best friend, hooked it up for me. It listens to me, Peabody. It does what I tell it to do."

"That's great, sir. I know you'll be very happy together."

"Okay, fun's over." She picked up her coffee, jerking her thumb toward the AutoChef so Peabody knew she was welcome to a cup of her own. "I did a run-through on Draco's apartment last night."

"I didn't know you planned to do that. I would have adjusted my personal time."

"It wasn't necessary." Eve had a nasty image of the scene in Areena's apartment if Peabody *had* come along.

"Draco kept a stash of illegals in his penthouse. A variety pack that included nearly an ounce of pure Wild Rabbit."

"Creep."

"You bet. Also a number of inventive sex toys, some of which were out of the scope of even my wide range of experience. He had a collection of video discs, and a large percentage of them are personal sexual encounters."

"So we have a dead sexual deviant."

"The toys and the discs are personal choice, but the Rabbit shuffles him over into SD territory. It could go to motive, or motives, since they're piling up like Free-Agers at a protest rally. No offense."

"None taken."

"We've got, as potentials, ambition, personal gain, money, sex, illegals, woman or women scorned, and all-around general dislike. He enjoyed preying on women, generally pushing members of both sexes around. He had a regular illegals habit. He was also an irritating son of a bitch, and had everyone who knew him wanting to string him up by his intestines. It doesn't cut the list by much. But."

She shifted in her chair. "I started running probabilities last night. Made some headway. My handy new XE-5000 will copy that data to you so you can continue to run scans. I have a consult with Mira shortly. That may help shave the working list down. Set up a conference with our pals in EDD for eleven."

"And the interviews this afternoon?"

"Go as scheduled. I'll be back in an hour, two at most." She pushed away from her desk. "If I get held up, contact the lab and nag Dickhead into verifying the illegals I sent down this morning."

"A pleasure. Bribe or threat?"

"How long have you worked with me now, Peabody?"

"Almost a year, sir."

Eve nodded as she strode out. "Long enough. Use your own judgment."

Mira's area was more civilized — Eve imagined that was the word — compared with the warrens and hives of the majority of Cop Central. A bubble of calm, she supposed, especially if you didn't know what went on behind the doors of Testing.

Eve knew, and she hoped eons passed before she was forced to step through them again.

But Mira's individual space was a world away from the depersonalizing and demoralizing cage of Testing. She favored shades of blues in her cozy scoop chairs, in the soothing ocean waves she often set on her mood screen.

Today she was dressed in one of her soft and snazzy pastel suits. A hopeful green, the color of spring leaf buds. Her hair waved back from a face of composed beauty Eve constantly admired. There were teardrop pearls at her ears that matched the single dangle on a gold-linked chain at her throat.

She was, to Eve's mind, the perfect example of gracious femininity.

"I appreciate you fitting me in this morning."

"I feel a vested interest," Mira began as she programmed her AutoChef for tea. "Being a witness. In all my years attached to the NYPSD, I've never witnessed a murder." She turned with two cups of floral-scented tea in her hand and caught the dark flicker in Eve's eyes. "Richard Draco was not a murder, Eve. It was an execution. An entirely different matter."

She took her seat, handing Eve the tea they both knew she'd barely sip. "I study murder. Murderers. I listen to them, and I analyze them. I profile them. And as a doctor, I know, understand, and respect death. But, having a murder take place right in front of my eyes, not to know it was real. Well, it's given me some bad moments. It's difficult."

159

"I was thinking ingenious."

"Well." A ghost of a smile curved Mira's lips. "Your viewpoint and mine come from different angles, I suppose."

"Yeah." And Eve's angle was often standing over the dead with blood on her boots. It occurred to her now she hadn't taken Mira's state of mind into consideration that night at the theater. She had simply drafted her onto the team and used her as it seemed most efficient.

"I'm sorry. I didn't think of it. I never gave you a choice."

"You had no reason to think of it. And at the time, neither did I." She shook it off, lifted her tea. "You were backstage and at work very quickly. How soon did you realize the knife was real?"

"Not soon enough to stop it. That's what counts. I've started my interviews, concentrating on the actors first."

"Yes, the crime's steeped in theatrics. The method, the timing, the staging." More comfortable with the analytical distance, Mira ran the scene in her mind. "An actor or someone who aspires or aspired to be one fits the profile. On the other hand, the murder was clean, well produced, carefully executed. Your killer is bold, Eve, but also cool-headed."

"Would they have needed to see it happen?"

"Yes, I think so. To see it, under the lights, on the stage, with the audience gasping in shock. That, in my opinion, was as important to this individual as Draco's death. The thrill of it and the ensuing act. Their own shock and horror, well rehearsed."

She considered. "It was too well staged not to have been rehearsed. Draco was touted as one of the greatest actors of our time. Killing him was one step. Replacing him, even if only in the killer's mind, was an essential second."

"You're saying it was professionally motivated."

"Yes, on one level. But it was also very personal. If we look at an actor, or an aspiring one, professional and personal motives could be easily blended."

"The only one to tangibly benefit from Draco's death, professionally, is Michael Proctor. The understudy."

"Logically, yes. Yet everyone onstage or attached to that performance benefits. The media attention, the names fixed in the minds of the public, that indelible moment in time. Isn't that what an actor aspires to? The indelible moment?"

"I don't know. I don't understand people

who spend their lives being other people."

"The work, the skill, is in making the viewing audience believe they are other people. The theater is more than a job to those who do it well, who devote their life to it. It is, just as your job is to you, a way of life. And on the night Draco was murdered, the spotlight shone a little brighter for everyone in that play."

"In the play, or involved with the play. Not in the audience."

"With current data, I can't eliminate audience members, but am more inclined toward a person or persons closer to the stage." Mira set her cup aside, laid a hand over Eve's. "You're concerned about Nadine."

Eve opened her mouth, shut it again.

"Nadine's a patient, and she's very open with me. I'm fully aware of her history with the victim, and I'm fully prepared, should it become necessary, to give my professional opinion that she isn't capable of planning and executing a violent crime. If she'd wanted to punish Draco, she would have found a way to do so through the media. She's capable of that, very capable."

"Okay, good."

"I've spoken with her," Mira went on. "I know you're interviewing her formally today."

"After I leave here. Just me, Nadine, and her lawyer. I want it on record that she came to me with the information. I can bury the statement for a few days, give her some breathing room."

"That will help." But Mira scanned Eve's face, saw more. "What else?"

"Off the record?"

"Of course."

Eve took a sip of the tea, then told Mira about the video disc in Draco's penthouse.

"She doesn't know," Mira said immediately. "She would have told me. It would have troubled and infuriated her. Embarrassed her. He must have taped it without her knowledge."

"Then the next line would be: What if he showed it to her when she went to see him the day he was murdered?"

"Housekeeping would have reported considerable damage to the suite, and Draco would have been forced to seek emergency medical care before his performance." Mira sat back. "It's good to see you smile. I'm sorry you've been worried about her."

"She was shook when we had our meet. Really shook." Eve pushed out of the chair, wandered to the mood screen, and watched the waves ebb and flow. "I've got too many people buzzing in my ears. It's distracting."

"Would you go back to your life as it was a year ago, Eve? Two years ago?"

"Parts of it were easier. I got up in the morning and did my job. Maybe hung out with Mavis a couple of times a week." She blew out a breath. "No, I wouldn't go back. Doesn't matter anyway. I'm where I am. So . . . back to Draco."

Eve continued. "He was a sexual predator."

"Yes, I read your updated report just before you arrived. I will agree that sex was one of his favored weapons. But it wasn't the sex itself that fulfilled him. It was the control, the package of his looks, his style, his talent, and sexuality used to control women. Women whom he considered his playthings. And through them, showing his superiority to other men. He was obsessed with being the center."

"And the illegal? A guy uses Rabbit on a woman because he doesn't think he's going to score with her. It takes away her right to choose."

"Agreed, but in this case, I would say it was just another prop to him. No different in his mind than candlelight and romantic music. He believed himself a great lover, just as he knew himself to be a great actor. His indulgences, in his mind, were no more than his right as a star. I'm not saying that sex doesn't play a part in the motive, Eve. I believe, in this case, you have layers and layers of motives, and a very complex killer. Very likely every bit as egocentric as the victim."

"Two of a kind," Eve murmured.

He had it figured. Actors, they thought they were so fucking brilliant, so special, so important. Well, he could've been an actor if he'd really wanted. But it was just like his father had always told him. You work backstage, you work forever.

Actors, they came and they went, but a good stagehand never had to go looking for work.

Linus Quim had been a stagehand for thirty years. For the last ten, he'd been top dog. That's why he'd been offered the head job at the New Globe, that's why he pulled in the highest wage the union could squeeze out of the stingy bastards of management.

And even then, his pay didn't come close to what the actors raked in.

And where would they be without him?

That was going to change now. Because he had it figured.

Pretty shortly the New Globe was going to be looking for a new head stagehand.

Linus Quim was going to retire in style.

When he worked, he kept his eyes and his ears open. He studied. Nobody knew what was what and who was what to who in a theater company the way Linus Quim knew.

Above all, he was an expert on timing. Cues were never missed when Linus was in charge.

He knew the last time he'd seen the prop knife. Exactly when and where. And knowing that left only one window of opportunity for the switch. And only one person, to Linus's thinking, who could have managed it so slick. Could have had just enough time to stick the dummy knife in Areena Mansfield's dressing room.

It had taken guts, he'd give 'em that.

Linus stopped by a corner glide-cart for a late-morning snack, loading down a pretzel with bright yellow mustard.

"Hey!" The operator snatched at the tube with a hand protected with ratty, fingerless gloves. "You gonna use that much, you gonna pay extra."

"Up yours, wigwam." Linus added another blob for the hell of it.

"You use twice too much." The operator, a battle-scarred Asian with less than three months on the corner, danced in place on tiny feet. "You pay extra."

Linus considered squirting what was left in the tube in the man's pruney face, then remembered his upcoming fortune. It made him feel generous. He dug a fifty-cent credit out of his pocket, flipped it in the air.

"Now you can retire," he said as the operator snagged it on the downward arc.

He sucked at the mustard-drowned pretzel as he strolled away.

He was a little man, and skinny, too, but for the soccer ball–sized potbelly over his belt. His arms were long for his height, and ropey with muscle. His face was like a smashed dish badly glued back together, flat and round and cracked with lines. His ex-wife had often urged him to spend a little of his hoarded savings on some simple cosmetic repair.

Linus didn't see the point. What did it matter how he looked when his job was, essentially, not to be seen?

But he thought he might spring for some work now. He was going to take himself off to Tahiti, or Bali, or maybe even to one of the resort satellites. Bask in sun and sand and women.

The half million he'd be paid to keep his little observations to himself would pump up his life's savings nicely.

He wondered if he should have asked for

more. He'd kept the payoff on the low end — nothing an actor couldn't scrape up, in Linus's opinion. He'd even be willing to take it in installments. He could be reasonable. And the fact was, he had to admire the guts and skill involved here, and the choice of target.

He'd never met an actor he'd despised more than Draco, and Linus hated actors with almost religious equality.

He stuffed the rest of the pretzel in his mouth, wiped mustard from his chin. The letter he'd sent would have been delivered first thing that morning. He'd paid the extra freight for that. An investment.

The letter was better than a 'link call or a personal visit. Those sorts of things could be traced. Cops might have everybody's 'links bugged. He wouldn't put it past the cops, who he distrusted nearly as much as actors.

He'd kept the note simple and direct, he recalled.

I KNOW WHAT YOU DID AND HOW YOU DID IT. GOOD JOB. MEET ME AT THE THEATER, BACKSTAGE, LOWER LEVEL. ELEVEN O'CLOCK. I WANT $500,000. I WON'T GO TO THE COPS. HE WAS A SON OF A BITCH ANYWAY.

He hadn't signed it. Everyone who worked with him knew his square block printing. He'd had some bad moments worrying that the note would be passed to the cops, and he'd be arrested for attempted blackmail. But he'd put that possibility away.

What was half a million to an actor?

He used the stage door, keying in his code. His palms were a little sweaty. Nerves and excitement. The door closed behind him with a metallic, echoing clang. Then he breathed in the scent of the theater, drew in the glorious silence of it. He felt a tug at his heart, sharp and unexpected.

After today, he'd be giving this up. The smells, the sounds, the lights, and lines. It was all he'd really ever known, and the sudden realization of love for it rocked him.

Didn't matter a damn, he reminded himself, and turned to the stairs that led below the stage. They had theaters on Tahiti if he wanted a busman's holiday. He could even maybe open his own little regional place. A theater-casino palace.

That was a thought.

The Linus Quim Theater. Had a ring to it.

At the base of the stairs, he turned right, down the twisty corridor. He was humming now, happy in his own space, bubbling lightly with anticipation of what was to come.

An arm snaked out, hooked around his neck. He yelped, more in surprise than fear, started to turn.

Fumes poured into his mouth and nose. His vision blurred, his head rang. He couldn't feel his extremities.

"What? What?"

"You need a drink." The voice whispered in his ear, friendly, comforting. "Come on, Linus, you need a drink. I got the bottle out of your locker."

His head drooped down, weighing like a stone on his skinny neck. All he could see behind his eyelids were bleeding colors. His feet shuffled over the floor as he was gently led to a seat. He swallowed obediently when a glass was held to his lips.

"There, that's better, isn't it?"

"Dizzy."

"That'll pass." The voice stayed soft and soothing. "You'll just feel very calm. The tranq's mild. Hardly more than a kiss. You just sit there. I'll take care of everything."

"Okay." He smiled vaguely. "Thanks."

"Oh, it's no trouble."

The noose had already been prepared from a long length of rope culled from the fly floor. Gloved hands slipped it smoothly around Linus's neck, snugged and straightened it.

"How do you feel now, Linus?"

"Pretty good. Pretty damn good. I thought you'd be pissed."

"No." But there was a sigh that might have been regret.

"I'm taking the money and going to Tahiti."

"Are you? I'm sure you'll enjoy that. Linus, I want you to write something for me. Here's your pen. That's the way. Here's the pad you always use to make your notes. You never use an e-pad, do you?"

"Paper's good enough for me, goddamn it." He hiccupped, grinned.

"Of course. Write this down, would you? 'I did it.' That's all you have to say. Just write 'I did it,' then sign your name. Perfect. That's just perfect."

"I did it." He signed his name in a stingy little scrawl. "I figured it out."

"Yes, you did. That was very clever of you, Linus. Are you still dizzy?"

"Nope. I feel okay. I feel fine. Did you bring money? I'm going to Tahiti. You did everybody a favor by wasting that stupid bastard."

"Thank you. I thought so, too, Let's stand up now. Steady?"

"As a rock."

"Good. Would you do me a favor? Could you climb up the ladder here? I'd like you to loop this end of the rope over that pole and tie it off. Nice and snug. Nobody ties knots like a veteran stagehand."

"Sure thing." He went up, humming.

On the ground, his killer watched with heart-thrumming anticipation. There had been fear when the note had arrived. Tidal waves of fear and panic and despair.

Those were done now. Had to be done. Only mild irritation and the spur of challenge remained.

How to deal with it? The answer had come so smoothly, so clearly. Eliminate the threat, give the police their killer. All in one stroke.

In moments, only moments now, it would all be done.

"All tied off!" Linus called. "She'll hold."

"I'm sure. Oh no, Linus, don't walk back down."

Confused, he shifted on the ladder, looked down at the smiling face below. "Don't walk down?"

"No. Jump. Jump off the ladder, Linus. Won't that be fun? Just like jumping into the pretty blue water in Tahiti."

"Like in Tahiti? That's where I'm going once I'm flush."

"Yes, like Tahiti." The laughter was delighted, encouraging. A careful ear might have heard the strain beneath it, but Linus only laughed in return. "Come on, Linus. Dive right in! The water's fine."

He grinned, held his nose. And jumped.

This time death wasn't quiet. The panicked, kicking feet knocked the ladder down with a thunderous clatter. It hit the bottle of brew in an explosion of glass. Choked gasps forced their way through the tightened noose, became rattles. For seconds, only seconds, but the air seemed to scream with them.

And then there was only the faint creak of the rope swinging. Like the creak of a mast in high seas, it was curiously romantic.

chapter eight

"Weighing in Mira's profile of the killer, the scales drop on the side of a performer. An actor," Eve continued. "Or someone who wants or wanted to be one."

"Well, you got your headliners." Feeney stretched out his legs. "Your second string, your extras. Add them all up, you still got more than thirty potentials. You add the wanna-bes to that, and Christ knows."

"We divvy them up and cut them down. The same way Baxter should cut down audience members."

Feeney spread his lips in a grin. "We heard his whining all the way over in EDD."

"Then my job there is done. We factor in connections to the victim," Eve went on, "placement during the last act. We haul the most probables into Interview and start sweating them."

McNab shifted in his chair, lifted a finger. "It's still possible that the killer was someone in the audience. Somebody who knew Draco, had theater experience. Even working Baxter and whoever he drags into it with him twenty-four/seven on probabilities and backgrounds, it'll take weeks to eliminate."

"We don't have weeks," Eve shot back. "This is high profile. Pressure's going to build on The Tower," she said, referring to the office of the commissioner. "That means it's going to squeeze us, and squeeze us soon. We run the audience as Baxter passes on potentials, and keep running them until we whittle it down. Meantime, we focus on the stage."

She moved to the board where the stills of the murder scene, the body, the graphs and charts from the probability scans and background checks run to date were already tacked.

"This wasn't a spree killing. It wasn't an impulse. It was planned, staged. It was performed. And it was recorded. I've got copies of the discs for everyone. We're going to watch the play, each of us, study it until we know the lines, the moves, so well we could go on the road with it ourselves.

"It's about twisting the law," she murmured. "About playing with it. And in the end, it's about a kind of justice. The murderer might see Draco's death that way. A kind of justice."

Feeney rattled the sugared nuts in the bag in his pocket. "Nobody loved him."

"Then we figure out who hated him most."

The boy's name was Ralph, and he looked both terrified and excited. He wore a battered Yankees jacket over his dull brown janitorial uniform. He either had a very bad haircut or, Roarke supposed, was sporting some new fashion. Whichever, he was forced to blow, sweep, or shake the ragged streams of dark hair out of his eyes on a continual basis.

"I didn't think you'd come yourself, sir." Part of Ralph's panicked excitement came from the idea of speaking face-to-face with the legendary Roarke. Everybody knew the man was totally ice. "Orders are to report anything out of the ordinary to control, so when I saw how the stage door wasn't locked and coded, I figured how I should report it right off."

"That's right. Did you go inside?"

"Well, I . . ." Ralph didn't see any point in admitting his overactive imagination hadn't let him get two feet beyond the door. "I started to, you know. Then I saw how there were lights on that aren't supposed to be on. I thought it was smarter to stay out here and . . . be guarding the door, like."

"Good thinking." Roarke crouched down,

studied the locks, glanced up idly at the security camera. Its indicator light was off, and it shouldn't have been. "Do you usually work alone?"

"Oh no, sir. But since, you know, the building's closed because of that guy getting dead and stuff, my super asked one of the cleaning crew to volunteer for light maintenance. With the whole deal on opening night, nobody ever got to cleaning the bathrooms and stuff. The super, he said how the cops gave us clearance to go back in since they got what they needed already."

"Yes." Roarke had been informed only that morning that certain areas of the building were not cleared.

"We're not supposed to pass the police barriers onstage or back. Super said they'll give you a bitch of a shock if you try to mess with them."

"Super is quite correct."

"So, I'm just supposed to deal with the bathrooms is all. I popped for it 'cause I can use the money, you know?"

"Yes." Roarke straightened, smiled at the boy. "I know very well. Well then, Ralph is it? We'll just go in and see what's what."

"Sure." There was an audible gulp as Ralph stepped inside behind Roarke. "You know, they say a murderer always returns, like, to the scene of his crime."

"Do they?" Roarke's voice was mild as he scanned the area. "You'll learn there's very little *always* in the world, Ralph. But it's possible they could be right this time around."

The rooms beyond the anteroom were dark, but there was a backwash of light shining up the stairs from the lower level. Roarke started down, tucked a hand in his pocket where he'd slipped a small, illegal-for-civilian-use stunner when he'd gotten the call of a potential break-in.

He followed the glow toward the under-stage area.

He smelled home brew, the just-going-sour punch of it, and a nasty undertone he recognized as death.

"Yes, I'm afraid they're right this time," he murmured, then turned the corner.

"Oh, shit. Oh, man." Ralph's voice jumped over the words, and his eyes goggled at the figure dangling from a stout length of rope. "Is that a guy?"

"It was. If you're going to be sick, there's no shame in it, but find another place."

"Huh?"

Roarke glanced back. The boy's face was sheet white, his eyes going glassy. To keep it simple, Roarke simply pressed a hand on Ralph's shoulder and lowered him to the floor. "Put your head down, take slow breaths. That's the way, son. You'll do fine."

Turning from the boy, Roarke walked to the hanged man. "Poor, stupid bastard," he thought aloud, and took out his palm 'link to call his wife.

"Dallas. What? Roarke, I can't talk to you now. I'm up to my neck here."

"Speaking of necks. I'm looking at one now that's been considerably stretched. You'll need to come to the theater, Lieutenant, lower level. I've found another body for you."

Death demanded routine, even if the primary investigator's husband discovered the body.

"Can you identify him?" she asked Roarke, and signaled for Peabody to record the scene.

"Quim. Linus Quim. I checked the employment records after I called you. Head stagehand. He was fifty-six. Divorced, no children. He lived on Seventh — alone, according to his file."

"Did you know him personally?"

"No."

"Okay, stand by. Peabody, get me a ladder. I don't want to use this one until we've done a full sweep. Who's the kid?" she asked Roarke.

"Ralph Biden. One of the janitorial team. He was going to work solo today, saw the stage door was unlocked, and called it in."

"Give me times," Eve demanded as she studied the angle of the fallen ladder, the pattern of shattered glass from the broken brew bottle.

After one long stare, Roarke took out his log. "He contacted maintenance control at eleven twenty-three. I was alerted six minutes later and arrived on-scene at noon, precisely. Is that exact enough to satisfy, Lieutenant?"

She knew the tone and couldn't help it if he decided to be annoyed. Still, she scowled at his back and he walked away to take a small stepladder from Peabody.

"Did you or the kid touch anything?"

"I know the routine." Roarke set the ladder under the body. "Nearly as well as you by now."

She merely grunted, shouldered her field kit, and started up the ladder.

Hanging is an unpleasant death, and the shell left behind reflects it. It bulges the eyes, purples the face. He hadn't weighed more than one-twenty, Eve thought. Not enough, not nearly enough for the weight to drop down fast and heavy and mercifully snap his neck.

Instead, he'd choked to death, slowly enough to be aware, to fight, to regret.

With hands coated with Seal-It, she tugged the single sheet of cheap recycled paper out of his belt. After a quick scan, she handed the paper down. "Bag it, Peabody."

"Yes, sir. Self-termination?"

"Cops who jump to conclusions trip over same and fall on their asses. Call for a Crime Scene team, alert the ME we have an unattended death."

Chastised, Peabody pulled out her communicator.

Eve logged time of death for the recorder and examined the very precise hangman's knot. "Why self-termination, Officer Peabody?"

"Ah . . . subject is found hanged to death, a traditional method of self-termination, in his place of employment. There is a signed suicide note, a broken bottle of home brew with a single glass. There are no apparent signs of struggle or violence."

"First, people have been hanged as an execution method for centuries. Second, we have no evidence at this time the subject wrote the note found on-scene. Last, until a full examination of the body is complete, we cannot determine if there are other marks of violence. Even if there are not," Eve continued, backing down the ladder, "a man can be coerced into a noose."

"Yes, sir."

"On the surface, it looks like self-termination. It's not our job to stop at the surface and assume but to observe, record, gather evidence, and eventually conclude."

Eve stepped away, studied the scene. "Why would a man come here to an empty theater; sit and drink a glass of brew; write a brief note; fashion himself a nice, tidy noose; secure it; walk up a ladder; then step off?"

Since she understood she was expected to answer, Peabody gave it her best. "The theater is his workplace. Self-terminators often take this step in their place of employment."

"I'm talking about Quim, Linus. Specifics, Peabody, not generalities."

"Yes, sir. If he was responsible for Draco's death, which could be the meaning of the note, he may have been overcome by guilt, and he returned here, to where Draco was killed, balancing the scales by taking his own life under the stage."

"Think of the profile, Peabody. Think of the original crime and its method of execution. I find calculation, ruthlessness, and daring. Tell me, where do you find guilt?"

With this, Eve strode off to where Ralph was sitting, pale and silent in a corner.

"Screwed that up," Peabody muttered. "Big time." She blew out a breath, trying not to be embarrassed she'd had her wings pinned in front of Roarke. "She's pissed now."

"She's angry. Not at you, particularly," Roarke added, "nor at me." He looked back at the corpse, the pathetic waste of it, and understood his wife perfectly. "Death offends her. Each time. Every time she deals with it."

"She'll tell you that you can't take it personally."

"Yes." He watched Eve sit beside Ralph, automatically shielding his view of death with her body. "She'll tell you that."

He could be patient. Roarke knew how to wait, to choose his time and his place. Just as he knew that Eve would seek him out, would find him, if for no other reason than to assure herself he hadn't stuck his fingers too deeply into her work.

So he sat on the stage, still dressed with the final courtroom set. An odd place for a man with his background, he thought with some amusement, as he used his personal

183

palm computer to scan updated stock reports and revise a departmental memo.

He'd turned the stage lights on, though that had simply been for convenience. When she tracked him down, he sat in the dock under a cool blue spot, and he looked as seductive as a condemned angel.

"They ever get you that far?"

"Hmm?" He glanced up. "You've seen my records. No arrests."

"I've seen what's left of your records after you played with them."

"Lieutenant, that's a serious accusation." Still, a smile flirted with his mouth. "But no, I've never had the pleasure of defending myself in a court of law on a criminal matter. How's the boy?"

"Who? Oh. Ralph. A little shaky." She climbed the stairs to the dock. "I had a couple of uniforms take him home. We shouldn't need to talk to him again. And after he recovers, he'll have all his pals buying him a beer to hear the story."

"Exactly so. You're a fine judge of human nature. And how's our Peabody?"

"What do you mean?"

"You're a good teacher, Lieutenant, but a fierce one. I wondered if she'd recovered from the bruising you gave her."

"She wants to make detective. She wants

to work murders. First rule, you go on a scene, you don't bring anything with you. No preconceptions, no conclusions. And you don't take what you see at first glance on face value. You think Feeney didn't slap me upside the head with that a few times when he was my trainer?"

"I imagine he did and had plenty of bruises of his own when he hit the rock of it."

"If that's a fancy way of saying I'm hardheaded, it doesn't insult me. She'll learn, and she'll think more carefully next time. She hates screwing up."

He reached up idly to brush his knuckles over her cheek. "I thought the same myself. Now, why don't you think this is self-termination?"

"I didn't say I didn't. There are a number of tests to be run. The ME will make the call."

"I wasn't asking for the medical examiner's opinion but yours."

She started to speak, then set her teeth and jammed her hands in her pockets. "You know what that was down there? That was a fucking insult. That was a stage carefully set for my benefit. Somebody thinks I'm stupid."

Now he did smile. "No. Someone knows

you're smart — very smart — and took great care, right down to the bottle of what will undoubtedly turn out to be Quim's own home brew."

"I've checked his locker. You can still smell the stuff. He kept a bottle in there, all right. What did he know?" she muttered. "Head stagehand? That means he'd have to know where everything needs to be and when. People, props, the works."

"Yes, I'd assume so."

"What did he know?" she said again. "What did he see, what did he think? What did he die for? He wrote down stuff in this little notebook. The handwriting on the death note looks like a match. If the ME doesn't find something off, he's likely to rule it self-termination."

Roarke rose. "You'll be working late."

"Yeah. Looks like."

"See that you eat something other than a candy bar."

Her mouth went grim. "Somebody stole my candy bars again."

"The bastard." He leaned down, kissed her lightly. "I'll see you at home."

If Eve's preconception that theater people led richly bohemian lives had taken a dent after a look at Michael Proctor's living quarters, it suffered a major blow when she reached Linus Quim's excuse for an apartment.

"One step up from street-sleeping." She shook her head as she took her first scan of the single, street-level room. The antiburglar bars covering the two grimy, arrow-slot windows were coated with muck and caged out whatever pitiful sunlight might have struggled to fight its way into the gloom.

But bars and muck weren't enough to keep out the constant clamor of street traffic or the uneasy vibrations from the subway that ran directly under the ugly room.

"Lights on," she ordered and was rewarded with a flickering, hopeless yellow glow from the dusty ceiling unit.

Absently, she stuck her hands in her jacket pockets. It was colder inside than it was out in the frisky, late-winter wind. The entire place, such as it was, smelled of old sweat, older dust, and what she assumed was last night's dinner of hash and beans.

"What did you say this guy pulled down a year?" she asked Peabody.

Peabody pulled out her PPC, scanned. "Union scale for his position is eight hundred and fifty a show, with ascending hourly wage for put-ups, tear-downs, turnaround, and overtime pay. Union takes a twenty-five percent bite for dues, retirement, health plans, and blah-blah, but our guy still raked in about three hundred thousand annually."

"And chose to live like this. Well, he was either spending it or stashing it some-where." She strode across the bare floor to the computer unit. "This piece of crap's older than the piece of crap I just got rid of. Computer on."

It coughed, wheezed, snorted, then emitted a sickly blue light. "Display financial records for Quim, Linus."

Password required for data display . . .

"I'll give you a password." Halfheartedly, she rapped the unit with her fist and recited her rank and badge number.

Privacy Act protects requested data. Password required . . .

"Peabody, deal with this thing." Eve turned her back on it and began riffling through the drawers in a cabinet that had the consistency of cardboard. "Arena ball programs," she announced while Peabody tried to reason with the computer. "And more notebooks. Our boy liked to bet on the games, which might explain where his salary went. He's got it all written down here, wins and losses. Mostly losses. Petty-ante stuff, though. Doesn't look like he was spine-cracker material."

She moved on to the next drawer. "Well, well, look at this. Brochures of tropical islands. Forget the financials, Peabody. See if he went searching for data on Tahiti."

She moved onto the closet, pushed through a handful of shirts, feeling the pockets, checking for hiding places in the two pairs of shoes.

As far as she could see, the guy had kept nothing — no mementos, no photographs, no personal discs. Just his notebooks.

He had a week's worth of clothes, obviously old, which included one wrinkled suit. His cupboards turned up several dehydrated single packs of hash, several bottles of brew, one jumbo bag of soy chips, as yet unopened.

She took the bag out, frowned over it. "Why does a man so obviously tight with his money spring for a jumbo bag of chips, then hang himself before he eats them?"

"Maybe he was too depressed. Some people can't eat when they're depressed. Me, I head right for the highest caloric content available."

"Looks to me like he ate last night and again this morning. Autopsy will confirm that, but his recycler's overstuffed." Wincing, she reached into the slot and pulled out an empty bag. "Soy chips. My guess is he finished them off yesterday and had his backup bag ready for his next nutritious meal. There's a half bottle of brew chilling in his friggie box, and two backups in the cupboard."

"Well, maybe . . . Good call on Tahiti, Dallas." Peabody straightened. "It was his last data search. We've got pictures, tourist data, climate scans." As she spoke, the machine began to play exotic music, heavy on the drums. "And half-naked dancing girls."

"Why does our urbanite do scans of far-away islands?" Eve walked back over, watched the native women shake impressively in some tribal dance. "Computer, replay most recent search for transpo choices and costs from New York City to Tahiti."

Working . . . Last search for transpo data initiated oh three thirty-five, twenty-eight March, 2059, by Quim, Linus. Data as follows: Roarke Airlines offers the most direct flights daily . . .

"Naturally," Eve said dryly. "Computer

hold. Quim spent time just this morning re-searching flights to Tahiti. Doesn't sound like a guy suffering from guilt and depression. Computer, list Quim, Linus, passport and/or visa data."

Working . . . Quim, Linus: Request for passport initiated fourteen hundred hours, twenty-six March, 2059.

"Going on a trip, weren't you, Linus?" She stepped back. "What did you see, what did you know?" she murmured. "And who were you going to tap for the money to pay for your island vacation? Let's take this unit in to Feeney, Peabody."

Eliza Rothchild had made her debut on stage at the age of six months as a fretful baby causing her parents distress in a drawing room comedy. The play had flopped, but Eliza had been the critic's darling.

Her own mother had pushed her, pulled her, from audition to audition. By the age of ten, Eliza was a veteran of stage and screen. By twenty, she'd been a respected character actress, with a room full of awards, homes on three continents, and her first — and last — unhappy marriage behind her.

At forty, she'd been around so long no one wanted to see her, including producers. She claimed to be retired rather than used up, and had spent the next decade of her life traveling, throwing lavish parties, and fighting excruciating boredom.

When the opportunity arose to play the nagging nurse Miss Plimsoll in the stage production of *Witness*, she'd pretended reluctance, allowed herself to be wooed, and had privately wept copious tears of relief and gratitude.

She loved the theater more than she had ever loved any man or any woman.

Now, as her security screen announced the arrival of the police, she prepared to play her role with dignity and discretion.

She answered the door herself, a sternly attractive woman who didn't bother to disguise her age. Her hair was a rich auburn threaded with silver. The lines around her hazel eyes fanned out without apology. She wore a hip-skimming tunic and sweeping trousers over a short, sturdy body. She offered Eve a hand glittering with rings, smiled coolly, and stepped back.

"Good afternoon," she said in her smooth voice that held the granite of New England. "It's comforting to see the police are prompt."

"I appreciate your time, Ms. Rothchild."

"Well, I don't really have a choice, do I, but to give it to you."

"You're free to speak through or with a lawyer or representative."

"Of course. My lawyer is standing by, should I decide to do so." She gestured toward the living area. "I know your husband, Lieutenant. Quite the most fatally attractive man I've ever encountered. He may have told you I was reluctant to come out of retirement and accept the role of Miss Plimsoll. But quite frankly, I couldn't resist him."

She smiled again, sat in an elegant high-backed chair with a tapestry seat, rested her elbows on the wide arms, folded her hands. "Who could?"

"Roarke persuaded you to come out of retirement."

"Lieutenant, I'm sure you're aware there's nothing Roarke couldn't talk a woman into. Or out of."

Her eyes measured and judged Eve, then shifted idly to Peabody. "Still, you're not here to discuss Roarke but another fatally attractive man. Though, in my opinion, Richard lacked your husband's charm and underlying . . . we'll say *decency*, for lack of a better word."

"Were you and Richard Draco involved romantically?"

Eliza blinked several times, then laughed. The sound was a steady, bubbling gurgle. "Oh, my dear girl, should I be flattered or insulted? Oh me."

With a sigh, she patted her breast, as if the bout of humor had been a strain on the heart. "Let me say that Richard would never have wasted that particular area of his skills on me. Even when we were young, he considered me much too plain, too physically ordinary. 'Too intellectual,' I believe was one of his terms. He considered cultural intellect a flaw in a woman."

She paused, as if realizing she'd gone too far in the wrong direction, then opted to finish it out. "Gallantry was not one of his talents. He often made snide little jokes about my lack of appeal. I chose to be neither amused nor offended as what it came down to was simple. We were of an age, you see. Which meant I was years too old for his taste. And if I may say, several notches too self-reliant. He preferred the young and the vulnerable."

And that, Eve thought, had come out in a flood, as if it had been dammed up quite some time. "Then your relationship with him would have been strictly professional?"

"Yes. We certainly socialized. Theater people tend to be an incestuous little group — metaphorically, and literally as well, I suppose. We attended many of the same parties, performances, and benefits over the years. Never as a couple. We were civil enough, as we both knew he wasn't interested in me in a sexual manner, it took away that tension."

"Civil," Eve repeated. "But not friendly."

"No, I can't claim we were ever friendly."

"Can you tell me where you were on opening night, between the scenes that took place in the bar and the courtroom? The scene where Christine Vole is called back as a witness."

"Yes, of course, as it's as much a routine as what I do onstage. I went back to my dressing room to check my makeup. I prefer doing my own makeup, as most of us do. Then I was backstage for a time. My next scene has me in the balcony, watching the courtroom — and Sir Wilfred — along with the character of Diana and a number of extras."

"Did you see or speak with anyone between those scenes?"

"I'm sure I did." Eliza lifted her fingers, making a little steeple. Then collapsed them. "A number of the technical crew would have been backstage, and I might have exchanged a word or two. Carly and I passed each other."

"Passed each other?"

"Yes. As I was coming out of my dressing room, she was going toward hers. Hurriedly, as our cue was coming up shortly. Did we speak?"

She paused, pursing her lips, searching the ceiling as if for the memory. "I believe we did. She made some offhand complaint about Richard. I think she said he'd given her ass a bit of a pinch or pat. It annoyed her, as well it should, given his treatment of her."

She continued to sit, regally, her eyes bright and fixed on Eve's. "I find it hard to sympathize, as she's smart enough to know better than to get involved with a man of his nature. I believe I made just that sort of comment to Kenneth before I started up to the second level of the set to take my mark."

"You saw him as well."

"Yes, pacing about, muttering to himself. He often does so before a scene. I couldn't tell you if he heard me or noticed. Kenneth tries to stay in character and he works very hard to ignore Nurse Plimsoll."

"Anyone else?"

"Well, I . . . Yes, I saw Michael Proctor. He

was in the wings. I'm sure he was dreaming of the night when he might have his chance to play Vole. Not that I believe for a moment he arranged to do so. He has such a helpless air, doesn't he? I can see this business devouring him whole in another year or so."

"And Areena Mansfield. Did you see her as well?"

"Certainly. She made the dash to her dressing room. She had a full costume and makeup change between those scenes. She raced right past me. But honestly, Lieutenant, if you want the positions and activities of the cast between scenes, you don't want to talk to one of us. You want Quim. He's head stagehand, a rumpled little man with sneaky eyes that miss little to nothing. He's everywhere."

"Not anymore," Eve said quietly. "Linus Quim was found hanged this morning in the theater. Lower level."

For the first time, Eliza's polished veneer cracked. Her hand went to her heart, trembled there. "Hanged?" The well-trained voice was husky on the single word. "Hanged?" she repeated. "There must be a mistake. Who would kill a harmless little toad like Quim?"

"It appeared to be self-termination."

"Nonsense." Eliza got to her feet. "Why, that's nonsense. It takes great bravery or great cowardice to end your own life. He had neither. He was just an irritating little man, one who did his job well and never seemed to enjoy it. If he's dead, someone killed him. That's two," she said almost to herself. "Two deaths in the theater. Tragedies come in threes. Who's next?"

She shuddered, lowered herself to her chair again. "Someone's killing us." The avid interest in her eyes was gone, the play of amusement around her mouth turned down to worry. "There's another play, Lieutenant Dallas, by the late Dame Christie. *And Then There Were None*. Ten people, subtly linked, who are murdered one at a time. I don't intend to have a role in it. You have to stop this."

"I intend to. Is there a reason anyone would wish you harm, Ms. Rothchild?"

"No. No. I have no enemies on the scope that leads to murder. But there will be at least one more. It's theater, and we're a superstitious lot. If there's two, there must be three. There will be three," she said. "Unless you do something about it."

She jolted when her security beeped. The lobby clerk's face came cheerfully onscreen. "Ms. Landsdowne is here to see you,

Ms. Rothchild. Shall I send her up?"

"I'm engaged at the moment," she began, but Eve held up a hand.

"Please, have her come up."

"I —" Eliza lifted a hand to her hair, patted it. "Yes, yes, please send her up."

"Does Carly often drop by?" Eve asked.

"Not really. She's been here, of course. I enjoy entertaining. I don't recall her simply popping in this way. I'm really not up to chatting with her at the moment."

"That's all right. I am. I'll get the door," Eve said when the buzzer sounded.

Eve took a moment to study Carly's face on the security screen. Frantic would have been her description. She watched it change to shock, then smooth out quickly to careless curiosity after she opened the door.

"Lieutenant. I didn't realize you were here. Apparently I've chosen a bad time to pay a call on Eliza."

"Saves me tracking you down for a follow-up interview."

"Too bad I don't have my lawyer in my pocket." She stepped inside. "I was just out shopping and decided to drop by." She caught Eve's speculative look at her empty hands. "I had a few things sent on to my apartment. I do hate lugging parcels. Eliza."

Carly swept in, arms spread, and met

Eliza in the center of the living area. They exchanged light hugs and double-cheeked air kisses. "I didn't realize you were entertaining the NYPSD. Shall I leave you alone?"

"No." Eliza gripped her arm. "Carly, the lieutenant's just told me Quim's dead. Linus Quim."

"I know." Turning, she linked arms with Eliza. "I caught the news on-screen."

"I thought you were shopping."

"I was." Carly nodded at Eve. "There was a young man entertaining himself with a palm unit while his young woman tried on half the wardrobe in sportswear and separates. I heard the name."

She lifted a hand, appeared to struggle with herself briefly. "It upset me — panicked me, frankly. I didn't know what to think when I heard the report. I was just a few blocks away, and I came here. I wanted to tell someone who'd understand."

"Understand what?" Eve prompted.

"The report said it's believed his death is linked to Richard's. I don't see how it could be. Richard never took notice of techs or crew. As far as he was concerned, the sets were dressed and changed by magic. Unless there was a problem. Then he'd abuse them verbally or physically. Quim never missed a cue, so Richard wouldn't have known he existed. How could there be a link?"

"But you noticed him?"

"Of course. Creepy little man." She gave a delicate shudder. "Eliza, I hate to impose, but I could really use a drink."

"I could use one myself," she decided and rang for a serving droid.

"Did you notice Quim on opening night?" Eve asked.

"Just that he was doing what he did in his usual silent, scowling way."

"Did you speak to him?"

"I may have. I don't recall. I'd like a vodka, rocks," Carly added when the droid appeared. "A double."

"You didn't appear this upset when Draco was killed, and in front of your eyes."

"I can think of a dozen reasons any number of people would want to kill Richard," Carly snapped back.

"Including yourself."

"Yes." She took the glass from the droid, took one quick sip. "Most definitely including myself. But Quim changes everything. If their deaths are connected, I want to know. Because the idea scares me."

"Tragedies happen in threes," Eliza stated, her voice round and full and passionate.

"Oh, thanks, darling. Just what I needed to hear." Carly lifted her glass, drained the contents.

"Weird. These people are fucking weird." Eve got in her vehicle and headed back to Central. "One of their associates gets stuck in the heart basically at their feet, and they're like — my goodness, would you look at that. A tech is hanged, and they fall apart."

She flipped on her car link and contacted Feeney.

"No home 'link calls in or out in a forty-eight-hour period," he reported. "No calls to anyone on your list, period. He had bi-weekly contact with a bookie for bets on arena ball, kept it under the legal limit."

"Tell me something interesting, I'm dozing off here."

"He put a hold on a royal-class ticket to Tahiti but didn't book it. One way, heading out a week from Tuesday. Also put a hold on a VIP suite at the Island Pleasure Resort. A full month's stay. Made some inquiries about real estate, looking into some cliff-side house in the neighborhood of two mil. The guy's financials add up to about a quarter of that. The ticket and the suite would have gobbled most of that up."

"So he was looking to come into a nice pile."

"Or he was a hell of a dreamer. Can't find anything on his unit to indicate he did previous scans, you know, like a hobby."

"Blackmailing a murderer might net you a nice pile."

"Or a noose," Feeney added.

"Yeah. I'm heading by the morgue to nag Morse."

"Nobody does it better," Feeney said before Eve cut him off.

chapter nine

"Ah, Lieutenant Dallas." Chief Medical Examiner Morse's dark eyes glittered behind his microgoggles. Above the serviceable lenses, his eyebrows arched in two long, slim triangles. At the peak of the left was a small, shiny silver hoop.

He snapped his fingers, held out his sealed hand, palm up. A grumbling assistant flipped a twenty-dollar credit into it. "Dallas, you never disappoint me. You see, Rochinsky, never bet against the house."

The credit disappeared into one of the pockets of his puke-green protective jumpsuit.

"Win a bet?" Eve asked.

"Oh, yes indeed. A small wager with my associate that you would show up in our happy home before five P.M."

"It's nice to be predictable." She looked down at the middle-aged, mixed-race woman currently stretched out under Morse's laser scalpel. The Y cut had already been made.

"That's not my dead guy."

"Very observant. Meet Allyanne Preen, Detective Harrison's dead gal, who was several slots ahead of yours. Licensed companion, street level. She was found stretched out in an abandoned '49 Lexus coupe, in the great automotive morgue we call long-term parking, La Guardia."

"Trouble with a john?"

"No outward signs of violence, no recent sexual encounters." He scooped out her liver, weighed and logged it.

"She's got a faint blue tinge to her skin." Eve bent down to examine the hands. "Most noticeable under the nails. Looks like an OD, probably Exotica and Jumper."

"Very good. Any time you want to switch to my side of the slab, just let me know. I can promise, we have a lot more fun around here."

"Yeah, word's out on you party animals."

"The reports of the Saint Patrick's Day celebration in the ice room were . . ." His eyes laughed behind his goggles. "Accurate."

"Sorry I missed it. Where's my guy? I need his tox report."

"Mmm-hmm." Morse poked at a kidney before removing it. His hands were quick and skilled and seemed to keep time to the beat of the rebel rock music playing over the speakers. "I assumed you'd be in a hurry. I gave your guy to young Finestein. He just started here last month. Has potential."

"You gave mine to some rookie?"

"We were all rookies once, Dallas. Speaking of which, where's the stalwart Peabody?"

"She's outside, doing some runs. Listen, Morse, this is a tricky one."

"So they say, all the time, every time."

"I'm betting on homicide, but it was set up to look like self-termination. I need good hands and eyes on my guy."

"I don't take on anyone without them. Relax, Dallas. Stress can kill you." Unruffled, he strolled over to a 'link, put out a call for Herbert Finestein. "He'll be right along. Rochinsky, run this young lady's internals to the lab. Start the blood work."

"Morse, I've got two bodies, and the probability is that they're linked."

"Yes, yes, but that's your area." He wandered to a detox bowl, washed the soiled sealant from his hands, ran them under the radiant heat in the drying hood. "I'll look over the boy's work, Dallas, but give him a chance."

"Yeah, yeah, fine."

Morse pulled off his goggles and mask, smiled. His black hair was intricately braided to hang down to the middle of his back. He disposed of his protective suit to reveal the stunning pink of his shirt and electric blue of his trousers.

"Nice threads," Eve said dryly. "Going to another party?"

"I'm telling you, every day's a party around here."

She imagined he habitually chose snazzy clothes to distance himself from the starkness of his job, the brutality of it. *Whatever works,* Eve thought. Wading through blood and gore and the misery human beings inflicted on each other on a daily basis wore on you. Without an escape valve, you'd explode.

And what was hers?

"And how's Roarke?" Morse asked.

"Good. Fine." Roarke. Yes, he was hers. Before him there had just been work. Only been work. And would she have, one day, reached the limit, felt her own soul shatter?

Hell of a thought.

"Ah, here's Finestein. Be nice," Morse murmured to Eve.

"What am I?"

"An ass-kicker," Morse said pleasantly and laid a friendly hand on her shoulder. "Herbert, Lieutenant Dallas would like an update on the DOS I assigned to you this afternoon."

"Yes, the Dead on-Scene. Quim, Linus, white male, fifty-six years. Cause of death strangulation by hanging." Finestein, a skinny mixed race with black skin and pale eyes, spoke in quick, piping tones and fiddled nervously with a small forest of pencils tucked in a breast pocket protector.

Not only a rookie, Eve thought with frustration, *a nerd rookie.*

"Did you want to review the body?"

"I'm standing here, aren't I?" Eve began, then relented with a quick gnashing of teeth when Morse's long fingers squeezed her shoulder. "Yes, thank you, I'd like to review the body and your report. Please."

"Just this way."

Eve rolled her eyes at Morse as Finestein hurried across the room. "He's fucking twelve years old."

"He's twenty-six. Patience, Dallas."

"I hate patience. Slows everything down." But she walked over to the floor-to-ceiling line of drawers, waited while Finestein uncoded one, pulled it open with a frigid puff of cold gas.

"As you can see . . ." Finestein cleared his throat. "There are no marks of violence on the body other than those caused by the strangulation. No offensive or defensive wounds. There were microscopic fibers of the rope found under the subject's nails, indicating he secured the rope personally. By all appearances, the subject willingly hanged himself."

"You're handing me self-termination?" Eve demanded. "Just like that? Where's the tox report, the blood work?"

"I'm — I'm getting to that, Lieutenant. There were traces of ageloxite and —"

"Give her the street names, Herbert," Morse said mildly. "She's a cop, not a scientist."

"Oh, yes, sir. Sorry. Traces of um . . . Ease-Up were found in the victim's system, along with a small amount of home brew. This mix is quite commonly ingested by self-terminators to calm any nerves."

"This guy didn't pull his own plug, damn it."

"Yes, sir, I agree." Finestein's quiet agreement cut off Eve's tirade before it could begin.

"You agree?"

"Yes. The victim also ingested a large pretzel with considerable mustard less than an hour before death. Prior to this, he enjoyed a breakfast of wheat wafers, powdered eggs, and the equivalent of three cups of coffee."

"So?"

"If the subject knew enough to mix a cocktail of Ease-Up and alcohol before termination, he would have known that coffee can potentially counteract and cause anxiety. This, and the fact that the alcohol consumed was in very small proportion to the drug casts some doubt on self-termination."

"So, you're ruling homicide."

"I'm ruling suspicious death — undetermined." He swallowed as Eve's eyes bored into him. "Until more evidence weighs in on either side, I feel it's impossible to make the call."

"Just so. Well done, Herbert." Morse nodded. "The lieutenant will feed you details as she finds them."

Finestein looked relieved, and he fled.

"You give me nothing," Eve complained.

"On the contrary. Herbert's given you a window. Most MEs would have slammed it shut, ruling ST. Instead, he's cautious, exacting, and thorough, and he considers the attitude of the victim rather than only the cold facts. Medically, *undetermined* was the best you were going to get."

"Undetermined," Eve muttered as she slid behind the wheel.

"Well, it gives us a window." Peabody glanced up from her palm unit, caught the coldly narrowed stare Eve aimed at her. "What? What did I say?"

"Next person says that, I'm throwing them *out* the goddamn window." She started the car. "Peabody, am I an ass-kicker?"

"Are you asking to see my scars, or is that a trick question?"

"Shut up, Peabody," Eve suggested, and headed back to Central.

"Quim had a hundred on tonight's arena ball game." Peabody's smile was thin and self-satisfied. "McNab just relayed the data. A hundred's his top bet. Odd he'd place a bet a few hours before offing himself, then not even wait around to see if he won. I've got the name and address of his bookie here. Oh, but I'm supposed to shut up. Sorry, sir."

"You want more scars?"

"I really don't. Now that I have a sex life, they're embarrassing. Maylou Jorgensen. She's got a hole in the West Village."

Peabody loved the West Village. She loved the way it ran from bohemian chic to pinstriped drones who wanted to be bohemian chic. She liked to watch the street traffic stroll by in ankle dusters or buttoned-up jumpsuits. The shaved heads, the wild tangles of multicolored curls. She liked watching the sidewalk artists pretend they were too cool to worry about selling their work.

Even the street thieves had a veneer of polish.

The glide-cart operators sold veggie kabobs plucked fresh from the fields of Greenpeace Park.

She thought longingly of dinner.

Eve pulled up in front of a tidy, rehabbed warehouse, double-parked, and turned on her On Duty sign.

"One of these days, I'd like to live in one of these lofts. All that space and a view of the street." Peabody scanned the area as she climbed from the car. "Look, there's a nice, clean deli on the corner there, and a 24/7 market on the other."

"You look for living quarters due to the proximity of food?"

"It's a consideration."

Eve flashed her badge at a security screen in working order, then entered the building. The tiny foyer boasted an elevator and four mail slots. All freshly scrubbed.

"Four units in a building this size." Peabody heaved a sigh. "Imagine."

"I'm imagining a bookie shouldn't be able to afford a place in here." On a hunch, Eve bypassed the buzzer for 2-A and used her shield to gain access to stairs. "We'll go up this way, surprise Maylou."

The building was utterly silent, telling her the sound-proofing was first-rate. She thought of Quim's miserable flop a few telling blocks away. Bookies apparently did a lot better than the majority of their clients.

"Never bet against the house," Morse had said.

Truer words.

She pressed the buzzer on 2-A, waited. Moments later, the door swung open in front of an enormous redhead and a small, white, yapping dog.

"About time you —" The woman blinked hard gold eyes, narrowed them in a wild and striking face the tone and texture of alabaster. "I thought you were the dog walker. He's late. If you're selling, I'm not buying."

"Maylou Jorgensen?"

"So what?"

"NYPSD." Eve held up her badge then found her arms full of barking fur.

"Well, hell." Eve tossed the yelping dog at Peabody, then charged into the loft. Leaping, she tackled the redhead as the woman scrambled for a wide console, studded with controls and facing a wall of busy screens.

They went down like felled trees.

Before Eve could catch her breath, she was flipped to her back, pinned under a hundred eighty-five pounds of panicked female. She took a knee to the groin, spit in the eye, and only through lightning reflexes managed to avoid the rake of inch-long blue nails down her face.

Instead, they dug rivers in the side of her neck.

The smell of her own blood irritated her.

She bucked once, swore, then swung up, elbow in the lead. It slammed satisfactorily into Maylou's white face. Her nose erupted with blood.

She said, quite clearly: "Eek!"

Her gold eyes rolled up white, and her considerable weight flopped lifelessly on Eve.

"Get her off of me, for Christ's sake. There's a ton of her, and all of it's smothering me."

"Give me a hand. Dallas, she's like a slab of granite. Must be six-three. Push!"

Sweating, liberally sprayed with blood, Eve shoved. Peabody pulled. Eventually, Maylou was rolled onto her back, and Eve came up, gasping for air. "It was like being buried under a mountain. Jesus, shut that dog up."

"I can't. He's terrified." Peabody glanced over, with some sympathy, as the little dog backed his white butt into a corner and sent out high, ear-piercing barks.

"Stun it."

"Oh, Dallas." Peabody's tone was a whisper of utter horror.

"Never mind." Eve looked down at the blood spray on her shirt and jacket, gingerly lifted a hand to her raw neck. "Is much of this mine?"

"She made some mag grooves," Peabody announced after a quick exam. "I'll get the first aid kit."

"Later." Eve crouched down, frowned at the unconscious woman. "Let's roll her over and get the restraints on her before she wakes up."

It took some time, brought on more sweat, but they managed to secure her wrists behind her back. Eve straightened, studied the console.

"She's got something going on here. Thought we were a bust. Let's see what I remember about Vice and Bunko."

"Do you want me to call for a warrant?"

"Here's my warrant." Eve rubbed her fingers over her throbbing neck as she sat at the console. "Lots of numbers, lots of games. So what? Names, accounts, bets wagered, money owed. Looks clean enough on the surface." She glanced back. "Is she coming around yet?"

"Dead out, sir. You knocked her cold."

"Go find something to stuff in that dog's mouth before I use my foot."

"He's just a little dog," Peabody murmured and went to search out the kitchen.

"Too many numbers," Eve said to herself. "The pool's too damn deep for a nice little betting parlor. Loan-sharking. Yeah, I bet we got some loan-sharking here, and where you got sharks, you've got spine crackers. What else, what else?"

She turned, saw Peabody cooing to the dog and holding out a biscuit of some kind. Eve slipped out her pocket-link and called the one person she knew who could cut through the ocean of numbers and ride the right wave.

"I need Roarke a minute." She hissed it to his assistant when she came on-screen. "Just one quick minute."

"Of course, Lieutenant. Hold please."

"There's a sweet little dog, there's a nice little doggie. Aren't you pretty?"

Instead of razzing Peabody over the baby talk, Eve left her at it.

"Lieutenant." Roarke's face filled the screen. "What can I —" Instantly his easy smile vanished, and his eyes were bright and hard. "What happened, how badly are you hurt?"

"Not much. Mostly it's somebody else's blood. Look, I'm in a private betting parlor, and something's off. I've got some ideas, but take a quick look, give me your take."

"All right, if your next stop is a health center."

"I haven't got time for a health center."

"Then I haven't time for a consult."

"Goddamn it." She was tempted just to cut transmission, but took a steadying breath instead. "Peabody's going to get the first aid kit. I got a couple of scratches, that's all. I swear."

"Turn your head to the left."

She rolled her eyes but complied.

"Get them seen to." He snapped it out, then shrugged as if in acceptance. "Let me see what you're looking at."

"Lots of numbers. Different games," she began as she turned her unit so that he'd have her view. "Arena ball, baseball, the horses, the droid rats. I think the third screen from the right is —"

"Overdue loans on bets. Interest compounded well above legal limits. The screen directly below is outlay, for loan collection. On the screen beside that, you have what looks like private games — casino style. Look on your console, see if you find a control that's linked to that screen. If it's simple, it'll be something like 3-C, for the placement of the screen in the grid."

"Yeah, here."

"Give it a flip. Ah," he said as the screen switched to monitor and played a busy casino, full of smoke and tables and glassy-eyed patrons. "What kind of building are you in?"

"Loft, West Village, two levels, four units."

"I wouldn't be surprised if the other level isn't very busy at this moment."

"This area isn't zoned for gambling."

"Well then." He grinned at her. "Shame on them."

"Thanks for the tip."

"My pleasure, Lieutenant. See to that injury, Darling Eve, or I'll be seeing to it myself first chance. I won't be happy with you."

He cut her off before she could make some snippy remark, which she figured was just as well. She turned and caught Peabody, the little white dog nestled in her arms, watching her with speculation.

"He knows a lot about illegal gambling runs."

"He knows a lot about legal ones, too. He gave us a lever with Maylou here. Do you care how or why?"

"No." Peabody rubbed her cheek on the

dog's fur, smiled. "It's just interesting. You going to bust the operation?"

"That's going to depend on Maylou here." Eve rose as the woman began to moan and stir. She made bubbling sounds, coughed, then began to buck, her enormous butt humping up, her surprisingly small feet kicking.

Eve simply crouched down. "Assaulting an officer," she began in an easy voice. "Resisting arrest, loan-sharking, spine cracking, running an illegal gambling facility. How's that for starters, Maylou?"

"You broke my nose."

At least that's what Eve assumed she said as the words were muffled and slurred. "Yep, looks like."

"You have to call the MTs. It's the law."

"Interesting, you refreshing me on the law. I think we can hold off on the broken nose a little while. Of course, the broken arm's going to need attention."

"I don't have a broken arm."

"Yet." Eve bared her teeth. "Now, Maylou, if you want medical attention and want me to consider looking the other way as regards your enterprise downstairs, tell me all there is to tell about Linus Quim."

"You're not here to bust me?"

"That's up to you. Quim."

"Penny-ante. Not a gambler, he just plays at it. Like a hobby. He's lousy at it. Costs him an average of a hundred K a year. Never bets more than a hundred bills straight, and usually half that, but he's regular. Jesus, my face is killing me. Can't I have some Go-Numb?"

"When did you talk to him last?"

"Last night. He likes to do the e-betting deal rather than over the 'link. Transmits twice a week, minimum. Last night, he laid a hundred on the Brawlers on tonight's arena ball — and that's rich, for him. Said he was feeling lucky."

"Did he?" Eve leaned closer. "Did he say that, exactly?"

"Yeah. He says, put me down a hundred on the Brawlers for tomorrow night. I'm feeling lucky. He even smiled, sort of. Said he was going to double it and let it ride on the next night once he won."

"In a good mood, was he?"

"For Quim, he was doing a happy dance. Guy's mostly a pain in the ass, a whiner. But he pays up, and he's regular, so I got no beef with him."

"Good thing. Now, that wasn't so bad, was it, Maylou?"

"You're not going to bust me?"

"I don't work Vice or Bunko. You're not

220

my problem." She released the restraints, hooked them in her back pocket. "If I were you, I'd call the MTs and tell them I walked into a wall — tripped over your little dog."

"Squeakie!" Maylou rolled over to her ample butt, threw open her arms. The dog leaped out of Peabody's hold and into Maylou's lap. "Did the nasty cop hurt Mama's baby girl?"

With a shake of her head, Eve headed out. "Give it two weeks," she told Peabody, "then call Hanson in Vice and give him this address."

"You said you weren't going to bust her."

"No, I said she wasn't my problem. She's going to be Hanson's."

Peabody glanced back. "What's going to happen to the dog? Hey, and the apartment. Maybe the bust will drive down the rent. You should see the kitchen, Dallas. It's mag."

"Keep dreaming." She got in the car, then scowled when Peabody popped the dash compartment. "What are you doing?"

"First aid kit."

"Stay away from me."

"It's either me or the health center."

"I don't need a health center. Don't touch me."

"Stop being a baby." Enjoying the role of

nurse, Peabody chose her tools. "Ass-kickers aren't afraid of a little first aid kit. Close your eyes if you don't want to see."

Trapped, Eve gripped the wheel, closed her eyes. She felt the quick, biting sting of the antiseptic before the numbing properties took hold. The smell of it spun in her head, rolled into her belly.

She heard the low hum of the suture wand.

She started to make some sarcastic comment to take her mind off the annoyance of the procedure. Then suddenly, she was sucked back.

The dim and dingy health center ward. The hundreds of stings as hundreds of cuts were treated. The vile buzz of the machines as her broken arm was examined.

"What's your name? You have to give us your name. Tell us who hurt you? What's your name? What happened to you?"

I don't know. In her mind she screamed it, again and again. But she lay still, she lay silent, trapped in terror as strangers poked and prodded, as they stared and they questioned.

"What's your name?"

"I don't know!"

"Sir. Dallas. Hey."

Eve opened her eyes, stared into Peabody's wide ones. "What? What is it?"

"You're really pale. Dallas, you look a little sick. Maybe we should swing by a health center after all."

"I'm all right." Her hands fisted hard until she felt herself steady again. "I'm okay. Just need some air." She ordered the window down, started the car.

And pushed the helpless young girl back into the darkest corner of her mind.

chapter ten

Needs must when the devil drives. I can't remember who said that, but I don't suppose it's important. Whoever it was is long dead now. As Linus Quim is dead now.

Needs must. My needs must. But who was the devil in this coupling? Foolish, greedy Quim or myself?

Perhaps that's not important either, for it's done. There can be no going back, no staging events to another outcome. I can only hope events were staged convincingly enough to satisfy those sharp eyes of Lieutenant Dallas.

She is an exacting audience and, I fear, the most severe of critics.

Yes, with her in the house, I fear. My performance must be perfection in every way. Every line, every gesture, every nuance. Or her view will no doubt ruin me.

Motive and opportunity, Eve thought as she walked to her own front door. Too many people had both. Richard Draco would be memorialized the next day, and she had no doubt there would be a lavish display of grief, passionate and emotional eulogies, copious tears.

And it would all be just another show.

He'd helped seduce Areena Mansfield into drugs and put a smear on her rise to stardom.

He'd stood in the spotlight Michael Proctor desperately wanted for his own.

He'd humiliated and used Carly Landsdowne in a very public fashion.

He'd been a splinter under the well-manicured fingernail of Kenneth Stiles.

He'd considered Eliza Rothchild too old and unattractive to bother with.

There had been others, so many others it was impossible to count, who had reason to wish Richard Draco ill.

But whoever had acted on it, planned and executed the murder, had enough cool, enough will to have lured a greedy theater tech into a hangman's noose.

She wasn't looking for brutality or rage but for cold blood and a clear mind. Those qualities in a killer were much more difficult to root out.

She wasn't moving forward, she thought with frustration. Every step she took simply pushed her further into the artifice of a world she found mildly annoying.

What kind of people spent their lives

dressing up and playing make-believe?

Children. It struck her as she closed her hand around the doorknob. On some level, wasn't she looking for a very clever, very angry child?

She gave a half laugh. Great. What she knew about children wouldn't fill the pinhole made by a laser drill.

She flung open the front door, intending to throw herself into a blisteringly hot shower, then back into work.

The music pierced her ears, rattled her teeth. She all but felt her eyes jiggle in her head. It was a screech of sound, punctuated by a blast of noise, layered with braying waves of chaos.

It was Mavis.

The irritable mood that had come through the door with Eve didn't have a chance. It exploded in the sheer volume and exuberance of Mavis Freestone's unique musical style. Eve found herself grinning as she stepped up to the doorway of what Roarke referred to as the parlor.

There in all the splendor, the elegance, the antiquity, Mavis danced — Eve supposed that was the closest word for it — bouncing and jiggling atop graduated stacked heels that lifted her tiny frame a full six inches from the floor. Their swirling pink and green pattern matched the hair that flew in yard-long braids around her flushed, delighted face and fairy body.

Her slim legs were green, with little pink butterflies fluttering up in a spiral pattern, then disappearing under the tiny, flippy skirt of fuschia that barely covered her crotch. Her torso was decorated in a criss-cross of the two colors with one pretty breast in pink, another in green.

Eve could only be relieved that Mavis had chosen to go with the green for both eyes. You just never knew.

Roarke sat in one of his lovely antique chairs, a glass of straw-colored wine in one hand. He was either relaxing into the show, Eve thought, or he'd lapsed into a protective coma.

The music, such as it was, crescendoed, led by a long, plaintive wail from the singer. Blessed silence fell like a cargo ship of bricks.

"What do you think?" Mavis tossed back the mop of bicolored braids. "It's a good follow-up number for the new video. Not too tame, is it?"

"Ah." Roarke took a moment to sip his wine. There'd been a moment when he'd been mildly concerned that the decibel level would shatter the crystal. "No. No indeed.

Tame isn't the word that comes to mind."

"Mag!" She bounced over, and her little butt wriggled with energy as she bent down to kiss him. "I wanted you to see it first since you're, like, the money man."

"Money always bows to talent."

If Eve hadn't already loved him, she'd have fallen face first then and there, seeing the absolute joy his words put in Mavis's eyes.

"It's so much *fun!* The recordings, the concerts, the way iced costumes Leonardo gets to design for me. It's hardly even like work. If it weren't for you and Dallas, I'd still be scraping gigs at joints like the Blue Squirrel."

She did a quick spin as she spoke, spotted Eve, and beamed like sunshine. "Hey! I've got a new number."

"I heard. Totally mag."

"Roarke said you'd be late, and you — Oh wow, is that blood?"

"What? Where?" Because her mind had switched channels, Eve whipped her gaze around the room before Mavis leaped toward her.

"It's all over you." Mavis's panicked hands patted Eve's breasts, shoulders. "We should call a doctor, a medi-unit. Roarke, make her lie down."

"And there is my constant goal in life."

"Har har. It's not my blood, Mavis."

"Oh." Instantly, Mavis's hands jumped back. "Ick."

"Don't worry, it's dry. I was going to shower and change at Central, but I weighed the potential of a piss stream of chilly water against a flood of hot and came home instead. Got another of those around?" she asked Roarke with a nod toward his wine.

"Absolutely. Turn your head."

She made a sound of annoyance, but tilted her head to show the treated scratches already healing.

"Man-o," Mavis said with admiration in her voice. "Somebody swiped you good. Musta had mag nails."

"But bad aim. She missed the eyes." She took the wine Roarke brought her. "Thanks for the tip before," she told him. "It panned out."

"Happy to oblige. Tilt your head up."

"Why? I showed you the nail rakes."

"Up," he repeated, nudging it back himself with the tip of his finger, then closing his mouth warm and firmly over hers. "As you can see, I have excellent aim."

"Awwww. You guys are so cute." With her hands folded at breast level, Mavis beamed at them.

"Yeah, we're just like a couple of puppies." Amused, Eve sat on the arm of a sofa, sipped at her wine. "It's a great new number, Mavis. All you."

"You think? I ran it for Leonardo, and now you two, but nobody else's seen it."

"It's . . ." Eve remembered Whitney's comment. "Got juice."

"That's what I thought. Roarke, can I tell her?"

"Tell me what?"

Mavis bit her lip, looked to Roarke for agreement, then, at his nod, drew two deep breaths. "Okay. My last disc cut, *Curl Your Hair*, Roarke got early word that it's hitting in the top five of next week's *Vid-Tracks*. Dallas, I'm fucking number three, right behind the Butt-Busters and Indigo."

She might not have had a clue who Butt-Busters or Indigo might be, but Eve knew *Vid-Tracks* was Mavis's bible. "That's fabulous." Eve rose quickly, gave Mavis a hard hug. "You kick ass."

"Thanks." Mavis sniffed, wiped a tear off silver-tipped lashes. "You're the first person I've told. I started to call Leonardo, but I want to tell him up-face, you know. And I'm glad I got to tell you first, anyhow. He'll understand."

"He'll go nuts."

"Yeah. We've got some serious cele-brating to do. I'm really glad you weren't late after all, so I could tell you and so you didn't miss the girl deal."

Instantly, warning flags sprang up in Eve's gut, fluttered nervously. "Girl deal?"

"Yeah, you know. Trina's already down in the pool house setting up. Figured we could use a swim and a spin in the relaxation tank. We're up for the full treatment."

"Full treatment?" *No,* was all Eve could think. *Not the full treatment. Anything but that.* "Look, Mavis, I just came home to work. I've got this case —"

"You've always got a case." Undeterred, Mavis poured herself a glass of wine, then brought the bottle to top Eve's off as Roarke lazily lighted a cigarette and smiled. "You've got to take time for you, or your internal or-gans get all shriveled and your skin goes saggy. I read all about it. Anyway, Trina's got some outrageous new body paint."

"No. Absolutely. I don't do body paint."

Mavis rolled her eyes. "For me, Dallas. We know you. But I think you should give it a try one of these days. I bet Roarke would really go for the Gold-Dust. It does amazing things for the boobs. Makes them sparkle."

"I don't want sparkling boobs."

"It's flavored, too. Frangipani."

231

"Really?" Roarke blew out a stream of smoke. "I'm very fond of tropical flavors."

"See? Anyway, you can think about that after you're all relaxed and your hair's gooped up. Summerset made snacks."

"Goodie. But really, I — oops, there's the door. I'll get it."

She escaped, forcing herself not to simply break into a run, bowl over whoever was at the door, and just keep running until she reached the sanctuary of Cop Central. She beat Summerset there by half a step.

"I'm getting it."

"Greeting and escorting guests falls into my job requirements," he reminded her. "Miss Furst is here to see you." So saying, he bumped Eve aside and opened the door.

"I should have called." Nadine knew just how Eve felt about reporters in her home. "I'm not here for 75," she continued quickly. "It's personal."

"Good. Fine. Come in." To Nadine's surprise, Eve clamped a hand on hers and all but dragged her toward the parlor.

"I've taken a couple of days off," Nadine began.

"I noticed. I didn't much care for your on-air substitute."

"He's a putz. But anyway, I wanted to

come by and tell you . . ." She paused, pulled herself back. "Oh, hi, Mavis."

"Nadine, hi! Hey, it's practically a party." However flighty Mavis seemed on the surface, she had a solid core of sense, with compassion and loyalty wrapped tightly around it. It took less than two seconds for her to see the strain in Nadine's eyes.

"Listen, I'm just going to run down and see how Trina's doing. Back in a flash." She went out in one, dashing through the door in a blur of color.

"Sit down, Nadine." Roarke was already up, leading her to a chair. "Would you like some wine?"

"I would, thanks, I would. But I'd really like one of those cigarettes."

"I thought you were quitting," Eve said as Roarke offered one.

"I am." Nadine sent Roarke a look of gratitude as he flicked on his lighter. "I quit regularly. Listen, I'm sorry to bust in on you both this way."

"Friends are always welcome." He poured the wine, gave it to her. "I assume you want to talk to Eve. I'll leave you alone."

"No, don't feel you have to go." Nadine took another long drag of the pricey tobacco. "Jesus, I forget you have the real thing. A bigger kick than herbals. No, don't go," she said again. "Dallas tells you every-thing anyway."

Roarke's face showed surprise. "Does she?"

"No," Eve said definitely but lowered to the arm of a chair. "I did tell him about your problem because of his connection to Draco. And his connection to you."

"It's all right." Nadine managed a weak smile. "Mortification builds character."

"You have nothing to be embarrassed about. Life would be awfully dull if we could look back without regretting at least one affair."

Her smile relaxed. "You plucked a winner here, Dallas. Nothing like a man who says the right thing at the right time. Well, Richard Draco is my regret. Dallas." She shifted her gaze to Eve's. "I know you don't have to tell me, couldn't obviously during the interview earlier. Maybe you can't tell me at all, but I have to ask. Am I in trouble?"

"What did your lawyer say?"

"Not to worry and not to talk to you without him present." She smiled grimly. "I'm having a hard time following his advice."

"I can't scratch you off the list, Nadine. But," she added as Nadine closed her eyes and nodded. "Since you're coming in dead last, I'd give taking the first part of your lawyer's advice another try."

Nadine huffed out a breath, sipped her wine. "First time I've ever been happy to be a loser."

"Mira's opinion weighs heavily, and she doesn't believe you're capable of calculated murder. Neither does the primary on a personal level or, considering the current evidence, on a professional one."

"Thank you. Thanks." Nadine lifted a hand to her head, pressed her fingers to the center of her brow. "I keep telling myself this is going to go away soon. That you'll wrap it up. But the stress is like a spike through my brain."

"I'm going to have to give you just a little more. Were you aware Draco had a video of you?"

"Video?" Nadine dropped her hand, frowned. "You mean of my work?"

"Well, some people consider sex work."

Nadine stared, eyes blank with confusion. Then they cleared, and Eve saw exactly what she wanted to see: shock, fury, embarrassment. "He had a video of . . . He took — he had a camera when we —" She slammed down the wine, surged to her feet. "That slimy son of a bitch. That perverted bastard."

"I'd say the answer's no," Roarke murmured, and Nadine whirled on him.

"What kind of man takes videos of a woman in his bed when she doesn't consent? What kind of sick thrill does he get from raping her that way? Because that's just what it is."

She jabbed a finger in his chest, for no other reason than he was a man. "Would you do that to Dallas? She'd kick your butt from here to Tarus III if you did. That's just what I'd like to do to Draco. No, no, I'd like to take his puny dick in my hands and twist it until it popped right off."

"Under the circumstances, I'd prefer not to be his stand-in."

She hissed out a breath, sucked one in, then held up her hands, palms out. "Sorry. It's not your fault." To find control again, she paced, then turned to face Eve.

"I guess that little display of temper moved me up the list a few notches."

"Just the opposite. If you'd known about the disc, you'd have attempted a quick castration. You wouldn't have let someone else stick him. You just verified your own profile."

"Well, good for me. Yippee." Nadine dropped into the chair again. "I guess the disc's in evidence."

"Has to be. No one's going to view it for thrills, Nadine. If it helps, you don't show up that much. He angled things so he's in the spotlight, so to speak."

"Yes, he would. Dallas, if the media gets hold of that —"

"They won't. If you want my advice, go back to work. Keep your mind busy, and let me do my job. I'm good at it."

"If I didn't know that, I'd be on tranqs."

Inspiration struck. "How about a girl night instead?"

"Huh?"

"Mavis and Trina are all set. I don't have time for it, and there's no point in Trina dragging her whole bag of tricks over here and not putting it to full use. Take my place. Go have the works."

"I could use some relaxation therapy."

"There you go." Eve hauled her out of the chair. "You'll feel like a new woman in no time. Go for the body paint," she suggested as she pulled Nadine out of the room. "It'll give you a fresh outlook and sparkling boobs."

Moments later, Eve came back into the parlor, dusting her hands.

"Well done, Lieutenant."

"Yeah, that was pretty slick. They're all down there cooing like . . . what coos?"

"Doves?" he suggested.

"Yeah, like doves. Now everybody's happy, and I can go back to work. So, you up for a video?"

"Nadine's? Can we have popcorn?"

"Men are perverts. No, not Nadine's, funny guy. But the popcorn's a good idea."

She'd intended to set up in her office, to keep it official. She should have known better. She ended up in one of the second-level lounging rooms, snuggled into the sinfully soft cushions of the mile-long sofa, watching the taped play on a huge wall screen, and with a bowl of popcorn in her lap.

The size of the screen had been Roarke's selling point. It was impossible to miss even the smallest detail when every feature was larger than life.

It was, she realized, almost like being on-stage herself. She had to give Roarke points for that one.

Eliza, she noted, had embraced her role of the fussy, irritating nurse assigned to monitor Sir Wilfred. Her period costume was anything but flattering. Her hair was scraped back, her mouth a constant purse. She affected an annoyingly lilting voice like the ones Eve had heard some parents use on recalcitrant offspring.

Kenneth hadn't stinted on his portrayal of the pompous, cranky barrister. His movements were jerky, restless. His eyes sly. His voice would, by turns boom loud enough to shake the rafters, then drop into a crafty murmur.

But it was Draco who owned the play during the first scenes. He was undeniably handsome, outrageously charming, carelessly amused. Yes, she could see how a vulnerable woman would fall for him — as Vole or as himself.

"Freeze screen." She pushed the bowl at Roarke and rose to move closer to the image of Draco. "Here's what I see. The others are acting. They're good, they're skilled, they're enjoying the roles. He *is* the role. He doesn't have to act. He's an egocentric, as arrogant and as smooth as Vole. It's a part tailored for him."

"So I thought, when I put his name forward for the play. What does that tell you?"

"That whoever planned his murder probably thought the same thing. And saw the irony of it. Vole dies in the last act. Draco dies in the last act. A dramatic bit of justice. Executed, before witnesses."

She walked back to sit. "It doesn't tell me anything new, really. But it solidifies the angles. Resume play."

She waited, watched. Areena's entrance, she saw now, was brilliant in its timing. That was the writer, of course, the director, but the *style* of it had to come from the actor.

Beautiful, classy, mysterious, and coolly sexy. That was the role. But that wasn't the true character, Eve remembered. The real Christine Vole revealed herself to be a woman consumed by love. One who would lie for the man she knew to be a murderer, who would sacrifice her dignity, her reputation to save him from the law. And who, in the end, executed him for dismissing that love.

"It's acting on two levels," Eve murmured. "Just as Draco is. Neither of them show the face of their character until the last scene."

"They're both very skilled."

"No, they're all skilled. All used to manipulating words and actions to present an image. I haven't chipped through the image yet. Sir Wilfred believes he's defending an innocent man, and in the end learns he was duped. That's enough to piss you off. If we're correlating life and make-believe. It's enough to kill for."

He'd thought the same himself, and nodded. "Go on."

"The character of Diana believed every bullshit line Vole fed her. That his wife was a cold bitch, that he was innocent, that he was going to leave her."

"The other woman," Roarke put in. "The younger one. A little naive, a little grasping."

"In the end, won't she figure out she was duped and used and be mortified? Just as Carly learned she was duped and used and mortified. As Christine learned. And there's Michael Proctor standing in the wings, hungry to take it all on."

She studied the faces, listened to the voices, measured the connections. "It's one of them, one of the players. I know it. It's not some tech with a grudge, or with dreams of being in the lights. It's someone who's been in the lights and knows how to wear the right face at the right time."

She fell silent again, watching the play progress, searching for some chink, some instant when a glance, a gesture indicated the feelings and plans beneath the facade.

But no, they were good, she mused. Every one of them.

"That's the dummy knife, first courtroom scene. Freeze screen, enhance sector P-Q, twenty-five percent."

The screen shifted smoothly, with the evidence table enlarging. The knife on it was in clear view from this angle, and enlarged, Eve could see the subtle differences between it and the murder weapon.

"The blade's nearly the same size and shape, but the handle's a bit wider, thicker. It's the same color, but it's not the same material." She let out a breath. "But you wouldn't notice it unless you were looking for it. You expect to see the prop, so you see it. Draco could have looked right at it, hell, he might have picked it up himself, and he wouldn't have noticed. Resume normal play."

Her head was beginning to throb lightly. She barely noticed when Roarke began to rub her shoulders. She watched the change of scenes, the curtain drop, the soundless circling of one set for another. A few techs slipped across behind the curtain, nearly indistinguishable in their traditional black.

But she spotted Quim. He was clearly in charge now, in his element. He gestured, a kind of theater sign language that meant little to her. She saw him consult briefly with the prop master, nod, then glance downstage left.

"There." Eve leaped to her feet again. "He sees something, something that doesn't fit. He's hesitating, yeah, just for a second, studying. And now he's moving off in the same direction. What did you see? Who did you see? Damn it."

She turned back to Roarke. "That was the switch. The real knife's on the courtroom set now. Waiting."

She ordered the disc to reverse, then set her wrist unit to time, and replayed. "Okay, now he spots it."

Behind her, Roarke rose, moved to the AutoChef and ordered her coffee. When he stepped beside her, she took the cup without realizing it, drank.

On-screen, extras moved out to their marks. The bartender took his position, techs vanished. Areena, dressed in the cheap and gaudy costume that suited a mid-twentieth-century barfly, took her seat on a stool at the end of a bar. She angled herself away from the audience.

A train whistle blew. Curtain up.

"Two minutes, twelve seconds. Time enough to stash the knife. Right in the roses, or somewhere no one would notice until it could be moved. But it's close. Very close. And very ballsy."

"Sex and ambition," Roarke murmured.

"What?"

"Sex and ambition. That's what killed Leonard Vole, and that's what killed Richard Draco. Life imitates art."

★ ★ ★

Peabody wouldn't have said so, at least not if she used the animated painting she was currently trying to study. And pretend she understood. She sipped the champagne Charles had given her and struggled to look as sophisticated as the rest of the guests at the art show.

She was dressed for it, at least, she thought with some relief. Eve's Christmas present to her had been her gorgeous undercover wardrobe designed by Mavis's wonderful lover, Leonardo. But the shimmering sweep of blue silk couldn't transform the Midwestern sensibility.

She couldn't make head nor tail of the creeping movement of shape and color.

"Well, it's really . . . something." Since that was the best she could come up with, she drank more champagne.

Charles chuckled and gave her shoulder an affectionate rub. "You're a sweetheart for putting up with me, Delia. You must be bored to death."

"No, I'm not." She glanced up at his marvelous face, smiled. "I'm just art-stupid."

"There's nothing stupid about you." He bent down, gave her a light kiss.

She wanted to sigh. It was still next to impossible to believe she could be in a place like this, dressed like this, with a gorgeous man on her arm. And it galled, *galled* to think that she was much more suited to take-out Chinese in McNab's pitiful apartment.

Well, she was just going to keep going to art shows, operas, and ballets until some of it rubbed off on her, even if it all made her feel as if she was acting in some classy play and didn't quite have her lines down.

"Ready for supper?"

"I'm always ready for supper." That line, she realized, came straight from the heart. Or the gut.

He'd reserved an intimate private room at some swank restaurant with candlelight and flowers. He was always doing something like that, Peabody mused as he pulled out her chair at a pretty table with pink roses and white candles. She let him order for both of them because he'd know just the right thing.

He seemed to know all the right things. And all the right people. She wondered if Eve ever felt so clunky and out of place when she found herself with Roarke in posh surroundings.

She couldn't imagine her lieutenant ever feeling clunky.

Besides, Roarke loved her. No, the man adored her. Everything had to be different when you were sitting across candlelight with a man who thought you were the most vital woman in the world. The only woman in the world.

"Where have you gone?" Charles asked quietly.

She jerked herself back. "Sorry. I guess there's a lot on my mind." She picked up her fork to sample the saucy seafood appetizer. The perfection of it on the tongue nearly had her eyes crossing in ecstasy.

"Your work." He reached across the table to pat her hand. "I'm glad you were able to take a break from it after all and come out tonight."

"We didn't work as late as I thought we would."

"The Draco matter. Do you want to talk about it?"

It was just one more perfect thing about him. He would ask and listen if she chose to unburden herself. "No, not really. Can't anyway at this stage. Except to say Dallas is frustrated. So many levels and angles make it slow going."

"I'm sure it does. Still, she seemed her usual competent self when she spoke to me."

Peabody's hand froze as she reached for her wineglass. "She spoke to you? About the case?"

Caught off guard, Charles set his fork down. "She didn't mention it to you?"

"No. Did you know Draco?"

Charles cursed himself, briefly considered dancing around the truth, then shrugged. He'd never been anything but honest with Peabody and didn't want that to change. "No, not really. I happened to be with Areena Mansfield the other night when Dallas and Roarke dropped by to speak with her. I was working."

"Oh." Charles's profession didn't bother Peabody. He did what he did, just as she did what she did. Maybe if they'd been lovers, she'd have a different attitude, but they weren't.

Damn it.

"Oh." She said again, because his profession did a lot more than bother her lieutenant. "Shit."

"Put simply, yeah. It was awkward, but Dallas and I came to terms."

"What kind of terms?"

"We talked. Delia, I've tried not to say too much because it puts you in the middle. I never wanted that."

"You never put me there," she said immediately. "Dallas did."

"Because you matter very much to her."

"My personal life is —"

"A concern to her, as a friend, Delia."

The quiet censure in his tone made her wince, then give up. "Okay, I know it. I don't have to like it."

"I think things should be smoother now. She had her say, I had mine, and we both felt better for it. And when I explained to her that we weren't having sex, she —"

"What?" The word squeaked out as Peabody jumped to her feet. Sparkling silver, glittering crystal danced on the white linen cloth. "You told her that? *That?* Good God. Why don't you just strip me naked and push me into the squad room?"

"I wanted her to know we had a friendship, not a professional agreement. I'm sorry." Recognizing his misstep too late, Charles rose, lifted his hands. "I didn't mean to embarrass you."

"You tell my immediate superior that I've been seeing a professional for what, nearly three months, and haven't done the mattress dance. No, no, jeez, what could be embarrassing about that?"

"I didn't realize you'd wanted sex to be part of our relationship." He spoke stiffly now. "If you had, you had only to ask."

"Oh yeah, right. I say, how about it, Charles, and I'm a client."

The muscles in his belly went taut as wire.

"Is that what you think?"

"I don't know what to think." She dropped into her chair again, briefly held her head in her hand. "Why did you have to tell her that?"

"I suppose I was defending myself." It was a tough admission to swallow. "I didn't think beyond it. I'm very sorry." He moved his chair over so that he could sit close and take her hand. "Delia, I didn't want to spoil our friendship, and for the first stages of it, I was hung up on someone who couldn't, who wouldn't be with me because of what I am. You helped me through that. I care very much about you. If you want more . . ."

He lifted her hand, brushed his lips over the inside of her wrist.

Her pulse gave a little dance. It was only natural, she supposed. Just as it was natural for her blood to go warm, very warm, when he shifted that skilled mouth from her wrist to her lips.

But doubts churned inside of her, side by side with simple lust. It was infuriating to realize not all the doubts were directed at Charles.

"Sorry." She broke the kiss, eased back, and wondered when she'd lost her mind. There was a gorgeous man she liked very much, and who knew all there was to know about sexual pleasures, ready to show her just what could be done to the human body, and she was playing coy.

"I've hurt your feelings."

"No. Well, maybe a little." She drummed up a smile. "Fact is, this is a first for me. I've completely lost my appetite. All across the board."

chapter eleven

Working out of her home office could be an advantage. The equipment, even counting her new computer system at Central, was far superior. There were fewer distractions. And it was next to impossible to run out of coffee.

Eve chose to do so from time to time, even if only to have a fresh view to clear her mind.

Her plan today was to start the morning with something fulfilling. She stood in the center of her home office, smirking down at her old, despised, computer.

"Today," she told it, "death comes to all your circuits. Will it be slow and systematic or fast and brutal?" Considering, she circled it. "Tough decision. I've waited so long for this moment. Dreamed of it."

Showing her teeth, she began to roll up her sleeves.

"What," Roarke asked from the doorway that connected their work areas, "is that?"

"The former bane of my existence. The Antichrist of technology. Do we have a hammer?"

Studying the pile on the floor, he walked in. "Several, I imagine, of various types."

"I want all of them. Tiny little hammers, big wallbangers, and everything in between."

"Might one ask why?"

"I'm going to beat this thing apart, byte by byte, until there's nothing left but dust from the last trembling chip."

"Hmmm." Roarke crouched down, examined the pitifully out-of-date system. "When did you haul this mess in here?"

"Just now. I had it in the car. Maybe I should use acid, just stand here and watch it hiss and dissolve. That could be good."

Saying nothing, Roarke took a small case out of his pocket, opened it, and chose a slim tool. With a few deft moves, he had the housing open.

"Hey! Hey! What're you doing?"

"I haven't seen anything like this in a decade. Fascinating. Look at this corrosion. Christ, this is a SOC chip system. And it's cross-wired."

When he began to fiddle, she rushed over and slapped at his hands. "Mine. I get to kill it."

"Get a grip on yourself," he said absently and delved deeper into the guts. "I'll take this into research."

"No. Uh-uh. I have to bust it apart. What if it breeds?"

He grinned and quickly replaced the housing. "This is an excellent learning tool. I'd like to give it to Jamie."

"What're you talking about? Jamie Lingstrom, the e-prodigy?"

"Mmm. He does a little work for me now and then."

"He's a kid."

"A very bright one. Bright enough that I prefer having him on my team rather than competing with him. It'll be interesting to see what he can do with an old, defective system like this."

"But I want it dead."

He had to smother a chuckle. It was as close to a whine as he'd ever heard from her. "There, there, darling. I'll find you something else to beat up. Or better," he said, wrapping his arms around her, "another outlet entirely for all that delightful natural aggression."

"Sex wouldn't give me the same rush."

"Ah. A dare." He accepted it by leaning down and biting her jaw. When she swore at him, he took her mouth in a hot, hungry, brain-sucking kiss.

"Okay, that was pretty good, but just what are you doing with your hands back there?"

"Hardly anything until I lock the door, and then —"

"Okay, okay, you can have the damn thing." She shoved away from him, tried to catch her breath. Her system was vibrating. "Just get it out of my sight."

"Thank you." He caught her hand, lifted it, nibbled on her fingers as he watched her. One taste of her always made him crave another. And another. He tugged her forward, intending to nudge her into his office.

Peabody walked in.

"Sorry." She averted her eyes, tilting her head to study the ceiling. "Summerset said I should come right up."

"Good morning, Peabody." Roarke gave his wife's furrowed brow a quick brush of his lips. "Can we get you some coffee?"

"I'll get it. Don't mind me. Just a lowly aide." She muttered it as she crossed the room, giving Eve a wide berth as she aimed for the kitchen.

"She's upset about something." Roarke frowned toward the kitchen area as he listened to Peabody muttering as she programmed the AutoChef.

"She just hasn't had her morning fix yet. Take that heap of junk out of here if you want it so much. I have to get to work."

He hefted the system, discovered he had

to put his back into it. "They made them a lot heavier back then. I'll be working from home until noon," he called over his shoulder, then his door closed behind him.

It was probably shallow, it was definitely *girlie* to have gotten such a rise out of watching that ripple of muscle. Eve told herself she wouldn't have noticed if he hadn't stirred her up in the first place.

"Peabody, bring me a cup of that."

She went behind her desk, called up the Draco file, and separating it into suspects, witnesses, evidence gathered, and lab reports, ordered all data on the screens.

"I reviewed the disc of the play last night," she began when she heard the sturdy clop of Peabody's hard-soled cop shoes cross the room. "I have a theory."

"Your coffee, Lieutenant. Shall I record, sir?"

"Huh?" Eve was studying the screens, trying to shift and rearrange data in her mind. But Peabody's stiff tone distracted her. "No, I'm just running it by you."

She turned back and saw that once again Roarke was right. Something was up with her aide. She ordered herself not to poke into the personal, and sat. "We've pretty well nailed down the time of the switch. The prop knife is clearly visible here. Computer,

Visual Evidence 6-B, on screen five."

"You've marked and recorded this VE?" Peabody asked, her voice cold as February.

"Last night, after my review." Eve moved her shoulders. The snipe was like a hot itch between her shoulder blades. "So?"

"Just updating my own records, Lieutenant. It is my job."

Fuck it. "Nobody's telling you not to do your job. I'm briefing you, aren't I?"

"Selectively, it appears."

"Okay, what the hell does that mean?"

"I had occasion to return to Central last night." That just added to her slow burn. "In the process of reviewing the file, assimilating evidence and the time line, certain pieces of that evidence, marked and sealed for Level Five, came to my attention. I was unaware, until that point, that there were areas of this investigation considered off limits to your aide and your team. Respectfully, sir, this policy can and will hamper the efficiency of said aide and said team."

"Don't use that snotty tone on me, pal. I marked Level Five what, in my judgment, required Level Five. You don't need to know every goddamn thing."

Little spots of heat bloomed on Peabody's cheeks, but her voice was frosty. "So I am now aware, Lieutenant."

"I said knock it off."

"It's always your way, isn't it?"

"Yeah, damn right. I'm your superior, and I'm the primary on this investigation, so you bet your tight ass it's my way."

"Then you should have advised subject Monroe, Charles, to keep his mouth shut. Shouldn't you? Sir."

Eve set her teeth, ground them. *Try to spare feelings,* she thought, *and you get kicked in the face.* "Subject Monroe, Charles, has, in my opinion, no connection to this investigation. Therefore any communication I've had with him is none of your goddamn business."

"It's my goddamn business when you interrogate him over my goddamn personal relationship with him."

"I didn't interrogate him." Her voice spiked with frustrated fury. "He spilled it all over me."

They were both standing now, leaning over the desk nearly nose-to-nose. Eve's face was pale with temper, Peabody's flushed with it.

When McNab walked in, the scene had him letting out a low, nervous whistle. "Um, hey, guys."

Neither of them bothered to so much as glance in his direction, and said, in unison, at a roar: "Out!"

"You bet. I'm gone."

To insure it, Eve marched over and slammed the door in his fearful and fascinated face.

"Sit down," she ordered Peabody.

"I prefer to stand."

"And I prefer to give you a good boot in the ass, but I'm restraining myself." Eve reached up, fisted her hands in her own hair and yanked until the pain cleared most of the rage.

"Okay, stand. You couldn't sit with that stick up your butt, anyway. One you shove up it every time Subject Monroe, Charles, is mentioned. You want to be filled in, you want to be briefed? Fine. Here it is."

She had to take another deep breath to insure her tone was professional. "On the evening of March twenty-six, at or about nineteen-thirty, I, accompanied by Roarke, had occasion to visit Areena Mansfield's penthouse suite at The Palace Hotel, this city. Upon entering said premises, investigation officer found subject Mansfield in the company of one Charles Monroe, licensed companion. It was ascertained and confirmed that LC Monroe was there in a professional capacity and had no links to the deceased or the current investigation. His presence, and the salient details pertaining to it, were noted in the report of the interview and marked Level Five in a stupid, ill-conceived attempt by the investigating officer to spare her fat-headed aide any unnecessary embarrassment."

Eve stomped back to her desk, snatched up her coffee, gulped some down. "Record that," she snapped.

Peabody's lip trembled. She sat. She sniffled.

"Oh, no." In genuine panic, Eve stabbed out a finger. "No, you don't. No crying. We're on duty. There is no crying on duty."

"I'm sorry." Knowing she was close to blubbering, Peabody fumbled for her handkerchief and blew her nose lavishly. "I'm just so mad, so embarrassed. He told you we've never had sex."

"Jesus, Peabody, do you think I put that in the report?"

"No. I don't know. No." She sniffled again. "But you know. I've been seeing him for weeks and weeks, and we've never . . . We never even got close to it."

"Well, he explained that when —" At Peabody's howl of horror, Eve winced. Wrong thing to say. Very wrong. But what the hell was the right thing? "Look, he's a nice guy. I didn't give him enough credit. He likes you."

"Then why hasn't he ever jumped me?" Peabody lifted drenched eyes.

"Um . . . sex isn't everything?" Eve hazarded.

"Oh sure, easy for you to say. You're married to the mongo sex god of the century."

"Jesus, Peabody."

"You are. He's gorgeous, he's built, he's smart and sexy and . . . and dangerous. And he loves you. No, he adores you. He'd jump in front of a speeding maxibus for you."

"They don't go very fast," Eve murmured and was relieved when Peabody gave a watery laugh.

"You know what I mean."

"Yeah." Eve glanced toward the connecting doors, felt a hard, almost painful tug. "Yeah, I know. It's, ah, it's not that Charles isn't attracted to you. It's that . . ." Where the hell was Mira when she needed her? "That he respects you. That's it."

Peabody crumpled her handkerchief and moped. "I've had too much respect, if you ask me. I know I'm not beautiful or anything."

"You look good."

"I'm not really sexy."

"Sure you are." At her wit's end, Eve came around the desk, patted Peabody's head.

"If you were a guy, or into same-sex relationships, would you want to have sex with me?"

"Absolutely. I'd jump you in a heartbeat."

"Really?" Brightening at the idea, Peabody wiped her eyes. "Well, McNab can't keep his hands off me."

"Oh man. Peabody, please."

"I don't want him to know. I don't want McNab to know that Charles and I haven't been hitting the sheets."

"He'll never hear it from me. I can guarantee it."

"Okay. Sorry, Dallas. After Charles told me, and I went back to work to take my mind off it, and found those sealed files . . . It kept me up most of the night. I mean, if he didn't say anything relevant, I couldn't figure out why you had two reports and a video disc sealed."

Eve blew out a breath. Interpersonal relationships were tough, she thought. And tricky. "One of the reports and the disc don't involve Charles." Damn it, Peabody was right about one thing, covering them up hampered the investigation. "They involve Nadine."

"Oh. I thought something was up there."

"Look, she had a thing with Draco years ago. She came to me about it. He used her, dumped her, in his usual pattern. When

261

Roarke and I went through his penthouse, we found those personal discs. The one I sealed —"

"Oh. He recorded sex with Nadine. Scum." Peabody sighed. "She's not a suspect, at least not one we're looking at, so you wanted to spare her the embarrassment. Dallas, I'm sorry. All around sorry."

"Okay, let's forget it. Go wash your face or something so McNab doesn't think I've been slapping you around."

"Right. Boy, I feel like an idiot."

"Good, that bucks me right up. Now, go pull yourself together so I can pry McNab out of whatever corner he's hiding in, and we can get to work."

"Yes, sir."

By the time they were assembled in her office, Feeney had arrived. He'd reviewed the video of the play himself, had enlarged, refocused, enhanced, and worked his e-magic so that the team was able to confirm the time frame of the switch.

The two courtroom scenes were side by side on a split screen, with Feeney in front, showing the minute difference in the shape of the knife, its angle of placement from one to the other.

"Whoever did the switch copped a knife

that so closely resembled the dummy nobody would have noticed it without picking it up and giving it a good looking over."

"The prop master?" McNab asked.

"He'd have no reason to do more than check to see that the knife was still on its mark. The courtroom set stayed — what do you call it — dressed throughout the performance. He'd have noticed if the knife was missing," Feeney added. "According to his statement, he checked the set immediately after the scene change and immediately before it changed again. He had no reason to check otherwise."

"That gives the perpetrator approximately five minutes." Eve tapped her fingers on her mug. "However, we narrow that if we follow the line that Quim saw something or someone suspicious, as it appears he did during the scene break. Under three minutes to get the dummy knife hidden and be back wherever he needed to be. Onstage or in the wings."

"Then the perp had to wait." Peabody narrowed her eyes. "Wait, and count on no one making the switch through the next courtroom scene, through the dialogue and action. Wait out the play until Christine Vole grabs it up and uses it. That's about thirty minutes. A long time to wait."

"Our killer's patient, systematic. I think he or she enjoyed the wait, watching Draco prance around, emoting, drawing applause, all the while knowing it was his last act. I think the killer reveled in it."

Eve set down her coffee, sat on the edge of her desk. "Roarke said something last night. Life imitates art."

Peabody scratched her nose. "I thought it was the opposite."

"Not this time. Why this play? Why this time? There were easier, less risky, more subtle ways to off Draco. I'm thinking the play itself meant something to the killer. The theme of love and betrayal, of false faces. Sacrifice and revenge. The characters of Leonard and Christine Vole have a history. Maybe Draco had a history with his killer. Something that goes back into the past that twisted their relationship."

Feeney nodded, munched on a handful of nuts. "A lot of the players and techs had worked with him before. Theater's like a little world, and the people in it bump into each other over and over."

"Not a professional connection. A personal one. Look, Vole comes off charming, handsome, even a little naive, until you find out he's a heartless, ruthless opportunist. From what we've uncovered, this mirrors

Draco. So who did he betray? Whose life did he ruin?"

"From the interviews, he fucked over everybody." McNab lifted his hands. "Nobody's pretending they loved the guy."

"So we go deeper. We go back. I want you to run the players. Look for the history. Something that pops out. Vole destroyed a marriage or relationship, ruined someone financially. Seduced someone's sister. Set back their career. You look for the data," she told McNab and Feeney. "Peabody and I will chip away at the players."

Eve decided to start with Carly Landsdowne. Something about the woman had set off alarms in her head since their first conversation.

The actress lived in a glossy building with full security, glitzy shops, and circling people glides. The expansive lobby area was elegantly spare, with water-toned tile floors, modest indoor shrubbery, and a discreet security panel worked into an arty geometric design in the wall.

"Good morning," the panel announced in a pleasant male voice when Eve approached. "Please state your business in The Broadway View."

"My business is with Carly Landsdowne."

"One moment, please." There was a quiet tinkle of music to fill the silence. "Thank you for waiting. According to our logs, Ms. Landsdowne has not informed us of any expected visitors. I'll be happy to contact her for you and ask if she is able to receive guests at this time. Please state your name and produce a photo ID."

"You want ID? Here's some ID." Eve shoved her badge up to the needle-sized lens of the camera. "Tell Ms. Landsdowne Lieutenant Dallas doesn't like waiting in lobbies."

"Of course, Lieutenant. One moment, please."

The music picked up where it had left off, and it had Eve gritting her teeth. "I hate this shit. Why do they think recorded strings do anything but cause annoyance and an urgent desire to find the speakers and rip them out?"

"I think it's kind of nice," Peabody said. "I like violins. Reminds me of my mother. She plays," Peabody added when Eve just stared at her.

"Thank you for waiting. Ms. Landsdowne will be happy to see you, Lieutenant Dallas. If you would proceed to elevator number two. You have been cleared. Have a safe and happy day."

"I hate when they say that." Eve strode to the proper elevator. The doors opened, and the same violin music seeped out. It made her snarl.

"Welcome to The Broadway View." A voice oozed over the strings. "We are a fully self-contained, fully secured building. You are welcome to apply for a day pass in order to tour our facilities, including our state-of-the-art fitness and spa center, which offers complete cosmetic, physical, and mental therapies and treatments. Our shopping area can be reached through public or private access and welcomes all major debit cards. The View also offers its patrons and, with proper reservations, the public, three five-star restaurants as well as the popular Times Square Café for those casual dining needs."

"When is it going to shut up?"

"I wonder if they have a swimming pool."

"If you are interested in joining our exclusive community, just press extension ninety-four on any house-link and request an appointment with one of our friendly concierges for a tour of our three model units."

"I'd rather have all the skin peeled from my bones," Eve decided.

"I wonder if they have efficiencies."

"Please exit to the left and proceed to

apartment number two thousand eight. We at The View wish you a pleasant visit."

Eve stepped out of the car and headed left. The apartment doors were widely spaced down a generously sized hallway. Whoever'd designed the place hadn't worried about wasted space, she decided. Then she had the uncomfortable feeling she was going to discover her husband owned the building.

Carly opened the door before Eve could buzz. The actress wore a deep blue lounging robe, her feet bare and tipped with ripe pink. But her hair and face were done and done well, Eve noted.

"Good morning, Lieutenant." Carly leaned against the door for a moment, a deliberately cocky pose. "How nice of you to drop by."

"You're up early," Eve commented. "And here I thought theater people weren't morning people."

Carly's smirk wavered a bit, but she firmed it again as she stepped back. "I have a performance today. Richard's memorial service."

"You consider that a performance?"

"Of course. I have to be sober and sad and spout all the platitudes. It's going to be a hell of an act for the media." Carly gestured toward an attractive curved sofa of soft green in the living area. "I could have put on the same act for you, and quite convincingly. But it seemed such a waste of your time and my talent. Can I offer you coffee?"

"No. It doesn't worry you to be a suspect in a murder investigation?"

"No, because I didn't do it and because it's good research. I may be called on to play one eventually."

Eve wandered to the window wall, privacy screened, and lifted her brows at the killer view of Times Square. The animated billboards were alive with color and promises, the air traffic thick as fleas on a big, sloppy dog.

If she looked over and down, and it was the down that always bothered her, she could see the Gothic spires of Roarke's New Globe Theater.

"What's your motivation?"

"For murder?" Carly sat, obviously enjoying the morning duel. "It would, of course, depend on the victim. But parallelling life, let's call him a former lover who done me wrong. The motivation would be a combination of pride, scorn, and glee."

"And hurt?" Eve turned back, pinned her before Carly could mask the shadow of distress.

"Perhaps. You want to know if Richard hurt me. Yes, he did. But I know how to bind my wounds, Lieutenant. A man isn't worth bleeding over, not for long."

"Did you love him?"

"I thought I did at the time. But it was astonishingly easy to switch that emotion to hate. If I'd wanted to kill him, well, I couldn't have done it better than it was done. Except I would never have sacrificed the satisfaction of delivering the killing blow personally. Using a proxy takes all the fun out of it."

"Is this a joke to you? The end of a life by violent means?"

"Do you want me to pretend to grieve? Believe me, Lieutenant, I could call up huge, choking and rather gorgeous tears for you." Though her mouth continued to smile, little darts of angry lights played in her eyes. "But I won't. I have too much respect for myself and, as it happens, for you, to do something so pitifully obvious. I'm not sorry he's dead. I just didn't kill him."

"And Linus Quim."

Carly's defiant face softened. "I didn't know him very well. But I am sorry he died. You don't believe he killed Richard, then hanged himself, or you wouldn't be here. I suppose I don't, either, however convenient it would be. He was a little, sour-faced man, and in my opinion didn't think of Richard any more than he thought of the rest of us actors. We were part of his scenery. Hanging, it takes time, doesn't it? Not like with Richard."

"Yes. It takes time."

"I don't like suffering."

It was, Eve thought, the first simple statement the woman had made. "I doubt whoever helped him into the noose thought about it. Are you worried, Ms. Landsdowne, that tragedies come in threes?"

Carly started to make some careless remark, then looking into Eve's eyes changed her mind. "Yes. Yes, I am. Theater people are a superstitious lot, and I'm no exception. I don't speak the name of the Scottish play, I don't whistle in a dressing room or wish another performer good luck. But superstitious won't stop me from going back on that stage the moment we're allowed to do so. I won't let it change how I live my life. I've wanted to be an actor for as long as I can remember. Not just an actor," she added with a slow smile. "A star. I'm on my way, and I won't take a detour from the goal."

"The publicity from Draco's murder may just give you a boost toward that goal."

"That's right. If you think I won't exploit it, you haven't taken a good look at me."

"I've taken a look at you. A good look." Eve glanced around the lovely room, toward the staggering view from the window. "For someone who hasn't yet achieved that goal, you live very well."

"I like living well." Carly shrugged. "I'm lucky to have generous and financially responsible parents. I have a trust fund, and I make use of it. As I said, I don't like suffering. I'm not the starving-for-art type. It doesn't mean I don't work at my craft and work hard. I simply enjoy comfortable surroundings."

"Did Draco come here?"

"Once or twice. He preferred using his place. In hindsight, I see it gave him more control."

"And were you aware he recorded your sexual activities?"

It was a bombshell. Eve had her rhythm now, and recognized simple and utter shock in the eyes, in the sudden draining of color. "That's a lie."

"Draco had a recording unit installed in his bedroom. He had a collection of personal discs detailing certain sexual partners. There's one of you, recorded in February. It included the use of a certain apparatus fashioned of black leather and —"

Carly leaped off the sofa. "Stop. You enjoy this, don't you?"

"No. No, I don't. You were unaware of the recording."

"Yes, I was unaware," Carly snapped back. "I might very well have agreed to one, have been intrigued by the idea if he'd suggested it. But I detest knowing it was done without my consent. That a bunch of snickering cops can view it and get their kicks."

"I'm the only cop who's viewed it so far, and I didn't get any kick out of it. You weren't the only woman he recorded, Ms. Landsdowne, without her consent."

"Pardon me if I don't give a fuck." She pressed her fingers to her eyes until she could find a thread of control. "All right, what do I have to do to get it?"

"It's in evidence, and I've had it sealed. It won't be used unless it has to be used. When the case is closed, and you prove to be cleared, I'll see that the disc is given to you."

"I guess that's the best I can expect." She took a long breath. "Thank you."

"Ms. Landsdowne, did you employ illegals in the company of Richard Draco, for sexual stimulation or any reason?"

"I don't do illegals. I prefer using my own mind, my own imagination, not chemicals."

You used them, Eve thought. *But maybe you didn't know what he was slipping into that pretty glass of champagne.*

chapter twelve

Roarke had two holo-conferences, an inter-space transmission, and a head-of-departments meeting, all scheduled for the afternoon and all dealing with his Olympus Resort project. It was over a year in the works, and he intended for it to be open for business by summer.

Not all of the enormous planetwide plea-sure resort would be complete, but the main core, with its luxury hotels and villas, its plush gambling and entertainment com-plexes, was good to go. He had taken Eve there on part of their honeymoon. It had been her first off-planet trip.

He intended to take her back, kicking and screaming no doubt, as interplanetary travel was not on her list of favorite delights.

He wanted time away with her, away from work. His and hers. Not just one of the quick forty-eight-hour jaunts he managed to push her into, but real time, intimate time.

As he pushed away from his in-home con-trol center, he rotated his shoulder. It was nearly healed and didn't trouble him overmuch. But now and again, a faint twinge reminded him of how close both of them had come to dying. Only weeks before, he'd looked at death, then into Eve's eyes.

They'd both faced bloody and violent ends before. But there was more at stake now. That moment of connection, the sheer will in her eyes, the grip of her hand on his, had pulled him back.

They needed each other.

Two lost souls, he thought, taking a moment to walk to the tall windows that looked out on part of the world he'd built for himself out of will, desire, sweat, and dubiously accumulated funds. Two lost souls whose miserable beginnings had forged them into what appeared to be polar opposites.

Love had narrowed the distance, then had all but eradicated it.

She'd saved him. The night his life had hung in her furious and unbreakable grip. She'd saved him, he mused, the first moment he'd locked eyes with her. As impossible as it should have been, she was his answer. He was hers.

He had a need to give her things. The tangible things wealth could command. Though he knew the gifts most often puzzled and flustered her. Maybe because they did, he corrected with a grin. But underlying that overt giving was the fierce foundation to give her comfort, security, trust, love. All the things they'd both lived without most of their lives.

He wondered that a woman who was so skilled in observation, in studying the human condition, couldn't see that what he felt for her was often as baffling and as frightening to him as it was to her.

Nothing had been the same for him since she'd walked into his life wearing an ugly suit and cool-eyed suspicion. He thanked God for it.

Feeling sentimental, he realized. He supposed it was the Irish that popped out of him at unexpected moments. More, he kept replaying the nightmare she'd suffered through a few nights before.

They came more rarely now, but still they came, torturing her sleep, sucking her back into a past she couldn't quite remember. He wanted to erase them from her mind, eradicate them. And knew he never would. Never could.

For months, he'd been tempted to do a full search and scan, to dig out the data on that tragic child found broken and battered in a Dallas alley. He had the skill, and he had the technology to find everything there was to find: details the social workers, the police, the child authorities couldn't.

He could fill in the blanks for her, and, he admitted, for himself.

But it wasn't the way. He understood her well enough to know that if he took on the task, gave her the answers to questions she wasn't ready to ask, it would hurt more than heal.

Wasn't it the same for him? When he'd returned to Dublin after so many years, he'd needed to study some of the shattered pieces of his childhood. Alone. Even then, he'd only glanced at the surface of them. What was left of them were buried. At least for now, he intended to leave them buried.

The now was what required his attention, he reminded himself. And brooding over the past — there was the Irish again — solved nothing. Whether the past was his or Eve's, it solved nothing.

He gathered up the discs and hard copies he'd need for his afternoon meetings. Then hesitated. He wanted another look at her before he left for the day.

But when he opened the connecting doors, he saw only McNab, stuffing what appeared to be an entire burger in his mouth while the computer droned through a background search.

"Solo today, Ian?"

McNab jerked from a lounging to a sitting position, swallowed too fast, choked. Amused, Roarke strolled over and slapped him smartly on the back.

"It helps to chew first."

"Yeah. Thanks. Ah . . . I didn't have much breakfast, so I thought it'd be okay if I . . ."

"My AutoChef is your AutoChef. The lieutenant's in the field, I take it."

"Yeah. She hauled Peabody out about an hour ago. Feeney headed into Central to tie up some threads. I'm working here." He smiled then, a quick flash of strong white teeth. "I got the best gig."

"Lucky you." Roarke managed to find a French fry on McNab's plate that hadn't been drowned in ketchup. He sampled it while he studied the screen. "Running backgrounds? Again?"

"Yeah, well." McNab rolled his eyes, shifting so his silver ear loops clanged cheerfully together. "Dallas has some wild hair about there might be some way-back connection, some business between Draco and one of the players that simmered all these years. Me, I figure we already scanned all the data and found zippo, but she wants another run, below the surface. I'm here to serve. Especially when real cow meat's on the menu."

"Well now, if there is some bit of business, you're unlikely to find it this way, aren't you?"

"I'm not?"

"Something old and simmering, you say." Considering the possibility, Roarke hooked another fry. "If I wanted to find something long buried, so to speak, I'd figure on getting a bit of dirt under my nails."

"I don't follow you."

"Sealed records."

"I don't have the authority to open sealeds. You gotta have probable cause, and a warrant, and all that happy shit." When Roarke merely smiled, McNab straightened, glanced at the entrance door. "Of course, if there was a way around all that off the record —"

"There are ways, Ian. And there are ways."

"Yeah, but there's also the CYA factor."

"Well then, we'll just have to make sure your ass is covered. Won't we?"

"Dallas is going to know, isn't she?" McNab said a few minutes later, when their positions were reversed and Roarke sat at the computer.

"Of course. But you'll find that knowing and proving are far different matters, even to the redoubtable lieutenant."

In any case, Roarke enjoyed his little forays into police work. And he was a man who rarely saw a need to limit his enjoyments.

"Now you see here, Ian, we've accessed the on-record fingerprints and DNA pattern of your primary suspects. Perfectly legitimate."

"Yeah, if I was doing the accessing."

"Only a technicality. Computer, match current identification codes with any and all criminal records, civil actions and suits, including all juvenile and sealed data. A good place to start," he said to McNab.

Working . . . Access to sealed data is denied without proper authority or judicial code. Open records are available. Shall I continue?

"Hold." Roarke sat back, examined his nails. Clean as a whistle, he thought. For the moment. "McNab, be a pal, would you, and fetch me some coffee?"

McNab stuck his hands in his pockets, pulled them out, did a quick mental dance over the thin line between procedure and progress. "Um. Yeah, okay. Sure."

He ducked into the kitchen area, ordered up the coffee. He dawdled. McNab didn't have a clue how long it would take to bypass the red tape and access what was not supposed to be accessed. To calm himself, he decided to see if there was any pie available.

He discovered to his great delight that he had a choice of six types and agonized over which to go for.

"Ian, are you growing the coffee beans in there?"

"Huh?" He poked his head back in. "I was just . . . figured you'd need some time."

He was a sharp tech, Roarke thought, and a delightfully naive young man. "I think this might interest you."

"You got in? Already? But how —" McNab cut himself off as he hurried back to the desk. "No, I'd better not know how. That way, when I'm being charged and booked, I can claim ignorance."

"Charged and booked for what?" Roarke tapped a finger on a sheet of paper. "Here's your warrant for the sealeds."

"My —" Eyes goggling, McNab snatched up the sheet. "It looks real. It's signed by Judge Nettles."

"So it appears."

"Wow. You're not just ice," McNab said reverently. "You're fucking Antarctica."

"Ian, please. You're embarrassing me."

"Right. Um. Why did I ask for Judge Nettles for the warrant again?"

With a laugh, Roarke got to his feet. "I'm sure you can come up with some appropriately convoluted cop speak to justify the request if and when you're asked. My suggestion would be a variation on a shot in the dark."

"Yeah. That's a good one."

"Then I'll leave you to it."

"Okay. Thanks. Ah, hey, Roarke?"

"Yes?"

"There's this other thing." McNab shifted from foot to foot on his purple airboots. "It's kind of personal. I was going to work around to talking to the lieutenant about it, but, well, you know how she is."

"I know precisely." He studied McNab's face, felt a stir of pity wrapped around amusement. "Women, Ian?"

"Oh yeah. Well, woman, I guess. I gotta figure a guy like you knows how to handle them as well as you handle electronics. I just don't get women. I mean I get them," he rushed on. "I don't have any problem with sex. I just don't *get* them, in an intellectual sense. I guess."

"I see. Ian, if you want me to discuss the intricacies and capriciousness of the female mind, we'll need several days and a great deal of liquor."

"Yeah. Ha. I guess you're in a hurry right now."

Actually, time was short. There were a few billion dollars waiting to be shifted, juggled, and consumed. But Roarke eased a hip on the corner of the desk. The money would wait. "I imagine this involves Peabody."

"We're, you know, doing it."

"Ian, I had no idea you were such a wild romantic. A virtual poet."

Roarke's dry tone had McNab flushing, then grinning. "We have really amazing sex."

"That's lovely for both of you, and congratulations. But I'm not sure Peabody would appreciate you sharing that piece of information with me."

"It's not really about sex," McNab said quickly, afraid he'd lose his sounding board before he'd sounded off. "I mean, it is, because we have it. A lot of it. And it rocks, so that's mag and all. That's how I figured it would be if I could ever get her out of that uniform for five damn minutes. But that's like it, that's all. Every time we finish, you know, the naked pretzel, I have to bribe her with food or get her going about a case or she's out the door. Or booting me out, if we landed at her place."

Roarke understood the frustration. He'd

only had one woman ever try to shake him off. The only woman who mattered. "And you're looking for more."

"Weird, huh?" With a half laugh, McNab began to pace. "I really like women. All sorts of women. I especially like them naked."

"Who could blame you?"

"Exactly. So I finally get a chance to bounce on the naked She-Body, and it's making me crazy. I'm all tied up inside and she's cruising right along. I always figured women, you know, mostly they were supposed to want the whole relationship thing. Talking about stuff so you come up with all those nice lies. I mean, they know you're lying, but they go along with it because maybe you won't be later on. Or something."

"That's a fascinating view on the male/female dynamic." One, Roarke was certain, would earn the boy a female knee to the balls if ever voiced in mixed company. "I take it Peabody isn't interested in pleasant lies."

"I don't know what she's interested in; that's the whole deal." Wound up now, he waved his arms. "I mean, she likes sex, she's into her work, she looks at Dallas like the lieutenant has the answers to the mysteries of the universe. Then she goes off with that goddamn Monroe son of a bitch to the opera."

It was the last, delivered with vitriol, that had Roarke nodding. "It's perfectly natural to be jealous of a rival."

"Rival, my ass. What the hell's wrong with her, going around with that slick LC? Fancy dinners and art shows. Listening to music you can't even dance to. I ought to smash his face in."

Roarke thought about it a moment and decided, under similar circumstances, he'd be tempted to do just that. "It would be satisfying, no doubt, but bound to annoy the woman in question. Have you tried romance?"

"What do you mean? Like goofy stuff?"

Roarke sighed. "Let's try this. Have you ever asked her out?"

"Sure. We see each other a couple, three nights a week."

"Out, Ian. In public. In places where you're both required, by law, to wear clothes of some kind."

"Oh. Not really."

"It might be a place to start. A date, where you'd pick her up at her apartment at a time agreed upon, then take her to a place where food and entertainment are offered. While enjoying that food and/or entertainment, you might try having a conversation with her, one that doesn't directly involve sex or work."

"I know what a date is," McNab grumbled, and felt put upon. "I haven't got the credit base to take her places like that bastard Monroe."

"Ah, therein lies one of the wonders of the female mind and heart. Go with your strengths, take her places that appeal to her sense of adventure, romance, humor. Don't compete with Monroe, Ian. Contrast with him. He gives her orchids grown in greenhouses on Flora I, you give her daisies you picked from the public field in Greenpeace Park."

As the information, the idea of it, processed, McNab's eyes cleared. Brightened. "Hey, that's good. That could work. I guess I could try it. You're really into this shit. Thanks."

"My pleasure." Roarke picked up his briefcase. "I've always been a gambling man, Ian, and one who likes to win. If I were to wager on your little triangle, I'd put my money on you."

The idea pumped up McNab's mood so high he forgot about the pie in the kitchen and got straight to work. He was having such a good time planning out his first date with Peabody, he nearly missed the data that scrolled on-screen.

"Holy shit!" He jumped back up on his boots, did a little dance, and grabbed his communicator.

"Dallas."

"Hey, Lieutenant, hey. I think I've got something. Criminal charges, assault and a civil suit — bodily harm, property damage and blah blah, both filed by Richard Draco, June 2035. Charges were dropped, then sealed. Civil action settled to the tune of five million smackeroonies and sealed. Defendant in both cases was —"

"How did you access sealeds, McNab?"

He blinked, and his mind went blank. "How did I what?"

"Detective, how did you access sealed records without the proper authority or the orders of the primary investigation to obtain said authority?"

"I . . ."

"Where's Roarke?"

Even on the small communicator screen he could see flames leap into her eyes. "Roarke?" Though he had a bad feeling it was already too late, McNab tried to shift his expression into innocence, confusion, and righteousness all at once. "I don't know. I guess he's working somewhere. Um . . . did you want him for something?"

"Has he been playing with you?"

"No, sir! Absolutely not. I'm on duty."

Her eyes stared out from the communicator screen for a very long twenty seconds. He felt sweat begin to slip greasily down the center of his back.

"I . . . as to how I accessed data, Lieutenant, it occurred to me that, well, previous backgrounds had been negative, and your instincts, which I respect and admire and trust absolutely, indicated there *should* be something. So I took what you could call a shot in the dark. That's it, a shot in the dark, and communicated our position to Judge Nettles, who agreed to issue the proper authority. I have the warrant."

He picked it up, waved it. "It's signed and everything."

"I just bet it is. Is this going to spring back and bite my ass, McNab? Think carefully before you answer, because I promise you, if it bites mine, it's going to have a chew fest on yours."

"No, sir." He hoped. "Everything's in proper order."

"I'm ten minutes away. Hold everything . . . in proper order. And McNab, if I see Roarke's fingerprints anywhere, I'm going to wring your skinny neck."

The first thing Eve did when she walked back into the house was hit the house scanner. "Where is Roarke?" she demanded.

Roarke is not currently on the premises. He is logged, at this time, at his midtown offices. Shall I direct a transmission for you, Darling Eve?

"No. Sneaky bastard."

"It called you *darling*, sir. That's so sweet."

"One of Roarke's little jokes. And if I hear it repeated, I'll have to kill you."

She headed up the stairs out of habit. Peabody sighed again, knowing there were numerous elevators that would be delighted to save them the climb.

When they walked into the office, she smirked at McNab on principle, but she did offer up a quick little prayer for his skinny neck. She'd grown, however reluctantly, fond of it.

He sprang to his feet, leading with the warrant. "All proper and official, sir."

Eve snatched it away, took a good, hard look. The tension in her shoulders unknotted muscle by muscle. She was dead sure Roarke was behind this sudden bounty of data, but the warrant would pass muster.

"Okay, McNab. You can live for the time being. Contact Feeney, put him on a conference-link and let's see what we've got."

What they had was twenty-four years old, but it was violent, petty, mean-spirited, and provocative.

"So the sophisticated Kenneth whopped big time on one Richard Draco."

"Really big time," Peabody put in. "He knocked out two teeth, busted his nose, bruised his ribs, and managed to break several articles of furniture before security got through the door and pulled him off."

"It says in the civil action that Draco was unable to work for three weeks, suffered emotional damage, extreme embarrassment, physical trauma, and, this is my personal favorite, loss of consortium. Both the criminal charges and the civil action were taken against Stiles in his birth name, Stipple, which he legally changed to his current stage name immediately after the suit was settled."

Eve turned the new data over in her mind. "He made a deal with Draco to take the payment and I'm banking it was more than the aforesaid five million smackeroonies to agree to having all of it sealed. The media didn't get hold of it, and that had to cost, too."

"Twenty-four years ago," Peabody pointed out. "Neither of them were major names. But from what we know of Draco, he'd have whined to the press unless it was worth his while not to."

"He could have spewed it out any time. Could have continued to hold it over Stiles's head. Bad for the image developed." Still she shook her head. "I can't see Stiles being overly worried about this coming out now. He's an established celebrity. He could spin it into a positive. 'Ah, my wild youth' or some such thing. It's *why* he broke Draco's balls that's the key."

She checked her wrist unit, figured angles. "McNab, continue search and scan. If you turn up anything else interesting, relay it to me or Feeney. I'll be at Central. Feeney? Reserve us an interview room, first available."

"You hauling him in?" Feeney asked.

"Yeah. Let's see how he does on my stage. Peabody, have Dispatch send some uniforms to Kenneth Stiles's address. I want him to have a ride in a black and white."

She started out while Peabody dug for her communicator.

"Hey, Peabody, just a minute."

She hesitated, glanced over her shoulder. "I'm busy, McNab."

"Yeah, yeah." He grabbed her hand, gave her a tug.

"Cut it out." But her own hand reached back and gave his butt a quick squeeze. "I've got real cop work to do."

"You uniforms only wish you could dance the cop dance like us EDDs. Listen, you want to go out tonight?"

Being pressed against him always managed to get her lust quotient hopping. "I guess I could come by after shift."

He nearly let it go at that as an image of her out of that uniform swirled into his mind. Still, Roarke hadn't said they couldn't have sex *after* the date. "No, I was thinking we could go out."

"It's too cold to have sex outdoors."

He opened his mouth, closed it again as the image in his mind switched to rolling naked with Peabody in the shadows of Central Park. If they didn't get mugged, knifed, or murdered, it would be incredible.

"Is sex all you think about? Not that I'm against it, but how about we go to the Nexus Club, catch some music. I'll pick you up at eight."

"Pick me up? You'll pick me up?"

"That'll give you time to change." It was interesting, he thought, seeing her look at him as if he'd grown a third ear in the center of his forehead.

"Peabody! Move your ass!"

"You better go." He smiled as Eve's irritated voice boomed up the stairs. "I'll catch you later."

And because he was feeling lucky, he crushed his mouth down on hers, sucking until the kiss broke with a wet, sexy sound.

Peabody stumbled back and staggered out the door.

chapter thirteen

Eve grabbed a cup of coffee and was forced to settle for an energy bar as the candy thief had hit her again. The first chance she got, she was setting a trap for the sneaky bastard. But at the moment, she had other priorities.

She caught the glide to the interview area and picked up Feeney on the way.

"This guy likes to role play," Eve began. "I don't want to give him the chance to latch onto a character type. Let's mess with his rhythm."

"I want to be bad cop this time."

"Feeney, you're —" She stopped, sniffed the air. "What's that smell?"

Feeney hunched his shoulder. "I don't smell anything. I'm taking bad cop." He said it so decisively, Eve rolled her eyes, then shrugged.

"Okay, fine. I'll start off being pleasant and reasonable, then we'll jam him. If he's lawyered . . ." She sniffed again, scenting the air like a bloodhound as other cops and Central personnel streamed by. "It smells, I don't know, green," she decided. "Like a salad."

"I don't know what you're talking about. Let's keep focused, okay? A guy whips hell out of somebody like this one did, he's got a temper. Let's see if we can heat it up."

"Fine." As they stepped off the glide, she leaned in, sniffed at Feeney. "Hey, it's you."

"Shut up, Dallas."

She grinned now, as the back of the neck she'd just sniffed turned cherry red. "How come you smell like a fancy green salad, Feeney?"

"Quiet down, will you? Christ." He darted looks right and left until he was sure no one was close enough to hear. Then he lowered his voice to a mutter, just in case. "Look, my wife gave me this stuff for our anniversary."

"You're supposed to put salad dressing on lettuce and stuff, Feeney."

"It's not salad dressing, it's cologne."

"You smell good enough to eat."

His mouth found a spot between a snarl and a sneer. "Yeah, that's what she says. Keep it down, will you? I couldn't get out of the house this morning without putting it on, or I'd've hurt her feelings. You have to get pretty close to catch it, but the damn stuff lasts hours. I've been taking stairs and glides all day. I can't risk an elevator."

"Gee, that's really sweet, Feeney. Maybe

you could tell her you want to save it for special occasions."

"You think she'd tumble for that? Dallas, you don't understand women."

"Got me there." They turned the corner and saw Peabody outside Interview Three talking to another uniform. Eve recognized the tall young cop, sent him a nod when he turned, saw her, flushed.

"Well, it's Officer Trueheart. How's it going?"

"It's going good, Lieutenant. The suspect's inside."

"Subject," Eve corrected. "We're not calling him suspect at this point." She watched him process the difference in procedure. She could smell rookie on him as clearly as she could smell Feeney's cologne. "Did the subject request a lawyer or representative?"

"No, sir. I think —" He cut himself off, stiffened his already soldierly back. "I beg your pardon, Lieutenant."

"You're allowed to think, Trueheart. In fact, we encourage thinking around here." She remembered, with some bitterness, his first trainer who'd not only discouraged thinking, but humanity. "Give me your take."

"Yes, sir. Well, sir, I think he's too mad to

ask for representation at this time. Mad, Lieutenant, plus he wants to go a few rounds with you. In my opinion. The subject referred to you in . . . inflammatory terms during transport."

"And here I was planning to be nice to him. Stand by, Trueheart. You can go to Observation if you want. We'll need you to transport the subject, one way or the other, after interview."

"Yes, sir, thank you, sir. And I'd like to express my appreciation for your assistance in having me transferred from stiff-scooping detail to Central."

"The transfer was easy, Trueheart. Staying here will be up to you. Are we set?" she asked Peabody and Feeney.

She opened the door, strolled inside.

Stiles sat at the small table, his arms crossed, his face mutinous. He sent Eve one steely glare. "And what is the meaning of this outrage, Lieutenant Dallas? I want an explanation as to why I was removed from my home by two uniformed officers and shoved into the backseat of a police car."

"Peabody, make a note to speak with said uniformed officers. No shoving."

"So noted, sir."

"Record on," she said meandering to the table. "Interview with subject Kenneth

Stiles, regarding case number HS46178-C. Dallas, Lieutenant Eve, as primary. Also in attendance Feeney, Captain Ryan, and Peabody, Officer Delia. Mr. Stiles, have you been informed of your rights and obligations in this matter?"

"The cop with peach fuzz on his chin recited the standard. I want to know —"

"And do you understand these rights and obligations, Mr. Stiles?"

He showed his teeth. "I'm not a nitwit; of course I understand them. I insist —"

"I apologize for the inconvenience." She settled back, tried out a smile. There was no need to repeat the revised Miranda and remind him he could holler lawyer. "I realize this is unpleasant for you, again apologize for the inconvenience, and will try to expedite this interview."

Feeney gave a sharp snort so that Eve sent him a quick, worried look that had Stiles shifting in his seat.

"What is this about?" Stiles demanded. "I have a right to know why I've been dragged down here like a common criminal."

"You've been read your rights, Stiles." Feeney's voice was clipped and harsh. "Now we're the ones who ask the questions."

"I've already answered questions. I don't know anything other than what I've already told Lieutenant Dallas."

"I guess you don't know anything about that poor slob who ended up dangling by his neck a couple feet off the floor, either."

"Feeney." Eve held up her hands for peace. "Easy."

Feeney folded his arms over his chest and tried to look burly. "He keeps pulling my chain, I'm pulling his back."

"Let's take a minute. Want some water?"

Stiles blinked at her, baffled. He'd been ready to rip into Eve, and now she was giving him sympathetic looks and offering him water. "Yes, yes, I would."

"Why don't you offer him a snack while you're at it?"

Ignoring Feeney, Eve rose to fill a small cup with lukewarm water. "Mr. Stiles, some new information has come to light regarding your relationship with Richard Draco."

"What new information? I told you —"

"I said we ask the questions." Feeney came half out of his chair. "You didn't tell us squat. You didn't tell us you kicked Draco's face in, did you? A guy puts another guy in the hospital, maybe he finds a way to come back around and put him in the ground."

"I don't know what you're talking about." Stiles's voice was smooth, even, but his hand trembled lightly as he took the cup of water.

"Mr. Stiles, I'm going to warn you that there's a very stiff penalty for lying in interview." Eve leaned forward so that Stiles would focus on her face. "You don't want that kind of trouble; take my word for it. You cooperate with me, and I'm going to do what I can to straighten this out. If you're not straight with me, I can't help you. And it's going to be tough for you to help yourself."

"Guy's a coward," Feeney said in disgust. "Takes Draco out, but hides behind some poor woman to do it."

"I never —" The mutiny in Stiles's eyes turned to horrified shock. "My God, you can't believe I actually arranged Richard's death. That's absurd."

"At least he used to have some guts," Feeney went on, and deliberately cracked his knuckles in three nasty little pops. "Used his own hands to pound Draco's face in. Must've really ticked him off, huh, Stiles. You actor guys are fussy about your pretty faces."

Stiles moistened his lips. "I had absolutely nothing to do with Richard's death. I've told you everything I know about it."

Eve put a hand on Feeney's shoulder as if to restrain him, then with a sigh, rose. "The file, Officer Peabody. Hard copy."

"Yes, sir." Keeping her face blank, Peabody offered Eve a folder.

Eve sat with it, opened it, gave Stiles a chance to read as much as he could manage upside down. And watched his color drain. "I have documents here relating to both criminal and civil actions, which involve you, as defendant."

"Those matters were resolved years ago. Years. And sealed. I was assured they were sealed."

"This is murder, pal." Feeney's mouth twisted into a sneer. "Seal's broken."

"Let's give the guy a chance to settle into this, Feeney. Mr. Stiles, we were authorized to break the seal due to the course of this investigation."

"You don't owe him explanations."

"Let's just keep it smooth," Eve murmured to Feeney. "You were charged with assaulting Richard Draco, causing extensive bodily harm, mental and emotional trauma."

"It was twenty-four years ago. For God's sake."

"I know. I understand that. But . . . you indicated to me in your previous statement, on record, that you and the deceased had no overt difficulties. And yet . . ." Eve said, letting the silence hang a moment. "At one time you were driven to assault him seriously enough to result in his hospitalization, in your arrest, in a seven-figure civil suit."

The paper cup crumpled in Stiles's hand. Little drops of water flew. "It was all resolved."

"Look, Kenneth." She used his first name now, establishing intimacy. "The fact is, everything I've come up with on Draco points to him being a sorry son of a bitch. I have to figure you had cause to lay into him. Good cause. You were seriously provoked. You don't strike me as a violent man."

"I'm not." The sheen of sophistication had turned into a sheen of sweat. It gleamed on his face as he nodded at Eve. "No, I'm not. Of course, I'm not."

Feeney snorted again. "I'll buy that one. Didn't even have the nerve to stick Draco himself."

"I didn't kill Richard!" Stiles's voice rose, boomed as he looked at Feeney. "I had nothing to do with it. What happened before, good Lord, I was hardly more than a boy."

"I understand that, Mr. Stiles. You were young, you were provoked." Sympathy rang in Eve's voice. She got up, filled another cup with water, brought it back to him. "Tell me how it happened. Why it happened. All I want to do is clear this up so you can go home."

Stiles closed his eyes, drew air in slowly, released it. "We'd both begun to make our marks in theater, in small regional theaters. Not much of a mark, of course, but we were beginning. We were both aiming for New York. Broadway was enjoying a rich revival in those days."

His voice warmed a bit as he remembered his youth, that sense of anticipation, invulnerability. Color came back to his cheeks. "It was a return to the lights, the glamour, the brilliance after the destruction of the Urban Wars. People were looking for entertainment, for escape and, I suppose, for heros who didn't carry weapons. We were a tight and perhaps an arrogant circle. It was a heady time, Lieutenant, a renaissance. We were treated like royalty. Offstage, we lived very large lives. Excessive lives. Sex, illegals, lavish parties."

He picked up his water again, drank deeply. "It ruined some of us. I would say it ruined Richard. He reveled in the fame, in the excesses. It never affected his work, that was his genius, but offstage, he indulged in every possible vice. There was a cruelty to him, particularly toward women. He crushed more than one on his way. He liked to brag about it, to make bets about which woman he'd have next. I found it . . . unpleasant."

He cleared his throat, shoved his cup away. "There was a woman, a girl, really. We were seeing each other. It wasn't serious, but we enjoyed each other's company. Then Richard began the hunt. He stalked her, lured her, and in the end, ruined her. When he cast her off, it broke her. I went to her apartment. I don't know what instinct sent me there. When I found her, she . . . she was on the point of taking her own life. She had already slashed her wrists. I got her to a health center. I . . ."

He trailed off, hesitated, then continued with obvious difficulty. "They saved her, but something inside me snapped when I looked at her lying there, so pale, so used. I got drunk, then I went after Richard."

Stiles ran his hands over his face. "I might have killed him that night. I admit it. But people from the neighboring apartments stopped me. Afterward, I realized what a useless gesture it had been. It changed nothing and cost me a great deal. Instead of damaging Richard, I could have destroyed my own career, my own life. I put myself at his mercy, you see. He agreed to the settlements and the seals to protect his own image. I had reason to be grateful he was just that self-interested. It took me three years to pay off the suit, with merciless interest. Then I put it behind me."

"Seems to me you had plenty of reason to hate the son of a bitch," Feeney put in.

"Perhaps." Steadier now that the story was told, Stiles nodded. "But hate takes enormous amounts of time and energy. I prefer employing mine in more positive channels. I have everything I want; I enjoy my life. I would never risk it again on the likes of Richard Draco."

"Not such a risk when you put the knife in the hands of a woman."

Stiles's head snapped up. His eyes burned. "I don't use women. I've had nearly twenty-five years to learn a lesson, Lieutenant. Richard Draco stopped mattering to me a very long time ago."

"What happened to the woman?"

"I don't know." He heaved a huge sigh, full of regret. "She ceased to be part of my life. I believe the fact that I knew what had happened made it difficult for her to be around me, to maintain our friendship."

"Seems to me she'd have been grateful."

"She was, Lieutenant. But like me, she had to put the incident, all of it, behind her.

I went to London very shortly after the incident, worked there, and then in California, in Canada. We didn't keep in touch, and I never heard of her again."

Convenient, Eve thought. *Maybe just a little too convenient.* "What was her name?"

"Is that necessary?"

"It's a sad story you tell, Mr. Stiles. An effective one. But there's no one here to back it up. What was her name?"

"Anja Carvell." He looked back into the past, then down at his hands. "Her name was Anja. I've told you all I can."

"One more thing. Where were you yesterday morning between the hours of ten and eleven?"

"Yesterday? It's the hour I take my daily exercise. A brisk walk in the park."

"Can anyone verify that?"

"I was alone." His voice was cold again. The temper was coming back, but it was more controlled. "Am I to be detained any longer? I have a memorial service to attend."

"You're advised not to leave the city." Eve studied his face. There was something off, but she couldn't put her finger on it. "Any attempt to do so will result in an immediate warrant for your detention."

She rose, signaled toward Observation and Trueheart.

"An officer will take you back to your apartment. Oh, Mr. Stiles, one last thing. Did you ever have occasion to converse with Linus Quim?"

"Quim?" Stiles got to his feet, brushed the back of his fingertips down his lapel. "No. One didn't converse with Quim. He had a disdain for people in my profession. An odd little man. I wouldn't be surprised if you discovered he'd switched the knives. He really couldn't stand actors."

"Peabody, start tracking down Anja Carvell."

"I don't like the way it plays," Feeney commented. "Too slick."

"Yeah, I was waiting for the lights to come up and the music to start. Still, it could've gone down pretty much like he said."

"Even if it did, it doesn't change anything. He had a hard-on for Draco, a big, fat one. He strikes me as the type who'd chew on it for at least two decades."

"I like him for a long-term planner," Eve agreed. "Somebody who keeps slights and annoyances tucked in little boxes. And as someone who wouldn't want to get his hands dirty, not a second time."

But something was out of step. Details left out, or details added in. "We'll see how the

Carvell connection shakes out," she decided. "He was leaving holes, picking what he wanted to tell us, how he wanted it told. Ad-libbing," she mused. "Isn't that what they call it? He did a good job of it."

"I think he was in love with Anja." Peabody had her palm unit out but hadn't yet started the scan. "It makes a difference if he was."

Eve shuffled back her own thoughts, turned to her aide. "Where do you get that from?"

"It was the way he talked about her before he started to think it through, before he started picking his way. He got this look in his eyes. Wistful."

Eve hooked her thumbs in her front pockets. "He got a wistful look in his eye?"

"Yeah, just for a minute, he was really thinking about her, about the way it was, or the way he'd wanted it to be. I think she was the love of his life. When you've got one of those, it does stuff to you."

"Define *stuff*."

"It makes you think about them even when you're doing routine things. It makes you want to protect them, to make them happy and safe. You know," Peabody said with some frustration. "You've got one."

"One what?"

"Love of your life, jeez, Dallas. But see, you're the love of his right back. This wasn't the same way, because she threw him over for Draco. If you were to go insane and throw Roarke over for somebody, what do you think he'd do?"

"Before or after this somebody was no more than a smudge on the bottom of Roarke's shoe?"

"See?" Pleased, Peabody grinned. "If you've got a love of your life, you know." She paused, sniffed. "Something smells really good."

"Just keep going," Feeney ordered quickly. "If the theory is that Stiles was stuck on this Carvell woman, how does that change the picture?"

"Because you never get over the love of your life. That's the whole definition, isn't it? You only get one. So that bit about him losing touch with her was bull."

"I like it. If we find that Stiles had some contact with the woman, we've got a motive that spans a quarter century. The setup suits him in both murders. He had opportunity."

"It's all circumstantial," Feeney reminded her.

"Yeah, but we pile on enough, we might finesse a confession out of him. Find the woman, Peabody. If you run into snags, hook up with McNab on it. Feeney, how do you feel about going to a splashy memorial service?"

"My wife loves it when I rub elbows with celebrities."

"Peabody, we're in the field."

"Yes, sir." She watched them head off, and had a sudden craving for a big, chunky salad.

Feeney's wife was going to be delirious. Performers from every medium were in attendance. The service was held at Radio City. Though Draco had never performed there, its Art Deco glamour had just the right ambiance. Word was Draco's agent had hired the top Mourner's Association company to arrange the affair.

And as it was, technically, Draco's last performance, he'd skimmed off 15 percent of the gross.

Enormous screens flickered with Draco in dozens of images. There was a holo-performance running on a side stage, with Draco in full costume, defending country and womankind with sword and fancy footwork.

For two hundred and fifty dollars a pop, a thousand lucky fans could attend. The rest were invited guests.

There were seas of flowers, islands of people in sophisticated black, streams of gawkers who, despite the posted request, were busy immortalizing the event on disc.

On the main stage, atop a white pedestal, was Draco himself, resting in a coffin of pale blue glass.

"Hell of a show."

Eve just shook her head. "They're selling souvenirs. Did you see? Little Draco dolls, T-shirts."

"There's nothing like free enterprise," Roarke said from behind her. She turned, eyed him up and down.

"Why are you here?"

"Lieutenant, have you forgotten? The deceased met his end while starring in a play in my theater. How could I stay away? Besides . . ." He patted the pocket of his elegant suit. "I got an invitation."

"I thought you had meetings all day."

"The advantage of being in charge . . . is being in charge. I took an hour." With his hand lightly on her shoulder, he scanned the crowd, the lights, the screens. "Appalling, isn't it?"

"And then some. Feeney, let's split up, see what we see. I'll meet you at the main entrance, one hour."

"You got it." He spotted several faces he

knew from on-screen and a banquet table. No reason he couldn't see what he saw with his mouth full.

"Roarke, if I ditched you twenty-five years ago, would you still be hung up about it?"

He smiled, caressed her hair. "Difficult to say, as I'd have spent that time hounding you and making your life a living hell."

"No, seriously."

"Who said I wasn't?" He took her arm, led her through the crowd.

"Let's pretend you're someone less annoying."

"Ah. All right. If you'd broken my heart, I'd attempt to pick up the shattered pieces and rebuild my life. But I'd never forget you. What have you got?"

"Peabody's got a theory about love, the love of your life. I'm playing with it."

"I can tell you, you're mine."

"No kissing," she hissed, seeing the intent in his eyes. "I'm on duty here. There's Michael Proctor. Smiling. I went over his financials, and he paid over ten K for that dental work, while he lives in a sty. He's chatting with that slick-looking woman over there. He doesn't look so shook up or bumbling now."

"He's talking with Marcina, one of the top screen producers in the business. Could be your boy is hoping for a career shift."

"Less than a week ago, the stage was his life. Interesting. Let's see how he holds up."

She worked her way over, noted the instant Proctor saw her. His eyes widened, his head drooped, and his shoulders hunched in. *Presto-chango,* Eve thought, *from debonair leading man to fumbling second lead in a blink. The magic of theater.*

"Proctor."

"Ah, ah, Lieutenant Dallas. I didn't realize you'd be attending."

"I get around." Deliberately, she scanned the theater. "I guess Quim can't expect this kind of send-off."

"Quim? Oh." He had the grace, or the skill, to flush. "No, no, I suppose not. Richard was . . . he was known and respected by so many people."

"A lot of them sure are toasting him." She leaned over, studied the pretty bubbles in the glass he held. "With premium champagne."

"He would have expected no less." This from the woman Roarke had identified as Marcina. "This event suits him perfectly." She shifted her gaze over Eve's shoulder, then beamed. "Roarke! I wondered if I'd see you here."

"Marcina." He stepped up, lightly kissed

her cheek. "You're looking well."

"I'm very well. Dallas," she said after a moment, and pinned Eve with her sharp gaze. "Of course. This must be your wife. I've heard a great deal about you, Lieutenant."

"If you'll excuse me," Proctor said.

"Don't run off on my account," Eve told Proctor, but he was already edging away.

"I see a friend." He dived into the crowd like a man leaping overboard.

"I assume you're on duty?" Marcina skimmed a glance over Eve's trousers and serviceable jacket. "You're investigating Richard's death."

"That's right. Would you mind telling me what you and Proctor were talking about?"

"Is he a suspect?" Lips pursed, Marcina looked over to where Proctor had disappeared. "Fascinating. Actually, it was shop talk. Michael has the right look for a screen project I'm putting together. We were discussing the possibility of him coming out to New L.A. for a few days."

"And is he?"

"Perhaps. But he's committed to his current play. He's quite looking forward to taking Richard's place onstage. Not that he put it quite so tactlessly. My people will be talking to his people, as it were, over the

315

next week or two to see if we can work something out. He hoped that the theater will reopen very soon."

The minute Eve stepped outside, she took a deep gulp of air thick with the stink of smoke from glide-carts, screaming with the noise of street and air traffic. She preferred it over the sweetly perfumed air inside.

"Proctor isn't letting Draco get cold before he steps into his shoes."

"He sees an opportunity," Roarke commented.

"Yeah. So did the killer."

"Point taken." He traced a fingertip over the dent in her chin. "I might be a little late tonight. I should be home by eight."

"Okay."

"I have something for you."

"Oh, come on." When he reached in his pocket, she stuffed her hands in hers. "This isn't the time or place for presents."

"I see. Then I guess I'll just keep this for myself."

Instead of the jewelry case she'd expected, he pulled out a jumbo chocolate bar. Her hand whipped out of her pocket, snatched it.

"Then again," Roarke murmured.

"You bought me a candy bar."

"I know the way to your heart, Lieutenant."

She tore off the wrapping, bit in. "I guess you do. Thanks."

"It's not dinner," he said with a narrowed eye. "But if you can hold off, we'll have some together when I get home."

"Sure. You got transpo?"

"I'll walk. It's a nice day." He caught her face, kissed her before she could tell him not to.

Chewing her candy, she watched him walk away. And thought she understood exactly what Peabody meant by the love of a lifetime.

chapter fourteen

Mira studied the record of the interview with Kenneth Stiles. She sipped her tea while Eve paced. In another five minutes, she would have been on her way home. Eve had caught her as she'd been locking up.

Now she would be late. That thought shifted through the back of her mind as she focused on the interview. Her husband would understand, particularly if she made a quick detour on the way and picked up a carton of his favorite ice cream.

She'd learned long ago the tricks and balances of blending a demanding career and a successful marriage.

"You and Feeney are an excellent interview team," she commented. "You read each other well."

"We've been doing it awhile." Eve wanted to hurry Mira along but knew better. "I think he's been practicing that hard-ass look in the mirror."

That brought out a smile. "I imagine so. Given his comfortable face, it's surprisingly effective. Am I correct in assuming you don't believe Stiles told the whole truth?"

"Are you ever wrong?"

"Now and again. You're looking for this Anja Carvell?"

"Peabody's tracking her."

"He had, and has, strong feelings for her. I'd say she was a turning point for him. If it had been a storybook, the woman would have come to him after he defended her. Happily ever after. But —"

"She didn't want him."

"Or didn't love him enough, felt unworthy, humiliated, scarred." Mira lifted a hand. "There are countless reasons why she and Stiles didn't match. Without observing her, I couldn't say. Still, it's Stiles's emotional and mental state that interests you."

"Peabody's idea is that this woman was the love of his life, and because of that, he'd never have completely lost touch with her."

"I think Peabody has good instincts. He protected her, defended her. A man with his sense of theater or drama would tend to put himself in the role of hero, and she his damsel in distress. He may very well still be doing so."

"She's key," Eve murmured. "Maybe not *the* key, but a key." With her hands in her pockets, she wandered to Mira's window. She was feeling closed in today and couldn't say why. "I don't get it," she said at length. "The woman shrugs him off, sleeps with another guy, folds herself into this other guy so completely that when *he* tosses her away, she tries to self-terminate. And still Stiles is hung up on her. He beats hell out of Draco, gets himself arrested, gets skinned in a civil suit. And when he talks about her twenty-five years later, he goes soft. Why isn't he bitter? Why isn't he pissed? Is he jamming me here?"

"I can't say with absolute certainty. He's a talented actor. But my evaluation at this point is no, as far as his feelings for the woman, he's not jamming you. Eve, the human heart is a mystery we'll never completely solve. You're putting yourself in this man's place. That's one of the skills you have, what makes you so good at what you do. But you can't quite get into his heart. You would look at this woman and see weakness."

Mira sipped more tea as Eve turned. "She was weak. Weak and careless."

"And quite young, I imagine, but that's beside the point. You look at love differently because you're strong and because of where and in whom you found it. The love of your life, Eve, would never betray you or hurt you or, where it matters most, ever let you down.

He accepts who you are, absolutely. As much as you love him, I don't think you fully understand how rare and how precious that is. Stiles loved, and perhaps still loves, a fantasy. You have the reality."

"People kill for both."

"Yes." Mira ejected the disc, held it out to Eve. "They do."

All the talk about love and lifetimes got under Eve's skin and made her feel uncomfortably guilty. She played back what others had said and realized everyone who had mentioned her relationship with Roarke as an example had spoken of what he would do for her or wouldn't do to her.

It wasn't, she decided, a very pretty picture of her participation in the whole love and marriage deal.

She never really *did* anything, she thought. She still had a miserable time finding the right words, the right gesture, the right moment. Roarke seemed to pluck them out of the air as easily, as smoothly, as he plucked his fortune.

So she'd make an effort. She'd push the case onto the back burner, okay, the side burner, she admitted, and do something, Jesus, romantic.

In her current state of mind, she wanted

to avoid Summerset at all costs, so she actually put her car in the garage. Then, like a thief, she snuck in the house through one of the side doors.

She was about to plan her first intimate dinner.

How hard could it be? she asked herself as she jumped into the shower. She'd led tactical teams in hostage situations, tracked psychopaths, outwitted the deranged.

She was smart enough to put a fancy meal on a fancy table. Probably.

She zipped out of the shower and into the drying tube. Not in the bedroom, she decided, because that was, well, obvious, and she thought, most likely, romance should be subtle.

She'd use one of the lounging rooms.

As the hot air whirled around her, she began to plot.

Thirty minutes later, she was feeling both satisfied and frazzled. There were so many damn rooms in the house, she still didn't believe she'd been in all of them. And all the damn rooms had stuff, enormous amounts of stuff. How was she supposed to figure out what was needed?

Candles, she got that, but when she ran an inventory scan, she discovered a veritable forest of candles in several areas. Still, the satisfaction came from skulking through the house, evading the ever-watchful Summerset.

She decided on white, because color meant she'd most likely have to match it with more colors, and that was just more than she could handle. She spent another twenty minutes dealing with the menu, then had to face the frightening ordeal of selecting plates, flatware, crystal.

It had been a shock to run an inventory on something as basic as dinner plates and find her husband had over fifty types of varying material and patterns.

What kind of maniac needed over five thousand plates?

Her maniac, she reminded herself, then nearly choked when she ran the crystal.

"Okay, that's got to be wrong." She was at the point of choosing at random because her time was running short.

"Might I ask precisely what you're doing?"

A lesser woman would have yelped. Eve managed, just barely, to bite it back. "Get lost. I'm busy."

Summerset simply strode over, the cat at his heels. "So I observe. If you wish to know the contents of the house, I suggest you discuss it with Roarke."

"I can't because I've killed him, disposed of his body, and now I'm going to hold the biggest auction, on or off planet, in the history of civilization."

She jabbed a finger against something called *Waterford, Dublin pattern,* only because she recognized it as the city where Roarke had been born. Then she looked up with a scowl toward the hovering Summerset. "Go away."

But his attention had shifted from her to the table under the glass dome of the observation balcony. She'd used the Irish linen, he noted. An excellent choice, which was probably blind luck. The Georgian candlesticks, white tapers. There were dozens of other candles, all white, scattered around the lounging room, as yet unlighted.

Galahad the cat pranced over and leaped onto the satin pillows on the love seat.

"Jesus Christ, they're just forks and knives!"

The combination of horror and frustration in her tone had Summerset's lips twitching. "Which china pattern have you selected?"

"I don't know. Will you get out of here? This is a private party."

He tapped her hand aside before she could select, scanned her other choices, and ordered the proper flatware. "You've neglected to order napkins."

"I was getting to them."

He turned a pitying eye on her. She was wearing a cotton robe, had yet to enhance her face. Her hair was standing in spikes from the constant swipe of her fingers.

But he gave her points for the attempt. In fact, he was pleasantly surprised by her taste. Though some of her selections were unconventional in combinations, they managed to blend into a rather charming ambiance.

"When one plans a special meal," he said, taking care to look down the long line of his nose at her, "One requires the proper accompaniments."

"What am I doing here? Playing Space Attack? Now, if you'd just go slither under the door again, I could finish up."

"Flowers are necessary."

"Flowers?" Her stomach pitched to her feet. "I knew that." She wasn't going to ask. She'd saw her tongue off with her teeth before she asked.

For a humming ten seconds they simply stared at each other. He took pity on her, though he told himself he was simply maintaining his authority as majordomo. "I would suggest roses, the Royal Silver."

"I guess we've got those."

"Yes, they can be accessed. You'll also require music."

Her palms started to sweat. Annoyed, she rubbed them on the robe. "I was going to program something." *Or other.*

"I assume you intend to dress for the evening."

"Shit." She heaved out a breath, stared hard at the cat who was staring hard back at her. She suspected he was grinning.

"It's part of my duties to organize matters such as this. If you'll go put on something . . . more, I'll arrange the rest."

She opened her mouth to agree. Already the knots in her stomach loosened. Then she shook her head and felt them tighten right back up again. "No, I have to do it myself. That's the point." She massaged her forehead. She was getting a headache. Perfect.

His face remained stern, cold, but inside, he softened like jelly. "Then you'd better hurry. Roarke will be home within the hour."

She would, Summerset concluded as he left her alone, *need every minute of it.*

His mind was on business when he got home. His last meeting of the day had involved a textile conglomerate looking for a buyout. He had to decide if he was looking to buy.

The company, and most of its subsidiaries, had been sloppily run. Roarke had no sympathy for sloppy business practices. As a result, his initial offer had been insultingly low.

The fact that their negotiator hadn't been nearly as insulted as he should have been sent up red flags. He would have to do more research before he took the next step.

The problem would be on one of their two off-planet sites, he calculated. It might be worth a trip to study them firsthand.

There had been a time he would have simply arranged his schedule and done so. But in the past year it had become increasingly less appealing to leave home, even for the short term.

He had, he thought with some amusement at himself, become rooted.

He stopped by Eve's office on the way to his own, was mildly surprised not to find her there, neck deep in her current case. Curiosity had him setting his own work aside and moving to the house scanner.

"Where is Eve?"

Eve is currently in Lounging Room Four,

third level, south wing.

"What the hell is she doing in there?"

Would you like to engage monitor?

"No, I'll go see for myself."
He'd never known her to loiter in that area of the house. The fact was, he'd never known her to lounge unless he nagged, seduced, or conned her into it.

It occurred to him it might be pleasant to have their meal there, relax together with a bottle of wine, and shake their respective days from their minds.

He'd have to talk her into it.

Thinking this, he walked into the room. If she'd been looking in his direction, she would have caught one of the rare moments when her husband was completely flabbergasted.

The room was lit with dozens of white candles, and the fragrance of them waltzed with the tender perfume of dozens of silver roses. Crystal glinted, silver gleamed, and the romance of harp strings wept in the air.

In the midst of it, Eve stood in an alarm-red dress that left her arms and shoulders bare as it skimmed down her long, slim body like an avid lover's hungry hands.

Her face was flushed, her eyes bright with concentration, as she twisted the wire on a bottle of champagne.

"Excuse me." He saw her lovely shoulders jerk, her only sign of surprise. "I'm looking for my wife."

Her stomach jittered a little, but she turned, smiled. He had a face made for candlelight, she thought. For slow and simmering fires. Looking at it never failed to start one in her blood. "Hi."

"Hello." Glancing around the room, he walked toward her. "What's all this?"

"Dinner."

"Dinner," he repeated, and his eyes narrowed. "What have you done? You're not hurt?"

"No. I'm fine." Still smiling, she popped the cork, relieved when champagne didn't come spraying out.

He frowned as she poured champagne into crystal flutes. "All right, what do you want?"

"What do you mean?"

"I mean I know a setup when I see one. What do you want?"

Her smile wavered. It took a great deal of effort to keep it from turning into a snarl. Sticking to the steps she'd carefully outlined, she handed him his wine, gently tapped her glass to his. "What, I can't put together a nice dinner without ulterior motives?"

He thought about it. "No."

She set the bottle on the table with an ominous crack. "Look, it's dinner, okay? You don't want to eat, fine."

"I didn't say I didn't want to eat." She was wearing perfume, he noted. And lip dye. She'd fussed with her eyes. He reached out to toy with the tear-shaped diamond pendant he'd given her. "What are you up to, Eve?"

That tore it. "Nothing. Forget it. I don't know what came over me. Obviously, I lost my mind for a minute. No, for two sweaty, stupid hours. That's what it took to put this fiasco together. I'm going to work."

He caught her arm before she could march past him and wasn't the least surprised to see the quick flare of violence in her eyes. But he was surprised to see hurt.

"I don't think so."

"You want to keep that hand, pal, you'll move it."

"Ah, there she is. For a moment, I thought you'd been replaced by a droid. It gave me a bad start."

"I bet you think that's funny."

"I think I've hurt your feelings, and I'm

sorry." He brushed his lips over her forehead even as he flipped desperately through his mental calendar. "Have I forgotten an occasion?"

"No. No." She stepped back. "No," she said again, and felt ridiculous. "I just wanted to do something for you. To give you something. And you can just stop looking at me like I've fried a few circuits. You think you're the only one who can put this kind of deal together? Well, you're right. You are. I nearly stunned myself with my own weapon a half a dozen times tonight just to put myself out of my misery. Oh fuck it."

She picked up her glass again, stalked to the wide, curved window.

Roarke winced and began the delicate task of extracting his feet from his mouth. "It's lovely, Eve. And so are you."

"Oh, don't start with me."

"Eve —"

"Just because I don't do this kind of thing, because I don't take the time — hell because I don't think of it, doesn't mean I don't love you. I do." She spun around, and he wouldn't have described the look on her face as particularly loving. She'd gone back to fury. "You're the one who's always doing the things, saying the words. Giving . . ." She fumbled a moment. "Just giving. I wanted to give something back."

She was beautiful. Hurt and angry, passionate and pissed, she was the most beautiful creature he'd ever seen. "You steal my breath," he murmured.

"I've got this whole love of a lifetime thing in my head. Murder, betrayal, rage."

"I beg your pardon?"

"Never mind." She paused, took a deep breath. "The last couple of days people have said things that keep sticking in my brain. Would you jump in front of a maxibus for me?"

"Absolutely. They don't go very fast."

She laughed, relieving him considerably. "That's what I said. Oh hell, I messed this up. I knew I would."

"No, I took care of that." He moved to her, took her hand. "Do you love me enough to give me another chance at this?"

"Maybe."

"Darling Eve." He lifted her hand to his lips. "What you've done here means a great deal to me. You, you mean everything to me."

"See how you do that. Slick as spit."

He trailed his fingers over the curve of her shoulder. "I like the dress."

It was a good thing, she thought, he hadn't seen her frozen panic when she'd opened her closet. "I thought it would work."

"It does. Very well." He picked up her glass, then his own. "Let's try this again. Thank you."

"Yeah, well, I'd say it was nothing, but that would be a big, fat lie. Just tell me this one thing. Why do you have a million plates?"

"I'm sure that's an exaggeration."

"Not by much."

"Well, you never know who might be coming to dinner, do you?"

"Including the entire population of New Zealand." She sipped champagne. "Now, I'm behind schedule."

"Have we a schedule?"

"Yeah. You know, drinks, dinner, conversation. Blah blah. It all ends up with me getting you drunk and seducing you."

"I like the end goal. Since I came close to spoiling things, the least I can do now is cooperate." He started to pick up the bottle, but she laid a hand on his arm.

"Dance with me." She slid her hands up his chest, linked them behind his neck. "Close. And slow."

His arms came around her. His body swayed with hers. And his blood leapt with love, with lust, as her mouth brushed silkily over his.

"I love the taste of you." Her voice was

husky now, soft. "It always makes me want more."

"Have more."

But when he attempted to deepen the kiss, she turned her head, skimmed those heated lips along his jaw. "Slow," she said again. "The way I'm going to make love with you." She nibbled her way to his ear. "So that it's almost torture."

She threaded her fingers through his hair, all that gorgeous black, fisted them, drew his head back until their eyes met. His were deep and blue and already hot.

"I want you to say my name when I take you." She teased his mouth with hers again, retreated, felt his body tighten like a bow against hers. "Say it so that I know nothing exists for you but me at that moment. Nothing exists for me but you. You're all there is."

Her mouth took his now, a frantic mating of lips, teeth, tongues. She felt his moan start low, start deep, then merge with her own. She let herself tremble, let herself ache, then pulled back, pulled away a breath before surrender.

"Eve."

She heard the strain in his voice, enjoyed it as she picked up their glasses again. "Thirsty?"

"No." He started to reach for her, but she shifted away, thrust out his glass. "I am. Have a drink. I want to go to your head."

"You do. Let me have you."

"I will. After I've had you." She picked up a small remote, pressed a series of buttons. On the side wall, panels opened. The bed that had been tucked behind them was heaped with pillows. "That's where I want you. Eventually."

She took a long sip of champagne, watching him over the rim. "You're not drinking."

"You're killing me."

Delighted, she laughed, and the sound was like smoke. "It's going to get worse."

Now he did drink, then set his glass aside. "Praise God."

She walked back to him, slipped his jacket from his shoulders. "I love your body," she murmured, slowly working open the buttons of his shirt. "I'm going to spend a lot of time enjoying it tonight."

It was a powerful rush, she thought, to make a strong man quiver. She felt that dance of muscles as she traced a fingertip down his chest to the hook of his trousers.

Instead of releasing them, she smiled. "You'd better sit down."

There was a throbbing in his blood,

primal, edging toward violent. It took a great deal of effort not to yield to it, to drag her to the floor and answer that urgent beat.

"No, not here," she said, and lifting his hand, nipped lightly at his knuckles. "I don't think you'll be able to manage to cross the room when I'm done."

It wasn't the wine making his head swim. She guided him across the room, a kind of lazy, circling dance with her in the lead. When she eased him down to sit on the side of the bed, she knelt at his feet, brushed her hands slowly, intimately down his legs. And took off his shoes.

She rose. "I'll just go get the wine."

"I'm not interested in wine."

She walked away, tossed a glance over her shoulder. "You will be. When I start licking it off you."

She topped off the glasses, brought them back to set them on the small, carved table by the bed. Then, watching him, her eyes gold and full of the light from the candles, she began to peel the dress down her body.

He wondered that his system didn't simply implode.

"Christ. Christ Jesus."

The Irish had leaped back into his voice, as she knew it did when he was distracted, angry, aroused. The simple sign made her glad she'd taken the time and trouble to, well, dress for the evening.

The siren-red lingerie was an erotic contrast against her skin. The silk and lace body skimmer rode low over her breasts so they all but spilled out of the top. Then it cinched in, sheer and seductive, slicked over her hips. Her hose was sheer and shimmering, and braked to a teasing halt at mid-thigh.

She stepped out of the dress, kicked it aside with the toe of one spiked heel.

"I thought we'd have dinner first."

He managed to lift his gaze to her face even as his mouth fell open.

"But . . . I guess it'll keep." She stepped forward, planted herself between his legs. "I want you to touch me."

His hands burned to take, but he skimmed them lightly over her, following angle, curve. "I'm lost in you already."

"Stay there." She bent down, took his mouth.

She knew he held back, let her hold the reins. And because she knew it, she gave him everything she had.

The candlelight glimmered, warming the scent of the roses as she slid onto the bed with him. As she took her hands, her mouth over him. Erotic and tender, passionate and loving. She wanted to show him all, everything.

And as she did, he gave back. Long drugging kisses that weighed the limbs, lazy, lingering caresses that thrilled the blood.

The bed, with its thick mattress of gel, undulated beneath them.

She rolled, leaned away, so he contented himself with the flavor just above the silk hose on the back of her thigh.

Then she straddled him, drank from the glass of champagne. Upending it, she began to drink him.

His vision blurred, the breath clogging in his lungs to burning. She tormented him. Pleasured him. Her agile body slid and slithered over his while her mouth drove him to the verge of madness.

His control snapped, steel rending steel. The sound of silk tearing inflamed him as he ripped at it. And with a sound of greed, he filled his hands, his mouth with her.

She came, a wild, shock slap to her system. Her head fell back as she gulped for air. Her body shuddered as he feasted on it.

He said something she couldn't understand, in the language of his homeland that so rarely passed his lips. Then his face was pressed against her, his breath hot on her skin.

"I need you. Eve. I need you."

"I know." Tenderness washed into her, balm over a burn. She cupped his face, lifted it. Her lips met his, soft as a whisper. "Don't ever stop."

There were tears in her eyes. The shifting light caught the glint of them. He drew her closer, kissed them away. "Eve —"

"No, let me say it first. This time let me remember to say it first. I love you. I always will. Be with me," she murmured as she took him inside her. "Oh. Stay with me."

She wrapped herself around him, rose to him, matching stroke to stroke, beat to beat. Then his hands clasped hers, locked tight. Their eyes held in a bond just as fierce.

When she saw his, that wild blue, go blind, when she heard him say her name, her lips curved into a smile. And she surrendered.

chapter fifteen

She was sprawled across the bed, facedown, in a position Roarke knew she assumed when her system had, finally, shut down. He stretched out beside her, sipping what champagne was left and trailing a fingertip absently up and down her spine.

"I'll give you an hour and a half to stop that."

"Ah, she lives."

She stirred herself enough to turn her head and look at him. "You look pretty smug."

"As it happens, darling Eve, I'm feeling pretty smug."

"It was all my idea."

"And a fine one it was, too. Would I be risking my skin if I asked just what inspired you?"

"Well . . ." She curved her back into the brush of his finger. "You bought me a candy bar."

"Remind me to arrange for a truckload tomorrow."

"A truckload would kill us." She pushed

to her knees, shoved back her hair. She looked soft and used and content.

"I'll risk it."

With a laugh, she leaned over to rest her forehead to his. "One last mushy thing before it becomes a habit. You make me happy. I'm starting to get used to it."

"That's a very nice way to end the mush."

"I guess we should eat."

"I'd hate to think of you slaving over a hot stove and not have the results appreciated."

Her eyes slitted. "Is that a dig?"

"No, indeed. What's for dinner?"

"Lots of stuff with weird, fancy names."

"Yum."

"I figured if you didn't like it, it wouldn't be programmed." She scooted off the bed, stood naked, glancing around. "I don't guess there's a robe in here."

"Afraid not." He dug through the tangle of sheets and pillows and came up with the now tattered body skimmer. "You could wear what's left of this."

"Never mind." She picked up her discarded dress, shimmied into it.

"Well now, that stirs the appetite considerably."

"Even you couldn't go another round after that last one." When he grinned, she thought it wise to move out of reach.

★ ★ ★

She couldn't pronounce half the food she put in her mouth, but it was damn tasty. "What is this called again?"

"Fruit de le mer a la parisienne."

"I guess if they called it a bunch of fish in a fancy sauce, it wouldn't have the same ring."

"A rose by any other name." He refilled her water glass. "Lieutenant?"

"Huh?"

"You're trying not to think about your day. Why don't you just tell me about it instead?"

She stabbed another scallop. "I've got a lead on —" She cut herself off, sucked it in. "No, you tell me about your day."

"My day?" he asked in surprise.

"Yeah, what did you do today, how'd it go, that sort of thing."

"You're in a mood," he murmured, then shrugged. "I dealt with some financial reorganization."

"What does that mean?"

"I bought some stock on its way down, sold some that I believe had topped off, studied the daily analysis of several companies and adjusted accordingly."

"I guess that kept you busy."

"Enough, until about noon when I went

into the office." He wondered how long it would take until her eyes glazed over. "I had a holo-conference regarding the Olympus Resort. Cost overruns remain under the acceptable five percent. However, on a point-by-point project analysis, I find indications of a downturn in resource productivity that warrants closer study and a correction."

Ninety seconds, he calculated, watching her eyes. He'd figured she'd drop off at sixty. "Then, I bought you a candy bar."

"I liked that part."

He broke off a chunk of his roll, buttered it. "Eve, did you marry me for my money?"

"You bet your ass. And you'd better hold on to it, or I'm history."

"It's very sweet of you to say so."

That made her grin. "I guess we're finished talking about your day."

"I thought we were. What's your lead?"

"Love. At least that's where all the arrows are pointing right now." She filled him in while she polished off her meal.

"Kenneth Stiles attacked Draco and beat him badly enough for medical intervention." Roarke cocked his head. "Interesting, isn't it, when you compare the two men. Draco was taller, considerably heftier, and certainly, on the surface, a great deal tougher. No indication that Stiles was injured?"

"None. I thought about that, too. It comes down to the pussy and the pissed. Draco being the pussy, Stiles the pissed."

"And being the pissed cost Stiles several million dollars."

"And he didn't even end up with the girl."

"Anja."

"Peabody found a handful of Carvells in the city. Wrong age span, so we're widening the scan. My gut tells me she has some of the answers."

"Cherchez la femme."

"What?"

"Find the woman," he translated.

She lifted her glass in a quick toast. "You can count on it."

"Anja." He said the name softly, a bare whisper of sound. And heard the gasp of surprise and recognition that followed it. "Don't say anything. Please. Just listen. I have to speak with you. It's important. Not over the 'link. Will you meet me?"

"This is about Richard."

"It's about everything."

It took time. He was certain he was being watched and feared his own shadow. Stiles sat at the mirror in his dressing area and skillfully, painstakingly altered his appearance. He changed the color of his eyes, the shape of his nose, his jaw, the color of his skin. He covered his hair with a wig, a thick mane of deep brown. He supposed it was vanity that prevented him from using the more ordinary gray one.

He couldn't bear to look old in her eyes.

He added a slim mustache, a slender brush of beard in the center of his chin.

All of this came naturally, despite the anxiety. He had donned a hundred characters in his life, sliding into them as smoothly as a man slips into favorite slippers after a long day.

He added girth to his small frame — shoulders, chest, then covered the padding with a simple dark suit. The lifts in his shoes would give him another inch of height.

He took his time, studying the results in the long triple mirror, searching for any sign of Kenneth Stiles. For the first time in over an hour he allowed himself a small smile.

He could walk right up to Lieutenant Eve Dallas and kiss her on the mouth. He'd be damned if she'd recognize him.

Empowered, as he always was by a new role, Stiles swirled on a cape and went out to meet the woman he'd loved all his life.

She kept him waiting. She always had.

He'd chosen a small nostalgia club that had fallen out of fashion. But the music was low and bluesy, the patrons minded their own, and the drinks came quickly.

He sipped at gin and paged through the battered volume of Shakespeare's sonnets. It was their signal.

She had given him the book all those years ago. He had taken it for a token of love instead of the friendship she'd intended. Even when he'd realized his mistake, he'd treasured it. As much as he'd treasured her.

He'd lied to the police, of course. He'd never broken contact with her, had known where she was, what she was doing. He had simply assumed another role with her, that of confidant and friend.

And after a time, living the part for so many years, he grew comfortable with it.

Yet, when she slid into the booth across from him, held out a hand for his, his heart leapt.

She'd changed her hair. It was a glorious tangle of smoky red. Her skin was a pale, pale gold. He knew it was soft to the touch. Her eyes were deep, tawny, and concerned. But she smiled at him, a hesitant curve of a lush mouth.

"So, you still read it?" Her voice was soft and lightly French.

"Yes, often. Anja." His fingers flexed on hers, then deliberately relaxed. "Let me order you a drink."

She sat back, watching him, waiting, as he signaled a waiter and ordered her a glass of sauvignon blanc.

"You never forget."

"Why would I?"

"Oh, Kenneth." She closed her eyes a moment. "I wish things had been different. Could have been."

"Don't." He spoke more sharply than he'd intended. It could still sting. "We're beyond regrets."

"I don't think we ever get beyond them." She let out a small sigh. "I've spent more than half my life regretting Richard."

He said nothing until her drink was served and she'd taken the first sip. "The police think I killed him."

Her eyes went wide, and wine sloshed toward the rim of her glass as her hand jerked. "But no! No, that's impossible. Ridiculous."

"They know what happened twenty-four years ago."

"What do you mean?" Her hand darted out for his, squeezed like a vise. "What do they know?"

"Steady now. They know about the assault, my arrest, the suit."

"But how is that possible? It was so long ago, and all the details were put away."

"Eve Dallas. Lieutenant Dallas," he said with some bitterness as he lifted his own drink. "She's relentless. She managed to break the seal. They took me in, put me in a room, hammered at me."

"Oh, Kenneth. Kenneth, *mon cher,* I'm so sorry. It must have been hideous."

"They think I've harbored a grudge against Richard all this time." He laughed a little, drank. "I suppose they're right."

"But you didn't kill him."

"No, but they'll continue to dig into the past. You need to be prepared. I had to tell them why I attacked Richard. I had to give them your name." When the blood drained from her face, he leaned over, clasped both of her hands. "Anja," he said deliberately, "I told them I'd lost track of you, that we've had no contact in all these years. That I didn't know how to find you. I told them Richard had seduced you, then when he was certain you were in love with him, he cast you off. I told them about the attempt to take your own life. That's all I told them."

She made a small sound of despair and lowered her head. "It still shames me."

"You were young, brokenhearted. You survived. Anja, I'm sorry. I panicked. But the fact is, I had to give them something. I thought it would be enough, but I realize now, she won't stop. Dallas will keep searching, keep digging until she finds you. Finds the rest."

She steadied, nodded. "Anja Carvell has disappeared before. I could make it impossible for her to find me. But that won't do. I'll go to see her."

"You can't. For God's sake."

"I can. I must. Would you still protect me?" she said quietly. "Kenneth, I don't deserve you. I never did. I'll speak with her, explain how it was, how you are," she added.

"I don't want you involved."

"My dearest, you can't stop what Richard started a lifetime ago. You're my friend, and I intend to protect what's mine. Whatever the risk," she added, and her eyes hardened. "Whatever the consequences."

"There has to be more."

Roarke ran his hand over Eve's naked ass. "Well. If you insist."

She lifted her head. "I wasn't talking about sex."

"Oh. Pity."

He'd managed to peel the red dress off her again, and then it had been a simple matter of one thing leading to another. Now she

349

was sprawled over him, all warm and loose.

But apparently, she didn't intend to stay that way.

"They all hated him." She scooted up to straddle him and gave Roarke a very pleasant view of slender torso and firm breasts. "Or at least actively disliked him. Maybe feared him," she considered. "Nobody in that cast is particularly sorry to see him dead. Several of the actors had worked with each other before. Had histories, links, connections. To Draco, to each other. Maybe it was more than one of them."

"*Murder on the Orient Express.*"

"What's that? An Asian transpo system?"

"No, darling, it's yet another play by Dame Christie. She seems to be popping up. A man is murdered in his bed, in the sleeping car of a train. Stabbed. Repeatedly. Among the passengers is a very clever detective, not nearly as attractive as my cop," he added.

"What does a make-believe dead guy on a train have to do with my case?"

"Just enhancing your theory. In this fictional murder, there were a number of varied and seemingly unconnected passengers. However, our dogged detective refused to take such matters at face value, poked around, and discovered links, connections, histories. Disguises and deceptions," he added. "When he did, he discovered they all had motives for murder."

"Interesting. Who did it?"

"All of them." When her eyes narrowed, he sat up, wrapped his arms around her. "Each of them took a turn with the knife, plunging it into his unconscious body in return for the wrong he'd done to them."

"Pretty gruesome. And pretty cagey. No one could betray anyone else without betraying themselves. They back up each other's alibis. Play the role," she murmured.

"Very nearly a perfect murder."

"There are no perfect murders. There are always mistakes, with the murder itself the biggest of them."

"Spoken like a cop."

"I am a cop. And I'm going back to work."

She wiggled away, slid off the bed, and once again reached down for the dress.

"You put that red number back on, baby, I won't be responsible for my actions."

"Simmer down. I'm not strolling around naked. You never know where Summerset's skulking." She began pulling the dress up and glanced around the room. "I guess we should clean up some."

"Why?"

"Because it looks like we've —"

"Had a very enjoyable evening," Roarke finished. "This may shock you, but Summerset knows we have sex."

"Don't mention his name and sex in the same sentence. Gives me the creeps. I'm going to grab a shower, then work awhile."

"All right. I'll join you."

"Uh-uh. I'm not showering with you, ace. I know your games."

"I won't lay a hand on you."

He didn't say anything about his mouth.

"What do you do? Take a pill?"

Limber, refreshed, and utterly satisfied, Roarke buttoned his shirt. "You're stimulation enough."

"Apparently."

He took her hand, led her to the elevator, requested her office.

The cat was stretched across her sleep chair and gave a twitch of his tail when they walked in.

"Coffee?" Roarke asked.

"Yeah, thanks."

The minute he turned toward the kitchen, Galahad leaped down and bolted into the room ahead of him. Eve heard the single demanding meow.

She sat at her desk, stared at her computer, tapped her fingers.

"Computer, Draco case file. Cross-reference task. Find and list any and all connections, professional, personal, medical, financial, criminal, civil, between cast members."

Working . . .

"I assumed you ran that already."
She glanced over as Roarke came back with coffee. "I'm running it again, with a few added details.
"Computer, highlight any name with sealed files, all areas."

That information requires authorization. Please submit same . . .

"Would you like me to get around that little hitch for you?"
She made a low sound, a definite warning. Roarke merely shrugged and sipped his coffee.
"Authorization Code Yellow, slash Dallas, slash five-oh-six. Request from Dallas, Lieutenant Eve, regarding double homicide. You are authorized to flag sealeds."

Authorization correct. Sealeds will be flagged. Data contained in sealed files re-

quires warrant, signed and dated, for access . . .

"Did I ask you to access the data? Just flag the damned sealeds."

Working . . . Multitask process will require approximately eight minutes, thirty seconds . . .

"Then get started. And no," she said to Roarke. "We're not opening the sealeds."

"My goodness, Lieutenant, I don't believe I suggested anything of the kind."

"You think you and McNab scammed me on that warrant today?"

"I have no idea what you're talking about." He eased a hip onto the desk. "I did give Ian some advice, but it was of a personal nature. Man talk."

"Yeah, right." She tipped back in her chair, eyed him over her coffee cup. "You and McNab sat around talking about women and sports."

"I don't believe we got to sports. He had a woman on his mind."

Eve's sneer vanished. "You talked to him about Peabody? Damn it, Roarke."

"I could hardly slap him back. He's so pitifully smitten."

"Oh." She winced. "Don't use that word."

"It fits. In fact, if he took my advice . . ." He turned his wrist, glanced at the unit fastened there. "They should be well into their first date by now."

"Date? Date? Why did you do that? Why did you go and do something like that? Couldn't you leave it alone? They'd have had sex until they burned out on it, and everything would go back to normal."

He angled his head. "That didn't work for us, did it?"

"We don't work together." Then, when his eyes brightened with pure amusement, she showed her teeth. "Officially. You start mixing cops and romance and case files and gooey looks at briefings, you've got nothing but a mess. Next thing you know, Peabody will be wearing lip dye and smelly girl stuff and dragging body skimmers under her uniform."

She dropped her head in her hands. "Then they'll have tiffs and misunderstandings that have nothing whatsoever to do with the job. They'll come at me from both sides, and before you know it, they'll be telling me things I absolutely do *not* want to know. And when they break it off and decide they hate each other down to the guts, I'll have to hear about that, too, and why they can't possibly work together, or breathe the same air, until I have no choice, absolutely no choice, but to kick both of their asses."

"Eve, your sunny view on life never fails to lift my spirits."

"And —" She poked him in the chest. "It's all your fault."

He grabbed her finger, nipped it, not so gently. "If that's the case, I'm going to insist they name their first child after me."

"Are you trying to make me crazy?"

"Well, darling, it's so easy, I find it difficult to resist. Why don't you put the entire matter out of your mind before it gives you a headache? Your data's coming up."

She shot him one fierce look, then turned to the screen.

Connections within connections, she thought as she scanned. Lives bumping up against lives. And every time they did, they left a little mark. Sometimes the mark was a bruise that never fully healed.

"Well, well, this didn't come up before. Michael Proctor's mother was an actress. She had a small part in a play. Twenty-four years ago." Eve sat back. "And just look who was onstage with her. Draco, Stiles, Mansfield, Rothchild. That correlates to the trouble between Draco and Stiles. Where's Anja Carvell?" she murmured.

"Perhaps she had, or has, a stage name."

"Maybe. No sealeds on Proctor's mother." She ordered the computer to do a run on one Natalie Brooks.

"Interesting. This was her last performance. Retired, returned to place of birth. Omaha, Nebraska. Married the following year. Looks squeaky clean. Attractive," she added when she ordered the computer to show her ID picture from twenty-four years before. "Young, got a fresh sort of look. Right up Draco's alley."

"You think she might be Anja?"

"Maybe. Either way, I can't see Draco passing her up. That adds another layer to Michael Proctor. He didn't mention his mother knew Draco."

"He might not have been aware of it."

"Unlikely. Let's take a look at the flags. Hmm, Draco's got a few sealeds of his own."

"Money, prominence, connections," Roarke said. "It buys silence."

"You ought to know." She said it with a smirk, then jerked up in her chair. "Wait a minute, wait a minute. What's this? Carly Landsdowne's got a sealed."

"More secrets? More silence?"

"Not this time. I know this code. It's an old one. It was in use when I went into the system. A lot of the kids in state homes wanted that code more than they wanted to eat their next meal. It's the code for adoption. Sealed," she added. "With the birth mother's data inside. Look at the date."

"Eight months after Stiles's assault on Draco. It won't be a coincidence."

"This plays for me. Draco got Anja Carvell pregnant. She tells him, he dumps her. Dumps her hard. She falls apart, tries self-termination, but Stiles gets to her before she's finished. She has a change of heart and decides to complete the pregnancy. Gives the kid away, and pays a hefty fee for a seal."

"It wouldn't have been easy."

Eve's eyes went flat. "It's plenty easy for some. Kids are tossed aside every day."

To comfort her, he put his hands on her shoulders, rubbed. "By Stiles's account, she was in love with the baby's father and nearly destroyed by him. Yet she didn't terminate the pregnancy. She gave the child up, which is different, Eve, than giving the child away. She paid for the seal to protect the child."

"It protects her, too."

"Yes, but there are other ways. She could have sold the baby on the black market. No questions asked. She chose legal channels."

"Stiles knew. She'd have spilled it. We're

going to have to have another chat. Now, let's see. Which judge should I wake up for the warrant and authorization to crack the seal?" She looked up at Roarke. "Any suggestions?"

"Lieutenant, I'm sure you know best."

chapter sixteen

Before she roused a judge out of bed and risked irritating him, she tried to tag Peabody through her communicator.

"Off duty?" Sheer shock glazed Eve's eyes at the blinking red light on her pocket unit. "What the hell does that mean?"

"Why, the nerve!" Roarke clucked his tongue. "I bet she's got some insane idea that she's entitled to a life."

"It's your fault, it's your fault, it's your fault," Eve chanted under her breath while she sent the transmission to Peabody's palm 'link.

After six beeps, Eve was up and pacing. "If she doesn't answer, I'm going to —" Abruptly, Eve's desk 'link exploded with noise. Her angry yelp had the cat racing back into the kitchen.

"Peabody! For God's sake, where are you?"

"Sir? Sir, is that you? I can't really hear over the music."

The audio might have been chaos, but the video shimmered clear and gave Eve a close-up view of her aide, complete with fussy hair, lip dye, and slumberous eyes.

I knew it, was all Eve could think. *I just knew it.*

"You've been drinking."

"I have?" The vague eyes blinked at the information, then Eve heard what could only be described as a giggle. "Well, maybe. A couple. I'm in a club, and they have drinking here. Really rocking screamers. Is it morning already?"

"Hey, Dallas!" McNab's face pushed against Peabody's so the two of them, equally plowed by the look of things, shared the screen. "This band is ice. Why don't you get your main squeeze and come on down."

"Peabody, where are you?"

"I'm in New York City. I live here."

Drunk, Eve thought in frustration. *Drunk as a Station Caspian colonist.* "Never mind. Take this outside before I go deaf."

"What? I can't hear you!"

Ignoring Roarke's amused chuckle, Eve leaned into her 'link. "Officer Peabody, go outside, keep the transmission open. I need to talk to you."

"You're outside? Well, hell, come on in."

Eve sucked in a breath. "Go. Out. Side."

"Oh, okay, sure thing."

There was a great deal of fumbling, more

giggling, bumpy views of a crowd of what Eve decided were maniacs leaping and spinning as the band crashed out noise. To her great pain, she heard, very clearly, McNab's hissed suggestion of what would be fun to do in one of the club's privacy rooms.

"You have to give him points for imagination," Roarke pointed out.

"I hate you for this." Patience straining, Eve held the transmission while Peabody and McNab stumbled out of the club. The noise level dropped, but not by much. Apparently McNab's choice of club was in the core of Broadway's never-ending party district.

"Dallas? Dallas? Where are you?"

"Your 'link, Peabody. I'm on your 'link."

"Oh." She lifted it again, peered at the screen. "What are you doing in there?"

"Have you got any Sober-Up in your bag?"

"Betcha. You gotta be prepared, right?"

"Take some. Now."

"Aw." Peabody's cheerfully colored lips moved into a pout. "I don't wanna. Hey, that's Roarke. I heard Roarke. Hi, Roarke."

He couldn't resist and moved into view. "Hello, Peabody. You're looking particularly delicious tonight."

"Golly, you're pretty. I could just look at

you and look at you and —"

"Sober-Up, Peabody. Now. That's an order."

"Damn." Peabody rummaged through her bag, came up with the little tin. "If I gotta, you gotta," she said, plucking out two pills before shoving the tin at McNab.

"Why?"

"Because."

"Oh."

"Peabody, I need all current data on Anja Carvell, all search and scan results."

" 'Kay."

"Shoot them to my car unit. Then I want you to meet me, *in uniform,* at Kenneth Stiles's address. Thirty minutes. Understood?"

"Yeah, sort of . . . Could you repeat the question?"

"It's not a question. It's an order," Eve corrected and repeated it. "Got that now?"

"Yeah. Um, yes, sir."

"And leave your trained monkey at home."

"Sir?"

"McNab," Eve snapped, and cut transmission.

"Party pooper," Roarke murmured.

"Don't give me any lip." She rose, pulled her shoulder harness out of the desk drawer, strapped it on. "Go do some financial adjustments and point by point analyses."

"Darling, you were listening."

"I'm not laughing," she told him, and was annoyed because she wanted to. "Stay out of trouble."

He only smiled, waiting until he heard her jog down the stairs.

She was going to ease her way around the seal instead of breaking through it, he thought. There was no reason he should have the same limitations.

He strolled down the corridor to a private room. His voice and palm prints were checked and verified. The locks disengaged.

"Lights on," he ordered. "Full."

The room streamed with light, blocked from the outside by the secured privacy screens on the bank of windows. He crossed the wide squares of tile while the door behind him closed, resecured.

Only three people had entry to this room. Three people he trusted without reservation. Eve, Summerset, and himself.

The slick black control panel formed a wide U. The equipment, unregistered and illegal, hummed softly in sleep mode. The wide eye of CompuGuard couldn't restrict what it couldn't see.

He'd restructured most of his questionable holdings over the years. After Eve, he'd disposed of or legitimized the rest. But, he thought as he helped himself to a brandy, a man had to have some small reminders of the past that made him.

And in his rebel's heart, the idea of a system like CompuGuard that monitored all computer business was an annoying pebble in his shoe. He was honor bound to shake it out.

He stepped to the control, swirled his brandy. "System up," he ordered, and a rainbow of lights bloomed over black. "Now, let's have a look."

Eve left her vehicle in a second-level parking slot a half a block from Stiles's apartment. She'd walked half that distance when she spotted the figure trying to blend with the trees at the edge of the facing park.

"Trueheart."

"Sir!" She heard the squeak of surprise in his voice, but he'd schooled his face into calm lines by the time he stepped out of the shadows. "Lieutenant."

"Report."

"Sir, I've had the subject's building under surveillance since his return at eighteen-twenty-three. My counterpart is surveilling the rear exit. We have maintained regular communications at intervals of thirty minutes."

When she made no comment, he cleared his throat. "Subject lowered privacy screens on all windows at eighteen-thirty-eight. They have remained engaged since that time."

"That's good, Trueheart, gives me a really clear picture. Now, tell me if he's in there."

"Lieutenant, subject has not left the surveilled premises."

"Fine." She watched a Rapid Cab swing toward the opposing curb. Peabody, looking considerably more official in full uniform with her hair straight under her cap, climbed out. "Stand by, Officer Trueheart."

"Yes, sir. Sir? I'd like to take this opportunity to thank you for this assignment."

Eve looked up into his very young, very earnest face. "You want to thank me for duty that has you standing out in the dark, in the cold, for . . ." She glanced at her wrist unit. "For approximately five and a half hours?"

"It's a homicide investigation," he said with such reverence she nearly patted his cheek.

"Glad you're enjoying it." She headed across the street, where Peabody waited. "Look me in the eye," Eve demanded.

"I'm sober, sir."

"Stick out your tongue."

"Why?"

"Because you want to. Now, stop sulking." With this, Eve walked toward the building. "And no rolling your eyes at the back of my head."

Peabody's eyes stopped in mid-roll. "Am I to be informed of the reason I've been called back on duty?"

"You'll be informed. If all your surviving brain cells are in working order, you'll get the drift when I corner Stiles. I'll fill in the blanks when we're done."

She gave her badge and palm print to the night guard for verification, got clearance. Eve ran it through quickly on the way up.

"Wow, it's like one of those daytime serials. Not that I watch them," Peabody said quickly when Eve's eyes slid coolly in her direction. "One of my sisters is addicted though. She's totally hooked on *The Heart of Desire*. See, Desire's this small and charming seaside town, but under the surface, there's all this intrigue and —"

"Don't. Really."

She hurried out of the elevator to prevent any possibility of a rundown of anything called *The Heart of Desire*. She pressed the buzzer at Stiles's apartment, held her badge up toward the security peep.

"Maybe he's asleep," Peabody said a few moments later.

"He's got a house droid." Eve pressed the buzzer again and felt the ache of tension squeeze in her gut.

She'd assigned a rookie, a rookie for Christ's sake, to surveillance on a lead suspect in two homicides. Because she'd wanted to give the kid a break.

If Stiles had slipped past him, she had no one to blame but herself.

"We're going in." She reached for her master code.

"A warrant —"

"We don't need one. Subject is suspect, dual homicide, also potential victim. There's reason to believe subject has fled or is inside, unable to respond."

She bypassed the locks with her master. "Draw your weapon, Peabody," she ordered as she reached for her own. "Go in high, to the right. Ready?"

Peabody nodded. Her mouth might have been brightly painted, but it was firm.

At Eve's signal, they went through the door, sweeping opposite directions. Eve ordered lights, narrowed her eyes against the sudden flash of them, scanned, sweeping as she angled herself to guard Peabody's back.

"Police! Kenneth Stiles, this is Lieutenant Dallas, NYPSD. I am armed. You're ordered to step out into the living area immediately."

She moved toward the bedroom as she spoke, ears cocked for any sound. "He's not here." Every instinct told her the place was empty, but she gestured Peabody to the far side of the room. "Check that area. Watch your back."

She booted open the door, led with her weapon.

She saw a neatly made bed, a tidy sitting area, and the dark pool of the suit Stiles had worn to the memorial service on the floor.

"The droid's here, Dallas," Peabody called out. "Deactivated. No sign of Stiles."

"He's gone rabbit. Goddamn it." Still, she kept her weapon out and ready as she moved into the bath, through the adjoining door.

One look at the dressing room had her holstering it again. "I guess that lets Trueheart off the hook," she said to Peabody when her aide joined her. Eve fingered a pot of skin toner, then lifted a wig. "Stiles is probably damn good with this stuff. Call it in, Peabody. Suspect in flight."

"Sir." Trueheart stood stiff as a petrified

redwood in the entry to Stiles's dressing room. His face was white but for the high color skimming along his cheekbones. "I take full responsibility for the failure of the assignment given to me. I will accept, without qualification, any reprimand you deem appropriate."

"First, stop talking like that droid Peabody's reactivating. Second, you're not responsible for the flight of this suspect. That's on me."

"Lieutenant, I appreciate you taking my inexperience into consideration in my failure to perform my duty and complete this assignment in a satisfactory manner —"

"Shut up, Trueheart." Jesus God, spare her from rookies. "Peabody! Come in here."

"I've nearly got the droid up and running, Dallas."

"Peabody, tell Officer Trueheart here how I deal with cops who botch assignments or fail to complete same in what I deem a satisfactory manner."

"Sir, you bust their balls, mercilessly. It can be very entertaining to watch. From a discreet and safe distance."

"Thank you, Peabody. You make me proud. Trueheart, am I busting your balls?"

His flush spread. "Ah, no, sir. Lieutenant."

"Then it follows that in my opinion, you didn't botch this assignment. If my opinion was otherwise, you'd be curled on the floor, clutching said balls and begging for mercy, which Officer Peabody has succinctly pointed out I do not have. Are we clear?"

He hesitated. "Yes, sir?"

"That's the right answer." She turned away from him, studied the dressing area. The forest of clothes in different styles and sizes; the long, wide counter covered with bottles and tubes and sprays. Cubbyholes loaded with hairpieces, wigs. Drawers ruthlessly organized with other tools of the trade.

"He can make himself into anyone. I should've factored that in. Tell me who you did see leaving the building between eighteen-thirty and when I arrived on-scene. We'll verify with the security discs from the exits, but be thorough."

He nodded, and his eyes unfocused with concentration. "A couple, man and woman, white and white, thirty-five to forty. They hailed a Rapid and headed east. A single woman, mixed race, late twenties. She left on foot, in a westerly direction. Two men, black and white, early thirties. They returned within thirty minutes, carrying what appeared to be a twelve-pack of beer and a large pizza. A single man, mixed race, late forties, some facial hair."

He stopped when Eve held up a hand. She lifted a small bag to show him a few strands of hair she'd already sealed for evidence. "Is this a color match?"

He opened his mouth, then closed it again to press his lips together. "It's difficult to say with certainty, Lieutenant, as the light was going. But the subject in question appeared to have dark hair very similar in shade to the bagged evidence."

"Give me details. Height, weight, style of dress, appearance."

She listened, trying to paint a picture of the transformation from Trueheart's report.

"Okay, anyone else?"

He ran through the few people who'd left the building, but no one rang bells like the single mixed-race male.

"Was he carrying anything? A bag, a box, a parcel?"

"No, sir. He didn't have anything with him."

"Okay, then he's likely still running with the same look. Call it in."

"Sir?"

"Call in your description, Trueheart. Add it to the all-points."

His face lit up like a birthday candle. "Yes, sir!"

★ ★ ★

It was blind luck that he was spotted. Eve would think about that later, and for a long time after. Blind luck.

It was a twist of fate that the express running to and from Toronto experienced a malfunction on its way into Grand Central. The delay would make all the difference.

But when the break came, Eve jammed her communicator back in her pocket. "Grand Central. Let's move."

She was halfway to the apartment door when she shot a glance over her shoulder. "Trueheart, is there a reason you're not one step behind me?"

"Sir?"

"When the officer in command says to move, you get your bony butt in gear and move."

He blinked rapidly, then appeared to process the information that she wanted him on the team. A goofy smile spread over his face as he rushed to the door. "Yes, sir."

"Transit cops are blocking exits, spreading to all gates. Backup's on the way." Eve relayed the information as they headed down to street level. "Suspect's bought a one-way express to Toronto."

"It's cold up there." Peabody flipped up the collar of her coat as they ran down the block to Eve's vehicle. "If I were fleeing the country, I'd head south. I've never been to the Caribbean."

"You can point that out to him when he's in lockup. Strap in," she suggested when they dived inside. She shot down the parking ramp like a rocket, hit the sirens, and did a screaming two-wheel around the corner.

Flopping in the backseat, stomach at knee level, Trueheart was in heaven.

He was in pursuit, not of a scrounging street thief, not of a whiny traffic violation, but of a murder suspect. He gripped the chicken stick to keep his balance as Eve wove fast and nervelessly through traffic. He wanted to imprint every detail on his mind. The wild speed, the flash of lights, the sudden jolt and jerk as his lieutenant — God, wasn't she amazing? — shot the vehicle into a fast vertical lift to bypass a jam on Lexington.

He listened to Peabody's clear, practical voice as she coordinated with the backup on her communicator. To Eve's low, careless cursing as she was forced to swerve sharply to avoid a pair of "fucking brain-dead morons" on a scooter.

She squealed to a halt on the west side of the transpo center. "Peabody, Trueheart, with me. Let's see what the transit boys have for us."

There were two transit cops sealing the exit. Both came to attention when Eve held up her badge. "Status?"

"Your suspect's inside, Lieutenant. Level Two, Area C. There are a number of passengers in that area. The express for Toronto was sold out. There are several shops, eateries, and rest room facilities. Men are posted at all lifts, glides, and walkways leading in or out of the area. He's in there."

"Stand by."

She walked into the great sea of noise and movement.

"Lieutenant, Feeney and McNab approaching south side of the building."

"Give them the target location. We don't have data on weapons, but we go in assuming he's armed." She crossed the wide expanse of floor while people rushing home or away streamed past her. "Alert the commanding officer we're heading down."

"Captain Stuart, sir. Channel B on your communicator. She's standing by."

"Captain Stuart, Lieutenant Dallas."

"Lieutenant, we have our net in place. Traffic Control Center will continue to announce delays for the twelve-oh-five to Toronto."

"Where's my suspect?"

Stuart's face stayed blank and hard, but

her voice tightened. "We've lost direct visual of the subject. He has not, I repeat, has not exited the patrolled area. Our security cameras are executing a full sweep. We'll pick him up."

"Contact me, this channel, when you spot him," Eve said briefly. "Inform your men that NYPSD is now on-scene and taking charge. Their full cooperation and assistance is appreciated."

"This is my turf, Lieutenant. My command."

"Target is suspected of two homicides on *my* turf, Captain. That's an override, and we both know it. Let's get the job done. We can have a pissing contest later." Eve waited a beat. "We're approaching Level Two. Please inform your men. Weapons are to be programmed to lowest setting and to be deployed only in extreme circumstances and for the protection of bystanders. I want a clean snatch."

"I'm fully aware how to perform an operation of this nature. I was informed the target may be armed."

"We can't confirm. Use caution and minimal force. Minimal force, Captain; that's priority. The area is packed with civilians. I'll maintain this channel for further communications."

Eve tucked the communicator back in her pocket. "Hear that, Peabody?"

"Yes, sir. She wants the collar. 'This evening, the New York City Transit Authority, led by Captain Stuart, captured the primary suspect in Richard Draco's murder, in flight. Pictures at eleven.' "

"And what is our objective?"

"To identify, restrain, and incarcerate target. In one piece, and with no civilian injuries."

"You following that, Trueheart?"

"Yes, sir."

Eve noted the transit officers holding the perimeter of Area C. And the flood of people who milled, loitered, or rushed over the wide platform and through the snaking corridors that opened into shops and eateries.

She smelled the greasy aroma of fast food, the hot scent of humanity. Babies were crying. The latest urban rock was pumping out of someone's tune box in direct violation of the noise pollution code. A small band of sidewalk singers was struggling to compete.

She saw weariness, excitement, boredom on the sea of faces. And with mild annoyance, she saw a strolling pocket-dipper snag a wallet.

"Trueheart, you're the only one who got a look at him. Keep your eyes open. We want to take this down smooth, but we don't want to waste time. The longer that express is delayed, the more nervous Stiles is going to get."

"Dallas, Feeney and McNab at nine o'clock."

"Yeah, I see them." She saw them, the surging tide of civilians, the dozens of byways. "This place is like an insect hive. We're going to spread out. Peabody, troll the right. Trueheart, take the left. Maintain visual contact."

She took the center, cutting through the crowd, eyes scanning. Across the tracks, a southbound train shot down the tunnel with a hot whoosh of air. A panhandler, his beggar's license smeared with something indefinable, worked the passengers waiting for the delayed Toronto express.

She was about to overlap with Feeney, shifted her gaze to lock Peabody's position, turned her head to lock Trueheart's.

She heard the shout, a series of screams, an explosion of glass as the panel on one of the busy storefronts shattered. Even as she spun, she saw Stiles shove his way through the panicked crowd, pursued by a transit cop.

"Hold your fire!" She shouted it, grabbing both weapon and communicator. "Stuart, order your man to cease fire! Target is cornered. Do not deploy weapons."

She was using elbows, boots, knees, to fight her way through the surge of people fleeing the area. Someone fell against her, all wild eyes and grabbing hands. Gritting her teeth, she shoved him away, bulled through an opening.

The next wave of people swarmed like bees, screaming as windows on the storefronts spat glass. She felt heat on her face, something wet ran down her neck.

She saw Stiles leap over the fallen and the cowering. Then she saw Trueheart.

He had long legs, and they moved fast. Eve used her own, burst free. Out of the corner of her eye, she saw a jerk of movement.

"No! Hold your fire!" Her shouted order was drowned out in the chaos. Even as she jumped toward the transit cop, he shifted to shooting position and took aim. At the same instant, Trueheart bunched for a leap and tackle.

The shock of the beam hit him midair, turned his body into a missile that rammed hard against Stiles's retreating back. The forward force sent them both tumbling off the platform, onto the tracks below.

"No. Goddamn it. No!" She shoved the transit cop, spun to the side, and rushed to the edge of the platform. "Hold all northbound trains! There are injured on the track. Hold all trains! Oh Jesus. Oh Christ."

A tangle of bodies, a splatter of blood. She jumped down to the tracks, feeling the shock sing up her legs. Her breath panted out as she searched for the pulse in Trueheart's throat.

"Goddamn it. Goddamn it. Officer down!" Her voice cracked out of a dry throat and into her communicator. "Officer down! Require immediate medical assistance, Grand Central, Level Two, Area C as in Charlie. Deploy medi-vac units. Officer and suspect down. Hold on, Trueheart."

She yanked off her jacket, spread it over his chest, then used her hands to press down on the long gash running down his thigh.

Feeney, out of breath and sweating, landed beside her. "Ah, Christ. How bad?"

"Bad. He took a hit, jumped right into the fucking beam." She'd been a step too late. One step too late. "Then the fall. We can't risk moving him without stabilizers. Where are the MTs? Where are the fucking MTs?"

"On the way. Here." He unfastened his belt, nudged her to the side, and fastened a tourniquet. "Stiles?"

She ordered herself to maintain, crab-walked to where Stiles lay facedown, checked for a pulse. "Alive. He didn't catch the hit, and the way they went down, it looked like the kid broke the worst of his fall."

"Your face is bleeding, Dallas."

"I caught some glass, that's all." She swiped at the trickle with the back of her hand, mixing her blood with Trueheart's. "When I get done with Stuart and her hotshots —"

She broke off, looked back down at Trueheart's young, pale face. "Jesus, Feeney. He's just a kid."

chapter seventeen

Eve burst through the emergency room doors in the wake of the gurney and fast-talking MTs. The words were like slaps, hard and ringing. Under the barrage of them she heard something about spinal injuries, internal bleeding.

When they hit the doors of an examining room, an enormous nurse, her skin a gleaming ebony against the pale blue of her tunic, blocked Eve's path.

"Step aside, sister. That's my man down in there."

"No, you step aside, sister." The nurse laid a boulder-sized hand on Eve's shoulder. "Medical personnel only beyond this point. You've got some pretty good facial lacerations there. Take Exam Four. Someone will be along to clean you up."

"I can clean myself up. That boy in there belongs to me. I'm his lieutenant."

"Well, Lieutenant, you're just going to have to let the doctors do what they do." She pulled out a memo board. "You want to help, give me his personal data."

Eve elbowed the nurse aside, moved to the observation glass, but didn't attempt to push through again. God, she hated hospitals. Hated them. All she could see was a flurry of movement, green scrubs for the doctors, blue for the nursing staff.

And Trueheart unconscious on the table under harsh lights while they worked on him.

"Lieutenant." The nurse's voice softened. "Let's help each other out here. We both want the same thing. Give me what you can on the patient."

"Trueheart. Christ, what's his first name. Peabody?"

"Troy," Peabody said from behind her. "It's Troy. He's twenty-two."

Eve simply laid her brow against the glass, shut her eyes and relayed the cause of injuries.

"We'll take care of him," the nurse told her. "Now get yourself into Four." She swung through the doors, became part of the blue and green wall.

"Peabody, find his family. Have a couple of counselors contact them."

"Yes, sir. Feeney and McNab are monitoring Stiles. He's in the next room."

More gurneys were streaming in. The injured at Grand Central were going to keep the ER busy for the rest of the night with cuts, bruises, and broken bones. "I'll inform the commander of the current status." She stepped back from the glass so that she could give her report without wavering.

When she was done, she took her position by the doors and called home.

"Roarke."

"You're bleeding."

"I — I'm at the hospital."

"Where? Which one?"

"Roosevelt. Listen —"

"I'm on my way."

"No, wait. I'm okay. I've got a man down. A boy," she said and nearly broke. "He's a goddamn boy. They're working on him. I need to stay until . . . I need to stay."

"I'm on my way," he said again.

She started to protest, then simply nodded. "Yeah. Thanks."

The nurse pushed back through the doors, sent Eve one smoking look. "Why aren't you in Room Four?"

"What's Trueheart's condition?"

"They're stabilizing him. He'll be heading up to surgery shortly. Op-Six. I'll get you to a waiting area after you're treated."

"I want a full report on his condition."

"You want it, you'll get it. After you're treated."

★ ★ ★

The waiting was the worst. It gave her too much time to think, to replay, to second-guess. To spot every small misstep.

She couldn't sit. She paced, drank vile coffee, and stared out the window at the wall of the next wing.

"He's young. Healthy," Peabody said because she could no longer stand saying nothing. "That weighs on his side."

"I should've sent him home. I should've relieved him. I had no business taking a rookie on this kind of operation."

"You wanted to give him a break."

"A break?" She spun around, and her eyes were fierce, brilliant with emotion. "I put his life on the line, into a situation he wasn't prepared for. He went down. I'm responsible for that."

"The hell you are." Peabody's chin lifted mutinously. "He's a cop. When you put on the uniform, you take on the risk. He's on the job, and that means facing the potential of taking a hit in the line of duty every day. If I'd taken the left instead of the right, I'd have done exactly what Trueheart did, and I'd be in surgery. And it would seriously piss me off to know you're standing out here taking away from actions I took to do my job."

"Peabody —" Eve broke off, shook her head, and walked back to the overburdened coffee machine.

"Well done." Roarke moved over, rubbed a hand on Peabody's shoulder. "You're a jewel, Peabody."

"It wasn't her fault. I can't stand seeing her take it on."

"If she didn't, she wouldn't be who she is."

"Yeah, I guess. I'm going to see if I can tag McNab and get an update on Stiles's condition. Maybe you can talk her into taking a walk, getting some air."

"I'll see what I can do."

He crossed to Eve. "You keep drinking that coffee, you'll have holes in your stomach lining I could put my fist through. You're tired, Lieutenant. Sit down."

"I can't." She turned, saw the room was momentarily empty. Let herself crumple. "Oh God," she murmured with her face pressed to his shoulder. "He got this stupid grin on his face when I told him I was pulling him with me. I thought I had him covered, then everything went wrong. People trampling people, screaming. I couldn't get through fast enough. I didn't get to him in time."

He knew her well enough to say nothing,

just to hold on until she steadied herself. "I need to know something. You've got strings here," she said, easing back. "Pull a few, would you, and find out what's happening in surgery?"

"All right." He took the recycled cup out of her hand, set it aside. "Sit down for a few minutes. I'll go pull those strings."

She tried to sit, managed to for nearly a full minute before she was up and after the coffee again. As she drew another cup, a woman stepped into the room.

She was tall, slim, and had Trueheart's guileless eyes. "Excuse me." She looked around the room, back at Eve. "I'm looking for a Lieutenant Dallas."

"I'm Dallas."

"Oh yes, I should have known. Troy's told me so much about you. I'm Pauline Trueheart, Troy's mother."

Eve expected panic, grief, anger, demands, and instead stared blankly as Pauline walked to her, held out a hand. "Ms. Trueheart, I very much regret that your son was injured in the line of duty. I'd like you to know that he performed that duty in an exemplary fashion."

"He'd be so pleased to hear you say so. He admires you a great deal. In fact, I hope it won't embarrass you, but I think Troy has a little crush on you."

Instead of drinking the coffee, Eve set it down. "Ms. Trueheart, your son was under my hand when he was injured."

"Yes, I know. The counselors explained what happened. I've already spoken with the patient liaison. They're doing everything they can to help him. He'll be fine."

She smiled, and still holding Eve's hand, drew her toward the seats. "In my heart I'd know if it was otherwise. He's all I have, you see."

Eve sat on the table, facing Pauline as the woman lowered into a chair. "He's young and strong."

"Oh yes, and a fighter. He's wanted to be a policeman as long as I can remember. It means so much to him, that uniform. He's a wonderful young man, Lieutenant, has never been anything but a joy to me." She glanced toward the doorway. "I hate thinking about him in pain."

"Ms. Trueheart . . ." Eve fumbled, tried again. "I don't believe he was in pain. At least, he was unconscious when I reached him."

"That's good, that helps. Thank you."

"How can you thank me? I put him in this position."

"Of course you didn't." She took Eve's

hand again. "You must be an excellent commanding officer, to care so much. My son wants to serve. Serve and protect, isn't that right?"

"Yes."

"I worry. It's very difficult for those of us who love the ones who serve and protect. But I believe in Troy. Absolutely. I'm sure your mother would say the same about you."

Eve jerked back, bore down on the ache that centered in her gut. "I don't have a mother."

"Oh, I'm sorry. Well." She touched Eve's wedding ring. "Someone who loves you, then. He believes in you."

"Yeah." Eve looked over, met Roarke's eyes as he came in. "I guess he does."

"Ms. Trueheart." Roarke crossed to her. "I've just been informed that your son will be out of surgery shortly."

Eve felt the quick, light tremble of Pauline's fingers. "Are you a doctor?"

"No. I'm Lieutenant Dallas's husband."

"Oh. Did they tell you how — what Troy's condition is?"

"He's stabilized. They're very hopeful. One of the surgical team will speak with you in a little while."

"Thank you. They said there was a chapel

on this floor. I think I'll sit there until they're ready for me. You look so tired, Lieutenant. Troy wouldn't mind if you went home and got some rest."

When she was alone with Roarke again, Eve simply braced her elbows on her thighs and pressed the heels of her hands to her eyes. "Tell me what you didn't tell her. Give it to me straight."

"The spinal injury is giving them some concern."

"Is he paralyzed?"

"They're hopeful it's temporary, due to swelling. If it proves to be more serious, there are treatments with high success rates."

"He needs to be a cop. Can you get a specialist?"

"I've taken care of it."

She stayed in the same position, rocked a little. "I owe you."

"Don't insult me, Eve."

"Did you see his mother? See how she was? How can anyone be that strong, that brave?"

Roarke cuffed her wrists, drew her hands down. "Look in the mirror."

She shook her head. "It's love with her. She'll will him to be safe and whole and happy because she loves him. I think she'll pull it off, too."

"Mother love is a fierce and powerful force."

Steadier, she rolled her aching shoulders. "Do you ever think of yours? Your mother?"

He didn't answer immediately, and the hesitation had her frowning at him. "I was going to say no," he explained. "But that was knee-jerk. Yes, I suppose I do, occasionally. I wonder now and then what became of her."

"And why she left you?"

"I know why she left me." The steel was back in his voice, in his eyes. Cold steel. "I held no particular interest for her."

"I don't know why mine left me. That's the worst of it, I think. The not knowing why. The not remembering." She hissed out a breath, annoyed with herself. "And that's useless speculation.

"I guess I've got mothers on the brain. I need to talk to Carly about hers."

She got to her feet, shoved back the fatigue. "I want to check on Stiles's condition, interview him if he's conscious. I'm going to have to go into Central, file my report. I have a meet with the commander first thing in the morning."

He rose as well. Her face was pale, her eyes bruised. The nicks and scratches on her face stood out like badges of honor. "You need to sleep."

"I'll catch some at Central. Anyway, as things stand, it should be wrapped up in a few hours. I'll take some personal time when it is."

"When it is, let's take a few days. You could use some sun."

"I'll think about it." Because they were alone, she leaned forward to kiss him.

At oh seven ten, Eve stood in Whitney's office. He had her written report on disc and hard copy, was listening to her oral follow-up.

"The doctor over Stiles estimates midday before he can be questioned. At this point, he's sedated. His condition is stable. Officer Trueheart remains in serious condition. His lower extremities are not yet responding to stimuli, and he has not, at this point, regained full consciousness. I would like to recommend Officer Trueheart for a citation for his conduct. His quick actions and disregard for personal safety were directly responsible for the apprehension of the suspect. The injuries sustained by him during the operation were not due to any negligence on his part but on mine."

"So you state in your written report. I disagree with your analysis."

"Sir, Officer Trueheart displayed courage

and clear thinking under difficult and dangerous circumstances."

"I don't doubt that, Lieutenant." He leaned back. "You're admirably controlled in both your written and oral reports. Are you considering discussing the problems with the operation personally with Captain Stuart? Because if you are, I will have to issue a direct order that you make no contact with Captain Stuart. She is, at this moment, being reprimanded by her superiors. You don't think that's enough?" he asked after a moment of thrumming silence.

"It's not for me to say."

"Admirably controlled," he repeated. "She fucked it up. Through her disregard for your authority, your orders, the chain of command, and all reasonable common sense, she botched the entire situation, is responsible for dozens of civilian injuries, thousands in property damage, offered the suspect the opportunity to flee, and put one of my men in the hospital."

He leaned forward, spoke through his teeth. "Do you think I am not pissed?"

"You are admirably controlled, sir."

He let out a short blast of sound that might have been a laugh. "Did you advise Captain Stuart that you were in command, that you were on the scene, and had said scene under control, that all weapons were to be set to low stun and there was to be no discharging of same without extreme circumstance?"

"Yes, sir, I did."

"Captain Stuart will be dealt with, I promise you. She'll be lucky to work System Control when the internal investigation is complete. Be satisfied with that."

"Trueheart's twenty-two years old." And it weighed on her, like a stone on the heart.

"I'm aware of that. I'm aware of how it feels to have a man go down under your hand. Suck it in, Lieutenant, and do the job. Sit down."

When she obeyed, he set her written report aside. "When's the last time you got any sleep?"

"I'm all right."

"When we're done here, you'll take two hours. That's an order. Anja Carvell," he began. "Do you consider her an essential element in this case?"

"She's a loose thread. Any thread that isn't knotted off is an essential element."

"And her alleged relationships to Kenneth Stiles and Richard Draco?"

"The number of connections crossed in this case result in too many triangles to be ignored. It appears that Stiles arranged for

Draco's murder, and as a result, Linus Quim's. However, there are a number of others with motive and opportunity. It isn't absolute that Stiles acted, more, that he acted alone. Before I moved on him, I was on the point of requesting a warrant to break the seal on Carly Landsdowne's adoption."

"Take your two hours, then try Judge Levinsky. Most judges are reluctant to open seals on private adoptions. He may be your best bet, particularly if you catch him after he's had breakfast."

She intended to follow orders. Finding a flat surface and sprawling over it would help clear her mind.

She closed the door to her office, locked it, then simply stretched out on the floor. Before she could close her eyes, her palm 'link beeped.

"Yeah, what?"

"Good morning, Lieutenant."

"No nagging," she muttered and pillowed her cheek on her hand. "I'm lying down right now."

"Good." Roarke studied her face. "Though you'd be better off in a bed than on your office floor."

"Do you know everything?"

"I know you. Which is why I decided to contact you. I neglected to pass on some information last night. The name of the birth mother in Carly Landsdowne's file."

"What're you talking about? I told you to leave that alone."

"I disobeyed. I'll look forward to you punishing me later. It's listed as Anja Carvell. She gave birth at a private woman's clinic in Switzerland. The adoption was preset and legal. She was given the mandatory twenty-four-hour period to withdraw her decision, stuck with it, and signed the final papers. She listed the father as Richard Draco, and included, per law, a sworn document that he had been informed of the pregnancy, her decision to complete it, and the adoption. The document was verified by voluntary truth testing."

"Was he notified of the live birth?"

"Yes. The file's complete, and as efficient as one expects from the Swiss. He was aware he had a child, a daughter. Mandatory DNA testing verified he was the father. He made no objections to the adoption."

She shifted to her back, let the information slide into her brain. "The adoptive parents are entitled to all this information except for the names. They're given medical histories of the birth parents, their cultural and ethnic backgrounds, intellectual, artistic, technical skills. All that can paint a pretty clear picture. The adoptee is also entitled to all this data upon request, including the legal names of the birth parents."

"I didn't find any request for that data from the adoptee," Roarke told her.

"There are ways around it. Carly could have known. She could have put it together and suspected Draco was her father. There's physical resemblance if you know to look for it. How much did she know?"

"You'll find out. Get some sleep."

"Right. Remind me to slap you around later for electronic trespass."

"I'm excited already."

She drifted off, thinking of fathers and daughters, of deceit and murder.

And woke with the old nightmare screaming in her throat, her skin bathed with the sweat of it and a violent pounding in her head.

She rolled over, pushed up to her hands and knees to struggle against the nausea. It took her several trembling seconds to realize not all the pounding was in her head. Some of it was at her door.

"Yeah. Hold on. Damn it." She rocked back to her heels, forced herself to breathe. She pushed to her feet, braced a hand on the desk until her legs were steady again.

After flipping the locks, she yanked open the door. "What?"

"You didn't answer the 'link," Peabody said in a rush. Her face was still flushed from the morning chill. "I was — are you all right? You look —" *Haunted,* she thought, but followed instinct and amended the word. "Out of it."

"I was sleeping."

"Oh, sorry." Peabody unbuttoned her coat. In her latest attempt to lose weight, she'd taken to getting off the subway five blocks from Central. Winter had decided to come back for another kick that morning. "I just got in, and ran into the commander on his way out. He's heading to the hospital."

"Trueheart?" She gripped Peabody's arm. "Did we lose him?"

"No. He's conscious. The commander said he surfaced about twenty minutes ago, and here's the best part, he's responding to stimuli. There's no paralysis, and they've upgraded him to guarded condition."

"Okay." The relief shuddered through her on bat wings. "Okay, good. We'll stop by and see him when we go in to interview Stiles."

"The squad's chipping in for a flower arrangement. Everybody likes Trueheart."

"All right, put me down." She sat behind her desk. "Get me some coffee, will you? I'm punchy."

"You didn't go home at all, did you? You said when you sent me off that you were going home."

"I lied. Coffee. I've got some information from an anonymous source. We're going over to reinterview Carly Landsdowne."

Peabody sniffed and stalked over to the AutoChef. "I guess your aide's not supposed to ask the name of the source?"

"My aide's supposed to get me coffee before I bite her throat."

"I'm getting it," Peabody muttered. "Why Carly, at this stage of the investigation?"

"I've just verified Richard Draco was her father."

"But they were . . ." A dozen emotions flew across Peabody's face. "Oh, yuck."

"In words of one syllable." Eve grabbed the coffee. "I want a formal request put in to Judge Levinsky to break adoption seal. We have to make it official. Meanwhile —" She broke off when her desk 'link signaled an incoming.

"Homicide. Dallas."

"Lieutenant Eve Dallas?"

Eve studied the woman. "That's right."

"Lieutenant Dallas, my name is Anja

Carvell. I'd like to speak with you on a very important matter, as soon as possible."

"I've been looking for you, Ms. Carvell."

"I thought you might be. Would it be possible for you to meet me at my hotel? I'm staying at The Palace."

"Popular spot. I'll be there. Twenty minutes."

"Thank you. I think I can help you clear up a number of matters."

"Jeez." Peabody snagged her own coffee when Eve broke transmission. "We look for her all over hell and back, and here she just drops into our laps."

"Yeah, nice coincidence." Eve shoved away from the desk. "I don't like coincidence."

TO BE OPENED IN THE EVENT OF MY DEATH

Yes, that had a nice ring, a dramatic touch. One never wants to lose one's sense of style, even under pressure. Particularly under pressure. The pills are where they can be easily reached, should they be needed. A last resort, of course, but they'll be quick. They'll be gentle.

"Do not go gentle into that good night." Well, what the hell did he know? If it comes

down to death or prison, death is preferable.

Life is a series of choices. One twists into the next, and the path shifts. It never really rides straight, unless there are no joys, no sorrows. I would always prefer the road that wanders. I made my choices, for better or worse, they were mine to make. I take full responsibility for the results of those choices.

Even Richard Draco. No, especially Richard Draco. His life was not a series of choices, but a compilation of cruel acts, small and large. Everyone he touched was damaged somehow. His death does not weigh on my conscience. What he did, knowingly, deliberately, viciously, deserved extermination.

I only wish there had been pain, great waves of pain, huge sweeps of knowledge, of fear, of grief in that instant before the knife pierced his heart.

But in planning his execution, I had self-preservation in mind as well. I suppose I still do.

Should I be given the opportunity to do it over again, I would change nothing. I will not feign remorse for disposing of a leech.

I have some regret for luring Linus Quim to his death. It was necessary, and God knows he was an ugly, cold-hearted little man. My choice could have been to pay him off, but blackmail is a kind of disease, isn't it? Once the body is infected by it, it spreads and returns at inopportune moments. Why risk it?

Still, it brought me no pleasure to arrange his death. In fact, it was necessary to sedate my nerves and anxiety. I made certain he felt no pain, no fear, but died with the illusion of pleasure.

But that, I suppose, doesn't negate the act of ending yet another life.

I thought I was so clever, staging Richard's murder in front of so many, knowing that all those surrounding him had reason to wish him harm. There was such a whippy thrill at the idea of having the knife Christine Vole would plunge into the black, miserable heart of Leonard Vole be a real one. It was so beautifully apt.

I regret and apologize for causing my friends and associates any distress, putting them, even for the short term, under any suspicion. Foolish of me, foolish to have believed it would never go this far.

No one, I told myself, cared about Richard. His death would be mourned by no one who knew him except with crocodile tears turned to glimmer on pale cheeks for the audience.

But I miscalculated. Lieutenant Dallas cares. Oh, not about Richard perhaps. She *has certainly unearthed enough truth about him by this time to stir her disgust. But she cares about the law. I believe it's her religion, this standing for the murdered dead.*

I realized that very soon after looking into her eyes. After all, I've spent my life studying people, measuring them, mimicking them.

In the end, I've done what I set out to do, what I believe with all my heart and soul I had to do. I have, ruthlessly perhaps, righted incalculable wrongs.

Isn't that justice?

chapter eighteen

Anja Carvell was beautiful, with the curvy body style women sweat or pay for. And men fall for. Her mouth was full, sensuous, and painted with the gleam of polished copper. Her skin had the delicate sheen of gold dust so that with the smoked red of her hair, the tawny eyes, she resembled a flame barely banked to simmer.

She sent Eve a long, level look, shifted her gaze briefly to Peabody, then stepped back, widening the door into her modest suite.

"Thank you for coming so quickly. I realized after we spoke that I should have offered to come to you."

"It's no problem."

"Well, you'll forgive me, I trust, for not knowing the proper procedure in such matters as this. My experience with people in your profession is severely limited. I've ordered a pot of chocolate."

She gestured to the living area where a white pot and two matching cups sat on a low table. "Would you care to join me? It's so cold and gloomy out. I'll just get another cup for your assistant."

"Don't bother." Eve heard, and ignored, Peabody's soft, windy sigh at her back. "You go ahead."

"In that case, shall we sit down?"

Anja led the way to the sofa, smoothed her long bronze colored skirts, then lifted the pot. There was quiet music playing, something with a bird trill of piano. A squat vase of cabbage roses stood beside the lamp. Their fragrance, and the woman's, perfumed the room.

It was, Eve thought, a pretty and civilized scene.

"I came to New York only last night," Anja began. "I'd forgotten how much I enjoy the city. The rush and energy of it. The heat of it, even in this endless winter. You Americans fill all the spaces and still find more."

"Where did you come in from?"

"Montreal." She sipped her chocolate, balanced the cup with the same female delicacy Eve had often admired in Mira. "Lieutenant, I'm afraid Kenneth wasn't completely truthful with you during your discussion with him. I hope you won't blame him for it. He was thinking of me."

"Ms. Carvell, I need your permission to record this conversation."

"Oh." After one disconcerted blink, Anja nodded. "Yes, of course. I suppose it must be done officially."

"Record on, Peabody." As Eve recited the standard rights and obligations, Anja's eyes widened with surprise, then warmed again with what might have been amusement.

"Am I a suspect then?"

"It's procedure. For your protection. Do you understand the rights and obligations I've outlined for you?"

"Yes, you were quite clear."

"Ms. Carvell, why did you come to New York from Montreal yesterday?"

"Kenneth . . . Kenneth Stiles contacted me. He needed to see me. He was quite distraught and anxious. He believes you think he killed Richard Draco. Lieutenant Dallas, such a thing is not possible."

"And why is that?"

"Kenneth is a kind and gentle man."

"The kind and gentle man put Richard Draco in the hospital twenty-four years ago after a violent assault."

Anja made an impatient sound, and her cup clicked into her saucer. "The rashness of youth. Must a man be hounded by a single foolish act committed so long ago? An act committed out of love and concern?"

"Whatever we do follows us, Ms. Carvell."

"I don't believe that. I'm proof a life can be changed through will." Her hand curled tight a moment, as if making a fist of that will. "Lieutenant Dallas, when I saw Kenneth last night, he was frightened and upset. I can swear to you, he would never have called me if he had indeed done what you suspect he has done."

"When did you see him last?"

"About eight o'clock. We met in a little club. I believe it was called Alley Cat."

"Yes, I know it."

"We spoke over drinks. It was then he told me he's given you my name, that you would look for me in regard to my one-time relationship with Richard."

Her smile bloomed as beautifully as the roses beside her. "He wanted to warn me, you see, so that I could hide myself, spare myself the discomfort of a meeting such as this. I calmed him as best I could and told him I would speak with you."

"He hasn't contacted you again?"

"No. I hope to speak with him after we're done here, hope to be able to reassure him that you no longer believe he could have done this thing."

"Kenneth Stiles attempted to leave the city last night." Eve watched Anja carefully as she spoke. "When an attempt was made to detain him, he fled and was injured during apprehension."

"No. No, no." Anja's hand shot out, gripped Eve by the wrist. "Injured? How badly? Where have you taken him?"

"He's in the hospital. His condition is stable. His doctors expect a full recovery. Why, Ms. Carvell, does an innocent man attempt to flee?"

She released Eve's wrist, rose to walk to the shielded window. Her hand pressed against her lips, as if to hold words back, then dropped to twist around the top button of her dress. When she spoke again, her voice wasn't so cool, wasn't so steady.

"Oh, Kenneth. Perhaps you're right, Lieutenant. Perhaps what we do echoes back to us the whole of our lives. He did it for me, you see. Just as before." She turned back, stood framed by the gray sky. There were tears glimmering in her eyes, but they did not spill onto her cheeks. "Will I be allowed to see him?"

"Possibly. Ms. Carvell, was Kenneth Stiles aware that you carried and gave birth to Richard Draco's child?"

Anja's head snapped back, as if struck by Eve's fist rather than her words. She gave a shaky laugh. Then, composing herself, she walked back to sit. "I see you're very thorough. Yes, Kenneth knew. He helped me through a very difficult situation."

"Is he aware Carly Landsdowne is that child?"

"He would not have the name the child's parents gave her. The files were sealed. I told no one but the attorney who drew up the documents where the child was placed and with whom. That is the point of sealed files, Lieutenant. What does this child — no, she would be a young woman now — have to do with this matter?"

"You've had no contact with Carly Landsdowne?"

"Why would I? Ah, you think I'm a liar or cold-blooded."

Anja topped off her cup of chocolate. But she didn't drink. Her only outward sign of distress was the restless fingers at her throat.

"I think I'm neither," she said after a moment. "I discovered myself pregnant. I was very young, very much in love, or what I perceived as love. I gave myself to Richard Draco. He was my first. He enjoyed being the first. I was not as careful with conception control as I should have been."

She gave a little shrug of the shoulder, settled back. "Being young and in love, when I learned I carried Richard's child, I was thrilled, swept away with the romantic notion that we would marry. He soon turned that thrill into despair. There was no anger, no passionate quarrel, and certainly there were none of the tender words and promises I had so happily scripted for him to say to me. Instead, he looked at me with disinterest, a faint annoyance."

Her eyes hardened, her hand dropped once more into her lap. "I will never forget how he looked at me. He told me it was my problem, and that if I expected him to pay for a termination of the pregnancy, I should think again. I wept, of course, and pleaded. He called me a few vile names, claimed that my sexual skills had been mediocre at best, and that he was bored with me. He left me where I was, on my knees. Weeping."

She sipped her chocolate again with no apparent distress. "You can understand, I hope, why I don't mourn his death. He was quite the most detestable man I've ever known. Unfortunately, at that point in my life, I didn't see that so clearly. I knew he was flawed," she continued. "But with that blind and beautiful optimism of youth, I'd believed, until that moment when he turned from me, that I could change him."

"Then you stopped believing it."

"Oh yes. I stopped believing I could change Richard Draco. But I thought I couldn't possibly live without him. I was also very frightened. Barely eighteen, pregnant, alone. I had dreams of becoming a great actress, and these were dashed. How could I go on?"

She paused for a moment, as if looking back. "We're so dramatic at eighteen. Do you remember when you were eighteen, Lieutenant Dallas, how you believed, somehow, everything was acute, vital, and the world, of course, revolved around you? Ah well."

She shrugged again. "I tried to end my life. I fumbled that, thank God, though I might have gotten it right if Kenneth hadn't come. If he hadn't stopped me, gotten me help."

"Yet you didn't terminate the pregnancy."

"No. I had time to think, to calm. I hadn't thought of the child when I took the razor to my wrists. Only of myself. It seemed to me that I'd been given another chance, and the only way to survive now was to do what was right for the life I'd started inside me. I might not have gotten through that without Kenneth."

She shifted her eyes, eloquent eyes, to Eve's. "He saved my life and the life of the child. He helped me find the clinic in Switzerland and the child placement attorney. He lent me money and a supporting arm."

"He's in love with you."

"Yes." Her agreement was simple, and sad. "My deepest regret is that I couldn't, and can't love him back, in the way he deserves. His attack on Richard all those years ago was an aberration, and one that cost Kenneth dearly."

"And after you placed the child?"

"I got back to my life. I never picked up that dream of becoming an actress again. I didn't have the heart for it any longer."

"As birth mother, you have the right to make regular inquiries about the child you placed."

"I never executed them. I had done what was best for her, best for myself. She was no longer mine. What interest could we have in each other?"

"She had an interest in Richard Draco. Carly Landsdowne was onstage the night he was killed."

"Yes?" Surprise, consideration flashed over her face. "She is an actress? Here in New York? Well, how many circles run within the circle of one life? And she was in the play with Richard and Kenneth. How strange, and how apt."

Eve waited. Watched. "You don't ask any questions about her."

"Lieutenant, you want me to pretend

some connection, some spiritual bond? Your Carly Landsdowne is a stranger to me. I wish her well, of course. But the link between us, a tenuous and temporary one, was broken years ago. My only connection with those days is Kenneth."

"Were you acquainted with Areena Mansfield?"

"Slightly, yes. She was very promising, even so long ago. She's done quite well for herself, hasn't she? I believe Richard toyed with her as well at some point. Why do you ask?"

"She was also in the cast. Natalie Brooks?"

"Natalie Brooks?" A little smile curved her mouth. "There is a name I haven't heard in many years. Yes, I remember she had a small part in the play Richard was in when he and I were lovers. She was very young, too. Pretty, fresh in a country girl sort of way. And, of course, easy prey. He seduced her when he turned from me. Perhaps even before. It's difficult to know. Was she, too, in this play?"

"No, but her son was Draco's understudy."

"Fascinating." Her eyes danced with amusement. "Please, you must tell me who else."

"Eliza Rothchild."

"But yes! A delightful woman. So dignified and acerbic. She had no tolerance for Richard. Of course, she was hardly his type and he took no pains to disguise that. Yes, this is fascinating. So many ghosts of the past moving like shadows on the stage. And Richard in the center, where he liked it best.

"I no longer follow theater, but if I'd known, I might have bought a ticket. Yes, I might very well have paid to see that final performance."

"You've had no contact with any of these people in the last twenty-four years?"

"But for Kenneth, no, as I've already said. I realize Kenneth told you that he hadn't seen or spoken to me over the years, didn't know where I was. The lie was not for himself, but for me. And now that you've told me all who are involved, it comes even more clear why he did so. He would have worried that these ghosts would haunt me. I assure you, and will assure him, they don't."

"Did he tell you that Richard Draco and Carly Landsdowne had been lovers?"

The cup jerked to a halt before it reached her lips. With her eyes on Eve's, she lowered it slowly to the table. "What are you saying?"

"That your former lover and the child you

414

made together were intimate. They had a sexual affair that ended shortly before his death."

"Mother of God." Anja squeezed her eyes shut. "Is this the payment for a small sin committed so many years ago? You've disturbed me, Lieutenant." She opened her eyes again, and they were hard, glinting. "If that was your purpose, you've succeeded. Surely neither of them knew."

She rose, prowled the room. "She's young. Attractive?" she asked with a glance back at Eve.

"Yes. Very attractive."

"He would find her hard to resist. Would see no reason to resist. And he has always been able to lure women into bed."

"She might have lured him, knowing."

"What woman chooses to sleep with her own father?" Anja shot back. Her hands fisted, her body trembled once as she spun around. "Why would she have known? The files were sealed."

"Seals crack," Eve said mildly. "Any and all of the parties involved can request the file. Perhaps she was curious about who made her."

"I would have been informed if a request was made and granted. It is the law."

"Laws are broken. That's why I have a job.

415

Draco might have opened the file himself."

At this, Anja merely laughed, a cold and brittle sound. "For what purpose? He had no interest whatsoever at the time. It's unlikely he remembered a child existed after all these years."

"There was a resemblance, Ms. Carvell. She has his coloring, the shape of his eyes, his jaw."

"So." She drew a breath, nodded, ordered herself to sit again. "He might have looked at her and seen himself. Might have," she murmured, toying with her button again. "Might have. Then taken her to his bed for some narcissistic thrill. I can't say. I can't tell you. Richard has become as much of a stranger to me as the young woman you speak of. I don't know them."

"Kenneth Stiles did."

Eve watched the realization and the horror bloom on Anja's face. Color rushed into her cheeks and just as quickly drained away again. "No. Whatever he knew or suspected, he wouldn't have turned to murder. I tell you, the violence of twenty-four years ago was an impulse, a rage of the moment. You said that the affair had ended. Before Richard was killed. Kenneth wouldn't have harbored violence. He couldn't have maintained it."

"Maybe not. Maybe not without help. Where were you on the night of March twenty-fifth?"

"Ah. I see. I see," she repeated softly, and folded her hands. "I would have been at home. And quite alone."

"You saw no one, spoke to no one, during that evening?"

"Not that I recall. I have no proof that comes to mind that I was where I say I was."

"Your family, Ms. Carvell?"

"I have no one. I can only swear to you that I did not travel from Montreal to New York and conspire to cause Richard Draco's death." She rose. "Lieutenant, I believe at this point, I would like to consult an attorney. I have nothing more to say on any of these matters until I have done so."

"That's your right. Thank you for your cooperation. Record off, Peabody."

"Would you be so kind as to tell me which hospital is caring for Kenneth? I'd like to contact them and inquire about his condition."

"He's at Roosevelt." Eve got to her feet. "Your attorney, when you engage one, can reach me at Cop Central."

"Very well." Anja walked to the door, opened it. "Good day, Lieutenant." She said it quietly, closed the door, engaged the locks.

Then, covering her face with her hands, she let herself weep.

"Impressions, Peabody."

"She's cool, sophisticated, sure of herself. She either believes Stiles is innocent or is determined to protect him. Her concern about him came off as genuine to me. She doesn't have a lot of concern left over to spare for Carly."

Eve frowned through the windscreen as she slipped behind the wheel of her vehicle. "Should she?"

"Well, it just seems to me there should be some, you know, emotional connection."

"Why? She conceived, gestated, delivered. That's nine months out of her life. Where's the emotional connection in that?"

"Because the baby grew inside her. She felt it kick and move around, and . . . I don't know, Dallas. I've never conceived, gestated, and delivered. I'm giving you my take, that's all."

Peabody shifted uneasily, feeling out of her depth. There was a darkness in the air, swirling around Eve. She didn't know what to make of it. She cut her eyes toward Eve, then away again. Eve was still staring out of the glass, brooding. "If she's giving it to us straight," Peabody ventured. "She placed the baby, then walked away. I just don't buy it could be as cut and dried, as easy as that. I thought you were leading toward her being in on the murder."

"I haven't discounted it." But she'd let something slip because her own emotions had been rattled. "Go back in, find out when Carvell registered, if she prebooked, and when she's scheduled to leave."

"Right." With some relief, Peabody scurried out into the fresh air.

What sort of woman chooses to sleep with her own father?

Eve's stomach had been in knots since that question had been tossed at her. *What if there is no choice? What then?* She let her head fall back. There was another question: *What sort of man chooses to sleep with his own daughter?*

That was one she had the answer to. She knew that kind of man, and he still whispered his candy breath in her ear.

"What are you doing, little girl?"

The breath exploded out of her lungs. She sucked it greedily back in.

What about the mother? she asked herself and wiped her damp palms on the thighs of her trousers. What made a mother? She didn't believe it was the bulk of life stirring in the belly. Eve angled her head, looked up toward the windows where Anja Carvell sat with her pot of chocolate and her ghosts. No, she didn't believe it was as simple as that.

There was more. There had to be more.

Most rational, decent human beings would instinctively protect an infant, a helpless child. But the need to protect another adult stemmed from duty. Or love.

She straightened in her seat as Peabody climbed back in. "She checks out. Called in yesterday, after six, requested a reservation. She got into the hotel some time just before eight. She's scheduled to leave tomorrow, but arranged for an option to extend."

"Mother, father, devoted friend," Eve murmured. "Let's move on to child."

"Carly. We're going to go right by a couple 24/7s crossing town. Maybe we could stop and get some hot chocolate."

"That stuff they sell in those places is swill."

"Yeah, but it's chocolate swill." Peabody tried a pitiful, pleading look. "You wouldn't let her give us any of the good stuff."

"Maybe you'd like some cookies, too. Or little frosted cakes."

"That would be nice. Thanks for asking."

"That was sarcasm, Peabody."

"Yes, sir. I know. Responded in kind."

The easy laugh had the black cloud lifting. Because it did, Eve pulled over at a cross-street 24/7 and waited while Peabody ran in and loaded up.

"You know, I'm really trying to cut down on this stuff. But . . ." Peabody ripped into the pack of cookies. "Thing is, weird, McNab doesn't think I'm chubby. And when a guy sees you naked, he knows where the extra layers are."

"Peabody, do you have some delusion that I want to hear how McNab sees you naked?"

She crunched into a cookie. "I'm just saying. Anyway, you know we have sex, so you've probably reached the conclusion we're naked when we're having it. You being an ace detective and all."

"Peabody, in the chain of command, you may, on rare occasions and due to my astonishing good nature, respond to sarcasm with sarcasm. You are not permitted to lead with it. Give me a damn cookie."

"They're coconut crunchies. You hate coconut."

"Then why did you buy coconut?"

"To piss you off." Grinning now, Peabody pulled another pack of cookies from her bag. "Then I bought chocolate chip, just for you."

"Well, hand them over then."

"Okay, so . . ." Peabody ripped open the second pack, offered Eve a cookie. "Anyway, McNab's got a little, bitty butt, and hardly any shoulders. Still —"

"Stop. Stop right there. If I get an image of a naked McNab in my head, you're going back to traffic detail."

Peabody munched, hummed, waited.

"Damn it! There he is."

Hooting with laughter, Peabody polished off the last cookie. "Sorry. Dallas, I'm sorry. I couldn't help it. Kinda cute, isn't he?"

And, she thought, it had bumped whatever had been troubling her lieutenant out of the way.

"Button it up," Eve warned, but she had to swallow a chuckle along with her cookie. "Brush the crumbs off your shirt and try to find your dignity somewhere." She pulled to the curb in front of Carly's building.

The high-end neighborhood, the exclusive building, the plush lobby sent a different signal to Eve now. Anja Carvell had selected wealthy parents for the child. The kind of parents who could assure the child would grow up with privilege, security, luxuries.

Had she taken as much care in researching the kind of people they were? Stable, loving, wise, supporting?

"Peabody, we did the run on Carly Landsdowne's educational history? It was private schools, right?"

"Yes, sir, I believe so." To verify, Peabody pulled out her PPC as they entered the lobby elevator. "Private and top rated, pre-school through college. They sprang for a bunch of extras including drama, dance, music, voice. All private tutors."

"What do the parents do?"

"Father's a doctor, microsurgeon. Mother's a travel agent, her own company. But she filed as professional mother from 2036 until 2056, the full twenty years allotted per child."

"No siblings?"

"None."

"She picked winners. She was careful. It mattered," she said to herself as she stepped out and walked to Carly's door.

It took two long buzzes before the door opened. Heavy-eyed, her hair sleep-tumbled, Carly gave a careless yawn. "What now?"

"A moment of your time."

"At dawn?"

"It's after nine."

"I repeat, at dawn?" Then she shrugged, stepped back. "Don't ask me anything until I get a cup of coffee. That should be added to those rights and obligations you're so fond of spouting."

"Cranky," Peabody whispered as Carly strode away.

Eve scanned the room, listened to the beep of the AutoChef, then tried not to let her mouth water when she caught the scent of rich and real coffee.

"I saw you at Richard's memorial yesterday," Carly said as she breezed back in. Her robe slipped silkily off one shoulder as she sat, crossed long, bare legs. "You do get around."

"Some of the matters I'm here to discuss with you are of a personal nature. You might want to ask your companion to leave."

"My companion?"

"Two wineglasses," Eve pointed out, with a nod at the low table. "Crushed pillows on the end of the sofa." She reached under one, tugged out one sheer leg of black hose. "Undergarments in unusual places."

"So your clever deductive powers lead you to the correct conclusion that I had sex last night." She shrugged and her robe slid down a little lower. "Why do you think he's still here?"

"Because you were having sex this morning before I so rudely interrupted. That little mating bite on your neck's very fresh."

"Ah." She sighed with a sound of amusement. "I suppose he was feeling a little frisky. Why don't you come on out, sweetheart?" She lifted her voice and kept her eyes on Eve. "Lieutenant Dallas has spoiled the moment anyway."

A door creaked open. There was the hesitant pad of bare feet on the floor. Rumpled and flushing, Michael Proctor stepped into the room.

chapter nineteen

"Ah . . ." He cleared his throat, tried to find something to do with his hands, and ended up letting them dangle from his arms at his sides. He was rumpled, wrinkled, and had misbuttoned his shirt. "Good morning, Lieutenant."

Carly's long, delighted roll of laughter filled the room. "Oh, Michael, do better. At least try to look satisfied and defiant instead of embarrassed and guilty. She's not the morals police."

"Carly." Her name was a vocal wince.

She waved a hand. "Go get yourself some coffee, you'll feel better."

"Um . . . Can I get anyone . . . anything?"

"Isn't he sweet?" Carly beamed, like a proud mother over a well-mannered child. "Go on, darling."

She turned back to Eve as Michael shuffled from the room. Her expression transformed, like a mask removed, from silk to steel. "I believe sex between consenting adults is legal in this state, so shall we move on?"

"How long have you and Michael been lovers?"

Carly examined her nails, picked idly at a minute chip in the polish. "Since you tell me it's after nine, for about twelve hours. I'm afraid I can't give you the exact time the act was consummated. I wasn't wearing my wrist unit."

"You want points for attitude?" Eve said evenly. "Fine with me. We can take this down to Central and see who's the biggest hard-ass. Or you can give me straight answers on how Michael Proctor ended up sharing your bed this morning."

Carly's lips twisted, but the idea of a session at Cop Central had her reaching for control. "We ran into each other at the memorial, ended up going out for a drink, came back here. One thing led very enjoyably to another. Is there a problem with that?"

"Bury one lover, pick up a fresh one? That might be a problem for some people."

Temper flashed into Carly's eyes, but she kept her voice level. "Save your narrowminded view for someone who's interested. It happens that Michael and I have a great deal in common, some chemistry stirred, and we acted on it. Above that, I like him very much."

427

"One of the things you have in common is Richard Draco."

"True enough. But Richard's dead. We're not."

Michael walked slowly back in. "Carly, would you like me to go?"

"Not on my account." She patted the cushion beside her. "Sit down." It was as much a challenge as a request. When he sat, she gave a pleased smile, hooked her arm through his. "So, Lieutenant, you were saying?"

"Michael, you didn't mention your mother knew Richard Draco."

The cup jumped in his hand, sloshed coffee on his slacks. "My mother? What does she have to do with it?"

"She worked in a play with Draco."

"Your mother's an actress?" Carly angled her head.

"She was. She retired years ago. Before I was born." He set his cup down, rubbed ineffectually at his slacks. "Leave my mother alone. She hasn't done anything."

"Did I say she had?" Nerves, Eve thought. He couldn't keep his hands still for them. "You know then, that she had been intimate with Draco at one time."

"It was nothing. It was years ago."

"Your mother and Richard?" Carly drew

back to study his face. "Oh. Sticky." And there was sympathy in her eyes. "Don't let it rattle you, sweetie."

But it had, obviously. "Look, she had a bit part, that's all. She wasn't a serious actress. She told me. She and my father have been together ever since . . . She wouldn't have told me except she knew I admired him, that I was going to audition for his stand-in. He used her. He liked using women."

He looked steadily at Carly now. "She got over him. Smart women do."

His mother, Eve decided, or maybe women in general, was his weak spot. "Yeah, he liked using women. Young, pretty women. They were toys to him, and he got bored with his toys fairly quickly. Your mother gave up her career, her hopes for it, because of him."

"Maybe." Michael blew out a breath. "Maybe that was part of it. But she made a new life, she's happy in it."

"He hurt her."

"Yeah." His gaze flashed up, ripe with bitterness. "Yeah, he hurt her. You want me to say I hated him for it? Maybe I did, on some level."

"Michael, don't say any more," Carly warned.

"The hell with that." His voice took on

conviction as well as anger. "She's talking about my mother. She wasn't some cheap tramp, some toy he picked up then tossed aside. She was a nice, naive girl. He took advantage of that, of her."

"Did he give her illegals, Michael?" Eve asked. "Did he give her a taste for them?"

"No. He tried. The son of a bitch."

"Michael, you don't have to answer her questions."

"I'm going to straighten this out, right now." Heat rolled off him in violent waves. "She told me that she came into the room and he was putting drops of something in her drink. She asked him what it was, and he just laughed. He said . . . my mother doesn't use hard language, but she told me exactly what he said. It would make her fuck like a rabbit."

Muscles quivered in his jaw as he stared at Eve. "She didn't even know what it meant. But I knew, when she told me, I knew. The bastard tried to slip her Wild Rabbit."

"But she didn't drink it?"

"No, it scared her. She told him she didn't want anything to drink, and that's when he got mad. He called her names, tried to make her drink it. She realized then what kind of man he was and she ran. She was crushed, disillusioned. She went back home. She told me that was the best thing that ever happened to her, going home.

"He didn't even remember her," Michael added. "He didn't even have the decency to remember her name."

"You spoke to him about her?"

"I wanted to see how he'd react. He didn't even pretend to remember. She meant nothing to him. No one did."

"Did you tell him? Remind him?"

"No." He deflated, the heat evaporating. "No, I didn't see the point. And if I'd pushed it, I'd have lost the job."

"Don't. Don't let it hurt you."

Eve's eyes narrowed in speculation as Carly slipped her arms around him, soothed. They stayed narrowed and cool when Carly shot her a burning glare. "Leave him alone. Do you get your kicks picking on people weaker than you?"

"It's what gets me through the day." *You're not weak*, Eve thought. *Did the people who made you form you*, she wondered. *Or the people who raised you?*

"It must have been hard on you, Michael, knowing all that and seeing Draco day after day."

"I had to put it out of my mind. I couldn't change what had happened, could I?" He gave a shrug that tried to be defiant. "And nothing I could do would make any difference. And one day, I'd step out onstage in his place, and I'd be better. That would be enough."

"You've got that chance now, don't you? A chance to stand in his light. A chance to be with one of his lovers."

His tightly compressed lips trembled apart. "Carly. It wasn't like that. I don't want you to think —"

"Of course it wasn't." She put a hand over his. "The lieutenant has a foul mind."

"Ms. Landsdowne."

Carly ignored Eve for a moment and laid gentle kisses on both of Michael's cheeks. "You've spilled your coffee. Why don't you go back and get us both a fresh cup?"

"Yeah. All right." He got to his feet. "My mother is a wonderful woman."

"Of course she is," Carly replied.

When he went back into the kitchen, she turned to face Eve fully. "I don't like seeing Michael's vulnerabilities exploited, Lieutenant. The strong are supposed to protect the weak, not kick them in the face."

"Maybe you're not giving him enough credit for spine." Eve moved over, eased down on the arm of a chair. "He defended his mother very well. For some, family ties are the strongest. You didn't mention you

432

were adopted, Ms. Landsdowne."

"What?" Confusion clouded her eyes. "For heaven's sakes, why should I have? I don't remember it half the time. What business is that of yours?"

"It was a private adoption, at birth."

"Yes. My parents never hid it from me. Neither was it made a particular issue in our home."

"Did they give you the details of your heritage?"

"Details? Medical history, ethnicity, of course. I was told my birth mother arranged for my placement because she wanted the best for me, and so on and so forth. Whether that was true or not never mattered. I had my mother."

She paused, then asked, "Are you speculating that *my* mother had a relationship with Richard at one time?" She let out a rolling laugh and shook back her cloud of tousled hair. "I can assure you she didn't. My mother never met Richard Draco. She and my father have been happily married for nearly thirty years. Before I was born she was a travel agent, not an actress."

"You were never curious about the woman who gave you up?"

"Not particularly. I have wonderful parents whom I love, and who love me. Why

433

should I wonder about a woman who's nothing but a stranger to me?"

Like mother, like daughter, Eve thought.

"Many adoptees want contact, want answers, even a relationship with their birth parents."

"I didn't. Don't. There was no hole in my life to fill. I'm sure my parents would have helped me find her if I'd asked. If I'd needed that. I didn't. And it would have hurt them," she said quietly. "I would never hurt them. How is this relevant?"

"Do you recognize the name Anja Carvell?"

"No." She stiffened slightly. "Are you telling me that's the name of the woman who placed me? I didn't ask for a name. I didn't want a name."

"You have no knowledge, have had no contact with a woman by that name?"

"No, and I don't want any." Carly got to her feet. "You've no right to do this. To play with my life this way."

"You never asked about your birth father."

"Goddamn it, if she's nothing to me, he's less than nothing. A lucky sperm. You wanted a rise out of me, you got one. Now, what does this have to do with Richard Draco's death?"

Eve said nothing, and in the silence she watched denial, disbelief, then horror flash into Carly's eyes. "No, that's a lie. A revolting, vicious lie. You hideous bitch."

She grabbed the little pot of violets on the table, heaved them to shower glass and petals down the wall. "It's not true."

"It's documented," Eve said flatly. "Richard Draco was your birth father."

"No. No." Carly sprang at Eve, shoved her roughly against a table and upended a lamp. The china exploded like a bomb. Before Peabody could intervene, Eve signaled her back, and took the hard slap to the face without attempting to block.

"Take it back! Take it back!"

She shouted it, tears spurting out of her eyes. Her beauty was stark now, white face, dark eyes. She grabbed Eve's shirt, shook, then with a moan, collapsed on her.

"Oh God. Oh my God."

"Carly." Michael bolted in from the kitchen. One look at his face told Eve he'd listened, he'd heard. When he rushed to Carly, tried to turn her into his own arms, she shoved away, crossed her arms defensively over her breasts.

"Don't touch me. Don't touch me." Like a candle burned to wax, she slid to the floor in a shuddering puddle.

"Peabody, take Michael back into the kitchen."

He stepped back, stared at Eve. "It was cruel what you did. Cruel." He walked toward the kitchen with Peabody behind him.

Eve crouched. She could still feel the heat from the crack of Carly's hand across her face. But her gut was iced over. "I'm sorry."

"Are you?"

"Yes."

Carly lifted her face, and her eyes were ravaged. "I don't know who I loathe more at this moment: myself or you."

"If you were unaware of your blood tie to him, you have nothing to loathe yourself for."

"I had sex with him. I put my hands on him. Allowed him to put his on me. Can you conceive how that makes me feel? How dirty that makes me feel?"

Oh God, yes. She was suddenly and brutally tired. She fought off her own demons and stared into Carly's eyes. "He was a stranger to you."

Carly's breath hitched. "He knew, didn't he? It all makes such horrible sense. The way he pursued me, the way he looked at me. The things he said. We're two of a kind, he told me, and he laughed." She gripped Eve's shirt again. "Did he know?"

"I can't tell you."

"I'm glad he's dead. I wish I'd killed him myself. I wish to God almighty it had been my hand on the knife. I'll never stop wishing that."

"No comments, Peabody?"

"No, sir." They rode down in the elevator with Peabody looking straight ahead.

There was an ache, churning, pulsing, swelling, in every part of her body. "You didn't like the way I handled that."

"It's not for me to say, Lieutenant."

"Fuck that."

"All right. I don't understand why you had to tell her."

"It's relevant," Eve snapped. "Every connection matters."

"You punched her in the gut with it."

"So now it's my method that doesn't meet your standards."

"You asked," Peabody shot back. "If she had to be told, I don't see why you shoved it in her face the way you did. Why you couldn't have found a way to soften it."

"Soften it? Her father was fucking her. You tell me how you soften that. You tell me how you put that in a pretty box with a bow on it."

She turned on Peabody, and like Carly's, Eve's eyes were ravaged. "What the hell do you know? What do you know about it with your big, sprawling, happy, Free-Ager family where everybody gathers around the dinner table with clean faces and chirpy news of the day."

She couldn't breathe, couldn't draw in enough air. She was strangling. But she couldn't stop the words.

"When Daddy came in to kiss you good night, he didn't crawl into bed with you, did he, and put his sweaty hands all over you. Fathers don't jam themselves into their little girls in your tidy world."

She strode off the elevator, through the lobby, and out to the street, while Peabody stood stiff with shock.

Eve paced the sidewalk, barely restrained herself from kicking the duet of white poodles and the droid that walked them. A headache was raging, a rocket blast that screamed inside her skull. She could feel her hands tremble, even though they were balled into tight fists in her pockets.

"Dallas."

"Don't," she warned Peabody. "Keep back a minute."

She could walk it off, she promised herself. She could walk off the leading edge of the fury that made her want to scream and pound and rip. And when she had, all that was left was the headache and the sick misery deep in her gut.

Her face was pale but composed when she walked up to Peabody. "My personal remarks were over the line. I apologize for them."

"It's not necessary."

"It is. In my opinion, it was also necessary to be cruel up there. It doesn't make me feel any better about it. But you're not here to be a punching bag for my foul moods."

"That's okay. I'm kind of used to it."

Peabody tried a smile, then gaped with horror when Eve's eyes filled. "Oh, jeez. Dallas."

"Don't. Shit. I need some time." She bore down, stared hard at the face of the building. "I'm taking a couple of hours' personal time. Grab some public transpo back to Central." Her chest wanted to heave, to throw the tears up and out. "I'll meet you at Roosevelt in two hours."

"All right, but —"

"Two hours," Eve repeated and all but launched herself into the car.

She needed to go home. She needed to hold on and to go home. Not trusting herself, she set the car on auto and rode with her head back and her hands balled in her lap.

From the age of eight, she'd built a wall or her subconscious had mercifully built one for her to block out the ugliness that had happened to her. It left a blank, and on that blank she'd created herself. Piece by painful piece.

She knew what it was to feel that wall crumble, to have the cracks form so the ugliness oozed in.

She knew what Carly faced. And what she would go through to live with it.

The headache kicked like a tornado inside her skull by the time she drove through the gates. Her eyes were glazed with it, with the greasy churn of nausea in her belly. She ordered herself to hold on, to hold it in, and staggered up the steps.

"Lieutenant," Summerset began when she stumbled inside.

"Don't mess with me." She tried to snap it out, but her voice wavered. Even as she bolted upstairs, he moved to the house intercom.

She wanted to lie down. She'd be all right if she could just lie down for an hour. But the churning defeated her. She turned into the bathroom, went down on her knees, and was vilely ill.

When she was empty, too weak to stand, she simply curled on the tiles.

She felt a hand on her brow, cool. Blessedly cool. And opened her eyes.

"Roarke. Leave me alone."

"Not in this lifetime."

She tried to turn away from him, but he slipped his arms under her.

"Sick."

"Yes, baby, I know." She felt fragile as glass when he lifted her, carried her to bed.

She began to shiver as he drew off her boots, covered her with a blanket. "I wanted to come home."

He said nothing, only got a damp cloth and bathed her face. She was too pale, the shadows under her eyes too deep. When he held a glass to her lips, she turned her face away.

"No. No soothers. No tranqs."

"It's for the nausea. Here now." He brushed her damp hair back and hoped he wouldn't be forced to pour it down her throat. "That's all. I promise."

She drank because her stomach was quivering again, and her throat felt as if it had been raked by claws. "I didn't know you were here." She opened her eyes again, and the tears that burned in her chest flooded into her eyes. "Roarke. Oh God."

She pressed herself against him. Burrowed. As her body shook, he tightened his arms around her. "Get rid of it," he murmured. "Whatever it is, let it go."

"I hate what I did. I hate myself for doing it."

"Ssh. Whatever it was, you wouldn't have had a choice."

"I should have found one." She turned her head so that her cheek rested against his shoulder, and with her eyes closed, she told him everything.

"I know what went through her." She was better now, the worst of the sickness eased. "I know what she felt. And I saw myself in her when she looked at me."

"Eve. No one knows better than you, or I, what vileness there is in the world. You did what you had to do."

"I could've —"

"No." He leaned back, cupped her face so that their eyes met. There wasn't pity in his, which she would have hated. There wasn't sympathy, which would have scraped her raw.

There was simply understanding.

"You couldn't have. Not you. You had to know, didn't you? You had to be sure if she'd known who he was to her. Now you do."

"Yeah, now I do. No one's that good an actress. She'll see herself, again and again, together with him. Over and over."

442

"Stop. You couldn't have changed that, no matter how she found out."

"Maybe not." She closed her eyes again, sighed. "I swiped at Peabody."

"She'll get over it."

"I came close to losing it, right out on the street. I nearly —"

"But you didn't." He gave her a little shake before she could speak again. "You irritate me, Eve. Why must you beat yourself up like this? You haven't slept in over thirty hours. You've entered into a phase of this investigation that hits so close to a personal horror most people would run away or shatter. You've done neither."

"I broke."

"No, Eve. You chipped." He pressed his lips to her forehead. "Then you came home. Lie down for a bit. Close your eyes. Turn it off."

"I shouldn't have told you to leave me alone. I didn't mean it."

"It hardly matters." The innate arrogance in his voice nearly made her smile. "I wouldn't have. I won't."

"I know. I wanted you to be here." She slid into him before he could nudge her back. "I needed you to be. And you were." Her mouth turned to his. Seeking. "Roarke."

"You need to sleep."

"I'm empty, and it hurts." Her hands roamed up his back, kneading. "Fill me with something. Please."

Love filled the voids and hollows, no matter how deep, no matter how wide. He would give it to her, take it for himself. With patience, with tenderness.

His lips brushed hers, settled, sank, until he felt hers warm and yield. Gathering her, he trailed kisses over her face, her hair, her throat. First to comfort.

She turned into him, offering more. But his hands were light as wings, floating over her, slipping under her shirt to her flesh with long, slow strokes. Then to soothe.

And when she sighed, when her body melted back against the pillows, he undressed her. His lips followed the trace of his fingers, gently stirring pulses. Now to arouse.

She opened for him, as she never had for anyone else. For him, she could lay herself bare. Body, heart, and mind. And know, and trust, he would do the same.

Without heat or demands or urgency, he nudged her up, let her linger on the crest, slide over, until her system glowed with the pleasure of belonging.

Her heart swelled, matched its beat to his, and her arms wrapped around him like ribbons to draw him close.

"I love you." He watched her face as he slipped inside her. "Completely. Endlessly."

Her breath caught, sighed out again. She closed her eyes to hold on to the beauty of the moment. And let him bring her home.

She held him close, needing for just a bit longer to have his body pressed so intimately to hers. "Thanks."

"I hate to state the obvious, but it was my pleasure. Better now?"

"A lot. Roarke — no, just stay like this a minute." She kept her face turned into his shoulder. "When we're together like this, it's not like it's ever been with anyone else. It's like there never was anyone else."

"For me either."

She laughed, relieved that she could. "You've had a lot more anyones."

"Who's counting?" He shifted, rolling over so that she ranged over him. The fragility was gone, he noted. There was the smooth and agile flow to her movements that characterized her.

Her cheeks were no longer pale, but her eyes were heavy, bruised, exhausted. It made him regret not pouring a tranq into her after all.

"Cut it out." She scooped her hair back

and nearly managed a scowl.

"Cut what out?"

"Thinking about fussing over me. You don't have to take care of me." She didn't need the amused glint in his eyes to tell her how ridiculous that sounded under the circumstances. "All the time," she amended.

"Let's take a nap."

"I can't. I don't imagine you can, either. I've already messed up your day. You were probably buying a solar system or something."

"Only a small, largely uninhabited planet. It's not going anywhere. I can use a break, and you need to sleep."

"Yeah, I do, but I can't."

"Eve —"

"Look, I'll catch some downtime soon. You're one to talk. You haven't had much more than me lately."

"Our engines don't run at the same speed."

That stopped her from her slide off the bed. "What the hell does that mean?"

"Just that."

She frowned, considered. "It sounds like something that ought to piss me off. But I can't figure out exactly why. When I do, I might have to pop you one."

"I'll look forward to it. If you won't sleep, eat. You need something in your stomach.

And what are you grinning at?"

"You. You're such a wife," she said as she headed toward the shower.

He sat for a minute, stunned. "Now I'm pissed off."

"See, now you know how it feels. Well, order me something to eat," she called out. "Water on, one hundred and two degrees."

"Bite me," he muttered and ordered her some soup with a high-protein additive.

She ate every drop, as much to please him as to kill the hunger. Her mind clear again, she dressed, strapped on her weapon. "I have to go by the hospital, see what I can get out of Stiles."

"Why? You've already figured it out." When she just stared at him, he shrugged. "I know you, Lieutenant. You let it churn around while you were eating, settle into place. Now you're revving up to finish it."

"I haven't filled all the gaps yet. I want to cover a few more bases, and I need to run something by Whitney. It sort of involves you."

"And what might that be?"

She shook her head. "If he doesn't clear it, it won't matter. I'll be able to reach you, right? If I need to talk to you before I get back."

"I'll be available. I thought I'd bake some cookies."

The dry tone had her snorting as she picked up her jacket. "You do that, honey." She turned to kiss him, then yelped when he twisted her earlobe. "Hey!"

"Don't work too hard, darling."

"Man." Pouting, she rubbed her ear as she walked to the door. "If I did that every time you used the *W* word, you wouldn't have any ears left."

She stopped at the door, looked back. "But you're beautiful when you're angry," she said, and fled.

Peabody stood outside the hospital's main doors, shoulders hunched against the brisk wind, nose red from it.

"Why the hell didn't you wait inside?" Eve demanded. "It's freezing out here."

"I wanted to catch you before you went in. Can we take a minute?"

Eve studied Peabody's set and serious face. *Personal business,* she decided, *not official.* Well, she deserved it. "All right. Let's walk, keep the blood moving." She headed away from the ramps and glides, as sirens announced another unlucky resident of New York was about to enjoy the building's facilities.

"About before," Peabody began.

"Look, I was out of line, and you were the closest target. I'm sorry about it."

"No, that's not what I mean. I figured it out. Took me a while," she added. "What you did, telling her cold like that was because you had to see how she'd react. If she knew Draco was her father, well, it bumped up her motive. Either way, if she knew it before they . . . you know, or if she knew it after they got going, it went to her frame of mind."

Eve watched a medi-van whip past. "She didn't know."

"I don't think so either. If you'd eased her into it, it would've given her time to think, to figure out how best to react, what to say. I should've known that right off instead of working around to it an hour later."

"I could have clued you in before we got there." With a shake of her head, she turned around, started back. "I hadn't settled myself into it yet."

"It was a hard thing to do. I don't think I'd've had the guts for it."

"It has nothing to do with guts."

"Yeah, it does." Peabody stopped, waited for Eve to turn to face her. "If you didn't have feelings, it wouldn't have been hard. But you do. Guts can be the same thing as mean without compassion. It was hard, but

449

you did it anyway. A better cop would have realized that quicker."

"I didn't give you much of a chance since I was busy jumping down your throat. You worked it out, came around to it on your own. I must be doing something right with you. So, are we square now?"

"Yeah, all four corners."

"Good, let's get inside. I'm freezing my ass off."

chapter twenty

They went by to see Trueheart first. At Peabody's insistence, they stopped off in the shopping mall for a get-well gift.

"It'll take five minutes."

"We've chipped in on the flowers already." The forest of goods, the wide and winding trails that led to them, and the chirpy voices announcing the sales and specials caused Eve's already abused stomach to execute a slow, anxious roll.

She'd rather have gone hand-to-hand with a three-hundred-pound violent tendency than be swallowed up in a consumer sea.

"That's from everyone," Peabody explained patiently. "This'll be from us."

Despite herself, Eve stopped at a display of dull green surgical scrubs brightly emblazoned with the hospital's logo. For ten bucks extra, you could have one splattered with what appeared to be arterial blood.

"It's a sick world. Just sick."

"We're not going for the souvenirs." Though she thought the oversized anal probes were kind of a hoot. "When a guy's in the hospital, he wants toys."

"When a guy gets a splinter in his toe, he wants toys," Eve complained but followed Peabody into a game shop and resigned herself to having her senses battered by the beeps, crashes, roars, and blasts.

Here, according to the flashing signs, you could choose from over ten thousand selections for your entertainment, leisure, or educational desires. From sports to quantum physics programs and everything in between, you had only to key in the topic of your interest and the animated map, or one of the fully trained and friendly game partners, would direct you to the correct area.

The store menu pumped out screaming yellow light. Eve felt her eyes cross.

The clear tubes of the sample booths were all loaded with people trying out demos. Others trolled the store proper, their faces bright with avarice or blank from sensory overload.

"Don't these people have jobs?" Eve wondered.

"We hit lunch hour."

"Well, lucky us."

Peabody made a beeline for the combat section. "Hand-to-hand," she decided. "It'll make him feel in control. Wow, look! It's the new Super Street Fighter. It's supposed to be majorly mag." She flipped the antitheft box over, winced a little at the price, then noted the manufacturer.

"Roarke Industries. We oughta get a discount or something. Oh well, it's not so bad when you split it." She headed toward the auto-express checkout, glanced back at Eve. "I guess Roarke's got a whole factory full of these, huh?"

"Probably." Eve pulled out her credit card, swiped it through the scanner, pressed her thumb to the identi-plate.

Thank you for your purchase, Eve Dallas. One moment, please, while your credit is verified.

"I'll give you my half on payday, okay?"
"Yeah, whatever. Why do these things take so long?"

Thank you for waiting, Eve Dallas. The cost of your selection, Super Street Fighter, PPC version, comes to one hundred and sixteen dollars and fifty-eight cents, including all applicable taxes. Due to Authorization One, your account will not be debited for this selection. Please enjoy your day.

"What the hell are you talking about?

What's Authorization One?"

Authorization One, Roarke Industries. This level entitles you to select any items under this manufacturer's brand at no cost.

"Wow. We can clean house." Peabody turned her dazzled eyes to the shelves crammed with delights. "Can I get one of these?"

"Shut up, Peabody. Look, I'm paying for this," she told the machine. "So just bypass Authorization One and debit my account."

Unable to comply. Would you care to make another selection?

"Damn it." She shoved the game at Peabody. "He's not getting away with this."

Peabody had the wit to run the box through security release, then jogged to catch up with Eve. "Listen, since we're here anyway, couldn't I just have one —"

"No."

"But —"

"No." Eve gave the glide one quick, bad-tempered kick, then got on to ride to medical level.

"Most women would be happy if their husbands gave them blank shopping credit."

"I'm not most women."

Peabody rolled her eyes. "You're telling me."

Peabody might have sulked over the loss of her own imaginary game collection, but Trueheart's pleasure in the gift outweighed greed.

"This is great. It just came out."

He turned the box over in his good hand. His other arm was cased in a plasti-cast to knit the bone that had snapped in his fall.

There was a collar of the same material around his neck, an IV drip in his wrist, and a brutal bruise that crept over his shoulder and showed purple and black against the sagging neck of his hospital shift. His left leg was slightly elevated, and Eve remembered how his blood had pumped out of the gash there and onto her hands.

Machines hummed around him.

All Eve could think was if she were in his place, she wouldn't be so damn cheerful.

She left the small talk and conversation to Peabody. She never knew what to say to hospital patients.

"I don't remember much after I took the hit." He shifted his eyes to Eve. "Commander Whitney said we got him."

"Yeah." This, at least, was her element. "*You* got him. He's down on the next patient level. We'll be questioning him after we leave here. You did the job, Trueheart. He might have gotten by us if you hadn't reacted fast and taken him down."

"The commander said you put me up for a commendation."

"Like I said, you did the job."

"I didn't do much." He shifted, trying to find a more comfortable position. "I would have taken him down clean if that trigger-happy asshole transit jerk hadn't blasted off."

"That's the spirit. The trigger-happy asshole and his moronic superior are going to get kicked around plenty."

"Wouldn't have happened if they'd listened to you. You had it under control."

"If I'd had it under control, you wouldn't be here. You took a mean hit and a bad fall. If you're feeling shaky over it, you should see the department counselor."

"I'm feeling okay about it. I want to get back in uniform, back on the job. I was hoping, when you close the case, you'd let me know the details."

"Sure."

"Ah, Lieutenant, I know you've got to get going, but I just wanted to say . . . I know you saw my mother the other night."

"Yeah, we ran into each other. She's a nice woman."

"Isn't she great?" His face lit up. "She's the best. My old man ditched us when I was a kid, so we've always, you know, taken care of each other. Anyway, she told me how you hung around, waited until I was out of surgery and all."

"You went down under my watch." *Your blood was on my hands*, she thought.

"Well, it meant a lot to her that you were here. I just wanted to tell you that. So thanks."

"Just stay out of laser streams," she advised.

Down on the next level, Kenneth Stiles stirred in his bed, glanced toward the nurse who checked his monitors. "I want to confess."

She turned to him, smile bright and professional. "So, you're awake, Mr. Stiles. You should take some nutrition now."

He'd been awake for a considerable amount of time. And thinking. "I want to confess," he repeated.

She walked to the side of the bed to pat his hand. "Do you want a priest?"

"No." He turned his hand over, gripped hers with a strength she wasn't expecting. "Dallas. Lieutenant Dallas. Tell her I confess."

"You don't want to get overexcited."

"Find Lieutenant Dallas, and tell her."

"All right, don't worry. But in the meantime, you should rest. You took a nasty fall."

She smoothed his sheets, satisfied when he settled, closed his eyes. "I'll go see about your nutrition requirements."

She notated his chart and slipped out. She paused by the uniformed guard at the door. "He's awake."

From her uniform pocket, she took out her memo pad and informed Nutrition that Patient K. Stiles, Room 6503, required his midday meal. When the guard started to speak, the nurse held up a hand.

"Just a minute. I want to get this in so they get it up here before midnight. Nutrition's been running behind all week." Since the patient had neglected to fill in his lunch choices from the authorized menu, she ordered him a grilled chicken breast, mixed rice with steamed broccoli, a whole wheat roll with one pat of butter substitute, skim milk, and blueberry Jell-O.

"That should be up within the hour."

"Whoever brings it has to be cleared," the guard told her.

She gave a little huff of annoyance, took the memo out again, and made the necessary notation. "Oh, Patient Stiles was asking for someone named Dallas. Does that mean anything?"

The guard nodded, pulled out his communicator.

"He's got cop juice for blood," Peabody commented as they walked down the corridor.

"The juice is still green, but it'll ripen." When her communicator beeped, she dug it out of her pocket. "Dallas."

"Lieutenant. Officer Clark on guard duty, Kenneth Stiles. The suspect is awake and asking for you."

"I'm one level up and on my way."

"That's good timing." Peabody punched for the elevator, then sighed and followed Eve to the exit door. "I guess we're walking."

"It's one patient level."

"One level equals three flights."

"You'll work off the cookies."

"They're only a fond memory. You figure Stiles is ready to give us some straight talk?"

"I figure he's ready for something." She pushed through the doors to the next level, headed left. "He doesn't know we found Carvell or that we've identified Draco as Carly's father. We'll see how he plays it before we clue him in."

She stopped at the door. "Clark."

"Yes, sir."

"He have any visitors?"

"Not a soul. He was sleeping it off until a few minutes ago. The nurse reported he was awake and asking for you."

"Okay, take a fifteen-minute break."

"Thanks. I can use it."

Eve reached for the door, pushed it open. Then, with a curse, leaped inside. She grabbed Stiles's legs, hauled up and took his weight. "Get him down!"

Peabody was already scrambling onto the bed, fighting with the knot. Clark pounded in behind her.

"I've got him, Lieutenant." He moved in with his wide shoulders and took Stiles's dangling body up another three inches.

He'd hanged himself with a noose fashioned from his own bedsheets.

"He's not breathing," Clark announced when the body collapsed on him. "I don't think he's breathing."

"Get a doctor." Face fierce, Eve straddled Stiles, pressed the heels of her hands to his heart and began to pump. "Come on, you son of a bitch. You *will* breathe." She lowered her mouth to his, forced in air. Pumped.

"Oh my God. Oh my God. Kenneth!" At

the doorway, Areena Mansfield scattered the armload of flowers she carried at her feet.

"Keep back! Come on, come on." Sweat began to pour down Eve's face. She heard the sound of running feet, of alarms shrilling.

"Move aside. Move aside please."

She slid away, pushed to her feet, and watched the medical team work on him.

No pulse. Flat line.

Come back, Eve ordered. *Goddamn you, come back.*

She watched the slim pressure hypo of adrenaline jab against his chest.

No response.

Small disks were slicked with gel. There were orders to set, to clear, then Stiles's body bucked when the discs shocked his system. The heart line on the monitor stayed blue and blank.

For a second time the disks slapped against him, a second time his body jerked, fell. And now a low beep sounded, and the blue line wavered and went red.

Sinus rhythm. We have a pulse.

At the door, Areena covered her face with her hands.

"Give me his condition."

"He's alive." The doctor, a cool-eyed man with saffron skin, continued to make notes. "There was oxygen deprivation, and some minimal brain damage as a result. If we keep him alive, it's correctable."

"Are you going to keep him alive?"

"That's why we're here." He slipped his memo pad back into the pocket of his lab coat. "His chances are good. Another few minutes dangling there, he wouldn't have had any chance. We've come a long way in medical science, but bringing the dead back to life still eludes us."

"When can I talk to him?"

"I can't say."

"Hazard a guess."

"He may be functional by tomorrow, but until we complete the tests, I can't gauge the exact extent of the brain damage. It may be several days, or weeks, before he's capable of answering any but the most basic of questions. The brain finds ways to bypass damage, to reroute if you will, and we can help that process along. But it takes time."

"I want to know the minute he can talk."

"I'll make sure you're informed. Now, I have patients to see."

"Lieutenant." Clark stepped up. "This is the nurse you wanted to see."

"Ormand," Eve said, reading the ID

badge. "Talk to me."

"I had no idea he meant to try self-termination. I wouldn't have believed he was capable of it, physically I mean. He was weak as a baby."

"A man wants to do himself, he finds a way. Nobody's blaming you."

She nodded, relaxed her defensive stance. "I was in there for a routine check of his vitals. He was conscious, and he told me he wanted to confess. I thought he meant to a priest. We get a lot of that, even from patients who aren't Catholic or Egatarian. But he became agitated, and asked for you by name. Said I was to tell you he wanted to confess."

"To what?"

"He didn't say. I thought he killed that other actor. Richard Draco." When Eve didn't respond, the nurse shrugged. "I calmed him down, promised to find you. Then I told the guard after I arranged for the patient's afternoon nutrition. I don't know anything else."

"All right." She dismissed the nurse, turned back to Clark. "I need you to stand by up in the ICU. I'll arrange for a relief in an hour. If there's any change in Stiles's condition before that, I want to know."

"Yes, sir. His own sheets," Clark murmured. "That takes balls."

"It takes something." Eve turned on her heel and strode to the waiting area where Peabody had taken Areena.

"Kenneth?" Areena got shakily to her feet.

"They're moving him to Intensive Care."

"I thought he was . . . when I saw him, I thought . . ." She sank to her chair again. "Oh, how much more can happen?"

"Eliza Rothchild said tragedies happen in threes."

"Superstition. I've never been overly superstitious, but now . . . He'll be all right?"

"The doctor seemed optimistic. How did you know Kenneth Stiles was here?"

"How? Why, I heard it on the news just this morning. They're saying he was injured while trying to leave the city. That he's the prime suspect in Richard's death. I don't believe that. Not for a moment. I wanted to see him, to tell him that."

"Why don't you believe it?"

"Because Kenneth's not capable of murder. It's cold-blooded and calculating. He's neither."

"Sometimes murder's hot-blooded and impulsive."

"You'd know more about that than I. But I know Kenneth. He killed no one."

"Do you know a woman named Anja Carvell?"

"Carvell? I don't think so. Should I? Will they let me see Kenneth?"

"I don't know."

"I should try."

Eve got to her feet as Areena rose. "You realize, don't you, that if Kenneth Stiles did plan the murder of Richard Draco, he's the one who put the knife in your hand."

Areena shivered, and the faint color in her cheeks faded. "That's only one more reason I know it couldn't have been Kenneth."

"Why is that?"

"He's too much of a gentleman. May I go, Lieutenant?"

"Yeah, you can go."

Areena paused at the doorway. "You fought to save his life. I watched you. You believe he's a murderer, yet you fought to save his life. Why?"

"Maybe I didn't want him to escape justice."

"I think it's more than that. But I'm not sure what."

"Hell of a day so far," Peabody said when they were alone.

"We're just getting started. Up and at 'em, Peabody. We've got places to go."

She turned out of the room and nearly

walked into Nadine.

"Ambulance chasing?" Eve said mildly. "I thought you were too important for that routine."

"You're never too important for that routine. What's the status on Kenneth Stiles?"

"No comment."

"Come on, Dallas. I have a source in the hospital. I heard he tried to hang himself. Did he kill Richard Draco?"

"Which part didn't you get, the *no* or the *comment?*"

Nadine's fashionable heels made the rapid stride down the corridor tricky, but she managed to keep up with Eve. "Are you charging him with murder? Are there any other suspects? Will you confirm Stiles was injured during flight?"

"The media's already broadcasting that one."

"Sure, with *allegedly* and *believed to be* sprinkled all through the reports. I need confirmation."

"I need a vacation. Neither of us look to be getting our wish anytime soon."

"Dallas." Giving up, Nadine took Eve's arm, tugged her aside out of the way of Peabody and her own long-suffering camera operator. "I have to know something. I can't sleep. Give me something, make it off the record. I need to close this circle before I can move on."

"You shouldn't be on this story."

"I know it, and if it comes out that Richard and I were involved, I'll take a lot of heat for that, personally and professionally. But if I just sit around and wait, I'll go crazy with those options, I'll risk the heat."

"How much did he mean to you?"

"Entirely too much. That's been dead a lot longer than he has. That doesn't mean I don't need to close the circle."

"Meet me at Central, an hour. I'll give you what I can."

"Thanks. If you could just tell me if Kenneth —"

"An hour, Nadine." Eve skirted around her. "Don't push your luck."

In twenty minutes, they were inside Anja Carvell's suite. There wasn't a trace of her.

"She jumped." Peabody hissed at the empty closet. Then she frowned and turned to stare at Eve. "You knew she wouldn't be here."

"I didn't expect to find her. She's smart. Smart enough to know I'd be back."

"*She* killed Draco?"

"She's part of it." Eve wandered into the bath. Anja's scent was still there, coolly female.

"Should I contact the authorities in Montreal? Start arranging for extradition?"

"Don't bother. She'd be expecting that. If she ever lived in Montreal, she wouldn't go back there now. She's gone under," Eve murmured, "but she won't go far. So we play it out. Call for the sweepers."

"No warrant?"

"My husband owns the joint. Take care of it. I'm going down to security."

By the time Eve had finished at The Palace Hotel, returned to Central, and made her case to Whitney, she was late for her appointment with Nadine.

It irritated her, as it always did, to find Nadine already in her office.

"Why do they let you in here?"

"Because I bring donuts. Cops have been weak for them for generations."

"Where's mine?"

"Sorry, the squad descended on them like rats. I think Baxter licked up the crumbs."

"He would." She settled at her desk. "Where's your camera?"

"She's outside."

"Well, get her in here. I haven't got all damn day."

"But I thought —"

"Look, do you want a one-on-one or not?"

468

"You bet I do." She grabbed her palm-link and called her camera. "You could use a few layers of concealer on those tote bags under your eyes." She dug into the hefty and well-packed makeup kit in her purse. "Try this."

"Keep that crap away from me."

"Suit yourself, but you look like you haven't slept in days." Nadine flipped open a mirror, began to enhance her own face. "Still, it makes you look fierce and dedicated."

"I am fierce and dedicated."

"And it never fails to look good on-screen. Great sweater, by the way. Cashmere?"

Baffled, Eve looked down at her navy turtleneck. "I don't know. It's blue. Will this air tonight?"

"Bet your ass."

"Good." Someone, Eve thought, wasn't going to get a good night's sleep. And this time, it wouldn't be her.

Nadine fussed with the camera angles, looked in the monitor, and ordered a light adjustment.

"It's not a damn beauty contest, Nadine."

"Shows what you know about on-air reporting. There, that looks good. Can you cut out some of that air traffic, Lucy? It's like sitting in a transpo center."

"I'm filtering out most of it." The operator fiddled another moment, then nodded. "Ready when you are."

"We'll do the bumper back at the shop. Start record. This is Nadine Furst for Channel 75," she began, her eyes on the pinpoint lens. "Reporting from Cop Central and the office of Lieutenant Eve Dallas, the primary investigator in the murder of actor Richard Draco. Lieutenant." Nadine shifted, faced Eve. "Can you give us an update on your investigation?"

"The investigation is ongoing. The department is following a number of leads."

"Mr. Draco was killed onstage, in front of a packed house. You yourself were a witness."

"That's correct. The nature of the crime, its location, and execution have resulted in literally thousands of interviews and witness statements."

And because it was always best to pay your debts, Eve tagged on an addendum. "Detective Baxter of this division has reviewed the bulk of those statements and taken on the arduous task of elimination and corroboration."

"It's true, isn't it, that people often see the same event, but see it differently?"

"It's often true of civilians. Police officers

are trained to see."

"Does that make you your own best witness?"

"In a manner of speaking."

"Is it true that Kenneth Stiles, a colleague and acquaintance of Draco's who was in the cast of the play, is your lead suspect?"

"That individual has been questioned, as have all members of the cast. As I stated, we are following a number of leads, and as the focus of the investigation has narrowed, we expect to make an arrest within twenty-four hours."

"An arrest." It threw Nadine off stride, but only for one beat. "Can you give us the name of your primary suspect?"

"I'm not free to give that information at this time. I can tell you that the person who killed Richard Draco, who killed Linus Quim, will be in custody within twenty-four hours."

"Who —"

"That's all you get, Nadine. Shut it down."

Nadine might have argued, but Eve was already getting to her feet. "Shut it down, Lucy. That was a hell of a bombshell, Dallas. If you'd given me a head's up, we could've gone live."

"Tonight's soon enough. You got your

story, Nadine. You'll hit with it first."

"Can't argue with that. Can you give me any more, just some filler for the follow-up? Procedural details, some of the hard data. The exact number of interviews, number of man-hours, that kind of thing."

"You can get that from media relations." Eve glanced at the camera operator, pointed a finger, then jerked a thumb at the door.

With a look at Nadine for confirmation, Lucy hauled the equipment out.

"Off the record, Dallas —"

"You'll know everything you need to know tomorrow. I have a question for you. You didn't mention Roarke in your report, his connection to the theater, to the play, to me. Why?"

"It's been done. Overdone. I want the meat."

"Doesn't fly, Nadine. Roarke's name boosts ratings."

"Okay, consider it payback." She shrugged and hauled up her purse. "For the girl night."

"Okay." Eve reached into her back pocket, drew out a sealed disc. "Here."

"What's this?" But the minute it was in her hand, Nadine understood. Her fingers closed tightly around it. "It's the recording Richard did. Of me."

"It's been removed from the evidence log. It's the only copy. I figure it should close that circle."

As her throat filled with conflicting emotions, Nadine stared down at the disc. "Yes. Yes, it does. Better, it breaks it." Using both hands she snapped the disc in two.

Eve nodded with approval. "Some women wouldn't have been able to resist watching it. I figured you were smarter than that."

"I am now. Thanks, Dallas. I don't know how to —"

Eve took a deliberate step back. "Don't even think about kissing me."

With a shaky laugh, Nadine stuffed the broken disc in her bag. It would go into the first recyler she came across. "Okay, no sloppy stuff. But I owe you, Dallas."

"Damn right you do. So next time, save me a donut."

chapter twenty-one

She slept for ten hours, pretty much where she had fallen after giving Roarke the briefest of updates. She woke, recharged, clear-headed, and alone.

Since he wasn't around to nag her, she had an ice-cream bar for breakfast, washed it down with coffee while she watched the morning news reports on-screen. She caught a replay of her one-on-one with Nadine and, satisfied with it, considered herself set for the day.

She dressed, dragging on dung brown trousers and a white shirt that had narrow brown stripes. She had no idea how long the shirt had been there, but since Roarke had started filling her closet, she'd stopped paying attention.

He bought her a ridiculous amount of clothes, but it saved her from the torture of shopping.

Since it was there, and the weather promised to remain cool, she buttoned on a waist-length vest that appeared to go with the rest of the deal.

She strapped on her weapon, then she set off to find Roarke.

He was already in his office, the morning stock reports on one screen, off-planet trading on another, and what seemed to be a serious math problem on the third.

"How can you deal with numbers first thing in the morning?"

"I live for numbers." He tapped his keyboard, and the math problem shifted into tidy columns she had no doubt added up to the smallest decimal point. "And as it happens, I've been up for some time. You look rested," he said after a moment's study of her face. "And very well-tailored as well. You're a resilient creature, Eve."

"I slept like a slug." She came around the counter, leaned down, and kissed him. "You've been putting in some long days yourself." She patted his shoulder in a way that made his antenna quiver. "Maybe we need a little vacation."

He sent the figures on-screen to his broker for immediate application, then swiveled around in his chair. "What do you want?"

"Just some quiet time somewhere. You and me. We could take a long weekend."

"I repeat." He picked up his coffee, sipped. "What do you want?"

Irritation gleamed in her eyes. "Didn't I just say? Don't pull that crap on me again. You had to grovel the last time."

"I won't this time around. Do I look stupid?" he said in a conversational tone. "I'm not above a bribe, Lieutenant, but I like to know the deal. Why am I being softened up?"

"I couldn't soften you up with a vat of skin regenerator. Anyway, it's not a bribe. I'm a damn city official."

"And they are, as we know, complete strangers to bribes."

"Watch it, ace. Who says I can't want a break? If I want a favor, it doesn't have to connect."

"I see. Well then, here's what I'll bring to the table. I'll give you your favor, whatever it may be, in exchange for a week of your time anywhere I want to go."

"A week's out. I've got court dates, paperwork. Three days."

Negotiations, he thought, were his favorite hobby. "Five days now, five days next month."

"That's ten days, not a week. Even I can do the math on that. Three days now, two days next month."

"Four now, three next month."

"All right, all right." Her head was starting to spin. "I'll work it out."

"Then we have a deal." He offered his hand, clasped hers.

"So, are we going to the beach?"

"We can do that. The Olympus Resort has a stunning man-made beach."

"Olympus." She blanched. "Off planet? I'm not going off planet. That's got to be a deal breaker."

"Deal's done. Buck up. Now, what's the favor?"

She sulked. It was a rare attitude for her, but she was damn good at it. "It's not even a big favor."

"You should've thought of that before you tried to scam me. You might have, if you'd had a decent breakfast instead of ice cream."

"How did you —" She broke off, and the single word was a vicious hiss. "Summerset."

"Now, when a woman asks her husband for a favor, it's a lovely touch if she sits on his lap." He patted his knee.

"You won't have much of a lap if I break both your legs." Seriously annoyed, she sat on the counter. "Look, it's police business, and you always want to stick your nose in anyway. I'm giving you a chance."

"Now, there you are." Enjoying himself,

he lifted a hand, palm up. "If you'd presented it that way initially, put me in the position of being given a favor rather than giving one, you wouldn't have made what you consider a poor deal. And you wouldn't be cross."

"I'm not cross. You know I hate when you say I'm cross. And before I forget, what's the deal with this Authorization One shit?"

"Did you buy something?" He handed her the rest of his coffee. "I must make a celebrational note on my calendar. Eve Dallas went shopping. Strike up the band."

She scowled off into space. "I was in a pretty good mood before I came in here."

"See, you're cross. As to Authorization One, what sense does it make for you to pay for products manufactured by one of my companies?"

"Next time I'm going to a competitor. If I can find one." She huffed out a breath, brought herself back on track. "I'm going to close the case today. I've worked it how to smoke out the killer, get a confession. It's roundabout," she murmured. "I have reasons not to take the straight line. I had to do a tap dance for Whitney to clear it. If it doesn't work . . ." She trailed off.

"What do you need?"

"To start, I need your theater. And I need

you to help me script and produce a little performance."

An hour later, Eve was on her way to Central, and Roarke was making the first phone call.

In her office, Eve loaded the disc recording of the play in her computer. With her mind elsewhere, she barely noted how smoothly the disc was accepted, how clear the audio and video. When she ordered it to fast-forward to the final scene, it did so without a single bump.

There they were, she thought. Draco as Vole blithely confessing to a murder he could no longer be charged with. His face handsome, smug, as he drew Carly's hand, Diana's hand, through his arm.

And she stood by him, pretty and charming, with a loving smile.

Kenneth Stiles, the cantankerous and sly Sir Wilfred, stunned fury on his face, as the realization struck that he'd been used, exploited, manipulated. Eliza's fussy Miss Plimsoll standing beside him, outraged, her hands gripping the back of Kenneth's chair, and white to the knuckles.

Areena, the beautiful and multifaceted Christine, who had sacrificed everything, risked prison, to save the one she loved.

Michael Proctor, merely a shadow, watching from the wings, wondering when he would step into the spotlight and into the role of murderer.

And hovering over all was the ghost of Anja Carvell.

Eve didn't flinch as she watched murder done, as the knife that should have been harmless plunged deep into the heart.

There, she thought and froze the screen. *There it is.*

Ten thousand witnesses would have missed it.

Hadn't she?

The performance of a lifetime, she realized. In death.

"End program," she ordered. "Eject disc."

She bagged it, gathered others. She engaged her office link for interdepartmental transmission. "Peabody, alert Feeney and McNab. We're moving out."

With a final check of her weapon, she prepared to begin a performance of her own.

Eve's driving, Mira observed from the backseat, was a mirror reflection of her personality. Competent, direct, focused. And fierce. As the car whipped through traffic, bulling into gaps, challenging other charging bumpers, Mira quietly checked the tension on her safety harness.

"You're taking a risk."

Eve gave a quick glance in the rearview, met Mira's eyes. "A calculated one."

"I believe . . ." Mira trailed off, found herself falling back into childhood prayers as Eve shot into sharp vertical, swung hard to the right, and skimmed crossways over jammed traffic.

"I believe," she continued when she had her breath back, "you've assessed the situation correctly. Still, there's a wide margin for error, which you could eradicate by adhering to strict procedure."

"If I'm wrong, it's on me. Either way, the person who killed Draco and Quim will be in custody by the end of day."

The car dove into an underground parking tunnel, barely slacking speed. It winged like an arrow from a bow toward a reserved slot. Mira's mouth came open, she made some small sound, as they roared toward the security barricade. Eve flipped down her visor to display her ID pass.

Mira would have sworn the barricade emitted a terrified squeal as it leaped clear. They nipped under it, tucked into the narrow slot.

"Well," Mira managed. "Well. That was exciting."

"Huh?"

"It occurs to me, Eve, I've never done a ride-along with you. I begin to see why."

Peabody snorted, shoved open her door. "Take my word, Dr. Mira, that was a leisurely drive around the park."

"Something wrong with my driving?"

"Not that a case of Zoner wouldn't cure," Peabody said under her breath.

"In any case." Mira stepped out of the car, drew Eve's attention away from her aide. "I'm pleased you asked me to be here. Not only because I might be useful, but it gives me an opportunity to observe how you work in the field."

"You're going to have to stay out of the thick." Eve left her car in the secured slot Roarke had arranged, started out to the street and the theater.

"Yes, but I'll be monitoring."

"We've got a little while before the show starts." At the stage door, Eve punched in the code she'd been given. "You'll likely get bored."

"Oh, I sincerely doubt that."

They walked out on the stage, where preparations were already under way.

"Hey, Lieutenant! Heads up, She-Body!"

Twenty feet overhead, McNab swung by in a safety harness. He gave a kick of his shiny green boots and sailed in a very grace-ful arc.

"Stop that horsing around." Feeney squinted up, wincing when his detective pretended to swim through the air.

"What's he doing up there?" Eve demanded. "Besides making an ass of him-self."

"Overhead cams. You gotta be young to enjoy that kind of duty. Most of the equipment was already in place. Roarke didn't miss a trick. But he wasn't setting up for a police op. We're adjusting. We'll be able to monitor the action from all angles."

"Is Roarke on-scene yet?"

"Yeah, he's in control, showing a couple of my techs more than they'd ever hoped to know. The man's a genius with electronics. What I couldn't do with him in EDD."

"Do me a favor and don't mention it. He's hard enough to deal with. Auto-locks set on all exits?"

"Yep. Once everybody's in, nobody gets out. We've got three uniforms, two techs, you, me, and Peabody. And flyboy up there. McNab, get the hell down from there now! You sure you don't want a bigger team?"

Eve did a slow turn, scanned the theater. "We won't need it."

"Feeney." Roarke stepped from the

shadows onto the stage. "Your control appears to be set."

"I'll go look it over. McNab! Don't make me come up there. Christ, how many times did I say that to my kids?" With a shake of his head, he walked offstage.

"He's going to hurt himself." Torn between amusement and concern, Peabody nudged Eve's shoulder. "Tell him to come down, Dallas."

"Why me?"

"Because he fears you."

Because the idea of that was pleasing, Eve set her hands on her hips, scowled up, and shouted. "McNab, stop screwing around and get your ass down here."

"Yes, sir."

He came down in a whoosh, cheeks flushed with the thrill. "Man, you gotta try that. What a rush."

"I'm happy we could provide you with some entertainment, Detective. Why shouldn't we have a little fun and frivolity during the course of an elaborate and expensive police operation, particularly when we're employing multimillion dollar civilian equipment and facilities."

"Um," was the best he could do before he cleared his throat. The grin had already been wiped off his face. "The overhead cams are set and operational, Lieutenant. Sir."

"Then maybe you can make yourself useful elsewhere. If it's not too much trouble."

"No, sir. I'll just . . . go." *Somewhere,* he thought, and escaped.

"That ought to keep him straight for the next five minutes." She turned to Roarke.

"I don't fear you," he told her. "But I brought you a present." He handed her a mini-remote. "You can signal control," he explained. "For lights, sound, set change. You can direct from any location in the theater. The play's in your hands."

"Opening act's up to you."

"It's already in place." He checked his wrist unit. "You have just over an hour before curtain."

"I need to check all ops. Peabody, do a round. Confirm that all egresses leading below, back, or above stage are secure, then take and maintain your assigned position until further orders."

"Yes, sir."

"Roarke, would you show Dr. Mira her observation area?"

"Of course."

"Great." She flipped out her communicator. "Feeney, I want those — what are they — houselights on for a minute."

When they flashed on, illuminating the theater, she switched the communicator to blanket transmission. "This is Lieutenant Dallas. In thirty minutes, I want all operation personnel at their assigned stations. If I so much as smell a cop, he or she is on report. Civilian protection is first priority. I repeat, that is priority. Weapons are to remain harnessed, and on low stun. I will not have a repeat of Grand Central."

She pocketed the communicator. "Roarke, contact me when Dr. Mira is settled."

"Of course. Break a leg, Lieutenant."

"What? Oh. Right."

"She was born for this," Mira said as Eve strode off. "Not just for command, which fits her like skin, but for balancing the wrongs with the rights. Someone else, perhaps anyone else, would have finished this another way."

"She couldn't."

"No. It's already cost her. She'll need you when this is done."

"We're going away for a few days."

Mira angled her head. "How did you manage to persuade her?"

"The art of the deal." He offered his arm. "May I escort you to your seat, Doctor?"

★ ★ ★

"Lieutenant. McNab, Position Four. First subject approaching theater, stage door entrance."

"Copy." Eve turned from the backstage monitor to Roarke. "That's your cue. Try not to deviate from the outline, okay? I believe physical risk is minimal, but —"

"Trust me."

"I just want to go over —"

"Lieutenant, does it occur to you that I might know what I'm doing?"

"It occurs to me that you always know what you're doing."

"Well then, I repeat. Trust me." With that he left to take his mark.

On the monitor she watched him walk out on the bare stage, stand under the lights. She wondered if he'd ever considered acting. Of course he hadn't, she thought. Deals, shady and otherwise, had been his passion. But he had the face for it and the build, the presence, the grace.

And, she mused, he had an innate skill with a believable lie.

Wasn't that acting?

"Michael." Roarke offered a hand as Proctor entered. "You're prompt."

"I didn't want to keep everyone waiting." With an easy laugh, Michael glanced around. "The trouble with being prompt is you always wait for everyone else. I was really glad to get your call. I wasn't sure the cops would ever let the theater open again, at least not in time for you to put *Witness* back into production."

"They appear to have everything they need from the scene."

"I want to thank you for giving me the chance to play Vole. I realize you could call in another name actor to fill the part."

"No qualms?" No, Roarke thought, he didn't see qualms. But ambition. "Considering what happened to Draco, I wondered if you might be somewhat anxious about stepping into the role."

"No, I'm fine with it. I don't mean fine," he corrected and had the grace to flush. "It's terrible what happened to Richard. Just terrible. But —"

"The show must go on," Roarke said smoothly, then glanced over. "Ah, Eliza, and Areena. Ladies, thank you for coming."

"Your call saved me from boredom and brooding." Eliza stepped up, brushed her cheek to Roarke's. "The boredom of being between acts. And brooding over Kenneth. I still can't believe what I'm hearing on the news."

"Don't," Areena said. "There's a mistake.

There must be." She rubbed her chilly arms. "It's so odd to be here again. I haven't been back since . . . since opening night."

"Will you be all right with this?" Roarke took her hand, warmed it in his own.

"Yes. Yes, I must be, mustn't I? None of us have any choice but to go on."

"Why shouldn't we?" Carly made an entrance. A deliberate one. She'd applied dramatic makeup to go with an electric blue dress that scooped low at the breasts, stopped short at the thighs.

For power, she'd told herself. She was damn well going to be powerful.

"None of us gave a damn about the late, unlamented Richard Draco."

"Carly," Areena murmured it, a quiet censure.

"Oh, save the fragile sensibilities for the audience. He fucked us all over at one time or another. Some of us literally," she added with a tight, fierce smile. "We're not here to dedicate our next performance to his memory. We're here because we want to get back to work."

"He may have been a bastard, dear," Eliza said mildly, "but dead is dead. And now Kenneth's in the hospital, and under guard."

"Kenneth ought to be given a medal for

ridding the world of Richard Draco."

"They haven't charged him yet." Areena twisted her fingers together. "Can't we just discuss the play and get away from the ugliness for a little while? Is this a full cast call, Roarke?" She brushed a hand over her hair, looked around. "I was sure the director would be here by now."

"Difficult to arrange a full cast call at the moment." Roarke let the implications of that hang. "The part of Sir Wilfred will need to be recast."

"Couldn't we rehearse with a stand-in?" Michael asked. "I've never run through an entire act with the first cast. It would be helpful for me to do that as soon as possible."

"There you go, Michael." Carly laughed. "No moss growing on you."

"You just said we were here to work," he shot back. "There's no reason to snipe at me."

"Maybe I'm feeling snipey. You're just sulking because I kicked you out of my apartment instead of crying on your shoulder."

"I would've helped," he said quietly. "I would have tried."

"I don't need your help. I don't need anyone." Her eyes glinted with an inner fury that burned into her voice. "I slept with you. Big deal. Don't think you mean anything to me. No man is ever going to mean anything to me."

"Once more, sex rears its ugly head," Eliza muttered. "Must we forever have glands interfering with art?"

"Eliza." Areena stepped forward, laid a hand on Carly's arm. "Carly, please. We need to get along. We need to stick together." She tried a bolstering smile. "What must Roarke think of us, bickering this way?"

"I'd say you're all under considerable strain." He paused, skimming his eyes over the faces turned toward him. "And that if any or all of you feel unable to continue with the run of the play, I'd prefer to know sooner than later."

Carly threw back her head and laughed. "Oh please. Each and every one of us would claw through broken glass for a chance to perform in this one. The publicity will pack this house for weeks when we open again, and every one of us knows it. Nothing as irksome as murder will get in our way."

She tossed her hair back, stretching out her arms as she crossed the stage. "So bring on a stand-in for the inestimable Sir Wilfred, cast a goddamn droid in the role, it'll still be standing room only."

She whirled back, arms still lifted. "Go ahead, Roarke, throw open the doors. Let the play begin."

As cues went, Eve figured it was near to perfect. "It never stopped," she said, and moved from the wing's shadows to the lights.

chapter twenty-two

"Lieutenant Dallas." Carly lowered her arms slowly, let one hand rest on her cocked hip. "What an irritating surprise to see you again."

"Oh, Carly, do stop playing the diva," Eliza said irritably. "You're not nearly old enough to pull it off. Lieutenant, I hope you're here to tell us you've made the arrest you promised. You seemed very confident in your interview on Channel 75."

"An arrest is imminent."

"Not Kenneth." Areena pressed a hand to her heart.

"If it was Kenneth," Eliza put in, "I hope we can all be counted on to behave decently and stand behind him. I intend to." She brought her shoulders back, spoke grandly. "I don't desert my friends."

"That's admirable, Ms. Rothchild." Eve slipped her hands in her pocket, fingered the remote. "But Kenneth Stiles is no longer the primary suspect in this investigation. Richard Draco's killer is on this stage."

Even as she spoke, the houselights

dimmed, the stage lights glowed. And the courtroom set slid into view. A long-bladed knife lay on the evidence table. Eve crossed to it, picked it up to weigh it in her hand.

"The murder took place on this stage. And so will the arrest."

"Well, we'll have to give you points for the dramatic twist, Lieutenant." Carly breezed forward, arranged herself languidly in the witness chair. "Please go on. We're all riveted."

"Cut it out, Carly. It had to be Kenneth." Michael sent Areena an apologetic look. "I'm sorry, Areena, but it had to be. He tried to run, and then he tried to . . . well, escape permanently. If he wasn't guilty, why would he have done all that?"

"To protect someone," Eve said. "It's a recurring theme here." She touched the tip of the knife with her finger, then set it down again. "Miss Plimsoll fussing over Sir Wilfred to protect his health, no matter how many different ways he insults or evades her."

"Really, Lieutenant, that's a character." Eliza puffed up like a bird who'd just had its tail feathers plucked. "Surely you're not suggesting that I had anything to do with this."

"It's all about character." Eve studied

Eliza's outraged face. "Sir Wilfred, protecting his client, risking his health, only to learn in the end he's freed a murderer. Leonard Vole, pretending to defend his beloved wife, helping her to escape a crumbling Germany years before, only to use her again and again to protect himself. And Christine." Eve shifted her gaze to Areena. "Risking her reputation, sacrificing her freedom to cover for him. Out of love that was thrown back in her face in the cruelest and most careless of ways when she had served her purpose."

"We know the play," Carly said with a dainty yawn. "I suppose you'll say that while only the understudy, Michael was ranged with Richard, that is, Vole."

"That's right. And with Draco out of the way, he becomes Vole. What better way to right an old wrong, to avenge his mother's honor?"

"Just a minute. That's enough. I've had enough of this. I don't have to take that sort of thing from you." Michael's fists bunched at his sides as he took one threatening step toward Eve.

"Michael." Roarke's voice was quiet. He shifted so that he blocked Michael's reckless advance, and the actor came face-to-face with iced violence. "I could hurt you in ways you can't possibly imagine."

"Roarke," Eve would have cursed him for the interference, but it would have changed the mood.

"Step back, Michael," Carly advised, and only the grip of her hand on the chair indicated her concern. "You'll only embarrass yourself. You're running through our happy troupe rather quickly, Lieutenant."

Carly crossed her legs, all but purring to shift the attention to herself. "But you haven't touched on me or my character counterpart. I don't believe Diana was protecting anyone."

"She would have." Eve turned, walked slowly to the witness chair. "Wouldn't she have seen that, after it all came tumbling down? That she would have followed after Christine, being used, being exploited, then being cast off when he looked for fresher prey? I think she would have hated him for that. Hated him," Eve repeated, resting her hands on the arms of the chair, leaning down. "For spoiling her party, her pretty dreams, for making her see what a fool she'd been to fall for something despicable, disgusting."

The pulse began to hammer in Carly's throat. "You're giving the character more depth than she deserves."

"I don't think so. I think Vole underestimated her. People, particularly men, often underestimate beautiful women. They don't look past the surface. He didn't know you, did he? Didn't know what kind of strength and passion and purpose lives inside you."

A spotlight flashed on, bathed Carly in a cool, white glow.

"You don't frighten me, Lieutenant."

"No, you don't scare easy. And when someone bruises you, you hit back. Harder. I have to respect that. He thought he could toss you aside, like an LC after the hour's up. He thought he could humiliate you in public, right here, on this stage, in front of the cast and crew. So they'd look at you with scorn or pity. You wouldn't, couldn't swallow that. He had to pay for that."

"Stop hounding her." Michael gripped the edge of the evidence table. "Leave her alone. You know what she's been through."

"She's just grasping at straws." Her mouth was dust dry, but Carly managed to keep her voice level.

"Men don't toss you aside, do they, Carly?" Eve glanced back at Michael. "That's not allowed. Not tolerated. It was easy to plan it, really. Just step by step. And it was so beautifully tailored to suit. He

497

would die right here, almost at your feet."

"I want a lawyer."

"You can have a team of them." Eve stepped back, wandered to the evidence table, tapped a finger on the handle of the knife. "It was easy to get the knife out of the kitchen. Who notices a missing knife where there are so many? You knew the pace of the play, how much time between a change of sets. Even if someone saw you, it wouldn't matter. You belonged here, like part of the scenery or an important prop. Slip the dummy knife up your sleeve, set the murder weapon down, and walk away.

"Was it hard to wait?" She turned the knife in her hand so that it caught the lights, shot glints. "To say your lines, to listen to others, while in your head you could see that last scene play, the way the knife would drive into him, the shock on his face, when he was finally punished for what he did to you."

"It's ridiculous, and you know it. You can't prove any of it because it's not true. You're just going to end up looking like a fool."

"I'll risk it. Carly Landsdowne, you're under arrest for the murders of Richard Draco and Linus Quim. You have the right to remain silent," she continued as Peabody came out, moving toward Carly. "You have the right to an attorney and/or the representative of your choice. You have —"

"Get away from her!" The shout came as Peabody prepared to snap restraints over Carly's wrist. "Don't you dare touch her. She's done nothing!"

Areena shoved Michael aside, rushed to the evidence table. Her face was wild with fury as she grabbed up the knife. "You won't touch her. You won't do this. Damn you to hell."

She whirled on Eve. "She didn't kill Richard. I did. I only wish I'd done it years ago, before he ever laid his filthy hands on her."

"I know." Eve walked to her, eyes locked, and took the harmless knife out of Areena's hand. "I know it. Anja."

"Anja? Oh God. My God." Carly crossed her arms over her breasts, rocked.

"Peabody, move these people out of here. Carly, sit down. There's a story you need to hear."

"Let her go." Areena's voice was frantic as she ranged herself between Eve and Carly. "I'll tell you everything. Haven't you put her through enough? I waive my rights. I understand them and I waive them. Now let her go."

"You." Carly's eyes seemed to burn in her face. "You and Richard."

"I'm sorry. So sorry."

"You knew." Bracing herself, Carly got to her feet. "You knew all along. And did nothing when he . . ."

"No. Oh, Carly, you can't think that I'd have stood aside. Yes, I knew. When I saw you, when you were cast and I realized you were . . . who you were, I went to him. You're so much what he coveted. Young and beautiful and fresh. I told him who you were so that he wouldn't touch you in that way. That was my mistake."

She closed her eyes, took the weight. "I'll never know if he would have looked elsewhere for his pleasure. I thought I was protecting you, and instead . . . Instead, he seduced you, knowing it. Knowing it. You weren't to blame. You were never to blame."

"He knew." Carly pressed a hand to her midriff. "You both knew."

"When I found out what he'd done, what he was doing, I confronted him. We argued. Bitterly. I threatened him, threatened to expose him, to go to the press with the story. I couldn't have, of course, I couldn't have because of what it would do to you. He believed me, at least initially, and broke it off with you. He was cruel to you because he

500

knew it would hurt me."

"How did you know me?"

"Carly, I . . ." Areena trailed off, shook her head. "I never interfered with your life. I had no right to. But I was kept informed."

"Why did you care?" Carly demanded. "I was nothing but your mistake."

"No. No. You were a gift, one I couldn't keep. I gave that gift to your parents because I knew they would cherish you. They would protect you. As I tried to," she said wearily. "I would never have told you, Carly. Never. If there'd been a choice. But I can't let them accuse you, can't let them blame you for what I did."

She turned back to Eve. "You had no right to put her through this."

"We've all got a job to do."

"Is that what you call this?" Carly gasped. "To find out which one of us exterminated a roach, and why. Well, you've done it. I wonder how you sleep at night. I want to go." She began to weep. "I don't want to be here anymore. I want to go."

"Dr. Mira?"

"Yes." Mira walked onto the set, slipped an arm around Carly. "Come now, Carly. Come with me."

"I'm dead inside."

"No, only numb. You need to rest a little."

501

Mira sent Eve a long, quiet look, then guided Carly away.

"Look what you've done to her. You're no better than Richard. Abusing her, exploiting her. Do you know the nightmares that will haunt her? Scream through her head?" Eyes grim, Areena faced Eve. "I would have spared her from that. I could have spared her from that."

"You killed him after he'd stopped abusing her. Why did you wait until it was over?"

"Because it wasn't over." Areena sighed, gave into her trembling legs, and sat. "He came to see me a few days before we opened. He'd been using. He was always more vile when he was using. He threatened to take her back. If I wanted him to keep his distance, I'd have to take her place. So I did. It was only sex, it meant nothing. Nothing."

But her hand shook as she dug into her purse, found a cigarette. "I should have pretended to be hurt, outraged, terrified. Those emotions would have stimulated him, satisfied him. I could have made him believe it. Instead, I showed disgust and disinterest. He retaliated by suggesting a threesome, himself, me and Carly, after opening night. He reveled in telling me everything he'd done to her, with her. How he'd enjoyed it, how exciting it had been for him to pound himself into her, knowing she was his blood, his daughter. He was a monster, and I executed him."

She got to her feet. "I have no remorse, I have no regret. I could have killed him that night when he stood in my rooms, bragging about being man enough to take on both mother and daughter at once."

There was a skim of sickness coating Eve's throat. "Why didn't you?"

"I wanted to be sure. And I wanted, somehow, for it to be just. And . . ." For the first time she smiled. "I wanted to get away with it. I thought I would. I thought I had."

When she began to fight with her lighter, Roarke crossed to her, took it from her chilly hands. Her eyes met his over the flame. "Thank you."

He laid the lighter back in her palm, gently closed her fingers around it. "You're welcome."

With her eyes closed, Areena took her first deep drag. "Of all my addictions, this is the one I've never been able to beat." She let out a sigh. "I've done many unattractive things in my life, Lieutenant. I've had my bouts of selfishness, of self-pity. But, I don't use people I care about. I wouldn't have let Kenneth be arrested. I would've found a way around that. But who would suspect quiet, obliging Areena of cold-blooded murder? Such a public one."

"That was your cover, doing it right here, onstage."

"Yes, surely I wouldn't commit murder in front of thousands of witnesses. I saw myself being eliminated as a suspect right away. And naively, I believed none of the others, being innocent, would face more than the inconvenience of questioning."

She managed a little laugh. "And knowing them, I was certain they'd find the process diverting. Frankly, Lieutenant, I didn't think any investigator looking into Richard's life to solve his death would work overly hard on the case once they discovered the kind of man he was. I underestimated you, even as Richard underestimated me."

"Until the moment you put the knife in him. Then he stopped underestimating you."

"That's right. The look in his eyes, the dawning of understanding, was worth every moment of planning. Of fear. It happened very much as you'd said before, only with me in the role you'd cast Carly in."

She could replay it in her head, scene by scene, move by move. Her own intimate play. "I simply took a knife from the kitchen one day when Eliza and I went down to ask for sandwiches. I kept it in my dressing room until opening night. Until the change of scene. There were several of us moving from point to point backstage, cast and crew. I exchanged the knives and added the touch of planting the prop in my own dressing room when my dresser's back was turned. I planted it right under her very loyal nose. Another clever twist, I thought at the time."

"It might have worked. It nearly did."

"Nearly. Why nearly, Lieutenant?"

"Anja Carvell."

"Ah. A name from the past. Do you know where it comes from?"

"No. I've wondered."

"A small, insignificant role in a small insignificant play that opened and closed on the same night in a backwater town in Canada. It was never put on my credits nor on Kenneth's. But it's where we met. And I realized some years later, it was where he fell in love with me. I only wish I'd been wise enough to love him back. He would call me Anja from time to time, a kind of private connection between that very young girl and that very young man who both wanted to be great actors."

"You used it when you placed her."

"Yes, for sentiment. And to protect her, I

thought, should she ever try to find her birth mother. I had given her to good people. The Landsdownes are very good people. Kind, loving. I wanted what was best for her. I made certain she got it."

Yes, Eve thought, *you made certain. Dead certain.* "You could have let go then. Why didn't you let go?"

"Do you think because I only saw her once, because I only held her once, that I don't love her?" Areena's voice rose. Rang. "I'm not her mother. I'm fully aware of that. But there hasn't been a day in twenty-four years that I haven't thought of her."

She stopped herself, seemed to draw in. "But I'm circling the point. I was persuasive as Anja. I know it."

"Yes, very. I didn't recognize you, not physically. Emotions, Areena. Who had the strongest motive, not only to kill him, but to make him pay in front of an audience? To end his life, just as Vole's was ended? Who had been the most betrayed, the most used? Once I eliminated Carly, there was one answer: Anja Carvell."

"If you'd eliminated Carly, why did you put her through that horror?"

"Anja Carvell," Eve went on, ignoring the question. "She struck me as a strong, self-possessed, and very direct woman. But how

506

did she switch the knives? I imagine she'd have found a way, and still it didn't quite work. For one simple reason. She would have needed to hold the knife herself, to strike the blow for the child she'd given up to protect."

"Yes, you're right. I would have left it to no one else."

"When I thought of you and her, I saw it. You changed your look, your voice, your attitude. But there are things you didn't change, or couldn't. There," Eve said, gesturing. "You reach up as you're doing now, toying with a necklace — or as Anja, with the top button of your dress — when you're formulating what you're going to say and how best to say it."

"Such a small thing."

"There are others. They add up. You can change the color, even the shape of your eyes, but not the look in them when your temper spikes or grief grabs you. You couldn't hide the purpose in them, for that one moment, when you locked eyes with Richard onstage. That instant before you killed him. I only had to think of Anja and you to realize you were one person."

"So you outwitted me." Areena got to her feet. "You've solved the puzzle and upheld what you see as justice. Brava, Lieutenant. I imagine you'll sleep the sleep of the righteous tonight."

Eve kept her eyes locked on Areena's. "Peabody, escort Ms. Mansfield to the black-and-white unit waiting outside."

"Yes, sir. Ms. Mansfield?"

"Eve." Roarke murmured it as their footsteps echoed offstage.

She shook her head, knowing she had to hold him off, hold herself together. "Feeney, do we have the full record?"

"Clear as a bell, Dallas, and fully admissible. She waived her rights."

"We're done here. Close it up."

"Will do. Meet you at Central. Good job. Damn good job."

"Yeah." She squeezed her eyes shut as Roarke laid a hand on her shoulder. "Thanks for the help. We got through it. No muss, no fuss."

She resisted when he tried to turn her to face him. He simply stepped around her. "Don't do this."

"I'm fine. I have to go in, deal with this."

"I'll go with you." He tightened his grip when she started to shake her head. "Eve, do you think I would leave you alone at such a time?"

"I said I'm fine."

"Liar."

She gave up, gave in, let him hold her. "I looked at her, I looked in her eyes and I wondered how I would have felt, what it would have been like to have someone care so much about me, someone who'd have done anything to save me from him. And then, looking at her, I trapped her using the thing she loved most."

"No. You saved the thing she loved most. We both know that."

"Did I? No, that's Mira's job." She drew a deep breath. "I want to close this thing. I need to make it over."

Paperwork could be a soothing routine. She used it, writing her report with the dispassionate and brutal efficiency required. She filed it, adding all the evidence gathered.

"Lieutenant?"

"Shift's nearly over, Peabody. Go home."

"I will. I wanted you to know Mansfield's finished in booking. She's asked to see you."

"All right. Set it up, Interview One, if available. Then take off."

"Happy to."

Eve turned in her chair to where Roarke stood, looking at her miserable view. "Sorry. I have to do this. Why don't you go home?"

"I'll wait."

She said nothing, only rose and made her way down to Interview.

Areena was already there, sitting quietly at the small table. She quirked her lips in a sneer. "I can't say I think much of the wardrobe choices in this place." She fingered the collarless top of the dull gray state issue.

"We've got to get a new designer. Record on —"

"Is that necessary?"

"Yes, I'm required to put any conversations with you on record. For your protection and mine. Dallas, Lieutenant Eve, in Interview One with Mansfield, Areena, at her request. Ms. Mansfield, you've been given your rights, do you choose to implement any or all of them at this time?"

"No, I have something to say to you. You knew it was me," she said, leaning forward. "You were perfectly aware it was me, before we came into the theater today."

"We've been over this ground."

"I'm asking you if you had any proof before my confession?"

"What difference does it make? I have your confession."

"For my own curiosity. The attorney I intend to hire will be entitled to that information, which will be relayed to me. Save us the middleman."

"All right. Acting on my suppositions as regarded Anja Carvell, I ordered voice print analyses between your statements and hers. Though you had altered your tone, your rhythm, effectively disguising your voice to the naked ear, the voice prints were an exact match. As fingerprints are. Several of yours were found in the room registered to Carvell. Strands of hair, both from a synthetic wig matching the shade worn by Carvell and those of your shade, and your DNA, were found in the aforementioned suite. Both were also found, on a warranted sweep of your penthouse in the same hotel."

"I see. I should have researched police procedure. I was careless."

"No, you weren't. You were human, which makes it impossible to think of everything."

"You managed it." Areena leaned back now, a considering look in her eye as she studied Eve. "You had enough evidence to bring me in here for questioning, to throw my deception in my face, use my relationship with Richard, with Carly, to break me. Instead, you chose to do so at the theater. In front of Carly."

"You might not have broken here. I banked on it working the other way."

"No, you'd have broken me. We both

know it. I couldn't stand against you. You did it in front of Carly for a very specific reason. You did it for her."

"I don't know what you're talking about, and I'm off shift."

Before she could rise, Areena gripped her hand. "You did it for her. She has to live with knowing what the father who made her was capable of. What he did to her. Knowing what he was, and that what he was runs inside her could twist her, scar her."

"She'll live with it." *Every day,* Eve thought. *Every night.*

"Yes, she will. But you made sure she saw more than that. You showed her that the other part who made her would protect her at all costs. Would sacrifice her own freedom to insure hers. Could love her that much. You showed her that there's decency, loyalty, and strength of purpose in her blood. One day, when she's settled, when she heals, she'll realize that. She may think of me kindly. When she realizes that, Lieutenant Dallas, I hope she has the courage to thank you as I'm thanking you now."

She closed her eyes tightly, inhaled deeply. "Can I have some water, please?"

Eve walked over, drew a cup. "You'll both pay for what he did. There's no way to stop that."

"I know." Areena sipped, cooled her throat. "But she's young and strong. She'll find a way to beat it back."

"She'll have help. Dr. Mira will counsel her. She's the best."

"I appreciate knowing that. I was so proud of the way she faced you down today. She's tough. And she's lovely, isn't she?"

"Yes, very."

"I couldn't bear what he did to her. Couldn't bear thinking he might do so again." Tears rose, were battled back.

Fragile? Eve thought. *Not in this lifetime.*

"With Quim," Areena continued, "it was difficult for me. I was afraid. But he was an ugly little man, and I'd had my fill of ugly little men. Lieutenant?"

"Yes."

"Will you, when I'm in prison, will it be possible to get an update on Carly's state of mind, on how she is? Nothing intrusive. Just if there's a way I could be told she's all right."

"I'll see what I can do." Eve hesitated, swore. "Record off," she ordered, and blanked out the sound and visual to observation. "Get a lawyer who knows how to spin the media, not just one who's tough in court. Better, get one of each. You want to sway public opinion. You want people to hear the story, all of it, and feel sympathy for you, disgust for Draco. Stop waiving your damn rights, and don't talk to me again, or any other cop, without your attorney present."

Amused, Areena lifted her eyebrows. "Do you save everyone, Lieutenant?"

"Shut up and listen. Go for diminished capacity and extreme emotional distress. Even with the premeditation, it's not much of a stretch. You killed the man abusing your daughter, and a blackmailer. If it's played that way, it's going to generate a lot of media in your favor." And she could tap Nadine to see that it swung that way. "The DA's not going to want the mess of a long, public trial with mothers picketing outside the courthouse and city hall. And they will. He'll offer you a deal. You may spend time in a cage, but if you're lucky, you'll get a hefty stretch of home incarceration with a bracelet, and another chunk of severe parole."

"Why are you doing this for me?"

"Isn't there some saying about looking gift horses in the mouth?"

"Yes. Very true." Areena got to her feet. "I wish, well obviously, I wish we'd met under different circumstances." She held out her hand. "Good-bye, Lieutenant."

Eve clasped her hand, let the grip hold.

When she walked back into her office, Roarke was there. She picked up her jacket, her bag. "What do you say we get the hell out of here?"

"I like the idea." But he caught her hand, ran his gaze over her face. "You look lighter, Lieutenant."

"I am. Considerably."

"And Areena?"

"She's a hell of a woman. It's weird." As she puzzled it, she sat on the edge of the desk. "It's the first time in eleven years on the job I've ever come across a killer I admire, and a victim I couldn't . . ."

"Care about," Roarke finished.

"I'm not supposed to care one way or the other. I'm just supposed to do the job."

"But you do care, Lieutenant. Brutally, you care. And this time you ran up against someone you were obliged to stand for who deserved exactly what he got."

"Murder's never deserved," she said, then made a small sound of impatience. "Hell with it. Justice was served in a courtroom. It might have been onstage, but it wasn't make-believe. There was no pretense when Areena Mansfield picked up that knife and rammed it into the heart Richard Draco didn't have. And when she took that step, that stand, justice was served."

"She'll have the jury eating out of her hand. Before it's over, they'll canonize her rather than convicting her. You know that."

"Yeah. Hell, I'm counting on that. You know what I figured out, pal?"

"Tell me."

"You can't go back. Can't fix what broke. But you can go forward. And every step matters. Every one makes a difference." She pushed away from the desk, cupped his face in her hands. "From where I'm standing, you're the best step I ever took."

"Then let's take the next, and go home."

She walked out with him, and because it fit the mood, took his hand in hers. She would sleep that night. She would sleep clean.

The employees of Thorndike Press hope you have enjoyed this Large Print book. All our Large Print titles are designed for easy reading, and all our books are made to last. Other Thorndike Press Large Print books are available at your library, through selected bookstores, or directly from us.

For information about titles, please call:

(800) 223-1244
(800) 223-6121

To share your comments, please write:

Publisher
Thorndike Press
P.O. Box 159
Thorndike, Maine 04986